THE HONOUR CODE OF GREED

A NOVEL BY MICHAEL JONES

GILLIES
7127 STANLEY AVENUE
NIAGARA FALLS, ONT, L2M 7K
(905) 358-6532

Published in Australia by
Temple House Pty Ltd,
T/A Sid Harta Publishers
ACN 092 197 192
Hartwell, Victoria 3124

Telephone: 61 3 9560 9920
Facsimile: 61 3 9545 1742
E-mail: author@sidharta.com.au

First published in Australia 2003
Copyright © Michael Jones, 2002
Cover design, typesetting: Alias Design
Cover design by Alias Design
Editing: Robert N Stephenson
Proofreading: Kath Harper

The right of Michael Jones to be identified as the Author of the Work has been asserted by him in accordance with the Copyright, Designs and Patents Act 1988.

This book is a work of fiction. Names, characters, places, organisations, and incidents either are products of the author's imagination or are used fictitiously. Any resemblance to actual events, organisations, or persons living or dead, is entirely coincidental.
All rights reserved. No part of this publication may be reproduced, stored in a retrieval system, or transmitted, in any form or by any means without the prior written permission of the publisher, nor be otherwise circulated in any form of binding or cover other than that in which it is published and without a similar condition being imposed on the subsequent purchaser.
National Library of Australia Cataloguing-in-Publication entry:
Jones, Michael - .
The Honour Code Of Greed
ISBN: 1-877.059-14-5
Printed by Shannon Publishing
Typeset in Sabon.

Michael Jones

M ichael Jones was born in Sydney, educated at Sydney Grammar and University of Sydney, and was a solicitor there for ten years before deciding to leave and travel overseas. Since then he has lived and worked in Spain, France, Italy, Switzerland, the United States, England, India, Russia, Malaya and Portugal, mainly in the not for profit world, but also in the business and professional sphere. Following the publication of a number of articles on corporate management, this is the author's first novel constructed around this theme.

His three children live in Rome, London and Miami, and his four stepchildren in various parts of Australia and the United States. Michael returned to live in Australia in 2000 after almost 40 years, and now resides with his partner in Woollahra in Sydney where he is working on a new novel.

Dedication

*To wonderful Gillian,
without whom nothing would have happened.*

PART ONE

The Love Of Money
1967–1971

CHAPTER ONE

NEW YORK, N.Y.
1967

NICK BARTON OPENED THE door from the street on a late February afternoon in 1967, and stepped into the smoky and dangerous smog of BJ's Bar on 2nd Avenue. BJ himself caught Nick's eye immediately, and beckoned him over for a chat, which he did only with his favourite customers.

BJ put a Scotch and water, without ice, on the bar – Nick's drink – and gave him a disillusioned stare. He looked, Nick thought, rather like a Roman senator might have looked – proud, hawk-nosed, disdainful and full of power.

"Charles Bellamy has been asking for you," BJ said, furiously polishing a glass to shining perfection. Nick was amused by BJ's obsession with his clean glasses when the rest of the establishment was so tawdry and neglected.

"I'd be careful of him, if I were you, Nick. He looks okay but he's a nasty bit of work, that fellow. If ever I've seen a bad egg, it's him." He replaced the glass on the bar top and began on another.

Nick sipped his whiskey and looked around. He heard the piano, the singing at the back of the bar, and the hum of voices. It seemed to him, suddenly, in spite of the fierce cold outside, that things in his life were improving – that there was a hint of spring in the air. It was hovering out there, waiting to blow up from Florida, or Havana, or Jamaica, or wherever it was hiding. "I don't know anyone called Charles Bellamy," Nick said. "I know practically no one except my landlady and I could do without her, if you'd like to take her off my hands."

"Everyone in here knows Charlie," BJ said with a tight and unamused smile. "You must have seen him! The tall, fair chap with the English accent and the Savile Row clothes. Looks like a film star. You know, kind of shiny and smart-assed."

Nick recognized the description quickly enough. He had noticed the man several times, standing around in the occasional shaft of sunlight from the street window like a young prince, unlike the rest of the seedy crowd that frequented the bar. He had the optimistic look of a winner, golden and undefeated, as yet untouched by the woes of life. It would have been impossible not to notice him among BJ's disconsolate clientele, but Nick had neither met him nor spoken with him. He could not imagine how the man even knew his name, nor why he should be asking for him.

"So, just who is this Bellamy fellow, and what does he want with me?"

"God knows what he wants, but it won't be good, that I know!" BJ said with a shrug.

"Well, he knows nothing about me, that's for sure," Nick said with a sour laugh.

"Charlie knows everything and everyone," BJ said laconically, "or, at least, everything that's useful to him. Just be careful of him, that's all."

"So you've told me," Nick said, as he downed the rest of his drink. He was alone in New York and he felt flattered that he should have been noticed. It seemed to him to be a curious predicament, but he was not going to be easily deterred.

"So, what did he want?" Nick asked again.

"He wants you to meet him here at five o'clock on Friday. I'd be somewhere else if I were you."

"He appears harmless enough to me."

"Yes, he does, doesn't he?" BJ agreed, as if addressing a child who he hoped would go away and stop asking questions. "So does the Devil, even with the whiff of brimstone." He poured Nick another drink.

"It's on the house," BJ said, in answer to Nick's protests.

"If you advise against my meeting him, then why did you give me the message?" Nick asked, but he well understood that the giving and receiving of messages, and other less savoury information, was one of the true reasons for the bar's success.

BJ shrugged. "It would be a waste of time not to. If Charlie wants to find you, he'll find you, whether I give you the message or not," he said. "It's easier in the long run to do as he asks, but you look like a decent type so I offered a bit extra," he said with a shrug. "Do as you please."

Nick's curiosity was aroused, as if BJ had mentioned a banned book. He finished off his second whiskey. "Tell him that I'll be here on Friday."

"Of course," said BJ. "I knew you would be." He gave a disenchanted smile. "No one ever listens, but then, Charlie has that effect on everyone. Just don't come in here one day, Nick, and say I didn't warn you."

"I never blame other people for my mistakes," Nick said. "It impedes progress and emotional growth." He grinned at BJ. "And besides, it's a total waste of time." Nick took his third drink and went and sat at one of the small, dim booths along the wall. The smoke and the whispered conversations swirled around him. Shadowy couples emerged from, or disappeared into, the smoky air. Laughter was interspersed with the music in a manner that Nick found both erotic and mysterious. The air of the bar seemed both vaguely threatening and full of promise, like the city itself. It felt both dangerous and exciting, as if hope was still out there somewhere, even if a little out of reach.

But Vietnam was bad and the country was angry. There was a kind of menace in the city and, allied with the hope, it created a curious and palpable tension in the town itself and in the bar. Nick imagined that perhaps London had been like this, in 1940 during the Phony War, before the bombs started to drop, or in Berlin in the early '30s when Hitler and his thugs were gathering strength.

A New York bar, Nick had discovered since his recent arrival in the city, was a unique establishment, dedicated to the disenchanted and the disillusioned, full of smoke and sadness, and typified, most characteristically, by the songs of Frank Sinatra like "One more for my baby and one more for the road". Such a place bore no resemblance to the venues with which Nick was more recently familiar, such as Mon Petit Frere in Montparnasse, smart and cheerful with the promise of delicious food, or La Bella Ragazza in Trastevere, full of sunshine and shadows and pretty girls, and even less to an English pub, smelling of beer and spurious camaraderie.

BJ presided with a gloomy and majestic melancholy over a dark hole in a wall on 2nd Avenue, where he dispensed drinks and his own worldly brand of wisdom in roughly equal proportions to a selection of divorcees, disappointed job hunters and men on their way home to unsuccessful marriages from which there was no escape.

The place conveyed an atmosphere that was both hopeful and disillusioned. Nick had discovered it quite by accident on a snowy afternoon earlier in the month on his lonely arrival in New York, and sensed immediately that it would perfectly suit his mood. He understood that BJ himself could provide exactly the companionship he needed. The barman's downbeat humour and philosophic rambling on the condition of the world – not good – were the perfect antidote to the boredom of a lonely city, his own dissatisfaction with his life and his healthy uncertainty and gnawing anxiety about his immediate and for that matter, long term future.

Besides, Nick loved the walk from his apartment at the corner of 79th and Madison. His stroll across town, breathing the icy air, looking at the glittering shop windows, and admiring the sleek Manhattan women gave him, every afternoon, an intense, if vicarious, pleasure. He loved the lighted interior of the automobiles sliding east and west to the expensive hotels and apartment houses, and the look of wealth that these sleek streets exuded with their style and their air of heavy padded luxury.

As Nick was without fame or notoriety and had no money, no one in Manhattan was interested in making his acquaintance. He was merely a part of the flotsam that the New York tide washed in and then, in due course, washed out again. Gone without recognition. Nick was not accustomed to this anonymity. New York, he quickly realized, was not a city in which to be alone.

He knew, on that first afternoon when he had discovered BJ's, that here, among the other losers and dropouts, among those waiting for their divorces and those recovering from them, he would find at least a semblance of the companionship he craved.

Several afternoons a week, BJ himself would listen to Nick's troubles, just as the barman listened, in strict rotation, to the woes of his other customers. It was psychotherapy for the price of a drink. Nick realized immediately that there are not too many bargains in New York, but a good barman is one of them. The place was always packed. It was always warm and always filled with people who really didn't give too much of a damn, at that moment in their lives, for anyone but themselves. From the first day Nick had felt completely at home.

He could not claim that he was a regular BJ confidante. He was too recent a customer for that, but he and the barman had talked on several occasions when BJ had taken the opportunity to expound to Nick on the evils of those who practised the law, particularly if they had failed to make a fortune in such a pursuit, as Nick had so signally failed to do. BJ understood misery well enough, but he was hardly sympathetic to failure. He did not believe for one moment that sympathy was the cure for the ills of his clientele. It was simply good for business, and business was what interested BJ.

He was not running the bar for the good of his health, as he so often stated. BJ's bar was comfortable and it was fun, but it was also dangerous, for it brought together a clientele who were desperate for solutions and none too fussy where they found them. Finishing his drink, and thinking of these matters in the heavy, smoky warmth, Nick eventually hunched back into his greatcoat and went out into the freezing, windy street. He didn't blame BJ for being irritated, but he knew well enough, even then, that no one ever takes advice unless they have already made up their mind to do what is being advised. Charlie looked like a possible interesting friend, and anyway he was quite sure that he could look after himself. He was a lawyer, wasn't he, and thirty-five years old already. He was practically middle-aged, for God's sake! Besides, and more importantly, he recalled noticing that a very beautiful girl often accompanied this Charles Bellamy, and Nick felt that he could do with meeting a beautiful girl. In fact, meeting any girl would be an improvement on his present situation.

Nick hoped that the girl would also be there when he arrived on Friday evening at a little after five. However, although he found Charles Bellamy already waiting, he was alone. He did look patently English, Nick thought, but without that slightly moth-eaten look that so many Englishmen seemed to have in New York. His clothes had a London style about them. They were neither too new, nor yet too shabby, and the trousers were the right length, just breaking on his shoes. He came straight over to Nick, and shook his hand.

"I'm Charlie Bellamy," he said. "And you are Nick Barton, I know. It's whiskey and water, no ice, isn't it?"

Nick nodded. It was the kind of thing, he discovered, that Charlie always made it his business to know. Nick and Charlie sat in one of the dark and scruffy booths that lined the walls of the bar. Sitting opposite Charlie in the darkened booth, Nick felt a sensation similar to that which a man feels when he meets a woman with whom he knows he will fall in love, or at least go to bed. It is a kind of dismal fluttering in the brain, a cerebral warning transmitted to his guts that danger and trouble as well as other, and hopefully more enjoyable, experiences may well be in the offing. There was nothing sexual in the feeling at all, nothing erotic. It was merely his subconscious warning him of difficulties and complications yet to come. He ignored this warning, as most people do.

"You're an Australian lawyer," Charlie said. It was not a question. Nick nodded.

"Australians are amazing," Charlie continued "They are not naïve, or even unsophisticated – far from it, but they have a wonderful aura of innocence about them, as if they are not aware, or at any rate do not admit, that there is anything bad in the world." Charlie sipped his drink and looked around, as if expecting the bar to be full of Aussies who might dispute his opinion.

Nick said nothing. There seemed to him nothing appropriate to say. He did not feel that he was the possessor of any particular aura of innocence, or indeed, an aura of anything else that could be identified as a national trait.

"I suppose that's why they make such good con men," Charlie continued thoughtfully. "A European bent on mischief always so patently looks as if that's exactly what he's up to, and an American simply looks like a crook." He turned away from his perusal of the room and looked straight at Nick.

"Do you think this trait comes from having been founded as a gaol?" he asked. "I always think of Australia as the first gulag, don't you? I really do think, you know, that Australians feel that the world owes them a living. It's a feeling that one never has about America."

"You know Australia fairly well, then?" Nick felt slightly irritated by this critical philosophizing about his country.

"I sure do. I worked there for a couple of years." Charlie grinned rather ruefully. He had an attractive and disarming smile in a face still youthful and free of lines. "I fell in love with a girl a few years back. I followed her out there. We worked together in Sydney for a while. That was in my days as an idealist," he added sourly. "She cured me of that!"

"Ah!"

Yes, of course there would have to be a girl, Nick thought sadly. Somewhere there was always a girl involved. When men were together, particularly in a place like BJ's, there were always the stories of the girls they'd met somewhere, and the trouble that had resulted.

"Is she the one who comes in here with you sometimes?" Nick could easily understand why someone could fall in love with that girl. He was half in love with her himself, and he'd never even met her.

"You mean Laura?" Charlie laughed. "No, no, Laura is from Minnesota, or some such God awful part of America. The Australian girl was quite different. Married. Very ambitious! I was a fool in those days."

Yes, Nick thought dismally. Where women are concerned

perhaps all men are fools.

"It didn't work out, then?" he asked. He was not really interested. He assumed that this had nothing to do with any reason for his having been asked here for a meeting.

Charlie shrugged. "It's a long story. I bought a lottery ticket. It won, but I was out of Sydney, up in the Northern Territory, looking after my Aborigines up there. That's the kind of stuff I did in those days. Stupid, you know! You can't change the world with good intentions."

"Didn't Jesus?" Nick asked.

Charlie laughed again, rather sadly. Nick noticed that he had a habit of laughing at things that were not at all amusing. "So they say, but he had to be martyred to achieve his ends. I don't claim that kind of dedication," he said, "and, besides, it took several hundred years for Christianity to have any effect, and only then when they converted an Emperor and got their hands on some cash. I have no intention of waiting so long for success."

"Is it one of your ambitions to change the world?" Nick was curious. He had never met anyone with such a target in life.

"You know, it was then, it really was, " Charlie said, as if amazed that he could ever have been so foolish. "Anyway, the lottery was quite a bit of money – fifty thousand dollars. She found the ticket and cashed it and stole the prize. Naturally, she never told me any of this. Instead, she reported me to the immigration authorities, and they deported me as an illegal immigrant. She thought that I'd never find out what she'd done."

He signalled BJ to bring over two more drinks. BJ never waited on the tables, but he seemed prepared to do it for Charlie. He had that effect on people.

"I did find out, of course. I always find out everything. Later on I plan to even up that score, when I'm ready to deal a sufficiently lethal blow." He sipped his drink.

"In the meantime, here I was in New York a couple of years ago, in the middle of winter, with no money at all, and with my arse hanging out of my pants." He gazed rather suspiciously around the room, as if to ascertain if he were being followed or overheard. "Fortunately my old Mum happened to be in New York when I was born, which was a bit of luck for me. I have a US passport and so this is where the Immigration people in Australia dumped me."

He took a long swig of his drink, and added philosophically, "It's the best thing my Mum ever did for me, actually. It's so much better here than London. There's more opportunity here. You can do what you like in this place. You can get away with murder in New York."

Nick wondered, in a desultory fashion, whether getting away with murder was another of Charlie's ambitions, along with changing the world. He wondered what kind of home life he must have enjoyed if being born in New York was the best thing he considered his mother had ever done for him.

He sipped his whiskey, and made no comment but he was shocked. Nick had grown up in a household where he had never heard a voice raised in anger, let alone witnessed a dishonest act, or anyway one of which he was aware. *Pas devant les enfants*. Nothing in front of the children had been the rule. Now, sitting there with Charlie in that smoky room, half way around the world from where he had started out, Nick questioned, for the first time, whether such an upbringing had equipped him less well than he had previously realized to cope with the realities of life.

"That's worse than being divorced, in a way," Nick said mildly. "A horrible sort of betrayal, and all that money, too! Jesus Christ!"

For the first time a look of evil passed over Charlie's otherwise bland and handsome face. "Don't worry," he said. "I'll get even with that bitch, when I'm good and ready. But not yet."

"What are you going to do? Sue her?" Nick inquired.

Charlie grinned. "And waste my money on a pack of thieving lawyers? Never do that! There are so many more practical and speedy solutions to life's problems. No, I'm simply going to fuck up her life as she fucked up mine. Only in spades! Do unto others, you know, but do it better! And do it first, if possible!"

"Well, I can see why you come down to BJ's," Nick said.

Charlie looked around contemptuously. "I don't have any time for this bunch of losers," he said sourly, "but I like BJ himself, old cynic that he is, and I like the place. It suits me. Makes me feel good, and I can work here."

"Here? In the bar?" Nick was astonished. "What do you do in New York, then?" Charlie did not look like a millionaire, but he certainly no longer looked like someone who was broke, as he had apparently been when he arrived.

"Buy and sell. It's the only way to make a buck, really."

Nick looked at him with some admiration. He wondered how he would have made out in similar circumstances, without skills or resources in a strange, tough town. Not well, he thought. Not well at all. Even with such skills as he did possess, he wasn't doing at all well.

"Well," Nick said cheerfully, "it seems that you've been screwed even more than most of the people who come here."

"Yes," Charlie agreed with a small, private smile. "But I don't regret it. It taught me a few lessons that I needed to learn. Now I am a disillusioned idealist. I think it's not such a bad thing to be these days. You know, I used to believe in the kindness of women, and the sweetness of babies, and the amiability of a nice dog, in the essential goodness of mankind, and in doing some good in the world."

He leaned back and lit a cigarette, blowing expert smoke rings into the already thick air. "It's kind of sad, isn't it, the stuff they teach us to start out with in life? All so utterly useless when it comes to the crunch and real life accidentally crops up."

Nick reluctantly admitted to himself that it did not seem to have equipped him very adequately for some of the realities he had recently encountered.

"So what do you believe in now?" he asked Charlie. "Have you given up on the idea of reforming the world?"

"Not entirely. I still think the world needs a good kick in the arse, but I am revising my plans on how it can be achieved. I find that I must have a power base." He grinned. "You may be sure that I don't intend for something like that ever to happen to me again. No, sir! Power and revenge. The latter, I think, has amazing motivational strength. Then I shall reform the world, but I shall do it from the top down and not from the bottom up."

He spoke quite calmly, without a trace of anger or emotion, as if he were reciting a text he had read somewhere and by which he had been impressed, like how to get rich quick, or how to make friends and influence people. Some such rubbish. There was nothing violent in his tone, but Nick felt a small shiver of apprehension travel down his spine.

"How do you intend to get this power?" he asked.

Charlie grinned again. "Money, of course. Is there any other way?"

"There is nothing very original about that," Nick said. "Most men's lives are fuelled by greed – or lust!"

"Or despair," Charles said.

"You know that old BJ here warned me against you?"

"Yes, I suppose he would do that, but I didn't think that

you'd pay any attention. He doesn't trust me at all, you know. He thinks I'm up to no good."

"And are you?"

"What do you think?"

Nick shrugged. "I've come here for the meeting, haven't I?" he said. "What is it you wanted to talk to me about?"

Charlie leaned back, and watched Nick as he spoke. "You're a lawyer," he said, "but in spite of that, somehow you still have that wonderful look of innocence I was talking about earlier, that only Australia seems to produce. No lawyer in America or Europe has that. It's too old and too violent a world over here – too many bodies in the closet. And you're not a fool, in spite of being broke ..."

Nick interrupted. "That's easy enough to explain."

Charlie held up his hand. "Yes, yes. There's no need to get defensive! Men getting divorced are always broke. You don't need to explain. I know all about you!"

Nick relaxed for the first time in the meeting, and laughed. "Don't bullshit me, Charlie. How could you know all about me? We've never even met before."

Charlie again grinned his attractive, rather wolfish grin. "You don't suppose I'd have asked to meet you here to talk business before I checked you out, did you? Good God, I'd be dead in five minutes if I went about things in that way."

"Checked me out? That's pretty offensive." Nick started to stand up. "I'm beginning to think that maybe BJ is right. I don't think I need to know any more about this."

"Sit down and hear me out and don't be a bigger damned fool than you've been already," Charlie said roughly. "You're here to get a divorce. You can't work in the US because you don't have a green card. You've left your kids behind in Europe, where your wife is sitting on a pile of money that your pride won't let you touch." Charlie leaned back in the booth and looked straight at his companion.

"If you don't pull your finger out, mate, you'll be back in Australia again, starting from scratch, and that will be the last you'll see of your children. If you can't keep up financially, they'll just drift away into another world – one in which you won't be able to afford to compete at all. In fact, a world to which you won't even have access. And let me tell you something else," he added brutally, "you'll never make any serious money by yourself. You're not the type. You don't believe in it enough, and you're not sufficiently ruthless."

"And you can help me with these problems?" Nick asked angrily, but he settled back into his seat. "Why should you bother to do that?"

He might be as innocent as Charlie kept telling him he was, but he had learned enough to know that there were no gifts in the world. The lunch was never free, as they said in this town, and they ought to know.

"I've told you already, you can be very useful to me. You've a skilled mind and you're a lawyer. You're here on the spot where I need you, and you're hungry. It's serendipitous, and I believe in that kind of fate. Do you believe in fate?"

"Didn't the Greeks?"

"They said that character is fate, and so it is, I think," Charlie said. "Are you willing to listen to a proposition then, or are you going to plod off on your own virtuous way, and fall flat on your face? You've only one life, you know, Nick, no matter what they tell you, and it doesn't last forever. How many more mistakes do you think you can afford before you're destitute – or dead?"

"You don't pull any punches, do you?"

Charlie shrugged. "I tell it like it is. I used to be just like you, you know. I'll bet we were brought up on the same nursery stories." He waved his hand at the crowded and murky room. "But the world, as even you may have observed, is not full of polite, nice people, you know, sweet babies and rubicund old men with rosy cheeks, and little kids with Pooh Bears and Christopher Robin saying his prayers, like we were taught by Nanny and Granny and Mumsie to believe. Largely it's full of ruthless, dishonest shits. You either settle for what you've got, which in your case isn't much, or you fight on their turf, which means forgetting the crap you were raised on – or you lose the battle. Well?"

It would be impossible, ever afterwards, for Nick to plead innocence. He knew very well, right at that moment, that if he did not get up and leave, he would be walking across a line that he would never again be able to re-cross. And he knew, too, right then and with an absolute certainty, that he was going to cross the line. He was old enough and clever enough to know that life offers very few second chances.

"Very well. What do you want me to do?" he asked. He could feel his heart begin to pound in his chest with a dull, hard thud. He suddenly felt alive as he had not felt in weeks – maybe in years.

"You are going shortly to Juarez for your divorce. You'll fly to El Paso and a limousine will ferry you across the Mexican border to the courthouse in Juarez. After the case is heard, it will ferry you back to the airport or the hotel in the good old US of A. Right?"

Nick nodded. "That's what my lawyer tells me."

"I have a suitcase in Juarez which I want brought back. I can arrange for it to be in the trunk of your limousine. The border police know those cars, and they never search them."

"What's in the suitcase? If it's drugs, then the answer is no. I'm not such a fool as that!"

"Nothing will be in it except some valuable family possessions. I want to test different methods of bringing a suitcase into the States. I assure you that the customs never worry about the cars that cross for the divorces. They know them all, and I guess they think that you poor bastards have enough troubles already. I've checked it all out."

"And what can you do for me that would make the risk worthwhile? After all, whatever's in the suitcase, I would be breaking the law."

"Something which lawyers never do, of course," Charlie said sourly. "Shit! The hypocrisy of your profession never ceases to amaze me. My Dad was a country solicitor in Devon. He was a sanctimonious old crap artist!"

Charlie suddenly leant forward across the narrow table, and took Nick's arm in a vice-like grip. "I'll tell you what I can do for you! I can get you a green card, and I can give you a job with me that will keep you out of the gutter, and earn you enough to see your kids in Europe occasionally, and even maybe to have a decent life for yourself. Has anyone else made you a comparable offer?"

He let go of Nick's arm, and leant back in his seat. "For Chrissake, what else do you want, Nick? A lifetime guarantee of safety? You're proud and you're broke, but you're not a fool. All of that is a bad combination for you." He grinned malevolently " But it's perfect for me."

Nick looked around the dim, smoke-filled room. He looked for the first time into the sad and disillusioned eyes of the patrons, at their desperation, at the shabby saloon, and the worn-out clothes of the customers, and he felt again the mood of hopelessness that permeated the air. He knew that if he fell into that he would not know what to do about it. He would not survive.

Charlie was right. He would lose his children, because he would never be able to compete with the world in which they lived, and he would end up looking straight up the arsehole of the world from underneath. He did not relish the prospect of such a view. It was not the view of the world that he had anticipated seeing when he had started out, and he had no intention of settling for such a prospect now.

He recalled what his father always said when sitting down at the table for a game of poker: "Remember, it's not the fellow who wins at the beginning of the game who goes home with the money – it's the fellow who wins at the end." Life, he thought, was turning out to be not unlike a game of poker.

He reached out his hand to Charlie. "Okay," he said. "It's a deal, but how do I know I can trust you?"

Charlie shook his hand. "You don't," he said, "but it's an instinct you'll develop if you work for me. After all, everything in life is a gamble. You could be dead tomorrow. Lots of people will be."

"And how do you know you can trust me?" Nick asked.

Charlie laughed. "You have an honest face," he said. "It's going to be invaluable."

He stood up to leave. His blonde hair shone bright as a flag under the harsh glare from BJ's strip lighting along the ceiling. Nick wondered rather enviously from where this marvellous confidence came, this sureness with the world, this aura of invincible success that Charlie seemed to possess. He wondered if he would ever possess it, if he would ever be able to walk with such ease with his fellow men and to feel so comfortable among them.

Charlie looked at him and laughed again, as if he could read Nick's thoughts. "It's all bluff, Nick. It's all bluff. The fools see what they want to see, if you put it there in front of their nose. You must simply work out what it is they want to see and then show it to them, whether it's there or not."

"And what about the girl?" Nick asked.

"What girl?"

"The one who comes in here occasionally with you – Laura, you said?"

Charlie put his arm around Nick, and pulled him close. "You don't want to get involved with that," he said quietly. "You'll do no good there. Laura wants to be an actress. She won't look at you."

"She looks at you."

"Ah, yes, my friend! But I saw her first." He looked at Nick and shrugged.

"But if you want to meet her, what the hell! I suppose it will be this woman or another that you'll make a fool of yourself over, sooner or later." He shrugged himself into his heavy overcoat, and pulled a woollen cap down over his ears.

"I'll tell you what. I'll bring her in here one afternoon. Don't say I didn't warn you if you burn your fingers. If I were you, Nick, I'd put the money in the bank first. Once you've made enough money, you can have a thousand Lauras. You can have anything you want."

Nick shook his head. "A thousand girls, maybe, but I have a feeling about this one, Charlie. I think maybe she's unique."

Charlie looked at him sadly. "Shit, Nick, isn't that what you thought the last time you fell in love? And the time before that? Isn't that what we all think, every time, with every new girl? Just stick to making money, my friend, and buy what you want. Take my advice – if it flies, floats or fucks, rent it! It's much safer."

"Even people?"

"Especially people."

He gave a wave with his hand to BJ. "I'll be in touch," he

called from the door, and disappeared into the snowy gloom of 2nd Avenue. Inside the bar, Nick thought, it seemed as if a bright light had suddenly gone out.

CHAPTER TWO

NEW YORK, N.Y.
1967

"Nick is already in love with you," Charlie said to Laura as they sat down in a booth in the shadowy rear of the bar, where all the lovers sat. "He's seen you in here before, with me."

"Cut it out, Charlie." Nick felt a hot rush of blood to his face. He felt a fool. He had not blushed since he was twelve and his pants had fallen down in the street.

Laura looked him over critically and coolly, and quite clearly found him wanting. He was absolutely and obviously not what she was seeking at that particular time of her life, but she was a kind girl, properly brought up by her Swedish parents in Minnesota, and she could not be brutal. She had noticed his blush, and had been touched by it. She did not meet many men in New York who still blushed.

Laura Bergman had arrived in New York with the fresh beauty of her Scandinavian heritage and with all the belief in her own destiny that any pretty girl from Minnesota should have when she's been considered the most popular and successful girl in college; when she has received the award for the best amateur actress on the campus, and when she has been adored by her father and her brother, and admired by every guy she's come in contact with, and never in her life heard an unkind or defamatory remark. She knew that she could not fail, and that was how she looked and how she walked when she arrived.

She had met Charles Bellamy that first winter, in 1965, when they were both new in town and lonely, and when she still had the dew fresh upon her, and her face was like a flower, waiting to be picked. Laura had believed, that first winter, that nothing else but this invincible belief in herself would be necessary for success; that it was all there in the wings, breathlessly waiting for her to arrive.

Now, two years later, on the evening in early March when she came with Charlie to BJ's to meet Nick as had been promised, her beauty was more defined, sharper and more arresting than it had been when she had first arrived in New York, supremely confident in her own talent to amaze. Now she no longer looked like a girl fresh from college. She was a girl who'd been in New York for two years, and knew her way around. But the beautiful and arrogant assurance, the sure confidence of that earlier girl who had believed the world would roll over and succumb to her charms, was no longer there in her eyes or in her walk. Instead there was a touch of vulnerability, a small loss of faith, a yearning, perhaps, for the innocence that she had lost, and all of this made her both lovelier and sadder than that other younger girl who had now disappeared.

It meant that she was learning what the world could be like, how cruel and careless it could be if one wished to mount that perilous and treacherous ladder to the top. Beauty, Laura now understood, would not be enough. There were many lovely girls in Manhattan. Talent would not be enough, unless it was unique and outstanding and combined with a steely determination to succeed at any cost, and to pay whatever price was necessary in a ruthless world. You could pave the streets of Manhattan with talented young kids from the provinces waiting to be discovered. Most of them went home.

The knowledge that she might not have the necessary talent or beauty she might have been able to accept, but the possibility that she lacked the necessary determination, the required streak of steel in her soul, disturbed her deeply and undermined that otherwise certain faith.

The change was subtle and, of course, it passed unnoticed by Nick who had not known her in that earlier and more hopeful time. Charlie, however, knew and clearly understood that she was now both tougher and more desperate than she had been two years earlier, less sure of herself, less arrogant and more ready to take risks she would not then have considered necessary or advisable. This suited his purpose admirably. All his life Charlie had always known, by some subtle and mysterious instinct, the moment when people had become sufficiently desperate to be bent to his own purposes.

Laura sat between the two men and ordered a white wine spritzer. She had seen Nick's blush and to compensate for the fact that she had no interest in him, she smiled brilliantly into his eyes. She did not like to upset anyone if she could help it.

"I don't know why Charlie comes here," she said to Nick. "It kind of makes me feel gloomy."

"Why is that?" Nick asked.

"Look at their faces," Laura said. "So sad, all of them!"

"I come here," Charlie said, "because I can meet people like Nick – and you, too. Remember, Laura, this is where we met when we were both down and out."

"Speak for yourself," she said. "I was not down and out. I was just poor and starting out. It's quite a different thing, isn't it, Nick?"

Nick agreed that it was quite a different thing.

She gave Charles a shrewd look. "But yes, you're right!

You come here to find people who are desperate, so they can be useful to you when you're ready to use them."

Charlie shrugged. "Isn't that what we all do? And I can be useful to them, too. It's two-way traffic here. Given your choice, you'd be at some bar full of producers and casting directors."

"That's called networking," she said, but she had too much humour not to smile.

"It's called meeting people who can be useful, and getting to know them in case they can be used at some future date," he said. "Let's call a spade a spade, at least between ourselves."

"Fair enough, Charlie darling," she agreed, pleasantly enough. "But there's no need to call it a fucking shovel. We're only doing what everyone else is doing."

"And that, of course, makes it okay, I suppose? To do what everyone else is doing, and to call it by some trendy name?"

"For Chrissake, Charlie," Laura said irritably. "Let's not have one of your philosophical evenings."

She turned to Nick. The smoke swirled around them in the golden, lamp-lit air, and the booth smelled of bourbon and tobacco, of hot leather against hot bodies and old romances that had long gone sour; of cheap scent and sweat, a smell that was on the edge of despair. Nick wondered why he hadn't noticed it before.

Somewhere up the front of the long room a girl with a high, sweet confident voice was singing "Up, up and away in my beautiful balloon" to the accompaniment of the old upright piano which BJ kept near the bar and occasionally allowed his favourite customers to use.

"Charlie says you're here to be divorced. That's too bad," Laura said. "I'm never going to be divorced."

"First it's necessary to be married," Charlie said.

"Up yours, too, darling." She turned back to Nick. "Are you staying in New York, then?"

"Maybe," Nick said. "Charlie is going to offer me a job."

A swift, warning glance, subtle as a moth's wing, passed between Charlie and the girl, but nevertheless all she said was, "Is that wise, do you think?"

"Wise? Why not? I need the money and he says he needs me. It could be a perfect fit."

Laura glanced again at Charlie, another warning, enigmatic glance. "We know he always knows what he wants," she said. "But surely this is a question of what you want."

"What I want?" Nick repeated the words on a note of some surprise.

He didn't suppose, now that he thought of it, that anyone in his whole life had ever asked that question of him. He father had told him what he should want. His wife had told him what she did want, and his children had merely asked for him to be there and to love them, a task at which he considered he was currently not succeeding very well. Nick had never considered what it was that he himself might want. So far, it seemed to him that he had spent his life meeting other people's expectations.

He looked at Laura. "Do you know what it is that you want?"

"Oh, yes, that's easy. I want to be a wonderful actress, and to be as famous as Marilyn Monroe and Jackie O combined."

"Well, that shouldn't be hard. You are more beautiful than either. You are younger than Jackie, and Marilyn's dead, so she shouldn't give you too much competition. How about you, Charlie?"

The girl at the bar was now singing "They're singing songs of love, but not for me" in her sad and haunting contralto, reminiscent of Polly Bergen's wonderful rendition of the same song, the words dipping and swaying around the room full of people who knew only too well that the love songs were not for them, but who had still not entirely lost hope. Nick remembered the same song from Italy, Venice, perhaps? The Lido? Listening now to that song in this sad and smoky room made him determined that he would never be as vulnerable again as he had been then, no matter what he might have to do.

Charlie said, "I want to be the richest man in America, maybe in the whole world – and to stay out of gaol, of course. That's where Nick will come in. He will provide the respectable façade that I shall need."

"Modest ambitions, both of you," Nick said.

"And you, then, Nick," Laura demanded. "You still haven't told us what you want."

"Well, I suppose what I want is to be a free man."

They all laughed. "Well," Charlie said, "you're the only one at this table who doesn't stand even a chance of success."

Laura reached across the table suddenly and put her hand on top of Nick's where it lay on the tabletop. She flicked her eyes in the direction of Charlie's handsome, laughing face under the mop of shining blonde hair.

"Are you sure you're tough enough for all of this?" she asked softly. "You do know what our debonair corsair does, don't you?"

"Oh, yes, sure," Nick said. "He buys and sells." She gave him a quizzical look but said nothing further.

"You know," Charlie said, "it would not surprise me if, one day, Nick succeeds more than any of us. He has that look about him, don't you think, Laura? The look of the successful martyr? The genuinely concerned and harassed modern man?"

Laura put her hand out to Nick again. "Don't tease him too much, Charlie. I have a feeling that one day you might get more than you bargained for from Nick."

"Oh, I always get more than I've bargained for," Charlie said casually. "And so will Nick, I hope – one day soon."

Some afternoons, over the next few weeks, Laura came alone to the bar. If Nick was there they would sit together in one of the dark and intimate booths at the back of the bar, listening to one of BJ's cronies play the piano and sing the songs of the day. Laura did not drink much, as she was saving her skin for better things.

"Alcohol will give me veins on my nose," she said.

"You will be so rich and famous by then it won't matter."

She shrugged. "It will always matter," she said. "Out there, it's a jungle, didn't you know?" She laughed as if she enjoyed the thought of that jungle which awaited her.

Nick was lonely. He was in a strange town where he knew no one and he missed the life he had recently had, which had gone and was as irrecoverable as life at Versailles. It was a life he knew would never come again, because he would never again be as young and trusting as he had once been. He missed his children and he was very vulnerable. He told Laura one afternoon that he was falling in love with her.

"Please don't," she said. "I'm not the right girl for you. I'm much too tough for you, my darling Nick, but I'll tell you what I do know. I know that one day I am going to need a friend, and I'll count on you to be the one who will save me when I do."

"There will always be plenty of people to save you," he said. "The world will be full of them."

She shrugged, a very worldly gesture on her young shoulders. "The higher you climb the harder you fall," she said laconically. "There are not always people to save you when they're needed, particularly if you're falling from a very high perch. They are more inclined to push than to save! No, Nick, you will be the one."

Nick laughed uncertainly. He knew it would come to nothing, and that Laura did not want a man with no money and no influence. She did not want a man who was burdened down with all the excess emotional baggage that he was already dragging behind him. He also knew, in the way men know these things, that he would be a little in love with her all his life, unrequited or not, and no matter what she did, he knew that this love would be important to him in a way that it would never matter to her. There would be someone else for her, one day, who would fulfill that role and provide her with the anguish that would form her life.

"I'm in love with Charlie, I suppose," she told him one afternoon. "God help me! That bitch in Australia seems to have screwed him up for good, and all he cares about now is money, money, money – and getting his revenge. He certainly doesn't intend to hitch himself to anyone as unimportant as me. There's no future with Charlie, but I can't help it."

"No," Nick agreed. "One never can. I wonder why?"

All this took place during the sad afternoons while Nick was waiting to hear from his lawyers about the divorce in Juarez. While they talked in the dim and dubious shadows of BJ's, the New York spring gathered its beauty and its excitement all around them, like a magic cloak, and Charlie, secretly and quite unknown to either of them, held his first meetings with Sebastian Ventura y Cortez in a café over in Brooklyn, away from anyone he might know. He had no wish that anyone should see him with Sebastian Ventura, who was a dangerous man, and already notorious.

Finally, the journey to Juarez came around and Nick headed down at the end of April, briefed by his lawyer in New

York. He flew into El Paso to wait until his case was called, and then crossed over the bridge into the seedy Mexican splendor of Juarez in the limousine that had been organized for him. It all worked exactly as Charlie had told him that it would, and when he came out from the courtroom into the blazing Mexican sunshine, the driver gave him a big wink, and nodded to the cases which were now in the trunk of the car – two of them, Nick noted, not one – battered and heavy old leather cases, covered with faded labels from Nice and Monte Carlo and Capri and Venice. They looked as if someone's parents had taken them on their honeymoon in the '20s.

When Nick returned to his apartment in New York, he rang Charlie and told him to come around and collect the suitcases. He was not pleased. The cases were heavy, and had cost him more than one hundred dollars in excess baggage, in spite of the fact that he had travelled first class.

Charlie climbed the stairs up to the first floor of the old house on Madison at 79th Street to Nick's rented rooms, and breezed into the apartment with his usual sunny good humour and his wide and cheerful smile. He looked around with disgust at the shabby room and the awful furniture, and the sofas covered in stained black corduroy velvet.

"Jesus, Nick! Don't tell me that you can persuade influential and desirable girls to come up here."

"Influential, no," Nick said. "But occasionally I can persuade one who is fun."

"It's no use wasting your time on girls who are fun in this town," Charlie said. "You'll never get anywhere that way. First you must get rich, and then you must have an influential wife, and then you can have all the fun girls you could ever need. I see you have my suitcases."

"And you owe me a hundred dollars for excess baggage charges. Hell, Charlie, you said there would only be one case, and they weigh a ton. What've you got in these bags for Chrissake? Gold bricks?"

"Something much more useful to both of us than that, my friend. Cocaine." He held out two fifty-dollar notes.

Nick took the money and laughed. "Oh, sure, Charlie, and I suppose you've got the English Crown Jewels as well. You told me just personal stuff, no drugs. Just a test run, you said."

Charlie grinned. "Quite so, but surely you didn't believe me, Nick? Even you can't be quite so naive. A bad mistake! But no Crown Jewels. Those we don't need, at least not just yet. Just the cocaine."

"You're kidding me?"

Charlie shrugged. "I never kid about things like money, Nick. Open them and see."

He threw a bunch of keys across the room to Nick, who opened one of the cases. It was full of little plastic bags, which were filled with a white powder, which he supposed was what Charlie said it was.

"Fucking hell, Charlie," Nick shouted. He felt the blood rushing to his face and he was very angry, but he also felt that sinking feeling which told him he could not fool himself, and that he had really always known that the suitcases contained drugs, or at any rate something equally suspect.

Nevertheless he said, "I'm a respectable lawyer, for Chrissake, Charles, and an honest man! I could be in gaol now if they'd found this stuff in the car."

"Oh, stuff it up your arse, Nick," Charlie said with a small laugh. "There is no such thing as a respectable lawyer and an honest man. You don't suppose I would believe you if you tried to tell me that you had no idea what you were doing."

"Of course I had no idea," Nick lied. "Do you imagine that I'd get mixed up in a thing like this?"

"So innocent and so convincing," Charlie said admiringly, looking at him with a mocking expression. "Didn't I tell you that you would be just perfect, Nick. You could fool anybody."

"You don't imagine that I'm going ahead with all this, do you?"

Charlie sighed loudly. "Too late, Nick, too late! Of course I imagine it. You no longer have any choice in that matter. All I need to do is to pick up the phone and call the police, and you will be in gaol for the next twenty years."

Nick stared at him. "You don't suppose they would believe you?" he asked. At this time Nick still believed that the police would be interested in truth, justice and the American way.

Charlie laughed nastily. "You are a penniless, jobless tourist in a grubby, cheap apartment, with no apparent means of support. Of course they would believe me." He walked over to the window and looked down into the dreary courtyard at the rear of the building.

"In any case, I pay them a considerable amount of money every month to make sure they believe everything I say. You would have a lot of trouble proving yourself innocent. Or," he reached into his pocket and brought out a small but very lethal-looking revolver that he pointed casually in Nick's direction, "I could simply shoot you, and save you all the trouble of trying to defend yourself against police who are being paid by me. If I were you, I think the bullet would be preferable and more pleasant. A pretty young chap like you wouldn't do too well in an American gaol, unless you fancy constant sexual intercourse with a lot of very unattractive guys. Besides, it would be an awful waste, Nick, after all the trouble I've taken, and when I think how useful you're going to be."

Nick stared at the small gun. The fact that it had been produced so casually, and was being held so professionally, convinced him that Charlie would have no difficulty in using it. For the first time in his life he felt afraid. It was a steely, cold curdling feeling in his guts, which sank down into his testicles. It was a feeling of which he felt deeply ashamed, as it melted his bowels, and he felt that any moment he would shit his pants. It seemed somehow to emasculate and diminish him.

He knew then that he had acted like a fool, and more than that, he knew without doubt that he had understood from the beginning that this was not a legitimate deal. He understood clearly that he had been persuaded by greed and laziness to do what Charlie had asked, and had simply hoped that it would be okay.

Charlie stood across the room, still casually holding the gun and smiling the same bland and handsome smile which he displayed to BJ down at the bar. In spite of his fear, Nick said, "Just because one woman has screwed you around, are you going to take it out on the rest of the world?" He was surprised that his voice appeared normal, surprised in fact that any sound at all issued from his throat.

"No, Nick, not quite. Ten years ago, I started out to try and do a bit of good in a world that I thought then was pretty shitty. I ended up in gaol, deported and penniless, and treated by all and sundry like a piece of worthless trash. That is never going to happen again. Nevertheless, I am going to change the world. It's just that I now understand, as you will come to understand, that money is the only weapon, not goodwill or youth or faith or belief. Certainly not goodness. Simply power."

"You're crazy as a snake," Nick said.

Charlie laughed out loud, a free and carefree laugh as if he were at a funny movie downtown.

"Sticks and stones, Nick," he said. "You'll find out soon enough that this is the way to settle all your scores, I can assure you."

"And what about all the kids who'll die to make your fortune?"

"Oh, come on, Nick, don't tell me you're a bleeding heart? Do you imagine that it's kids who buy my very expensive cocaine and heroin? They are all on some far more dangerous and cheaper rubbish, I can assure you, and none of that cheap shit is supplied by me. I may have many faults, but hanging around school gates is not one of them!"

He moved around the room and looked with some distaste at the stained sofa before choosing a small chair and sat down.

"And what about the kids who are killed in stupid wars, like Vietnam, sent there by Kennedy and Johnson?" he asked. "I won't kill that many kids in ten lifetimes, and in the end I'll do better than either of those two hypocrites – or any other politician. Have you any idea what the world trade in drugs is worth?"

Nick shook his head. "Fifty million dollars?"

"One hundred billion last year. By the end of the century it will be four or five hundred billion dollars – all tax-free. You can buy a lot of protection with that kind of dough. You can buy anyone or anything in the world, and you can make any dream come true, Nick. So, are you joining me, or do I use my gun and leave you here with the blowflies and the mice?"

Nick looked at Charlie, so debonair, so carefree, so clever and so crazy, and knew with absolute certainty that if he refused now he would be shot. He decided that, for the time being, he had no alternative other than to agree. Later, he thought, when this crisis is over, there will be time to think about how to get out, but not now.

"Will you keep your side of the bargain, then?" Nick asked.

"A green card? A job with me? Sure, Nick. I always keep my side of the bargain. It's the secret of my success, and while you work for me, you will always do the same."

He glanced down at the suitcases lying on the floor. "It might be some consolation to your wounded and outraged conscience, Nick, if I tell you that this lot is worth around two million on the street, and your share is 10 percent."

He put the pistol away in his jacket pocket and looked up at Nick. "That's two hundred thousand dollars for you, my friend. Not bad for an afternoon's work! And while we're on the subject, I'd use some of it to get a decent apartment, if I were you."

He stretched out his foot and flipped the suitcase lid closed.

"If you're going to work on the wrong side of the law, you need to look very respectable indeed. Perfect clothes, perfect background, which we can arrange, and a perfect address. I must say that at least you already look respectable, Nick. That's a start. Now you must also look prosperous. I'd suggest Park Avenue, or something nice on Central Park South, around the corner from the Plaza, or maybe Beekman Place. You can't stay here, in this dump. We'll move you into the Pierre this afternoon, I think."

Nick remembered that his mother had said never to plan for the future, for life can turn on a penny. He wished, for a moment, that she were still around to see this particular turn. In a way he almost felt that she might approve, but then she had always been a gambler. Am I a gambler too, Nick wondered, or am I just a fool?

"I don't have the faintest idea what to do with this stuff," Nick said, pointing at the suitcases on his floor.

"Of course you don't, my dear chap. That's not your

department at all. You're in charge of investment, Nick. You think up the foolproof schemes. You will be the legitimate side of our partnership. Tomorrow I will introduce you to our corporate lawyers, and you can start from there. You will see to it that our affairs are always strictly kosher, my friend. Then a substantial gift from you to ... perhaps the New York City Ballet? The Metropolitan Opera? A very respectable and socially prominent charity? It's not hard, in this town, to establish your credentials if you have money, and a few good manners. I suggest that you give it some immediate thought. After all, you're my ambassador."

The following week, Nick moved from the Hotel Pierre into an apartment at 555 Park Avenue, and the meetings were held with Charlie's lawyers that set in motion the formation of the companies that Nick would manage and expand.

CHAPTER THREE

NEW YORK, N.Y.
JULY 1969

CHARLES BELLAMY WAS 32 years old on that hot summer afternoon, two years after he had recruited Nick, when he walked along Central Park South on his way to visit Laura in her apartment on W 68th Street. He had the style of a duke, and the looks of a film star, and he now exuded an aura of prosperity. It was a powerful combination. Already he had about him a slight look of disillusionment and a touch of ruthlessness that was foreign to so young a man in those easy and careless years. This served only to enhance, rather than to spoil, his otherwise certain attraction, redeeming him from looking like just another pretty and successful young man around the town.

To his right, in the park, the trees hung heavy and dark green with the weight of their summer burden and the New York humidity. They were, Charles thought, like the heavy hearts of women disillusioned in love. A faint haze of dust and heat softened the harsh shine of the late afternoon sun. Lined up against the wide entrance to Central Park opposite the side entrance to the Plaza, a line of carriages stood, with sleepy drivers snoozing under umbrellas while their listless horses flicked their tails at flies. They waited patiently for tourists who rested instead in the cool of air conditioned hotel rooms, too exhausted to ride in the park.

He turned the corner and made his way north to Laura's apartment house, where he trudged irritably up the four narrow and grubby flights leading to her apartment, cursing the heat of the July afternoon, and the fact that the building had no elevator, and no cooling. Charles hated Laura's apartment building. It was hot and grubby and it smelt of poverty – of overcooked food and under-loved people. Poverty, he knew, had its own special smell of defeat and disillusionment. And fear, too. He knew that smell from his first days in New York, and he understood that it could undermine the hopes of even the strongest if they sniffed it for too long. It was like some potent and addictive drug that pulled one down instead of lifting up, and it drained the energy and the initiative from even the healthiest and most active contestants in life's little play. Charles feared the smell of poverty as he feared nothing else in life.

Over the years since they had met, he and Laura had been occasional lovers, in the manner of their generation and their promiscuous and careless decade. They met now and then, without commitment, to make love on those nights when they believed they might console each other for the moments of quiet desperation in their lives. More importantly, and perhaps rarer in New York, they had become friends. They saw each other when neither of them had anything better lined up, or more important to undertake, and they dealt honestly with each other, according to their perceptions of the matter. None of this, however, prevented Charles from planning to use her when the time came, as he had always known that he would, and as he used everyone in his own desperate march to success.

With Laura, that something more important than making love with Charlie had by now come to mean not the theatre, nor her work as an actress, nor the meeting of agents and producers, those matters which had occupied her time when she first arrived in New York. These days that something more important meant having a date with a man whose money or position impressed her, or who could help her to escape the ever-present fear of losing her youth and looks without having achieved something adequate by way of compensation; the fear, simply, of having to return home and admit that she had failed. Having come painfully to terms with her current lack of success, Laura was now digging for gold in a more old fashioned manner. She was looking for a rich husband. To date, so far as Charles was aware, she had enjoyed little success. Plenty of takers for the bed but none for any arrangement more permanent, and certainly no lavish check writers in sight, nor any diamond rings. Hence the terrible apartment.

New York ate up kids like her for breakfast, and spat them out, and once they were spat out, most of them didn't look too good any longer. They went home to wherever they had come from, and settled down and married the boy next door whom they had gone to New York to escape, if he were still available. Laura was determined that this would not be her fate, although there was a nice boy waiting for her back in Minnesota. There usually was a nice boy waiting for these girls back home somewhere, half hoping that New York would defeat them and they would return home and settle for a cottage and two kids and a Chevy in the driveway.

After four years in town, Laura understood very clearly that she was no longer new and fresh by New York standards. She had lost that first wonderful bloom, that first fresh magic which makes the new girls a little different, and now there was a whole new batch of younger, fresher and maybe prettier or more talented girls pushing along from behind, and more arriving daily.

No. Laura was no longer a pretty ingénue, Charlie thought, as he grimly mounted the stairs to her apartment in the hot afternoon, but something less, and something very much more. Less successful than she had anticipated but more beautiful, less hopeful but more mature, sadder certainly, but less vulnerable and far more worldly. Tougher too and, Charles sensed and hoped, altogether more desperate. That would be perfect for his own plans. That was what he had been waiting for. It was as if fate had been keeping her waiting in the wings just for him, for the perfect moment to use her beauty and her intelligence to his own advantage. For hers, too, of course, although that was a consideration of infinitely less importance. It always was, with Charles.

He let himself in with the key she allowed him to keep, and he discovered her in the bedroom, at the moment of disillusioned but realistic assessment of herself that every woman experiences as she stares into her looking glass. She was expertly applying lipstick to her mouth, which she now held up like a flower for his inspection and enjoyment, and to be kissed.

"Charlie! How nice! What brings you here so early in the evening?" She was pleased to see him. She was always pleased to see him, for he made few demands on her and had never before offered her anything but light-hearted praise and jocular approval.

"It's fucking hot up here!" Charles looked around with disapproval at the peeling walls and sad paintwork of the bedroom walls.

"So sweet you always are, Charlie darling! The fan's on in the sitting room. There's a beer in the icebox if you want. Why don't you wait in there?"

"No, thanks. I came by to ask you out to dinner."

"You might have called first to see if I were free."

She was always slightly piqued by his assumption, whenever he felt like seeing her, that she would have nothing better to do. "As you see, I am already engaged for dinner." She was wearing a pink pin-tucked satin cocktail dress, and some fake pearls.

"Well, you can disengage," he said, flinging himself onto

the bed and taking off his shoes. "You wouldn't want to be seen anywhere decent in that dress, anyway."

"I paid $125 for this at Filene's," Laura said. "It's a Dior copy!"

"Well, it looks like shit on you," he said, thoughtfully. "I thought you had better taste than that!"

She shrugged. "I don't dress to please myself," she said.

She was accustomed to his insults, thrown at her rather in the mode of an interested but critical younger brother who was fond of her and wished her no harm. She knew that his remarks were not meant seriously to disturb her equilibrium. It was too hot, anyway, to get into a state about his customary and all too familiar brusqueness.

"And what moron have you managed to unearth who would want you to wear something which suits you so little?" He continued to lie flat on her bed, gazing at the ceiling, as if he would find her future, or perhaps his own, inscribed there, clear and uncomplicated, drawn like some map among the cracks and lines in the old and stained plaster.

"I am going to have dinner with Freddie Hartington," she said, and then added, "the third," as if to impress him further.

"Ah! Well that explains it, but why waste your time? Freddie is a genuine arsehole, and you know it as well as I do. He's the type of man who has pimples on his butt."

"How would you know? Have you seen his butt? I didn't think you were into that kind of thing."

"Don't have to see it," Charlie said laconically. "What a horrible thought! I know the type. Pudgy, unhealthy, pimples on his buns underneath those Brooks Brothers suits; probably doesn't wash properly, either. You fucking him?"

"It's none of your damned business," she said. She continued calmly to apply her makeup. She would not permit him to annoy her on this sultry evening.

"So!" he said morosely. "You're fucking him! He'll never marry you, you know. He's the kind that fucks all the new young girls around town, and makes them promises." He gave her a penetrating look.

"Ah! I see that he's made you promises. Well, when he's ready, he'll break them without a qualm. He'll marry some tough little debutante of whom his mother approves, and who is only interested in the money, because she's screwing the tennis coach at the Club for her serious fun. Mother would never approve of you, and she's in control of the dough, you know."

"You are crude and disagreeable," Laura said equably. "And, anyway, how do you know all of that?"

He shrugged. "It's the kind of thing I know," he said. "Cut the date with Freddie and come to dinner with me. I've a serious business proposition for you."

"Oh, you and your business propositions!" she laughed. "Pushing drugs on the street, I suppose? If you think I'm interested in selling shit on a corner in the Village to those jerks and junkies down there, when I can go out with Freddie, and have dinner at 21, you've another think coming. I've told you before, I won't get into that sort of thing."

She was well aware of Charlie's activities. She neither approved nor disapproved. She considered that he met a community need that someone else would service and profit from if he did not. Whatever he was doing seemed to her no worse than selling tobacco or booze, but she had never had the least interest in becoming involved with his drug pushing. She had seen enough of what happened to the young men and women who worked for Charlie and the others like him.

"I don't do that sort of thing any more," he said primly. "That was years ago, when we first met."

"Well, whatever it is you do now, I'm not interested in

anything to do with drugs. I'd rather take my chances with Freddie, Mother or no Mother."

He lay back on the bed again, lit a cigarette, and resumed his perusal of the ceiling.

"So ... have you taken a look at yourself lately, then, my old friend?" He spoke slowly and deliberately and blew a series of smoke rings up at the ceiling. "I gather you're still kidding yourself that you're an actress, but really, you know, you're just another New York hooker, with a use-by date which is rapidly approaching for that kind of work."

"So sweet you always are, Charlie! And you're a small time pusher in the Village. It hardly puts you in a position to criticize, and even less to moralize, to me."

"Now that's just where you're wrong."

He sat up and pushed the pillows behind him so that he could see her face, and his own, too, reflected in the spotted and smeared dressing-table mirror. "You may have descended the greasy New York pecking pole since you arrived in town as a promising ingénue but I, on the other hand, my old chum, have climbed up a rung or two. I am not small time at all ... not any more! Besides, pushing shit doesn't wear one out like selling the body."

"Not unless you end up in gaol. They'd rape a pretty chap like you until you didn't look too good any more."

He ignored her, having no wish to admit that there was a good deal of truth in what she said, and recalling that this was exactly the advice he had given to Nick, a year or two ago, when threatening him.

Instead he asked: "Have you any idea how short a time it will be before no one wants you, Laura, my darling, even for a one night stand? And then what? Back to Minnesota and the garage mechanic you left behind, two kids and a life of shattered dreams and sour regrets?"

She turned around on the dressing table stool and gave him a long, considered look.

"You really are a dead shit, you know, Charlie." She understood, clearly enough, that what he was saying might be the truth, but she was wounded that he should care so little that such a fate might be in store for her. She had always known he cared little for anyone but himself, in spite of his charm, but she had persuaded herself, every time, that he would change; that there was room somewhere in that handsome chest cavity for a heart to grow, even if there was no sign of one at the moment. It never had, and now she had given up any hope that it would. Besides, she had learned since coming to New York that what you see is what you get. People don't change, let alone improve as the years go by, for God's sake! She would be a fool to hold out hope for that in a big town – or anywhere, she supposed.

He shrugged. "Someone has to tell you, my sweet. It's no use getting angry with the message bearer. If you try spending any more time with the Freddie Hartingtons of this world, I'll begin to look like the Archangel Gabriel." He stood up and stretched and wandered over to the window to peruse the sight of the back windows of a smoke-stained apartment across the yard.

"Now, why don't you take off that awful pink garment, throw it in the incinerator where it belongs, pull on some jeans and give Freddie a ring. I'm sure the town is full of other silly girls who will fuck Freddie for a chance to dine with him at 21. Women are such fools!"

"I wouldn't count on that assumption if I were you, Charlie," Laura said tartly. "It has led better men than you to make some grave mistakes."

He ignored her. "And then you can listen to what I have to say, for a change."

"I am always listening to what you say, and you are very crude most of the time!"

"But realistic, you must admit," he said with a smirk.

"Freddie is worth at least ten million dollars."

"Small beer these days!"

She looked at him with amazement and some contempt. "Now look who's talking! Since when did you get such big ideas?"

She had known Charlie now for more than four years. She had never heard him talking big like this before. He rarely talked about his work, or business, or whatever it could be called, and he never made claims that were anything other than modest.

"Besides, I already told you," Charlie said. "It's Freddie's mother who is worth at least ten million, and that's a very different thing. Freddie is not worth shit unless he does as he's told. One of the certain things in life is that he will be told that he can't marry you, even if that's what he has in mind, which I doubt very much."

He gave her a considered look, and flicked the ash of his cigarette into a saucer on her bedside table. "Have you any idea what the annual world trade in illegal drugs is worth at this moment?"

"I told you, I'm not interested in drugs!"

"But have you any idea?"

She shrugged impatiently "How the hell would I know a thing like that? A hundred – two hundred million?"

"Maybe a hundred billion this year, every year, and rising. I estimate three hundred billion by 1990! Even more by the end of the century, and you and I will still not be too old by then to enjoy ourselves. We shall still be in the prime of life, you might say."

"So? It's not mine and it's not yours, and it's illegal!"

He laughed. "So is whoring, I believe!"

"I am looking for a nice guy to marry," she said primly, but she laughed. The trouble with Charlie was that he eventually made her laugh, even when she was angry with him, like now. Most especially when she was angry.

"Let me explain to you a simple fact of life, Laura, my darling," Charlie said patiently. "Nothing as big as two hundred billion dollars a year, tax free, is illegal. Something as big as that eventually runs the world."

"Governments run the world."

"Until now, perhaps, but by making all those drugs illegal, the governments of our lovely Western democracies have signed their own death warrants. They will shortly go down the drain. They have passed control of events over to the merchants. They are empowering people like me, who are responsible to no one, who do not have to be elected and who are without moral scruples of any kind. We can now afford to buy anyone and anything we want, and that's exactly what we shall do. It's what we are already doing! The day of everyman is almost over. Next will be corporate dictatorship."

She looked at his reflection in the mirror as she continued with her make-up. She thought he had flipped his lid, but such a conclusion hardly surprised her.

"The government will stop you."

"Don't be a fool. The government doesn't even want to stop us. Many countries I could tell you about depend on their illegal drug income to balance the budget. In most of the others, including this wonderfully hypocritical US of A, our one and only Land of the Free and Home of the Brave, there are already far too many snouts in our very generous trough."

He lit another cigarette and drew the smoke deep into his lungs. He crossed over to the window on the front side of the room and looked down into the hot and crowded street far below, pushing aside the dusty curtain with some distaste.

"They are very respectable and powerful snouts, too, if I may say so. They want everything to stay just as peachy and dandy and cozy as it is right now. They want the cash to keep flowing into their greedy and immoral little pockets, and I, and a few others like me, shall provide it for them."

"The gospel according to St Charles," she said. "You expect me to believe that you're a millionaire drug king?"

"Baron is the word, I believe. A millionaire drug baron is what the vulgar media is always yapping on about. Senselessly, usually, like most of the things that reporters yap about. Now why don't you just give that dismal turd Freddie a ring, and we'll be off to the Deli on 7th Avenue for a pastrami on rye and some serious talking."

"Is the Deli on 7th Avenue the place where the new millionaires in New York are dining these days?" She gave him a withering look that made Charlie laugh.

"We don't like to show off in case the IRS is watching," he said. "They have permanent spies in all the more expensive joints."

"Freddie won't date me again if I put him off!"

"Who gives a damn? If you do as I say, in a year or so you'll be able to buy and sell the Freddies of this world ten times over. You'll be able to fart in the face of his disgusting old snob of a mother, who has never done an honest day's toil in her life, though I suspect she's had a hand in some dishonest ones. Doesn't that prospect have some appeal for you?"

She smiled at him and picked up the phone. "I don't know why I let you persuade me to do things like this," she said. "I think you're all piss and wind. A hundred billion? Two hundred billion? Whoever heard of that kind of money?"

He shrugged. "You know perfectly well why you do as I

ask. You're ambitious, and you're proud, and you don't like sitting under the backside of the world looking hopefully upwards while it defecates on your pretty face."

"It would be nice to be on top for a change, I must say," she said. "But how do I know that you are the one who can put me there?"

"You don't really know anything about me yet," he said quietly. "Besides, I won't be putting you anywhere. You'll put yourself there, by using your brains and your style and your beauty, and all the knowledge of how bloody awful the world is."

He waved a languid hand towards the open window and the street below. He watched a motley crowd struggle home in the baking afternoon heat, weary and dispirited. No matter what he had to do, Charles swore, he would never again be a part of that ragged crowd.

"You will be using the knowledge that you've gained by surviving on the fringes of New York society with no other assets than a lovely face and at least a vestigial brain, which is more than most people have, believe me!"

She gave him a penetrating look.

"Here I am, cancelling the only decent date I've had all week, giving up dinner at 21, and going out to talk business with you. Funny business, too, by all accounts, I would think. Yet as you rightly point out, I don't really know a damned thing about you. Four or five years ago you arrived in New York, broke, and started pushing drugs. That's what I know about you. If I had even the vestigial brain you credit me with, I would kick you straight out the door!"

"It's better if we have no questions," he said. "No past. It's safer that way."

"That's too easy!" she said angrily. "I want to know what you did before New York. I want to know who you were and what you were then, and who you are and what you are now –

I think I deserve some kind of answer if I'm to even consider putting my life in your hands."

He laughed rather sourly. "Then? Then I was a naive kid," he said, "and now I am the worst kind of adult, a disenchanted idealist who wants to get rich quick. It's a dangerous combination. I told you all that a couple of years ago, one evening in BJ's. on 2nd Avenue."

"And who disillusioned you? That woman, I suppose?"

"Of course! Isn't it always some woman? But not in quite the way you imagine! And in another way I did it to myself, with my own stupidity. The basic rule in my business is never to blame anyone but yourself for your mistakes, and never, ever to believe your own lies! I shan't make those mistakes again."

"Maybe you won't, but there's always a new mistake to be made."

"You're too cynical for someone so young and pretty. Come on, now, ring up Freddie and get changed and we'll be off. It's far too hot to sit around in this bloody awful apartment any longer than we must."

"Go sit in the other room," she said. "I won't be long." She pulled off her pink dress and hung it in the closet. She pulled on her jeans and a cotton skivvy and sat down again in front of her mirror. After more than four years, she had no regular work. She had no money and she was still in this rotten apartment with no air conditioning and no elevator. Whatever Charlie was offering her, could it be worse than this? Her life was not turning out as she expected. Fame had so far eluded her and even a modest success had proven to be more difficult to achieve than she would have believed possible, dreaming in college of her future. She had learned, by now, that this was the usual story for pretty girls who came to New York to be actresses, but that was no consolation.

Laura did not consider herself to be just any young girl. A second-rate future was not what she had planned for herself and she was still too young and confident to consider failure an option, but she needed to review her choices. Perhaps it was time for a change, time to try to attack life from a different perspective. She looked around her bedroom and shuddered at the worn curtains and shabby spread on the bed. She gazed through the windows at the depressing West Side landscape where there was not a glimpse of a park, not even a leaf or a patch of blue sky unless she hung halfway out of the window.

She looked at the reflection in the mirror in front of her. She was happy enough with what she still saw there, but she had to admit that it was increasingly a work of art. The fresh young girl from Minnesota with the bloom of peaches in her cheeks and the gaze of starlight in her eyes was gone. Instead, she thought, I now look like a New Yorker, like a woman of the world who knows how things really work. She felt pleased to know how the world worked, but she was sad that the other girl, starry-eyed and idealistic and full of dreams, was gone, for she had rather liked her.

CHAPTER FOUR

FINCA DE LA MADONNA DE LA LUNA
NEAR MEDELLIN, COLOMBIA
JULY 1969

NICK BARTON ENTERED THE dining room of the Finca with some trepidation and looked around at the assembled Ventura y Cortez brothers, whom he had never met before. This was his first journey into the heartland from which they ran their own empire, rivals and partners of Charles Bellamy. Nick had developed a plan and now it was necessary to sell it to these educated thugs. Nick wondered how useful their Harvard degrees were going to be in helping them to see the benefits he was devising for their protection and for their profit. After two years together, and in partnership with these Ventura brothers, he and Charles were making serious money. It had not been difficult to persuade Charles that it had to be tidied up, moved around, and made to smell right. Too much of it, lying around in the open, would soon begin to stink in quarters where the smell could be dangerous.

The Finca de la Madonna de la Luna was lonely and remote, some thirty kilometres north-west of the city of Medellin in Colombia. It was hidden in the low mountain range, and it was impossible to approach without the knowledge of its occupants. The place was the perfect venue for illegal activities, if producing cocaine and heroin could be considered illegal in Colombia. Without it the country would go belly up in minutes.

The house was not old, although one wing had been there for decades, and perhaps for centuries, in one form or another. The rest of the considerable structure had been added more recently, to reflect the increasing wealth of the Ventura family. It rather resembled, Nick considered, a middle priced motel in New Mexico or Arizona, while the older wings looked like a stable building in one of the poorer towns in Mexico. The buildings were surrounded by several courtyards; all with fountains and gardens in the Andalusian manner, and these had been constructed and arranged with considerably more taste and knowledge than the house itself. Somehow the flowers and the trees and the courtyards held together the tawdry architecture. They gave the visitor the impression that he was approaching a country house of felicity and charm.

Judge Fabrizio Ruiz was reassured. He stopped his car and looked down at the vista below him. It was his first visit to the Finca since the death of his old friend Don Antonio Ventura, whose four sons now owned and ran the estate. He had not seen these sons many times since they were children, and he was frightened by the reputation they now had in Colombia. However, he admitted to himself that he was pleasantly surprised by what he now saw spread out in the valley below him. He had expected something far worse, something American and flashy; something more commensurate with what he had heard of the current style of the Ventura brothers.

Directly below him he saw a pretty valley, surrounded by several hundred hectares of green and lush pasture, dotted with cattle and bisected by a fast flowing river, with plenty of fresh water from the mountains. Beyond the pasture the country became rougher. It stretched from some low and wooded hills to the mountains beyond, and the Judge assumed that it was there those secret crops that were bringing such great wealth to the family of Ventura y Cortez could be found.

The Judge crossed himself at the memory of his old friend, Don Antonio. He was dead and his sons obviously had no respect for the traditional life of the land, nor in the long tradition of the careful husbandry of their ancestors. They seemed to care nothing for the carefully maintained and fragile links with the debilitated and impoverished aristocracy in Spain. It seemed to the Judge that they cared only for money.

His old friend had sent his sons away to America, and there, at Harvard University, they had learned the ways of financial management, business techniques and new methods of agriculture to enhance the productivity of this old, tired stretch of country. In addition, they had learned that there was a high lifestyle to be enjoyed beyond the sheltered confines of the Finca and the provincial pleasures of Bogotá. For those who were smart enough, there was wealth and power to be commanded on a scale undreamed of at the Finca de la Madonna de la Luna.

On the campus of Harvard and in the sophisticated circles of New York, Washington and Miami to which their birth gained them access through their father's connections, they discovered that there was an insatiable and rapidly growing demand for heroin and cocaine. This demand, they clearly saw, would only escalate as the baby boomers grew older and richer, and the foolish laws of the democracies pushed up the prices. The Ventura brothers understood that this was a demand that could be met by themselves and their beautiful farm in the remote hills behind Medellin.

They had returned to Colombia, first Jaime, then Jorge, then Sebastian and finally little Jesus, fresh from postgraduate studies in business management and international finance and banking and law. Together they set about restoring the family fortune. They had done well. All this passed through the Judge's mind as he returned to his car and headed down into the valley towards the low buildings in the distance.

In the dining room of the Finca, Nick sat with Jaime and his younger brothers. The room was large and handsome in the style of Southern Spain. Painted white, with a groined ceiling and splendid old tiles on the floor, which glowed now in the sunlight streaming in from the row of long windows overlooking a square patio, in the middle of which a splendid fountain sprayed trickles of water to give an illusion of calm and peace. The walls were hung with dark and impressive portraits of real or imagined family forebears and their long-nosed and high-corseted ladies. Three of the Ventura brothers seated around the table were dark and swarthy, but Sebastian was tall and fair, slender and handsome in the Scandinavian mould. A throwback, no doubt, to some passing lonely sailor washed ashore long ago along the coast of Spain, or perhaps, Nick thought irreverently, a passing fancy for a good-looking German waiter on one of their mother's many trips to Europe before the war.

"While we wait for the Judge," Jaime said quietly, "let's get on with the business at hand. The old fool may be hours yet. He's probably run his car off the road." The brothers laughed. The discomfort of other, and especially older, people was always a topic which amused them.

"The matter in hand, Don Jaime," Nick said, "is how we are going to handle the huge cash flow now being generated by us all in our current joint operations in the States, and the problem of how we can best clean it up and get it properly invested."

"The matter in hand, Mr Barton, is whether your organization is swindling us."

Nick had been at the Finca only since the previous day, but he had already learned that Jaime used all the techniques of a bully in his negotiations. He was always trying to get the opposition on the wrong foot, the opposition in this case being the Bellamy Corporation in the person of Nick. He had toughened up considerably in the two years he had worked with Charles, but he was unsure how to handle a guy like this, who was supposed to be on the same side, for God's sake!

Nick was pleased to have discovered, since his arrival, that he was really quite good at whatever game it was that Jaime had decided to play. Now he merely raised his eyebrows in astonishment and spoke in a deliberately low and calm voice.

"Swindling you? You really astonish me, Don Jaime," he said coolly. "Have we not paid every cent on every delivery that you have ever made, and even for those that, for one reason or another, we have ordered but not received? We have even paid for those deliveries that have been lost or confiscated through the carelessness or stupidity of your own people, I believe."

"Yes, yes," Jaime said impatiently, "that's not in dispute, but are you paying us a fair price?"

Nick shrugged. This kind of stupidity pissed him off. It was a waste of valuable time. "That's another matter. We are paying you the price agreed between us. If you want to try and re-negotiate the price, I'll discuss it with Charles, but let's have no further talk of swindling. We are partners, I seem to recall. The Bellamy Corporation wishes only to make as much profit as possible for us all."

"Lawyers, lawyers," Jaime muttered under his breath. "We do all the work, you take all the money."

"You are a graduate in law yourself, I understand, Don Jaime," Nick said.

"I am a simple farmer, sir," Jaime said stiffly.

Jaime liked to take this big, macho pose, but Nick judged him to be something of a fool. He was in love with his own increasing importance and the wealth that Charles was pouring into his lap, and the power that this huge influx of money gave him in the corrupt circles of government in Bogotá. This always made a man vulnerable, Nick knew, and it was his job, working for Charlie, to discover who was vulnerable and why. He knew that they would need this information to protect themselves, sooner or later.

"Come, come, Don Jaime," Nick said impatiently. "You know that what you are saying is not true. You grow the stuff and process it here, and you deliver it, with considerable help from us, I might add. We sell it, and develop new markets, and we hide it and invest it, so that in due course it comes out the other end smelling just wonderful."

"For a fat fee!" Sebastian said scornfully.

Jesus interrupted irritably. He was the youngest brother and, Nick assessed, the smartest of them all, the plainest and the least vain. Jesus at least appeared to have the advantage of not being totally and completely enamored of himself, and this made him dangerous.

"Jaime, this is all trivial nonsense," he said. "We have much more important matters to discuss while Nick is here. Bellamy and his organization have to cope with the Mafia, and the CIA and the FBI and all those fucking meddlers and do-gooders in the States, to say nothing of their greedy politicians, all of whom have to be paid a fortune to keep them off our backs. Besides, they can get their shit from Asia if they want. Let's not quarrel with our friends. We have enough trouble with our enemies, surely?"

Jaime gave his younger brother a surly look from his seat at the head of the table. He did not like being reprimanded in his own house by his baby brother, but Jesus was not afraid of him. He turned to Nick and said sharply, "Well, then, speak up!"

Nick took up the papers in front of him, although he knew their contents by heart. "Currently we are moving five million dollars a week out of America through our youth organization," he said.

"Your youth organization? That's a joke!" Sebastian laughed.

"Shut up, Sebastian," Jorge said. "Let him tell us. We're not in some Bogotá whorehouse now."

Nick smiled to himself. Let them disagree, he thought. It's all the better for Charles and me, in the long run, if they are at each other's throats. "We have set up a charitable trust," he continued patiently, "which sends young people to Europe for cultural visits. The trust pays their fares, they each take a courier parcel which contains anything up to one hundred thousand dollars and which is collected from them on arrival. That is untraceable. Then Charles has the import/export agency. Through that we can render false invoices from alleged suppliers and transfer funds legitimately in payments to overseas companies who are, of course, us. However, as you know, business is expanding quickly. We need to be more sophisticated in moving our funds. Our vaults at Bellamy Trust and at the Bellamy Foundation in Miami where we have recently relocated are stuffed with cash, some of which is yours, as you know. We don't want to send it here."

Jesus shrugged impatiently and turned again to his older brother. "Jaime, the money's no good to us unless we can launder it and re-invest it. Rooms full of dirty cash are useless, particularly here in Bogotá!"

"I know, I know! We have all the funds in bloody Bogotá that we can ever use, even to pay the bloody greedy politicians and the equally greedy priests," Jaime agreed. "Well, we have the casino in the Bahamas. We clear five million a week there, and bank it offshore."

"Peanuts," Jesus said to his brother. He turned to Nick. "What does Bellamy propose?"

"There are two small Florida banks currently for sale. One is in Naples on the Gulf Coast where there are many rich, but not so chic, retirees, and the other is in Miami. Charles is going to buy that one – the National Bank of Florida – for himself, and he suggests that you buy the Credit Naples Bank, and have Jesus go over there and run it for you. That way we can deal better with this mountain of cash, get it out of the country, tidy it up and invest it in our own offshore corporations. We can establish a legitimate banking relationship with banks in other countries where the rules can be more easily bent."

"Excellent," Jesus said. He approved of such an arrangement. It was, after all, what he had been trained for in America for all those years.

"I don't want Jesus in America," Jaime said. "I want him right here with the others, where I can keep an eye on him."

"Those days are gone," Jesus said impatiently. "For Christ's sake, we spent ten years growing the stuff here and selling it for nothing, getting our act together and establishing our markets. Now, thanks to Charles and to Nick here, we are finally free of all the local sharks who've ripped us off and we are making some serious money for ourselves which they can't touch. Those funds must never come to fucking Colombia! All the bastards here robbed us blind for years, and we paid them because we wanted to get started and we had no alternative. Until Sebastian found Bellamy and signed a deal with him we sold practically nothing in the United States, and now we're making millions."

"I don't trust him," Jaime muttered.

"Oh, fuck off, Jaime," Jesus said angrily. "This guy has opened up a whole world market for us. We're all selling drugs, for Chrissake, not oil! We're all criminals in the eyes of the world, and so I don't trust anybody! Not even you!" he shouted. "Let's just get on with it." He turned again to Nick, who liked his style. He saw clearly that Jesus was a man with whom he could deal. This was a man who could understand business, and whose mind was trained and whose ego was not one hundred per cent concentrated in his testicles – well, at least not all of the time.

"Give us some figures, Nick, as soon as you can," Jesus said. "I think the banks are an excellent idea, otherwise we could choke to death on our own cash flow. Pay no attention to Jaime. He'll do his job and I'll do mine. What else?"

"At the moment," Nick said, "we're really only on the street in the bigger cities. In New York, Chicago, Denver, Detroit, L.A. We're not even in Miami yet, except for our head offices. Someone else is making all the dough in the smaller places. It's time we moved in on them."

"We've talked about this before," Jorge said. He was tall and heavy, dark-skinned and with a surly and argumentative personality, another thug in reasonably decent clothes. "But it's been the distribution which was the problem, isn't that right?"

"Yes, Jorge, it was, but I think that we've solved that," Nick told them. "A lot of these difficulties are easier to solve now that we have so much cash to invest. There's a nationwide chain of supermarkets up for grabs. We can do a takeover. We'll form a new company to act as if we're a big public company doing a leveraged buy-out, but actually the cash will come only from your funds and ours, via a number of corporations that we shall set up offshore. It will all look like a kosher public company, but there really won't be any other shareholders. It's the Diggely-Doggely Supermarket chain."

Nick stood up and drew a quick diagram on the whiteboard, illustrating in simple terms what he planned to do.

"They're kind of at the lower end of the market, unpretentious, wouldn't attract too much attention, but they're in all the smaller cities, particularly throughout the South where we are very weak at the moment. They have branches everywhere. They have trucks delivering legitimate merchandise every day, all over the place. It would be perfect at our end, and we'd be in a position to double our orders with you, maybe even treble them within a couple of years, and we'd drive out a lot of our less aggressive competition."

"Sounds good for you, but that's sales and distribution. That's your end. You don't need to talk to us about that. You can do that whenever you like," Jesus said.

"We want you in on the investment," Nick explained. "There's a lot of money involved and it's a perfect launder. You'll own a legitimate share in a legitimate US corporation. We want you to use your own funds to take up forty percent of the equity."

"How?" Jaime demanded.

Nick looked impatient. "I've told you. You do it through a series of dummy off-shore companies and trusts which I shall set up in countries that couldn't give a stuff about this kind of thing. That's what I'm paid for!"

Jesus said, "If you treble your orders, how do we get the stuff to you? Our lines are overstretched now."

"Yes, yes, we know that. I'm coming to that," Nick said impatiently. "If we substantially increase our orders with you, and that doesn't include any expansion in Europe or Australia that Charlie is planning, then we want to know what plans you have for increasing deliveries. How will you get the merchandise to us? Have you given any thought to that kind of expansion?"

"He's right, you know," Sebastian said. He seemed to have recovered from his earlier surly and suspicious mood. "At the moment, we're using trucks through Mexico, and small craft in the Caribbean, into the Bahamas and one or two other rotten and corrupt little dumps. We lose about a third of the merchandise, one way or another, either because people are stupid or dishonest, or both. None of that would be any good if we had to increase our deliveries to the States, let alone deliver to Europe or Australia. The system would simply break down."

There was a knock at the door.

"Yes?" Jaime shouted impatiently. "What is it now?"

"Judge Ruiz is here."

"Oh, yes, the Judge! I'd forgotten all about him! Well, then, show him in!"

CHAPTER FIVE

AT THE NEW YORK DELI
JULY 1969

LAURA AND CHARLES WERE settled in the New York Deli, on 7th Avenue, with a pile of pastrami on rye in front of them, and two long, cold beers.

"Well, it isn't 21, but the company's more fun, I'll agree. And handsomer, too." Laura giggled. "And you're right. He does have pimples on his butt. So tell me, what's the deal that's going to change my life?"

Around them banged and clattered all the familiar noises of the big and popular deli, famous for its pastrami sandwiches and packed with eager and hungry customers. It was all a very New York scene.

"Have you ever heard of Jaime Ventura y Cortez or his brothers?"

She shook her head. "Never. They sound like some Hollywood studs. Should I have heard of them?"

"No. On the whole, Nick and I are making sure that as few people as possible hear of them. Jaime and his three younger brothers own an estate near Medellin, in Colombia, tucked away very privately in the hills. Their father went broke sending them all to Harvard, and then died, leaving them the farm."

"Very convenient for them," Laura said.

Charlie ignored her. "They come from an old Catholic family down there, well connected in Spain, I'm told. They had very little money until fairly recently, but they all have a very inflated idea of their own breeding and importance."

She laughed a little sadly. "Sounds familiar. It could be any of my New York playmates."

"There were two moles of equal birth,
But not alas of equal worth.
The one who said his blood was blue,
Was much the bloodier of the two."

"That's a little ditty my father taught me," she said.

Charlie rather agreed with the sentiments expressed.

"The boys went back to Colombia from Harvard with good degrees and very hungry for cash, after they'd seen the good life up here, as you might imagine, so they decided they'd grow and sell cocaine because, like you and me, they didn't like being poor. It killed their father, of course. This was not what he'd sent them to Harvard to learn. He thought they'd come back gentlemen. Well, he actually thought they already were gentlemen, but he hoped they would come back ready to do business in the modern world. Ha! He was right there. They did, but it wasn't the business he contemplated."

"And then they came all the way from Bogotá to the Village to get your advice and assistance?"

"Sarcasm does not suit you, Laura," Charles said tartly. "But as a matter of fact, yes, that's exactly what happened. Sebastian Ventura, the third brother, contacted me a couple of years ago. They wanted to expand their business into the States, and they wanted a partner who was clean. They wanted someone here who wasn't already tied up with one of the other cartels."

"An independent operator like yourself?"

"Exactly. I impressed them, you see. They were producing more stuff than they knew how to sell, so I offered my modest little organization and my superior brain and a deal to organize their entire US distribution network."

He leant back in his seat and fixed her with a steady gaze. "I said I'd do it, if they gave me an exclusive contract, and a share of the profits. Our mutual friend and colleague, Nick Barton, brought in my very first major delivery, via Mexico, although he wasn't very happy about it at the time. That was two years ago. We're doing pretty well, but now it's time for the next step."

"And what's that?"

"For me to take over. I have no intention of spending the rest of my life making millions for South American fuckwits with delusions of grandeur."

"Just like that, you take over? And maybe you're dead?"

He shrugged. "Maybe – and maybe they're dead, but I think not. For the time being we need each other. We are a team." He leant forward, tense with excitement, his eyes shining. Laura had never seen him like this before.

"I'm going down to Miami in a few days for a meeting with Sebastian Ventura. Nick's in Medellin right now, sorting out the legal problems, and trying to bully them into doing what we want so that we can make a fortune for them – and for ourselves, too, of course. There is nothing philanthropic about this. Sebastian's the brother who is ambassador for the family, and gets to travel and make contacts. We'll get hold of a nice little bank down in Florida, where the rules aren't too strict. We're awash with cash and it needs to be invested. We need to go legit, or at least look as if that's what we're doing!"

He laughed. "It's no use being rich in Bogotá. There's not much in Bogotá that anyone would want to spend his money on. Even the politics is more dependant on guns than money."

"So ...? That's all very interesting, but where do I come

in?" She took a large bite of pastrami and began to chew contemplatively.

"As I said, Jaime's brother, Sebastian, is coming to meet me in Miami. None of the boys is allowed to marry. Jaime thinks it would jeopardize their security." Charlie shrugged. "You know, families, women, children. Too easy for them to become distracted, or to be blackmailed or held for ransom. He has told them they must wait. The boys are tired of the putas in the Bogotá brothels. Sebastian likes American blondes. He should be a pushover for you. I want you to get him to take you back to Bogotá with him, and stay there with him as long as you can, and tell me everything that goes on. Everything they all do."

"To be his mistress there, you mean?"

He laughed, and put his hand over hers. "Laura, what a cute old-fashioned word. I didn't think anyone had mistresses in this liberated age, but perhaps they still do in Minnesota, if it's not too cold."

"Nevertheless, old-fashioned or not, that's what you want me to do."

Charlie's voice turned cold. "I want you to be his friend and his lover and his partner, and his confidante. And then I want you to spy for me, so that I know what's going on. I don't want to get killed simply because I'm not properly informed. I don't want to be outsmarted or swindled. You've got to keep an eye on devious shits like these lads with their Harvard education and their Latin morals, and their greed."

"What if I don't like him?"

"Laura, my darling, don't start gibbering at me like the heroine of a Barbara Cartland novel. You sound like a housemaid who fancies the second footman. If you're not careful, I'll begin to think I've overrated your intelligence. This is a business deal we're talking about, not a June wedding at the

Country Club. Besides, you don't really like Freddie, either."

"I don't have to live with Freddie."

"You would have to, at least for a while, if you were ever able to get him to marry you. And damned mean he'd be to you, I can assure you. And his mother would be meaner!"

She considered the truth of that statement. From the available evidence, she was forced to agree that this might well be the case. It was her experience that men on the whole behaved badly, even the unattractive ones, who should know better or at least have to make more effort.

"And if I get killed doing this? I presume there is a possibility that I might be killed?"

"I'll give you a very good funeral, if they don't put your body through the mincing machine, or throw it to the piranhas. I think the risk is minimal if you do your job properly, and keep your wits about you."

She gave him a considered look. "You are planning to swindle them out of their own business, aren't you?"

He grinned – a quick, rare smile that made him look young and guileless and very handsome. "There! I knew you really were a clever girl. Crudely put, but you have it in one hit. I don't like the word swindle. They will make a ton of money, but I do plan to get complete control of operations, when the time is right. I also plan to be seen by everyone in Miami, and New York, and London and Paris and Beijing and Sydney, as a very respectable banker, and a very rich one."

"Then you will have to marry before you're forty. Bachelors over forty are always suspect," she said. She knew that she would marry him if he asked, even though she believed it would make her unhappy in the long run, or maybe even sooner. But she knew that he would not ask, and she was both saddened and relieved by this knowledge, for she understood clearly that marriage to Charlie would be a mistake that she could not afford to make.

"Of course I must, but not yet. When the time is right I shall marry a woman who will open the right doors for me, so that I shall sit with those few people who actually run this world, instead of those stupid committees in Washington, which kid themselves that they do. All they do is what they're told and pocket the money that I, and others like me, give them. Or rather that, at the moment, Jaime and Sebastian and others like them give them."

Laura felt a tight contraction in her guts as she listened to what he told her. She recognized that feeling. She knew it was a combination of fear and excitement. It was the feeling of being on the edge, of being truly alive. She had felt it when she left home to come to New York, and she was pleased to find that it had not deserted her, as she believed that it might have done over the past few years of disappointments and failures. It was the gambler's instinct at work, telling her when to take a calculated risk. She had never desired to play safe with her life, and she had no intention of failing. She knew that she would rather be dead.

"Surely the government will become aware of all of this and stop it?"

"I've told you," Charlie said patiently. "The government is already aware of all this, as you call it, and is benefiting from it hugely. Or, at least, powerful individuals in the government are benefiting."

He signalled to the waitress and ordered two more beers.

"Why do you imagine that drugs pour into the United States in spite of all efforts to stop it? The government spends millions of dollars to no avail. No one has any intention of stopping it, even if it could be stopped – which would, in any event, be politically and practically impossible, as the government very well knows. The government, contrary to what everyone believes, is not stupid. It merely makes the mistake of assuming that all the rest of us are stupid!"

She looked at him thoughtfully. "Have you ever killed anyone?"

"Now that is a stupid question."

"Well, have you?"

"Of course I have. We're not playing gin rummy here, you know. How many people are killed on the roads each year, but do you think cars will be banned? How many people die of negligence in American hospitals every year, but are patients marching in the street in protest? How many people do you think the governments of the allegedly free world eliminate each year to protect what they allege are their interests, or their secrets, even when they don't have one of their nice, legitimate little wars going on?"

She considered that, and was prepared to admit that it was probably a considerable number. Nevertheless, she had no ambition to be one of them.

"Would I have to kill anyone?" she asked. "I don't think I could do that." She looked briefly around the restaurant at the ordinary American folk eating there; the tourists and theatregoers and out-of-town visitors. She could not believe in the reality of the conversation she was having. It seemed like a dream from which she would wake up tomorrow, apologize to Freddie and put up with his abuse and fix another date and get on with the ordinary, everyday, largely unsatisfactory and disappointing business of living.

"Very unlikely," he said. "But, just in case, I'll teach you how it's done. It isn't a difficult thing to learn."

"But to actually do?" Laura asked uneasily.

"Easy enough to do," he said, with a shrug, "when it's your life or his!"

"And what would I be paid?" she asked.

"So you're interested?"

"I didn't say that. You're right that I'm tired of being poor, but this kind of thing? I don't know. I think I'd be frightened of this. I don't want to spend the rest of my life being frightened."

"Nonsense," he said. "It's much easier than succeeding among the sharks in New York, particularly the theatrical sharks. No one will ask you to fuck them. They're not interested in that – at least not during working hours. That isn't the power game they want."

"I'd need to give it more thought," she said. "I can't just walk into this over dinner. I need to see this Sebastian. If I really don't like him, this would never work. Besides, what kind of a fool enters into a contract without knowing the pay and conditions?"

"I can tell you that. Fifty thousand in cash right now, off shore and tax-free. A new wardrobe for going with me to Miami, which I shall choose," he said pointedly, thinking of the pink satin. "That's another fifty grand. You can't go out with a man like Sebastian Ventura in something like that pink rag you had on this evening. If you don't like him, or he doesn't ask you to go with him, then the deal's off. You get to keep the clothes and the money and I'm a hundred Gs down the drain."

He sat back and looked around the crowded room, feeling pleased that he was able to make such an offer without a qualm. "If you go to Colombia, then it's another fifty immediately, and then fifty thousand a month for every month you stay with him in Bogotá, and a million dollars when he kicks you out, or you have to run for it. All of it will be paid tax free into a Swiss bank account." He gave her a self-satisfied smile. "That's a good deal of money for a girl who has nothing much."

She swallowed the last of her pastrami, and washed it down with a swig of her Heineken beer. She looked back at him for a long while, and then she threw back her head and laughed, loudly and clearly and with a carefree girlish glee. Even in that noisy and crowded room, many people turned and stared. Real, carefree and joyous laughter was as rare in New York as it was in Moscow.

"You talk to me about billions of dollars. Huge fortunes to be made, the kind of money that you tell me you're making already. You ask me to risk my life to help you make more, perhaps even to kill someone. Certainly to run the risk of being killed myself. The money won't do me much good if I am at the bottom of some South American river, being eaten by piranha fish. You must think I am a fool," she said. "I may be just an unsuccessful actress from no place at all, but you know, Charles, I don't much like being taken for a fool."

"What do you mean?"

Now it was he who was surprised, caught on the left foot, alerted to the possibility that she might be smarter than he had thought, or at least a good deal tougher.

"Let's be honest with each other, Charlie, if such a thing is possible between a man and a woman," she said sadly. "I don't understand how or why you got involved in this dirty business, but wrap it up however you like, we both know that I would perhaps be risking my life, and that I would be taking a walk on the wild side for ever more with a deal like this. You're asking me to consider living with a ruthless man whom I don't even know, in a town like Bogotá. You are asking me to play a very dangerous game in a very dangerous place. Even I know that a business like this is deadly, and no matter what governments may actually do about it, it's also illegal everywhere."

She took a deep breath and looked around the room, just to reassure herself that normal life was still going on around her.

"Earlier you told me that this business is worth billions of dollars a year. You tell me that you're setting out to tie up a good portion of the market for yourself. With my help, I might add! Then you offer me some small change. I might not have learned much on what you call the fringes of New York society, but I'd have thought that you, at least, would have learned that those outskirts are tougher than most people know. In five years, I've learned to know when I'm being used and when I'm not. I think women learn these things better than men – and quicker. Why not? We're used more often, aren't we? There isn't any old boys' club for women. We have no safety net held out in case we fall. I suggest that you go back on the streets and find some other sucker among what I'm sure is a wide acquaintance with street walkers, and others of dubious reputation."

"You'd rather go back to that lousy apartment, and spending nights with out-of-town salesmen?"

"I didn't say that and, anyway, you know I don't do that kind of thing, Charlie."

"Not yet, maybe," he said, "but the day will come, if you go on like you are."

She shrugged and looked at him calmly. She put up with a lot of crap from Charlie, because in her own way she loved the bastard, but she understood his faults and his ruthlessness with people, and she didn't like it all that much. She supposed, though, that in her own way she used men in much the same way as he was seeking to use her. She used them to get information, to gain access to other worlds, to succeed.

"What I'm saying is that I'd be a fool to go to war unless I'm properly paid."

Charles knew no one else in New York with the looks, style, intelligence or motivation to do what he was asking. At least, he did not know anyone who would be prepared to do the work, and whose skills and body were up for sale. In a way that he hadn't expected, Charles was impressed that she was driving so hard a bargain. His admiration for her increased, but it caused him to hesitate for a moment. There was a lot at stake here for someone like Laura, who had nothing, yet she was being cautious. She was tougher than he had anticipated, and smarter, too. He recalled ruefully that he had always underestimated how ruthless women could be when they were protecting their own interests, like lionesses with their cubs. He should at least have learned that much in Australia from Betty Wellington, but then he preferred not to think of Betty, at least for the time being.

"All right," he asked her. "How much do you want then?"

"I don't know yet, Charlie. I'm not a calculating machine, and I'm not a bitch, in spite of what you may think. I'll need some more information and I'll need you to be honest with me, or I'm out." She gave him a quick, uncertain smile.

"I am not risking my life on a useless project, no matter how rich it may make me. Dead people can't spend money! Off the top of my head, and this may not be my last figure, I would want one hundred thousand dollars a month, a million bonus at the end of every year, and twenty-five per cent of the total action when you've gotten rid of the Ventura family, or you have suitably neutralized them and I am out of a job."

"Don't you think that may be a little greedy?"

"It's horribly greedy, but it also sounds horribly dangerous. Think it over anyway. If you can find the right person who'll do it for less, I can live without Bogotá, even if I stay broke, which isn't certain, is it?"

He sat for some moments in silence. Finally he asked, "You want it in writing?"

Laura shook her head rather sadly. She understood that

here, in this ordinary New York Deli, she was making a decision which would change her life irrevocably, and suddenly she felt as she thought she might feel if she were already old, looking back over the years and wondering whether she'd done the right thing; wondering what her life might have been if she had decided differently, had taken another path.

"No, Charlie, nothing in writing. If I can't trust you, a deal like this on paper won't help me any more than it would help you. Besides, once I get to Bogotá, if I ever get there, you will have to trust me, my friend! If I tell these Ventura boys that I'm there as your spy, not only do I go down the drain, but you go with me. We'll be each other's insurance policy."

He shrugged. "That's okay with me. I like working on a percentage basis. That way if there's no action, I don't lose out. You'd better get out your atlas, and find out where Colombia is. Read up a little history, just for conversation on those long dull evenings that couples enjoy, you know."

Charlie was not often outmanoeuvred in a transaction, and he felt pissed off. He reluctantly admired her, but his ego was bruised and he was not happy that it should be so. He wondered momentarily if he were making a mistake, using Laura. Perhaps, after all, she might be too smart for her own good, or for his.

"No, I don't know, as I've not yet had the cozy, suburban pleasure of being a couple." She gave him a cool, hard look, a look he did not recognize as having seen before, and which he did not much like.

"Let's get one thing straight before we start, Charlie. You may, perhaps, be paying me a great deal of money in the future, and I shall be worth every penny of whatever it is, so don't underestimate me, and don't ever patronize me. I don't like men who patronize women. It's a fool's game, you know. We may not have that little bit of equipment dangling so uncomfortably between our legs, so we've discovered a better place to park our brains."

"Okay, okay! So, it was just a suggestion. Maybe you can watch videos," Charlie said angrily.

"Before we moved to live in Minnesota, my father was trade attaché at the Swedish Legation in Bogotá and I lived there for four years when I was growing up. I'll bet I know more about Colombia than you'll ever know, and I speak Spanish fluently. It was my major in college. Now, why don't we get out of this place, and go somewhere nice together for one last fling! And then I'll give you my decision. Right now I want to go to the Pierre."

"In jeans?"

"Well, I won't be in them for long, will I? And at least I know that you don't have any pimples on that very trim and handsome butt of yours, don't I?"

He patted her arm. "You are a constant surprise to me," he said.

All women, he thought, are a constant surprise. They were always tougher and harder and braver and more realistic than he expected, when the chips were down.

"At least we shall never be bored in this partnership."

"Never," she agreed. "Often surprised, maybe, but never bored, if there's to be a partnership. I haven't made a decision – yet."

They walked out into the traffic and the noise and the crowded sidewalk of 7th Avenue. Laura sniffed the air. It was hot and benzene-filled, throbbing with the city noise, and electric with the peculiar tension which seems only to affect the air in New York. The beaded, hippie crowd, loose and swinging, crammed the pavement.

"I love New York," she said. "I can smell the danger in the air."

"If you can afford to breathe it," Charlie said.

"Not everyone in New York is rich," she said, holding his arm.

"True, but if you go to the movies or read the papers, you'll find out that not everyone in New York is having fun, either," he said. "Fun is expensive, and the older you get the more it costs."

"Get a taxi, Charlie. I don't want to think about being old. I want to go to the Pierre before you make me too sad to make love."

CHAPTER SIX

AT THE FINCA DE LA MADONNA DE LA LUNA
JULY 1969

THERE WERE NO INTRODUCTIONS when Judge Ruiz came into the long dining room. He nodded silently at Jaime at the head of the table and looked curiously at Nick, whom he did not know, but he said nothing. Don Jaime indicated a large leather chair at the foot of the table, opposite himself.

"Sit down, Don Fabrizio," he said pleasantly. "It has been a long time since we had the pleasure of seeing you here at the Finca."

"Not since your father died. More than ten years," the Judge said.

"It's good of you to come all the way from town," Sebastian said pleasantly.

Nick smiled. As if the poor Judge had any choice in the matter, he thought.

"I was ordered to come here, wasn't I?" he asked.

"Not ordered, Judge. That is too ugly a word between friends. I prefer the word invited. You are an honored guest here, as a friend of our dear father, and indeed of all our family."

The Judge, although still wary, seemed pleased that good manners were being maintained and any question of compulsion glossed over, at least publicly. Perhaps, he thought, if they all acted like gentlemen, then gentlemen's decisions would be made. Nick watched fascinated as these thoughts passed transparently over the Judge's lined old face. Good manners, like good clothes, he had learned from Charles, could satisfactorily cloak all manner of devious and unattractive activities, a lesson that only a few criminals ever learned. Most of them were very suspicious of good manners, even if they recognized them, and their clothes, although often expensive, were rarely good.

"You saw my mother, Dona Isabella, in town?" Jaime inquired pleasantly.

The boys' mother distanced herself from their activities, but she was sufficiently a realist to accept their money. Above all things, except perhaps God, and even that was debatable, their mother respected the power of money. As Dona Isabella's respectability was important to the family, Jaime was prepared to spend a good deal of money to maintain it. She lived in considerable style in a handsome palacio in Bogotá.

"I had the pleasure of dining with her last week," the Judge said. "His Grace the Archbishop of Bogotá was there also, and Dona Caterina de Aragon, who is visiting from Madrid."

Jaime regarded the Church as both corrupt and venal, but he understood only too well what could be bought for cash in that institution, so his mother's contributions to Holy Mother Church were maintained at a very generous level. He wanted the use of the Vatican banking system, and therefore his connections in that tiny and powerful feudal state were carefully maintained to facilitate any future arrangements when such connections might be useful. Nick concurred with such tactics and Charles Bellamy also supported these donations generously.

"Yes," Jaime agreed tersely. "The Holy Father himself

was kind enough to receive my mother in Rome last month." And a pretty penny that cost, he thought grimly.

Those priests know where the money comes from and how high it smells Nick thought, but so long as it keeps coming they don't care about the source any more than we do. It was simply a good policy to keep them sweet. You never knew when they might be needed.

"Judge, we have been discussing and reviewing the matter of your courier services for us," Jaime said softly.

"Yes?" The Judge was cautious. He carried funds from the casino in the Bahamas to America and other destinations, in cash, in return for a handsome monthly fee that defrayed his gambling debts and the cost of his women. These expenses had become considerable.

"There has been a shortfall in the funds that you have been handling for us," Jaime said. His voice was still very soft, but it was pleasant no longer. It sounded, Nick thought, like a sharp blade being scraped over ice.

There was so much cash that surely they could not have noticed the small amounts that he had held back for himself, the Judge thought. He felt the first tiny tremor of fear stir deep down in his bowels, as thin and astringent as a fine needle being inserted slowly into his intestines.

"However, there is a much more serious matter to be discussed than the paltry question of your embezzlement, stupid and disloyal as that may be," Jaime said very slowly and in the same soft and icy tone. "We understand that reports of your activities on our behalf have been finding their way back to the secret police here in Colombia, and even to the CIA."

Don Fabrizio coughed. This was worse than he had expected. "There have been some inquiries as to my many and frequent journeys out of the country," he said.

"Well? You were briefed on how to answer such questions

when you agreed to act as a courier for our interests, were you not? And that was an arrangement which, may I remind you, we agreed to on the basis of your long friendship with our family, and in the light of your own urgent need for funds."

"Jaime ..." the Judge interrupted.

"Don Jaime, if you please," Jaime said with freezing formality.

The Judge coughed again and gave a supplicating glance in Nick's direction. Nick felt sorry for him, but there was nothing he could do to help the man. If the Judge had betrayed them, he was a fool, but Nick had the feeling that the performance was being played out in his presence for a purpose. They were showing him, first hand on his first visit, what happened to those colleagues who did not act in the best interests of the Ventura y Cortez family.

"Don Jaime," the Judge said slowly. "The police already knew what I was doing."

Jaime shrugged. "Of course they knew, my friend, and now you have given them the proof they required. As we all know, there are no secrets in Bogotá. All they wanted to know was whether they were getting the right percentage for themselves."

"I was afraid," the old man said softly.

He had, however, not been as afraid as he was now, facing this icy young man across the table. To his great embarrassment he voided his bowels into his underlinen, and the disagreeable stink began to penetrate the close atmosphere of the hot room. It was all the evidence of guilt that Jaime required. This was not, after all, a court of law.

"Don Fabrizio," Jaime said carefully, "you are a lawyer yourself. You have been a judge. More importantly than any of that, you have been a friend. You knew that you could have come to us, and that we would have protected you in this matter. We spend a great deal of money here in Colombia each year to secure just such protection for your colleagues and associates who provide other, similar services for us."

"I didn't know ... I wasn't sure. There was so little time." The old man's voice trailed off sadly. He sat there in his own stench, looking miserable.

Suddenly Jaime banged his huge fist on the table. Nick jumped, although he noticed that the brothers paid no attention. "You have betrayed us," he bellowed, "and you have stolen from us when we trusted you, and now you lie to us. You are contemptible. Do you know that you have condemned to death all those agents to whom you have spoken? Their lives have been forfeited and they will be on your conscience."

He stood up and strode across the room and yanked open the huge doors. The two guards outside straightened up and looked startled.

"Take the Judge out into the courtyard and shoot him," Jaime said quietly.

"Don Jaime, no!" The old Judge struggled to his feet. "No," he begged, "it was all a mistake. A mistake! The Bishop ..."

Jaime looked down his nose with utter contempt. "You have discussed these matters with the Bishop?" he demanded incredulously. "Surely not even you could be such a fool?"

"The Bishop already knew. He said ... he said ..."

Jaime turned his back. "Get rid of this piece of scum," he said, "and then drive his car back to Bogotá. Leave it parked outside his house. He has not been here today. No one has seen him here; do you understand? You know what to do."

The two guards lifted the Judge under the armpits, sniffing fastidiously at the smell that emanated from him. They dragged him whimpering from the room. The old man seemed unable to stand. There was silence for a moment.

"Was that performance undertaken here today to impress me?" Nick asked eventually.

"Open the windows, for God's sake. The stink of shit in here is unbearable," Sebastian said. He held a cologne-soaked handkerchief to his face.

"Was all of that really necessary, Jaime?" Jorge asked.

Jaime looked at his brother with furious contempt. "We're not running a nursery here, you know, Jorge. The rules are the same for everyone, even for friends of our mother, even for my brothers, if any of you betray us." Jaime lifted his eyes to Nick's face. "Even for Mr Barton," he said, with a trace of a smile.

Nick tried to keep his voice steady. "I do not work for you, Don Jaime. Your decisions do not apply for those of us who work for Charles."

Jaime laughed. "Brave words, my friend, but you are in my territory now, and Charles has no mandate here. My decisions apply, no matter who pays your monthly cheque. You can't apply to Charles Bellamy for help if you are buried here on my Finca."

"That's true," Nick agreed, "but if you hurt me, you only harm yourself. You lose Charles Bellamy, and with him would go your American market, and everything that you have been building up for years. I hardly think I'm worth it!"

"Come on, now," Jesus interrupted impatiently. "These matters don't concern Nick. Leave him alone, Jaime. And let's get on with our business. That old man was a fool, and he's got what he deserves, but for God's sake don't tell Mother. We'll never hear the end of it. What will we do about the Bishop?"

Jaime shrugged. "Leave that to me," he said. "If the Vatican can get rid of a pope, we can dispose of a bishop." He looked pompously round the table. "And what happens here in this room goes no further."

Like hell it doesn't, Nick thought.

"Let's get on with business," Jesus said again, irritably. "Go on, Nick. What were we discussing before we were so rudely interrupted by Jaime's theatrical performance?"

Jesus, Nick thought, might well turn out to be more lethal than Jaime himself, but he liked the way the man dealt with things. He was a good deal less crude. He worked with his brain and he kept his emotions, if he had any, reasonably under control. That was reassuring.

Jaime snorted with grim laughter. "Why is it that these old men think that because they go to Mass on Sunday and spill their guts to some ignorant priest, some peasant who has taken holy orders, that they can spend the rest of the week immune from even the rudiments of good sense, let alone loyalty?" He looked at Nick across the table. "Since you've not been here before, Nick, this is to let you know just how we treat traitors in Colombia."

Nick started back as coolly as he could manage. "And do you think for one moment that either Charles or I can afford to treat our enemies in any other way simply because we are in New York and not out here in the sticks? Would you like us to arrange a similar display for your benefit when you visit the States?"

"I shall not be visiting the States," he said. "I leave those risks to Sebastian."

"Come on, Nick," Jesus said impatiently. "Let's get on with it!"

Nick picked up his papers. "As I was saying, we form a corporation, several in fact, to make a take-over bid for the Diggely-Doggely Supermarkets, and the two banks. We want you all in on those deals to invest some of your cash. You're going to have to put it somewhere, and the shares will go straight through the roof as soon as it's known that Charles is involved." Nick placed a sheaf of papers back in his briefcase.

"Now, as to the planned expansion, and your own difficulties in getting adequate supplies through to us. The Mexican border cannot be overused. No matter what bribes we pay, there'll always be some officious little chap who wants to be honest. You've lost the use of the two small airports in Arkansas and the one in Alabama, due to the change of governors in those states. Charles and I suggest that we buy an airline."

"An airline?" Jesus raised his eyebrows. "An international airline?"

"There are several in difficulties at the moment," Nick said, "and their directors would look kindly on a well cashed-up take-over bid. We shall need one that has operating rights out of Bogotá and into the States." Nick smiled as he estimated how intrigued the brothers were by this idea. This would be their idea of glamour.

"Do you know," he asked quietly, "how they unload the lavatories on these new Boeing jets? Do you think that too many people are going to be poking around in the passenger's ordure when it comes off the planes? We simply design special facilities, and transport your drugs on scheduled flights in the lavatory receptacles."

Jaime laughed. "We carry the shit in the shit? I like it. Trust Charles Bellamy to think of something like that."

"Then we can stop worrying about the trucks and the light planes and the bribery of all those small airports in Mexico and Texas and Arkansas with the endlessly greedy personnel and all their corrupt local politicians. We simply buy the company that deals with the waste disposal from the planes, unload it onto the Diggely Doggely delivery vans and straight into our own stores all over the country."

Jesus said, "Yes, it sounds good to me. It has the virtue of complete simplicity, like all truly great schemes. We might have to get hold of a small commuter airline or two as well, to help spread the stuff around quickly."

"We'll work on the fine details and I'll let you have a business plan once we have your agreement to invest," Nick said. "I'm sure you understand that we'll be talking some very serious money here, but Charles can find additional funds if we need them to close the deals. He'll treble your business in the next three years and double it again in the three after that. And the shares in these companies will double, at least. But I must have your assurance that you can keep up with us, or should we look elsewhere? The Golden Triangle? Russia? Afghanistan? They all want our money!"

"Yes, to buy armaments," Jamie said sourly, "and to make stupid wars."

"So? Are we in a position to criticize?" Sebastian asked with a smile, but he looked at Nick unpleasantly. "So, you want to find someone else to work with, do you?"

"No, Sebastian, we don't. Charles and I are very happy with you guys, but we must have an assurance that you're willing to make the necessary investment to keep up with us. Charles would rather work with you. The fewer colleagues we have, the less chance of trouble, and we don't understand the Asiatics or the Russians so well. After all, you guys are practically American."

"Ha!" Jorge said. "As American as any Harvard graduate."

"Don't worry, Nick," Jesus said. "We'll keep up with you, no matter how quickly you expand. You have my word on it."

"Okay, then, work with Jesus on the details," Jaime said eventually. "It sounds good to me. We certainly need a better way of shifting the cash, now that we've so much of it. Whatever you say, Nick, so long as we get a fair deal and first cut of the action." His mood had now swung around from suspicion to brotherly love. "Let's go and get a drink, then. I'm parched and this room stinks. Have them air it out before we come back."

They walked through the great doors, which had been the gates of the old Finca, and into the grand courtyard. It looked out over the valley dotted with the prize cattle for which the estate was famous and over towards the river and the low mountains in the blue, hazy distance that hid the real source of their new wealth. Drinks were set out on a large tray under a pergola shaded by grape vines and wisteria.

Nick watched the brothers standing together, the three of them so dark and Spanish, and wondered about Sebastian, their ambassador, the brother who came and went, so tall and fair and Nordic. Here we have Jesus the intellectual, he thought, and Jaime the extrovert and Jorge the heavyweight and Sebastian – the playboy? Was he, Nick wondered, the weak link in the chain? Was that how Charles planned to loosen their grip when the time came, as sooner or later, Nick knew, it would?

As they stood there, drinking a glass of wine in the shade of the pergola, two men passed carrying the body of the Judge on a stretcher, headed for the chapel. Jaime had forgotten nothing, not even a priest to say a blessing over the body and to send the Judge's soul on its journey, hopefully in the right direction.

Sebastian came over. "Are you returning to Miami now?"

"Miami? No, I'm going to New York," Nick said, "to fix up our deals. Why do you ask?"

"I'm to meet with your boss in Miami, day after to-morrow. Didn't you know?"

"He doesn't tell me everything," Nick said, but he was annoyed. It made him look a fool, just when it was most important to have the appearance of complete authority with these men. However, it was a small but significant consolation to know that even Charles could make a mistake. But there must not be too many. The Ventura brothers might not be too bright, but they were very shrewd and quite ruthless. Together they made a very formidable combination, and there were four of them. There would be no room for mistakes.

"I'm going in to Bogotá," Sebastian said. "Do you want a lift to the airport?"

"Yes, thanks. As soon as we've finished our business here."

"Jaime has agreed to what you've asked," Sebastian said. "So your business is finished already. It's up to you to sort out the details and make sure that we get a fair deal."

"You always have," Nick said shortly. He shivered. He would be glad to leave. The Finca, although in beautiful country, depressed him. The whole of Colombia, he thought, was sad. The country felt as if it were moving backwards rapidly into a brutal past. He preferred America. Somehow, hurtling forward into a brutal future was preferable to going backwards. At least, Nick considered, in America, no matter how rough the journey, he was travelling in the right direction.

He nodded briefly to Sebastian. "Sure, whenever you're ready, then. Thanks."

CHAPTER SEVEN

FLORIDA YACHT CLUB, MIAMI, FLORIDA
JULY 1969

"REMEMBER, I DON'T WANT Sebastian to know that I brought you down here to meet him. It will make him suspicious," Charles said.

He wondered, for a moment, now that he had invested more than a hundred thousand dollars in the idea, whether Laura would be able to carry off the assignment, and whether, after all, he could trust her if she did indeed end up with Sebastian in Bogotá.

"I know, I know," she said impatiently. "I just walk by and I'm surprised to see you. I can do that, you know. I am an actress."

"Of sorts," he said unkindly.

"And you are a businessman – of sorts." Charles could not intimidate Laura.

"How do you get into a place like this, anyway? Isn't this a private club?"

They were lunching on the terrace of the Florida Yacht Club, overlooking the harbour and the wharves, at which were moored several huge cruise boats and, closer in, a mass of private yachts. Across the water lay Key Biscayne, and the long road and all the bridges that snaked their way down to Key West, only sixty miles from Cuba.

"We are here as guests," he said.

"But guests of whom?"

He smiled. Suddenly he felt in a better mood, felt that this would succeed.

"We are guests of a friend of mine. Never mind that. Just remember, Laura, that life is a one-way journey, and there are no happy endings. We all end up dead in the end – everyone. So you may as well go first class if you can. You don't get to practise and you don't get a second run."

"What about heaven?"

"I'll wait until I get there to make a judgment. If it's as comfortable as this place, I won't be complaining, except possibly about the company I may have to keep. Besides which, think of it! Practically everyone there will either be old or babies!"

She sat back in her chair and looked out over the water. For the first time in her life, she felt completely relaxed, perfectly dressed, absolutely right, down to the plain, heavy gold earrings and bracelet that Charles had bought for her at Van Cleef & Arpels before they left New York. They had cost a fortune and, in her experience, he was not given to generous gestures.

"Where did you learn to shop?" Laura asked.

"There's no trick to that," he said. "You simply go to the best shops, get the oldest and most experienced saleswoman, and listen to her advice. Women always know what other women should wear. Never take advice from a man. It's the old girls who will always tell the truth. Let them know that you're going to spend money and they want you to come back." He smiled. "You look great."

"It's not too hard, when you've the right gear and at least two thousand bucks to spend on every dress you buy. You wait until you see me this evening in that Chanel outfit. If I don't have this Sebastian jumping out of his seat, I'll want to know why."

The waiter placed a Waldorf salad in front of her and poured a glass of Sancerre.

When he had gone Laura said, "Tell me again. Four brothers, all educated at Harvard? So, are they very South American or very East Coast?"

"East Coast Spanish, I guess, from the look of them. I've only seen photos. Sebastian is the only one I've actually met," he said, after a moment's thought, "and he is very East Coast. He's completely Fifth Avenue and Palm Beach. He would certainly not pass unnoticed in this town. The other three look kind of dark and swarthy from their photographs, but I've picked the pretty one for you. Sebastian is tall and fair and quite presentable. He could be Scandinavian. I don't know where they got him. Some genes in the bloodline from a stray sailor, I guess. He's sophisticated. He knows his way around and is very plausible. Quite ruthless, of course, like all the rest of them."

"And you are not?"

"I'm not ruthless," he objected. "I'm just doing what I must do to try to make a better world."

She was astonished that he could believe this, but she had come to think that he really did, and she considered that his ability to think in this way made him very dangerous indeed.

"Mmmm," she said slowly. "That's what Robespierre said, too, and Hitler, and Lenin and Chairman Mao and all the rest of them who just knew they were right. Let's not kid ourselves, Charles. What we're doing will not make a better world for anyone, except possibly us. Let's not add hypocrisy to our other sins."

"You'll see what I can do when I'm ready," he said. He reached out and put his hand on her arm. She was touched by this show of concern, although she told herself that she should not allow it to affect her judgment.

"You do know, don't you, that you can't afford a mistake with these guys?"

She patted his hand. "It's all right, Charlie, I'm a big girl now, you know. You wouldn't be paying me as much as you are if this were going to be easy. If it comes to that, I know that I can't afford to make a mistake with you either, for all your high falutin' notions of making a better world."

"You don't pull your punches, do you?"

"In Minnesota, we weren't raised to mess around too much with the truth," she said, "even with a diplomat for a father." She smiled at him. "Money won't buy you everything, you know, Charlie."

"Perhaps not everything," he said. "Just everything I want, and everything the Ventura boys want, and even, I suspect, most of the things you want."

"And what if I want you?" Laura asked.

"Ah, well, my darling, you're quite right. Money won't buy that. At least not any more of me than you've already had, and that I gave away for free!"

"You know I'm in love with you," she said in a low voice.

He was untouched by her confession. "Don't be," he said. "You know as well as I do that it would be a mistake and I like you too well for that! And worse, it might affect your judgment."

"Every successful man needs a wife. I've told you that once before."

"When I marry, it won't be for love," he said.

"What for, then? If everything goes well, you won't need the money."

"For position," he said. "For power. To open those few secret doors that would otherwise remain closed to me, no matter how much money I have. Those last few magic doors.

That's something you can't buy, Laura, and I can't wait three generations to prize them open. I'm too impatient for that!"

"And what makes you think that kind of woman will look at you?"

"It will take time," he said, "but somewhere out there she's waiting. After all," he grinned, "I shall be very rich, and not too many very rich people are young and pretty, like me."

"Maybe not, but they have the same amount of vanity. Onassis didn't need to be young and pretty to get Jackie." She looked at him for a long while. "You know, Charlie, you've been hurt by one woman, and you're taking it out on all of us. You'd think you were the only man who ever got dumped."

"No," he said, "but I'm the only one I know who was dumped and shafted at the same time, and then deliberately tossed onto the trash heap. Besides, it's not time for me to marry yet, and you have other things to do."

"Perhaps I shall be rich and powerful one day, too," Laura said. "Perhaps I shall be able to open doors for you."

"You never know," he said. "It's a crazy world and anything can happen."

He did not take her seriously, she knew. I wonder, she thought, when he will realize that I am as determined to win this game as he is.

The waiter removed the plates, and served a lemon sorbet.

"What does Nick Barton do for you?" Laura asked.

"He's my lawyer. He does whatever I ask him to do."

"Anything at all?"

Laura liked Nick. She had liked him from the time they'd first met, in the bar on 2nd Avenue, when he had blushed, but she did not have a high regard for his ability to survive and prosper in this new world in which they all now lived. "Is he tough enough for that, do you think?"

"He might say the same about you. Are you questioning my judgment?"

"We can all make mistakes." She looked around, acknowledging the admiring glances from the men in the room.

"Do you think there's any way that governments can stop this trade in drugs?" she asked.

"Sure. Make it all legal and spend the cash on therapy instead of chasing mirages. Drugs are a medical and a social problem. We've just managed to turn them into a criminal one. They could stop it overnight, but they'll never do that. We are quite safe for a long while to come."

"Why is that?" She did not feel safe.

"Everyone is making too much money. They didn't learn any lessons from Prohibition, and they're not learning any now. Who was it that said 'those who know nothing about history are bound to repeat it?' That's the wonderful thing about democracy." He laughed. "They're all such slow learners, you see, and all so greedy, and such cowards. When they don't know what to do, they have a meeting, shifting the blame onto someone else," Charles said. "No matter what, whenever you want one of the bastards, they're having a meeting. And while they're doing that we're about to expand, my dear. It'll be a roller coaster! That's why Nick's been down in Medellin, just now, meeting with the boys. We're going to be real big, shortly. With your help."

"I should be very proud," she said with an edge of sarcasm.

"Now, don't be like that, Laura. You never know what may come out of this. The sky's the limit. If you give up now and go home to Minnesota, nothing will happen to you at all. You'll just have a life like everyone else. One must gamble."

"I might bring up a couple of nice kids."

"You might. You might do that anyway, but the world is full of nice kids. Maybe there are more important things to do."

"Like selling them drugs?"

"I've told you. This is a means to a better end."

She stood up, and kissed him lightly on the cheek. "Well, if you can convince yourself of that, I suppose I can. I'm going up to rest. What time shall I accidentally drift by?"

"Around eight," he said, "in the bar."

"We are all conspirators, Charles," she said, "and like all conspirators, we all have a secret agenda."

He wondered what she meant by that. He watched her cross the terrace. He watched the men watching her. The women's eyes watched their men watching her. She would do the job perfectly.

Later, in the evening, it would have been difficult to distinguish Sebastian and Charles from any of the aristocrats and millionaires lounging around their tables. The two men sat together in their immaculate dinner jackets and their understated Cartier watches. In fact, they looked better bred than the real thing, slimmer, healthier, handsomer and brighter. Charles was amused. It was the kind of thing he always found funny.

"I'm impressed," Sebastian said quietly. "This is much better than any hotel in town. There's no doubt about you, Charles. You know your way around."

Charles smiled. "You look pretty classy, too, Seb. Not like some South American spic at all."

Sebastian laughed. "Up yours, too, my friend. Where were you when I was at Harvard?"

Charles smiled. "Learning about the world, and how full of shit it all is!"

"Well done! That's pretty much what I learned at Harvard, but you probably got it for less."

Charles laughed ruefully. "Not much less, as it turned out!"

"Now," Sebastian said, "This plan of yours that Nick has

been discussing with my brothers down at the Finca. You know that Jaime has approved in principle?"

"Of course."

"Personally, I didn't think he'd would go for it."

"Oh? I didn't think we'd have too much trouble persuading him. He loves to bluster with us, but in the end he knows a good thing. When am I going to meet him?"

"One day soon, I guess. He doesn't like coming to the States. He's scared!" Sebastian pushed his chair back slightly and looked around the room. The mirrors on the apricot walls reflected the flowers set in the great porcelain bowls against the walls, and the jewels of the women, and the waiters serving the perfectly presented food, while beyond the huge windows the masts of the yachts swayed and turned lazily in the warm, tropical air. "Jaime would come to a place like this, I think," Sebastian said. "It would make him feel safe."

"He'll come when we get this thing going. The profits will be immense. Nick is back in New York already, working with the brokers and the lawyers. Jaime might seem like a donkey, Sebastian, but he's not a complete fool. I'd be careful if I were you, my friend. I wouldn't underestimate him. He knows that we must launder the cash and get it legitimately invested all over the world. That's what will give us real power, not making illegal cash on the fringes of society like a mob of Mafioso crooks. He'll go along with our plans."

"I don't think he has your social ambitions, Charles."

"No? But perhaps you do, otherwise what's the money for? I think Jaime wants power just as much as the rest of us, but for different reasons."

"So? How do we put it together then, Charles?"

The sommelier presented a bottle of Krug Imperial for their approval and poured it into the tulip-shaped glasses.

Charles raised his glass. "To our joint good fortune," he said. "Nick has a mass of lawyers on his staff. Let them sort it out. Corporations offshore, casinos, banks, dummy corporations in countries that don't ask too many questions. Accounts in Switzerland, Liechtenstein, the Bahamas, many places like that. They never care where the cash comes from so long as it comes in. It won't be much longer before computers will be moving money with the speed of light around a global economy. Most places won't give a shit where it comes from so long as they have their share. In the States, of course, we shall always be totally kosher, cleaner than a virgin's knickers. Offshore, we'll simply find the countries most easy to corrupt, and then we'll buy them."

"And the distribution here? These supermarket chains, and airlines and whatever? What about the opposition? What about the Mafia? What about the Chinese? They won't take too kindly to being pushed aside by a few jumped-up little shits like us."

Charles leaned back in his chair and sipped his champagne. He looked at Sebastian. "Do you remember when you approached me in the Village and first asked me to deal with you and set up a distribution network?"

"Sure I remember. It's less than three years ago."

"Why did you choose me?"

Sebastian shrugged. "We wanted a part of the action in a very dangerous game. You had style. You had the brains, and you had the balls, and you were greedy and ambitious enough to share it with us. It seemed to me an invincible combination."

"And have I performed?" Charles asked. He knew the answer to that.

Sebastian smiled. "You know you have, above and beyond the call of duty. We're making more money than I ever believed possible, and we've got those shits in Medellin and

Bogotá off our back, by processing the stuff ourselves and selling direct through you."

"And what advice did I give you then?"

"Charge the top price, sell the best quality, and only deal with the nobs!"

Charles smiled. "That left the shitty trade for the opposition."

"Has there been trouble?"

"Occasionally, but nothing I can't handle. No one wants a shoot out, you know."

"Except the press and a few gung-ho FBI chaps. A few arrests to make them all look good." They both laughed.

"The opposition would like to have the carriage trade," Charles said, "but they haven't a chance. What they don't know is that we are about to move in on their territory. That they won't like."

"Is it worth the trouble?"

"I want it all," Charles said shortly. "Or as much of it as I can grab. Nick will get the legal boys and the accountants to draw up a complete business plan for you to take back to Bogotá. We'll go to New York before you leave and get it all clear. I'll let the pilot know that we'll take the jet up tomorrow."

Charles leaned over and tapped him on the arm. "Sebastian! This is important, my friend. You're not paying attention!"

"I've just caught sight of the most gorgeous girl I've ever seen in my whole goddam life."

Charles grinned to himself. He knew from the glazed look in Sebastian's eyes that he had seen Laura. Charles turned around. Even he was surprised at how stunning she looked, in the long cream and black silk suit he had bought her at Chanel and the pearls. She had swept her hair up on top of her head and pinned it back with diamond clips. She looked like Audrey Hepburn pretending to be a princess in "My Fair Lady." Better, she looked like a princess pretending to be Audrey Hepburn. Sebastian was transfixed. Well, Charles thought, that's a good start.

"I know that girl," Charles said casually. "She's from New York." He waved, and Laura smiled a professionally delighted smile.

"Why, Charlie Bellamy! What a surprise! Whatever are you doing down in these unfashionable parts in the middle of summer?"

"Catching a few rays," he said. "How about you?"

"Escaping from New York when I should be there," Laura said. "But a girl can only go to so many parties. I'm waiting for the Nigels' yacht. We're all going to the Caribbean for a few days."

Sebastian stood beside him and jabbed him in the ribs. Charles turned, as if surprised to find someone there.

"Laura, may I present my friend, Don Sebastian Ventura y Cortez, from Colombia," he said. "Seb, this is Miss Laura Tessier, who is the loveliest girl in Manhattan."

Sebastian bent over her hand and brushed the tips of her fingers with his lips. "Enchanted, Miss Tessier." He gave Charles a kick in the shins, and grinned. Charles took the hint.

"Laura, we're all alone and miserable. Won't you join us for a drink?"

"Or for dinner?" Sebastian interrupted.

Laura laughed. "I'm sorry, boys. I don't believe I'll be free for dinner, but a glass of champagne perhaps." She turned to Sebastian and, in flawless Spanish, inquired where he lived and whether he played polo in Buenos Aires with the Mendoza brothers.

"I do so love to watch men play polo," she said. "The last

bastion of masculinity and privilege. Practically the only place, any more, where one sees both together."

"The only sport that combines money and balls," Charles said.

Laura gazed at him without a smile. "Crude as always, my dear Charles. I'm sure that Senor Ventura could manage something more subtle than that!"

She gave Sebastian a ravishing smile. This is too easy, she thought. And Charles was right, he is handsome, too.

Sebastian leaned over. "Can't we persuade you to cancel your dinner and stay with us for the evening, Miss Tessier?"

"Laura," she said, "please."

At the end of the week, when Sebastian returned from his meetings in New York, Laura left Miami with him, and went to live in Bogotá. As the plane took off, lifting out over the Keys and heading south across the lovely scattered islands of the Caribbean, she looked down at the sparkling innocent-looking sea scattered with those magical little patches of land, so beautiful and corrupt. She felt as if her old self had died, and some new person had been born, someone whom she did not yet know, and maybe would not like, someone tougher and more successful than the little college girl from Minnesota who had gone so naively to New York. A survivor.

It was a gamble, as Charles said, and she felt the gambler's fever under her skin.

Flying to Bogotá with Sebastian, she thought about Nick Barton. She thought about the rumours he was starting to put about in Bar Harbor and Palm Beach that Charlie was the illegitimate son of a marquis, or perhaps even of a member of the British Royal Family. Once she had been inclined to laugh, or to think all of it was crazy, and rather foolish. Now she understood that it was camouflage, a camouflage of style, and of money and glamour and rumour and envy, that would protect them all from the suspicion of doing anything wrong.

In a way, Charles is crazy, she thought. He sees himself as some kind of messiah, and I am frightened of messiahs. Anyone who believes he has the true word and the ear of God is a major danger to everyone.

She turned and looked at Sebastian's clean-cut collegiate profile in the seat beside her. So far as she could work out he regarded himself simply as a successful, rich businessman working no closer to the edge of the law than any aristocrat was entitled to do. And, of course, a first-rate lover. That I can handle more easily than a messiah, she thought. That at least I can understand.

And what do I think of myself? A spy? A fool? A successful tart? It was difficult to decide. I'm not being paid for the fucking, so I guess I'm not strictly a tart, she thought. It's just a means to an end, like a woman married for security to a man whom she does not love. A perfectly respectable arrangement. It's done all the time, sex and companionship and a well-run house in exchange for an adequate income.

In truth, she finally admitted to herself, I'm no different from Charlie and Nick or this handsome man sitting beside me. I'm prepared to do anything to succeed.

PART TWO

Along The Sparkling Foreshores Of Florida
April – July 1979

CHAPTER ONE

MIAMI, FLORIDA
APRIL 1979

CHARLES BELLAMY STOOD AT the window of his penthouse office on the top of the Miami Trust and Savings Building, and looked down over the blue expanse of Biscayne Bay, thinking how many years had passed since he had seen Laura, and wondering whether she was still so beautiful. It was almost ten years since she had gone to Bogotá with Sebastian Ventura, but he thought of her often. The view from his windows pleased him. Beyond those azure seas lay Colombia and the huge wealth of the Catholic and corrupt dictatorships of Central and South America. They were all so greedy, so disorganized, so rapacious, and so easy to do business with in these uncertain times.

Greed was good. Greed was fashionable. Business was almost too easy. No one seemed to care about illegality. Money was the new religion, and its vulgar altars were everywhere. Charles's self-satisfied contemplation of these succulent facts, and of the huge panorama below him, was interrupted by the low buzz of his desk telephone.

"Yes?"

It was Sydney Wallace, his vice-president for customer services. "Mrs van Breevoort would like to see you."

"Sydney, you know I never see private clients at the bank."

"She is most insistent, Mr Bellamy, and she brings us a lot of business."

"Very well – just for one minute, then."

Emily van Breevoort had the good fortune to combine in her ancestors both the old Dutch aristocracy that had founded New York, and the new money that succeeded them. She had a duplex apartment on Park Avenue, and a large mansion in Palm Beach, where she spent the winter. She came into the room now, dressed busily and fussily and full of her own consequence. She was ugly as a frog, but with the commanding presence of a queen. Charles felt that she was not a woman he would like to have as an enemy, and he had taken a great deal of care that she should not be one. He kissed her on the cheek, and she blushed.

"Now that's enough of that," she said, plainly enjoying herself.

"I suppose you've come for a donation to your Historic Homes Foundation, Emily." Charles was very generous to the favourite charities of these powerful dowagers. It had opened a lot of doors, and had brought the bank a lot of legitimate business of the right kind. Its reputation had been enhanced, and its respectability assured.

"Well, you suppose wrong for once, my dear Charles. I have come to ask you to a party at my house in Palm Beach. It will be my last party of the season before I go back to New York. It's to be a very special party."

"Oh? Why so special?" Emily considered all her parties to be special. In fact, they were usually very dull, and Charles avoided them unless he knew of a guest whom he particularly wanted to meet. No one of importance in America, or elsewhere for that matter, ever went to Palm Beach without being entertained by Emily van Breevoort.

She settled herself comfortably on one of his sofas, by the

long windows overlooking the bay.

"This is a charming room, Charles. Much too good for an office, and full of quite marvellous pictures." She surveyed the room with the practised eye of a connoisseur.

"Come, Emily, you don't visit me to discuss interior decoration."

"Since you came to Miami and bought this bank, and whatever other stuff you own, which seems to me to be plenty," she said, in her frank, outspoken manner, "you have been very good to me. Oh, I know that I'm a silly, tiresome old woman, so don't tell me that I'm not, because I won't believe you."

"Very well then, Emily," he said. "You are a silly, tiresome old woman."

She laughed. "I like you, Charles Bellamy. Some people around here say you are a royal bastard, in both senses of the words, and some tell me that you're a drug peddler and an undesirable character, and I shouldn't have anything to do with you!"

He smiled. "For anyone who succeeds, you know, Emily, there is always envy and gossip, and a million rumours, usually not very nice. None of it is ever true, more's the pity, or I should be a much more interesting man."

"Quite. The gossip in Palm Beach is frightful, but of course one would die of boredom without it, but that's not what I came to talk about." She leant forward on the sofa and tapped his knee. "I want to give you some good advice in return for all the money you've made for me," she said.

"Advice?" Charles was amused that this dowdy old woman should feel that he needed her advice.

"Over the years, you have given me a lot of excellent information. I can't think why you do it, or where you get it from, but I have become even richer than I was by listening to you, and I like that. Now I'm going to return the favour by interfering in your life. That's what rich, plain old ladies are for, you know. They arrange the lives of rich, handsome young men."

"I wondered what they did," he said. "I am pleased to know it is so innocent."

"Now, Charles, don't be naughty. This is a serious matter. You say the gossip doesn't matter, and that anyway it isn't true, but you are an ambitious man and, if you're not careful, it will damage you in just the places where you're most vulnerable. Eventually it may well prevent you from going where you want to go."

"And where is that?"

"To the top," she said flatly. "You can't afford a suspicious reputation up there. At least not until you are behind the sacred closed doors, and then, my dear, as we both know, you can get away with anything. Have you ever heard of the Countess de Trafford?"

"My dear Emily, everyone has heard of Lady de Trafford. She is as famous and as chic as Jackie O."

"Quite," she said with some disapproval. "All that vulgar publicity. I suppose it's all right for those Kennedy women, but my mother told me a lady's name should be in the newspapers only three times. When she is born, when she marries and when she dies. Unfortunately, my niece seems to have a talent for attracting undesirable attention from the less responsible media." She looked at him shrewdly. "You're not surprised?"

"Surprised by what?"

"That Edwina's my niece?"

He smiled. "Do you imagine I would be as successful as I am if I didn't know those kinds of things?"

"You are very provoking, Charles. I had hoped to surprise you. She is my late brother's daughter. He squandered his fortune and killed himself. He was a very foolish man. You know her husband was murdered?"

"Everyone in the English-speaking world knows about that, Emily. The newspapers have been filled with nothing else for months. As a matter of fact, I knew him quite well."

"You knew Marcus de Trafford?" Now it was Emily who sounded surprised, although she very quickly suppressed her tone, in case she should sound ill-mannered. "So you've met Edwina already?"

"No. Her husband and I were business associates only."

"Business associates? I wasn't aware that Marcus had any business."

"How do you imagine he earned enough money to restore that old castle of his and support such an expensive life-style and such a glamorous wife?"

"Yes, well, be that as it may, her life is a mess at the moment, as you can imagine. All kinds of scandal and innuendo. It is all very unpleasant. There has been far too much publicity and you know where that leads! Vulgar speculation! So I've asked her to come visit with me here. I think it would be nice if you met her." She gave him a rather arch look, and he laughed.

"Are you by any chance doing something else that rich, plain old ladies are alleged to do?"

"Exactly. I am trying to do a little matchmaking. To keep yourself clear of dirty talk you need to marry, my dear Charles. And you must marry well. You're much too smart not to know that. Edwina would be very suitable. Marcus seems to have been broke when he was murdered, apart from the entail, which, of course, she can't touch. It goes to some dreary nephew or cousin in Alberta. Anyway, she has position but no money. You have ..."

"Money but no family," he finished for her. "My goodness, Emily, you do get down to basics."

"The upper classes have not survived by beating around the bush in these matters," she said firmly.

"And what about love?"

"Love? Goodness me, Charles, you're not a pair of domestics. Edwina comes from one of the oldest and most distinguished families in America. Her uncle, who brought her up after her fool of a father killed himself in a car crash, was our Ambassador to the Court of St James. Her first husband was a Ponsonby. That was a disaster, but all the Ponsonbys are not impossible. They're no more raffish than the Churchills, and look at Pamela."

"Pamela is not a Churchill. She merely married one, some considerable time ago."

Emily ignored him. "And then Edwina married Marcus de Trafford, who was a cousin of the Queen, you know. Or was it the Queen Mother? One or the other, anyway. It's all the same to me."

"All very well and good," Charles said, "and I'm very much obliged to you for taking all this trouble, but she may not wish to marry me, or indeed anyone at all, after all this drama. What is more to the point, I may not wish to get married."

"She is broke," Emily said, "and you are very rich. At least, I suppose you are. And good-looking, too. I never cared for the way Marcus looked. Rather decadent, I thought, and seedy."

"So are you very rich, and you tell me that her uncle was an ambassador. She can hardly be destitute, and Marcus de Trafford must have left something, surely?"

"Debts! Why do you think Jackie married Onassis?"

"To be independent of the Kennedy clan?"

"Exactly!"

"Ah!"

She gave him a penetrating look. "Charles, I don't know why, but I am fond of you, so let me speak frankly," she said. Emily fanned herself with a magazine. She was finding this a little more difficult than she had thought. Charles was not easy to patronize. Attractive, yes, and quite relaxed, but really rather formidable when it came to the point.

"If what you've been doing up to now hasn't been speaking frankly, Emily, then I am at a loss to know what it is."

"Now, don't be provoking, Charles. We are worldly people, you and I. You are an ambitious man. Ambitious for power, I think, and position, not just for money, which you and I understand is merely a tool. Edwina would be the perfect wife. I would like you to meet her. In spite of what you may have read in those terrible newspapers, she is extremely nice and I love her dearly. Will you come?"

"Yes, of course, Emily. For you, anything, but I am making no promises. I am a confirmed bachelor."

"What utter nonsense," she said. "You are in the prime of life, as they say, and you need a wife. In fact, my dear Charles, to get where you want to go, you must have one, and whoever she is must be the right woman. Not so easy to find for a man like you," she added shrewdly. "The wrong marriage could undo everything. You know that."

He had a sudden vision of himself sitting on the terrace of the Yacht Club almost ten years ago with Laura, before she went to Bogotá, listening to the same conversation. He had not seen Laura since that day. Sebastian did not encourage her to travel. Nevertheless, a considerable part of the immense fortune he had made was due to the information Laura had given him, over those ten long years. She, too, would be rich when he had finished with the Ventura family, if she were still alive then, but he could never marry Laura. Emily was right. If he were to succeed in all his ambitions, he must choose the right wife. In matters such as these women were so much more powerful and important than most of them could be persuaded to believe.

"Yes," he said, "someone else told me that, many years ago. She wanted to marry me, too."

Emily sniffed. "I am surprised you have escaped."

He smiled. "It took determination," he said.

"So I shall expect you tomorrow evening. Black tie at seven thirty. I shall tell Edwina that you knew her husband."

"Not a good idea, I think," he said.

"Goodness, why ever not? She'll be so curious."

"Curious and surprised, I should think," he said, but he made no further demur.

After Emily left, Charles buzzed his secretary. "Have Jake do a flight plan to Palm Beach for tomorrow afternoon, for the small jet, and a car to meet me at the Palm Beach airport at seven o'clock," he asked.

"Will you stay the night in Palm Beach, Mr Bellamy?"

"No, I'll return after the party," he said.

He went back, after Emily's departure, to the contemplation of his view. He considered with some pleasure all those rapacious, ill-governed islands in the sun that enabled him to flourish so prosperously with their lax banking laws, and corruptible police and politicians. Miami sprawled around him in the sunshine. It was a city that suited him as if he had designed it for himself. Here, with his perfect clothes and perfect manners and his upper-class English voice, he had been accepted without question, as he would not have been, perhaps, in London or New York or Philadelphia, no matter how rich he might have become.

It was extraordinary that Emily should come, at that moment, to talk of marriage. It had been uppermost in his mind for some time, a marriage to someone totally invulnerable, who would carry his reputation should anything be suspect. It must be a marriage to a woman who could open the secret and innermost doors of international power and society for him. Edwina de Trafford came, certainly, from the right background, but her own reputation was a little battered. First a scandalous divorce from a playboy who had thought that she had more money than she had. Well, no one who mattered cared about that. Everyone was allowed one youthful indiscretion. Then a much grander marriage to a penniless peer with a very dangerous reputation, a cousin to the Queen and a well-known homosexual. Well, anyway, bi-sexual!

No one cared about any of that either, but they knew. Just as all the in-crowd had known, in London, and the South of France, that Marcus dealt in drugs to maintain that luxurious lifestyle, and to restore that horrible and uncomfortable castle of his in Scotland that had now passed to his heir in Canada.

But, thought Charles, the murder was another matter. Nasty. Very regrettable. It had been a huge mistake, and he did not care to make mistakes. He should have realized that smart and powerful people do not like their indiscretions made public, particularly sexual indiscretions. Hadn't Mrs. Pat Campbell said, eighty years ago, that you may do anything you like in England, so long as you don't do it in the street and frighten the horses. Still true, but he had forgotten it for one crucial moment.

Now he would have to think more about Edwina de Trafford. He did not care to upset Emily. She was a very powerful and determined woman, and he had no wish to offend her. He hoped he had not made a mistake in accepting her invitation. He laughed rather mirthlessly to himself. Where women were concerned, it seemed to him that he always made mistakes. He had become rich and powerful, but he was still a fool about women.

While he was puzzling over these matters, Nick Barton knocked on his door and came in from the private entrance before he could call out and tell him to bugger off.

"Good morning, Charles,"

"Afternoon, I think, Nick. To what do I owe this rather unceremonious interruption?"

Nick laughed. Charlie and he had been together long enough by now, more than twelve years, and he knew too much about his affairs to be impressed by this kind of stuff.

"Don't be so pompous, Charlie. It's only me, not His Holiness the Pope or the Miami Vice Squad. It seems we have a small problem."

"No problem is small if it's worthy of the name," Charles snapped irritably.

"That reporter fellow, Peter Francis ..."

"That shabby bastard. He can't even dress decently! Don't tell me he's snooping around again. I thought we had him fired from the *Miami Herald*."

"We did. He's freelancing."

"What's he living on?"

Nick shrugged. "Someone must be paying," he said.

"Well, Jesus Christ, Nick, do I have to do everything around here? Find out and stop it."

"He's working with Jerkovitz," Nick said.

"Lieutenant Stan Jerkovitz?"

"None other! How many Jerkovitzes do you know?"

"That dumb Polish cop in the Drug Squad?" Charlie laughed. "He and that Francis chap are both so stupid it's hardly worth worrying about them, but find out who is bankrolling them and stamp on it before it gets out of control."

"Ok, Charlie. And then there's Australia."

"God," Charles said. "That place is my nemesis. I'm not quite ready to push the Wellingtons into the picture yet. What about that chap Phillip Morgan-Smith in Melbourne?"

"We may have to activate the Wellingtons now, Charles. Phillip Morgan-Smith is dead. Drowned while sailing on a yacht in Port Phillip Bay. I believe a good deal of the Ventura family's money was sticking to his upper-class fingers."

"So it wasn't an accident?" Charlie shrugged philosophically. "Isn't that typical. I told you that they're all crooks down there. Did we arrange it?"

Nick shook his head. "No. It wasn't really our concern. I should imagine it was the Medellin crowd, possibly even Jaime himself."

"I wonder why? Was he dealing with someone else as well?"

Nick shook his head. "So far as I know he only bought through us, but anything's possible. He was probably too greedy, standing on the toes of the local Mafia."

Charlie laughed harshly. "There's nothing worse than an upper-class crook. They're so bloody self-righteous, as if they've a God-given right to do as they please!"

"I'm searching for more information, Charlie, but it seems to me that after so many years of plain sailing, a suspicious number of problems are cropping up."

"What are you trying to tell me, Nick?"

"Well, I just don't like the fact that things are going wrong. It's not an accident, Charlie. There are no coincidences in life. Well, anyway not in business! Someone knows more than they should about what we're doing and whoever it is, they are out to make trouble for us, I should think."

"What trouble?"

"Stan Jerkovitz and Peter Francis snooping around, and now Phillip Morgan-Smith goes off the rails."

Charlie shrugged. "Well, he wasn't really working for us. I don't see the problem."

"I just don't like the feel of it."

Charles looked at him. "You're right, Nick. You're always right when you get these feelings, and we can't afford to have trouble now. All right. Get to work on the Wellingtons. It's time I paid them back in their own coin. Put our Australian plan into action, then. And Nick?"

Nick turned as he was leaving.

"You may have to do something about Morgan-Smith's wife. She knows altogether too much for her own good – or ours!"

Nick shrugged. "Not now, Charlie. She's harmless. One thing at a time. What about the reporter, Peter Francis?"

"Just keep an eye on him. Let me know what's going on. I doubt that he can find out anything relevant, even with the help of that fool Jerkovitz, but we need to be careful. I don't want to have to get rid of a cop, unless we must. It always creates too many waves, but a reporter won't ruffle anyone's feathers."

Nick went out and closed the door behind him.

CHAPTER TWO

PALM BEACH FLORIDA
APRIL 1979

EDWINA CARLINGFORD PONSONBY de Trafford was dressing at Emily van Breevoort's house in Palm Beach on the evening following her aunt's meeting with Charles Bellamy. Her name was famous, perhaps even slightly notorious at that time. Her husband Marcus, the fifteenth Earl de Trafford, had been dead for more than a year, and some of the notoriety surrounding the sexually explicit manner of his murder had abated. Edwina felt that evening, for the first time since then, a delicious sense of anticipation as she prepared to re-enter, after a year's sabbatical to avoid unpleasant publicity, that world into which she had been born.

At least, she thought, if she no longer had houses and money, she still had a few decent jewels left over from the debacle of her life to date. She held up to her neck a necklace of rubies and pearls that Cartier had made for her two years ago, as a gift for her thirtieth birthday from Marcus. She knew they suited her dark hair and creamy skin. She wanted to look stunning this evening because the whole ugly business of Marcus' death had undermined her confidence. It had made her feel unsure of herself in a manner that she had never imagined would happen to her. She had, all her life, been too surrounded by privilege, and too beautiful and admired, to feel unsure.

She needed now to look her best. She knew, well enough, that it was all a trick, just an arrangement of a rag and a bone and hank of hair, and her jewels were so magnificent that she felt safe behind their splendid and impenetrable barrier. If people wished to see a legend, that is what they would see. Women like Jackie O, and Grace of Monaco and the Duchess of Windsor understood it. Why didn't she? Emily knocked at the door.

"Not ready yet?" she trilled. "May I come in?"

Without waiting for a reply, she opened the door and crossed the room, plump and plain, but loyal in a manner which Edwina had come to value. Emily dressed like the Queen Mother, in gowns of a dowdy and expensive complexity that she believed no one would be able to duplicate. The fact that no one would ever wish to do so never apparently entered her head. Nor the Queen Mother's either, Edwina imagined.

"My God, Edwina, you still have those marvellous beads," Emily said, picking up the strings of pearls and rubies. "That'll knock Sybell's eyeballs out."

"Sybell Torringford?"

Emily nodded rather guiltily. "I had to ask them, darling. They're staying with the Barfords, next door."

"She's such a bitch. She's the only one of Marcus' family who behaved really badly. Is Freddie with her?" Freddie was her husband, the Marquess of Torringford.

"Of course," Emily said. "She never lets him out of her sight in America. She's convinced that all the women are after him."

"She's probably right," Edwina said. "There are heaps of rich old girls, young ones, too, I should imagine, who'd even put up with Freddie in order to be a Marchioness. Almost anyone would be preferable to Sybell. I hope you haven't left us alone tonight with just the Torringtons and the Barfords, or I'm hiding up here."

Emily laughed. "Darling, I'm not a masochist. There's the Blanchards, and Billy and Pattie du Pont and Elaine and Pierre de Castellaine and Susy Wallingford and her bullfighter or whatever he is from Madrid, and Harry and Anne Rockefeller and the Foords, the young ones not the old fools, and Poppy von Mengersen and Billy and Peggy Whitford. Thank God we haven't too many women for a change. I wish all the men would stop dying off or running away with unsuitable girls, but I don't suppose there's much we can do about that. And then ..."

"Stop, stop," Edwina said, laughing. "How many have you got, for God's sake? The whole of Palm Beach?"

"Darling, it's your first real party since all that awful business with Marcus and everyone is dying to see you again, and you didn't come to Palm Beach to play bridge with all the old fogies, did you? And you do look wonderful. Not a day over twenty-five."

"Well, you'd better tell me the rest of the bad news."

Emily pulled a face. "Here I've gone to all this trouble and you're not a bit grateful."

Edwina laughed again. She felt curiously buoyant. "Go on. You know you've invited every old frump in Palm Beach. They all jump at your invitations to this marzipan palace of yours."

"Not everyone jumps. Charles Bellamy is very difficult. I had to work hard on him."

"You say he's Dickie Rotherham's cousin?"

"Well, no. That's what everyone else says. But he only goes to a very few houses, and he's awfully rich."

"Couldn't be anything to do with Dickie, then. Poor chap hasn't a bean. You say this fellow's loaded?"

"And nice, too. Not like most of the new people at all."

"Well, that'll be a change, anyway. No talk of margins

and take-overs, then, and how much he's paid for everything?"

"None. And he's very handsome."

"No matchmaking, Emily. I am not going to the altar again."

"Nonsense, darling. You're far too beautiful to waste."

Edwina said acidly, "I didn't say I'd be wasted. I said I wouldn't be married."

"Don't be foolish, Edwina. You have no money. Now hurry up, darling. I must go down. Don't be too long."

Edwina sat at her dressing table and gloomily reviewed the guest list.

She sighed, and clipped the second huge ruby into her ear. She adjusted the double row of enormous beads around her neck, and stood up. Charles Bellamy? Handsome and rich? One thing for sure, he was not a cousin of Rotherham's. There hadn't been more than one son grown to maturity in that family for four generations. Two sons killed in the Second War, four brothers killed in the First, and before that girls, girls, girls!

She wondered idly where his money came from, so quickly and in such huge quantities. LBOs? Junk bonds? Shady land deals? Drugs? Not the last, surely, or he would never have been invited here. Who cared? She would never see him again after tonight.

She stood for a moment at the top of the pink marble staircase and listened to the manic shrieks of laughter from below. Slowly she began to descend back into the world that, until Marcus was murdered, she had believed to be the only one that mattered. She sighed. She wished that she could feel that way again.

Emily's butler had known her since she was a girl, and she was a favourite of his. He was delighted to see her back where he believed she belonged, and determined that no one would dare to overlook her.

"The Countess de Trafford," he bellowed in tones so stentorian that they penetrated even the voices of twenty-three utterly self-absorbed human beings striving to make themselves heard above each other. It would be an exaggeration to say that there was a silence. However, it would be correct to say that a certain hush prevailed in that immense room for a moment or two while the occupants turned to be confronted by Edwina standing in the doorway. She was beautiful, elegant, faintly touched with scandal, a woman almost legendary in that small world in which she moved, and she was hung with a Nizam's ransom in pearls and rubies.

On that small hush, Edwina trod into the room, across the splendid rugs and into the arms of her hostess.

"My dear," Emily said, "you have done us proud. Those rubies!" She turned. "Sybell, you know our darling Edwina, of course, back in the swim again. And Freddie!"

Emily's Palm Beach drawing room ran from the front to the beach side of her pink stucco villa. It opened on three sides with French doors onto scented gardens and walled spaces filled with jasmine, orange blossom and wisteria. Beyond the garden the lawns swept down to the ocean. The room was a microcosm of late twentieth century American de luxe. It was fifty feet long and more than half as wide, and paved with pale pink marble bisected with Aubusson rugs and sofas like small islands upholstered in silk. The room was lit by two 18th century chandeliers made in Venice of pink glass convolvulus. At each end were huge vases of lilies and pink hydrangeas. On the walls Emily had hung paintings of spell-binding fascination, for each one of them was already famous, seen on cards and calendars for so long that it seemed impossible that somewhere there existed originals from which these myriad copies had been taken. As she turned to greet the disagreeable Sybell,

Edwina noted from the corner of her eye a splendid Monet, two Gauguins, a superb Renoir and at least two wonderful soft Manets, and an exquisite Matisse, her favourite, all of which she had known all her life, and somehow this familiar splendor gave her comfort.

Sybell gave her a chilly smile, and an envious glance at her jewels. Freddie planted a damp and disagreeable kiss on her cheek. He looked rather like a moth-eaten head on the wall of a hunting lodge, bright-eyed and pink-lipped, but nevertheless dead.

"Dear Freddie," Edwina said unenthusiastically. "I don't believe I've heard from you since you and Sybell stayed for the hunting at Roxby two years ago." She turned to Sybell with a sweet smile. "Or did you get in touch when Marcus died?"

She allowed her eye to rove over the room full of familiar faces from her youth. She wondered idly if this was what she would be doing for the rest of her life, being polite to people she did not particularly like in rooms so luxurious that they engendered in her a faint sense of guilt. She was accustomed to splendor. After all, she and Marcus had dined with the Queen in England, but she was out of touch with the smothering luxury of the American rich.

Emily touched her arm and she turned to look into the eyes of a man whom, like the paintings, she recognized instantly as having been a part of her life forever, but previously seen only in some inferior reproduction. Here undoubtedly was the original, as surely as those on the walls were by Monet and Picasso.

"Edwina, my dear, this is Charles Bellamy."

She held out her hand. "Mr Bellamy."

"Lady de Trafford." He bowed briefly over her hand. She passed on, but felt as if her fingers had been burnt, singed by some mysterious fire, although his lips had barely grazed them. He would not slobber on her, like Freddie Torringford.

It was not what Emily would have called a smart party. Emily did not give her smart parties in Palm Beach, where she came to relax with old friends. Smart parties were for New York, and involved entertaining a lot of 'in' people whom she had not known for years, or been to school with, or been a bridesmaid at their wedding. Emily did not, on the whole, like the 'in' people whom she considered rude and ruthless. Furthermore they required a good deal of effort, so she confined them to New York, where everything seemed to be a lot of effort, no matter what.

Edwina had known them all, at dances and debutante balls, at weddings and summer parties, since she was a child, all of them except Charles Bellamy. As she moved around the room she could feel a backwash closing in behind her, like ripples on the surface of a pond, and she knew that those ripples concerned her. They included speculation on her clothes, her jewels, her finances, how much she really knew about Marcus' unsolved murder and whether she was rich or poor. She was amazed, as once she would never have been, that these people, so rich, so powerful, so influential, should have nothing better to do than speculate on the tired and trivial gossip that surrounded her name. Only Charles Bellamy gave the impression of being concerned with anything more important than the world inside this hothouse room, and the people gossiping within it.

As Emily's position in society was unassailable, she had no need to pander to fashion. Everyone therefore sat around the immense table in her baronial dining room, and not around smaller tables, an arrangement that was considered much smarter. As far as Emily was concerned, any way in which she chose to entertain was good enough for anyone fortunate enough to be invited. She knew perfectly well that her trendier guests laughed at her old-fashioned food and her pompous old-fashioned servants, but no one ever refused her invitations. No one dared.

Edwina found, without surprise, that she was seated next to Charles Bellamy, but she was a little taken aback to find him next to the hostess herself. Emily must have a high regard for this man, she thought, to have afforded so singular an honour to so new an acquaintance. Billy du Pont was on Emily's right, and next to him was Poppy von Mengersen. On her own left was Billy Whitford, the old campus heartthrob. As she looked around the table, she could not suppress a small laugh. To her surprise, her neighbour on her right also laughed.

"I know," Charles said. "We all do look rather like a selection of well-groomed animals, don't we? Perhaps the Mad Hatter's Tea Party?"

She giggled. "Freddie looks just like a stuffed elk!"

"And me?" Charles asked.

"I don't know. Perhaps a jaguar, or something rather smooth and dangerous and certainly not dead yet. Much too well groomed to be moth-eaten. It isn't too often that I see a Savile Row dinner jacket next to me in America."

"And equally rarely that I find myself next to Chanel and Cartier, especially worn with such grace."

She laughed. "It's too early in the evening for such serious talk, Mr Bellamy, and Emily has already warned me to be on my guard."

He glanced around. "I think I'll manage to keep my end up," he said solemnly. "The competition doesn't look too challenging."

Across the table Poppy von Mengersen was telling a scurrilous story about a woman allegedly in Paris who Edwina knew to be in India. She knew that her own affairs were being attacked with the same total disregard for the truth. Poppy however had not survived successfully on both sides of the Atlantic for the past forty years without an uncanny nose for a rising star. She had thus identified Edwina, and she was about to take her side. Poppy could be a very powerful ally indeed.

On her left, Billy Whitford said, quietly, "It's nice to see you again, Edwina, after all these years."

She smiled. "Not so many years, really, Billy. It's just that we're no longer young like we once were." She had been so fond of Billy once. The memory of that youthful love brought back to her suddenly and poignantly, in all its brevity and sweetness, the innocence of her own youth in Pennsylvania with its dates and dances and crushes and flirting with handsome, promising young athletes such as Billy had been then, in those far off, halcyon days. She leant over and kissed him on the cheek.

"You look so well, Billy. It makes me feel young again."

"Katie got me off the booze, otherwise I reckon I'd be dead by now."

"Good luck," she said.

Somewhere a string quartet was playing some Mozart, but she couldn't quite hear the melody above the conversation. She wondered, suddenly and disconcertingly, what she was doing here, among these greedy and envious people. They really don't care if I drop dead, so long as I don't do it here and spoil their evening, she thought. And shortly we shall all be dead for the next ten million years, and none of this will matter. Marcus is already dead. Poor vain, silly Marcus, rotting up in Scotland among his dreary forebears, murdered, she supposed, by one of his greedy, ruthless and amoral friends. If the footman had not placed a dish in front of her, she believed that she might well have risen and fled from the house with its oppressive air of treasures hoarded and promises betrayed.

She caught the eye of her neighbour once again. "Don't run away yet," Charles said quietly. "We've hardly had a chance to talk."

"Are you a mind reader? That's the second time this evening you've guessed exactly what I was thinking." She picked up a heavy fork. Gilt or gold, she wondered. Surely Emily didn't have gold on the table? They would all be murdered in their beds.

"Emily tells me that you're a cousin of Dickie Rotherham's."

"Does she, indeed?"

Edwina smiled. "And are you a cousin of Dickie Rotherham's?"

"We happen to share the same family name, but as I have no interest in genealogy I have no idea. However, I imagine that I am about as likely to be related to Dick Rotherham as I am to the Pope." He smiled. "From what I hear, he would be far happier to have my assets than I would be to have his title."

"Tell me why you let everyone assume that you are his cousin."

"I am not in charge of what other people think, unfortunately. If it makes them happy to think they know a rich man in Florida who is related to an English marquis, why should I bother to disillusion them? The world is so foolish, and life so short and sad, I have no wish to spoil their fun."

He gave a short laugh. "It may interest you to know that you are the only person who has had the courage or the effrontery to ask me that question, and now you have the truth. So now you owe me one true answer."

"To what?"

"What is a woman like you doing in a place like this?"

She shrugged. "These are people I've known all my life.

Emily is my father's younger sister."

"She looked old enough to be your grandmother."

"Now you are being both ungallant and unkind," she said. To her complete amazement, he looked very disconcerted.

"No, no, I'm very fond of Emily. What I meant was, do you ever feel that life might offer something more challenging than being fashionable?"

"Once I thought that fashion and fun were everything. Now I'm not sure. I am getting old, perhaps, and too notorious."

"Let's say famous. It sounds better. Besides, you are a beautiful and intelligent woman in the prime of her life. Now you must spread your wings."

She looked at him sadly. "I thought that's what I'd been doing since I was eighteen."

"You haven't even started yet," he said.

"And are you proposing to teach me how it's done?"

"Why not? Is anyone else waiting to try?"

She shook her head.

"You simply put out your arms and fly, " Charles said.

"So easy?" She smiled at him. Much to her surprise she liked him. "But we can't talk here about spreading wings and flying," she said. "Why don't you meet for me for lunch at the Club tomorrow?"

"I never go to the Club."

"Never? Goodness! I thought everyone went there who could possibly get in the door. Has America changed so much, then, or are you Jewish?"

"They reprimanded CeeZee Guest for taking Helena Rubinstein to lunch. What stupidity, since we are all Jews anyway. Perhaps they would throw out Jesus, or His Mother." He smiled. "Who could be bothered with all that nonsense?"

"Most people would give their right arm to be so bothered," she said with a laugh. "And I don't think it was Helena Rubinstein."

"Whoever! And you and I are not most people. Most people allow others to dictate the terms on which they live. Do you do that?"

"Most people allow it, to a greater or lesser degree."

"I do not allow it!"

"Never?"

"Touché! But those days are over."

She shrugged. "So, no lunch then, since you are too big a snob to accept my invitation to the most fashionable place in Palm Beach."

He grinned, an unexpectedly charming and boyish grin that rather disconcerted her. She felt her heart give a dangerous lurch. "Certainly lunch, why not? I'll send the plane for you and we can have lunch in Miami. Do you accept?" He held out his hand and she took it. She felt again the burning sensation in the tips of her fingers. She turned to Billy. She felt profoundly disturbed.

After the party and in bed, Edwina could not sleep. Her whole life seemed suddenly so trivial, but she had no idea what to put in its place. She knew no other task. She felt adrift on some vast sea from which all the familiar landmarks had disappeared, and there was only a low and threatening horizon and no trace of land. What frightened her most was that the threatening cloud looked very like Charles Bellamy and she was not at all sure she was ready for that.

CHAPTER THREE

SYDNEY, NEW SOUTH WALES
APRIL 1979

THE CITY OF SYDNEY was enjoying a spell of perfect early autumn weather. Puffy, white clouds hung over the sail-like roof of the famous Opera House. The harbour was already filled with small craft and sailing boats, although it was barely nine o'clock in the morning.

Too good to be true, Harry Wellington thought as he eased his car off the Harbour Bridge and into the central business district. He parked in the basement of the towering block that held his offices. Gone were the days of the horrible damp little cottage in North Sydney where he and Betty had started out in business, and worked with that loony young Englishman.

He rose up in the lift to the thirty-fifth floor, with its sweeping views to the mountains in the west and across the blue waters of the harbour out to the headlands. Beyond that the huge expanse of the Pacific Ocean spread out under his window. He was chairman of his own group now, and his suite of offices could rival anything in the city. For the first time in many years he thought about those early days when they had been struggling for every buck and about the young Englishman, Charles Bellamy, who had followed them out from India and worked with them here in Australia, wanting to look after the Aborigines and make a better world.

He wondered why the kid had disappeared like that, without notice. Damned rude of him, now that he thought about it all. Well, the boy had always been a dreamer. He and Betty would never have made any money at all if they had gone on working with Charlie. Betty said he had gone back to England, and Harry supposed that was the truth of it.

They had never heard another word from him, ungrateful little sod. He and Betty had had to learn the hard way that they couldn't reform the world. Maybe Charlie had now learned the same lesson, in some dismal swamp in Africa or a desert in the Negev, or maybe he would never learn. Some kids didn't. They just went on hoping for a better world that never came until they just sank beneath the surface with everyone else.

Harry shrugged, trying to shake off the sinking feeling that accompanied the realization that so many years had gone by since the events he was thinking about. He could not get Charlie out of his head. In some ways those days seemed simpler. Happier. Thinking about them now left a sour note in the air, and spoiled this perfect morning and the feeling of security he received every day in his luxurious offices.

When the lift reached his floor he said to the receptionist, "No calls for an hour, Janet," and went into his office. He drank a glass of water. He began to feel calmer.

The phone on his desk buzzed. He picked it up. "I thought I said no calls for an hour, Janet," he said irritably.

"Miami has been trying to reach you all morning, Mr Wellington. They say it's very urgent."

"Did they leave a name?"

"A Mr Nicholas Barton. Alcon Corporation, they said."

"Alcon Corp?"

Harry was impressed. Alcon was very big business. Armaments, rockets, intercontinental ballistic missiles, space shuttles, all the super toys of the twentieth century.

"Did they say what they wanted?"

"No. They said they'd ring back to discuss the letter."

"Letter? What letter?"

"It's on your desk, Mr Wellington. It came this morning by special delivery."

There it was, this symbol of affluence. He slit open the envelope and pulled out the heavy sheets of paper. They must have chopped down half a rain forest to make this paper, he thought.

ALCON CORPORATION FLORIDA
18 April 1979
Mr Harry Wellington,
Managing Director and Chairman,
National Fundraising Consultants,
46 Bridge Street,
SYDNEY NSW AUSTRALIA

Dear Mr Wellington,

Our corporation will shortly be expanding its operations into the Southern Pacific region, with new corporate headquarters in Sydney, Australia.

You will, I am sure, appreciate that some of our products are sensitive in both a political and environmental context. We intend therefore to preface our entry into this new market with the creation of a substantial Foundation that will, we believe, serve to soften the image of our otherwise rather aggressive company.

Your success in this field and your reputation has preceded you. Our research in Australia has led us to believe that your company will be ideally placed to assist us in both setting up and in promoting our Foundation to the Australian community to maximum advantage.

While we understand that you are a busy man, we are eager to proceed as soon as possible with this project. We hope that you will be able to fly to Florida to discuss these matters with us without delay. Accordingly we have taken the liberty of placing at your disposal a first class return ticket to Miami via Los Angeles departing Sydney 20 April 1979.

Further we stand ready to remit a fee of $50,000 as an initial payment for consultations, and trust that these arrangements will be satisfactory. Please advise banking details by return so that a cash transfer may be effected. Unless we hear from you to the contrary we shall make arrangements for you to be met in Miami when you arrive here on 20 April 1979.

Yours sincerely,
Nicholas Barton
Executive Vice President

He was to be paid fifty grand for one week and a contract with Alcon Corporation? Jesus Christ! It was not like the old days he had just been thinking about in the car, when Alcon Corporation would never even have heard of his name. They would not have bothered to shit on him in the old days.

He buzzed his secretary. "Janet, ring United and check that they are holding a ticket to Miami in my name."

He sat back and re-read the letter. This contract would establish him as the leader in his field in Australia. Betty would be thrilled. She could have her new house that she wanted so badly. The phone rang.

"Yes, Mr Wellington. I have United reservations on hold. They are waiting for the ticket to be collected. One first class ticket on the non-stop service to Los Angeles with a connection to Miami. It leaves at 4.30 this afternoon. Shall I tell them you'll collect the ticket at the airport?"

Today? Jesus! Was it already the twentieth? No wonder the guy from Miami was telephoning. "Yes. Tell them I'll collect the ticket at Mascot, and cancel all appointments for the next week, Janet. Ring this Mr Barton and tell him I'll be on the plane. Get me some US dollars from the bank, and my passport, and get my wife on the phone."

Betty was not as thrilled as he'd expected. She was suspicious. "Who are these Alcon people? I don't like the sound of this at all," she said on the phone.

"Betty, they are one of the biggest companies in the world. We're absolutely made. Just pack a bag for me, there's a dear, and start looking for that big new house you want in Pymble."

"Harry, check it out first!"

"What's to check?"

"Very well," she said. "If you won't then I will."

"Do as you please," he said, "but pack a bag and send it to the office in a taxi. I'm going to Miami on this plane. It's the biggest break in my career."

Several hours later, when United Flight 110, non-stop across the Pacific from Sydney to Los Angeles lifted off the runway at Kingsford Smith Airport, Harry was settled in the front left hand seat in the first class compartment. He was going to a meeting that would place him firmly at the top of his profession. He had done good work. He had built up the company slowly and purposefully and he deserved to succeed. They no longer worked for nothing as they had when young Charlie was around. They charged large fees, but they raised large funds for their clients. There was nothing to be ashamed of in that. Nothing could be achieved without money. He would think no more about those old, idealistic days. Betty had been right all along. They needed to be tough and businesslike, not all soft and do-goody. Today was what mattered. Today, tomorrow, and success.

CHAPTER FOUR

KEY LARGO, FLORIDA
APRIL 1979

THE FLORIDA KEYS IS a chain of small islands hanging off the end of Florida like a fishhook, bent to the south and west and extending out into the blue Caribbean Sea. They are joined by a road and a series of amazing bridges which end at Key West, once the residence of Papa Hemingway before it became too crowded for him and he moved ninety miles further south, to Cuba.

Once, too, the Keys had been joined by a famous railway which had taken passengers to the wharf at Key West to catch the boats to Cuba for the gambling and the good times, which the island republic had offered in those corrupt and glamorously sinister days.

On Key Largo, closer to Miami, Charles Bellamy had built a small and lavish estate where, on the day following Emily's dinner, he awaited the arrival of Edwina de Trafford with an impatience that surprised him. At forty-two he had not expected to feel again such a youthful excitement over the presence of a new woman in his life. He found himself intrigued by her combination of sophistication and vulnerability; her hard exterior and what he believed might be a very much softer core.

Edwina took one of the cars from Emily's garage that

morning, and drove to the airport at Palm Beach, half inclined to believe that the invitation given so casually the previous evening would be forgotten. She was wrong. Promptly at 11.30 she was paged in the private lounge provided for persons travelling in their own jets, of whom there was always a number arriving and leaving at Palm Beach, and a uniformed pilot led her to the tarmac.

"Mr Bellamy has sent the helicopter, ma'am. He sends his apologies and hopes you won't mind, but it's so much quicker than the drive from Miami Airport. With the 'copter we can go straight to the house."

The helicopter was painted navy blue with the initials BC in red. Edwina was amused to realize that they stood not for Before Christ, but for Bellamy Corporation. She settled herself into the passenger compartment, and immediately the rotors began to whir. The machine rose up, shot across the inland waterway and started down the coastline. Edwina had always imagined that one of the few compensations of being Queen of England must be that everything starts the moment she arrives. Now she knew that feeling and she found it very satisfactory.

The helicopter raced down the shoreline towards Miami Beach and the Florida Keys. They sped offshore along the body-strewn beach past the vast hotels, and then turned west across the harbour and over Key Biscayne, then southwest to follow the line of the Keys as they curved out into the navy blue sea.

"Aren't we landing in Miami?" Edwina asked the pilot.

"No, ma'am, we're going straight through to the estate. Not much longer."

As the machine dropped down onto the landing pad, Edwina could see Charles Bellamy standing alone, waiting for her, and again she felt that profound malaise, as if she were stepping from a life she understood into a void, an unfamiliar world. Not only unfamiliar, but dangerous.

Don't be a fool, she told herself. There is no unfamiliar world out there. Just life! But the hint of danger simultaneously unnerved and intrigued her.

He took her hand as she stepped down. "I hope you didn't mind the helicopter. Some people hate it, but at the last minute I changed my mind and decided it would be more fun to have lunch down here. I hope it didn't make you nervous?"

"Everything you do makes me nervous."

"Does it really? How nice!"

"I had my nose pressed to the window the whole way down," she said.

He looked with some amazement at this beautiful and worldly woman and marvelled that she could still be thrilled by so simple an experience. For most of us, he thought, the ability to view the world with wonder and curiosity is soon over, gone with our childhood.

They crossed a wide paved courtyard and entered through a stone arch into a long gallery across the whole front of the house. In turn this opened onto a terrace from which the garden fell away to a private beach and the sea. A small boat rocked a few metres offshore, its bright red sails furled. Edwina noticed that the table was set, and food already on the sideboard.

"Am I late?"

"Not at all. When I'm down here I like to be alone. The servants do everything before I arrive. It will all be very simple."

It is quite perfect, she thought, looking around, and we are quite alone. She knew that it was the kind of simplicity that only a fortune could provide. She glanced around at the bamboo furniture hand-crafted in the high mountains of

Assam, and the pool set into the terraces. She looked behind her at the long room filled with modern American paintings, only some of which she recognized. There were some superb pieces of Chinese sculpture, each one fit for a museum. She raised her eyebrows.

"It takes a great deal of talent to create this kind of thing," she said. "Archie has done a wonderful job."

"Champagne?"

He poured the pale golden wine into two long thin glasses from Venice. "You knew straight away it was Archie?"

"Of course. No one else gets quite that look. Does it upset you that I recognize his work? I may have lived in Europe for a few years, but I'm not completely out of touch with America, you know."

He shrugged. "The pictures are my own choice. Or, at least, they are my choice of what I am advised to buy."

She was surprised. "But it does upset you! Anyone who knows Archie's work would recognize it straight away. It's charming, and perfect for here, by the sea. Aren't you happy about it?"

"Oh, I like his work well enough, but it's not foolish of me to think a man's home should reflect something of himself, surely?"

"As I don't know you at all, I wouldn't know what to look for," she said. "Besides, if that's what you want, you should never use so fashionable a decorator as Archie Spruce."

"You're right," he said with a smile. "But I don't have a choice. I'm too busy to do it myself. I wanted the best, and I liked his work at the Vanderbilts' cottage in Newport. I know nothing of things like that."

"Most people don't. That's why decorators get work. It would be a hard world for them if we could all do everything ourselves."

He laughed out loud. "People would still use them, just to show off. Look at all the money they waste on caterers and florists just so they can all have identical parties."

"Well, we can't cook the food and do the flowers and still look wonderful. If you expected that, you'd get some lousy food and some very bad-tempered hostesses."

"I get that anyway, often enough. That's what I like about Emily. She's so unfashionable. She serves the food she wants. She never uses caterers. She picks the flowers in her own garden and probably nothing has changed in twenty years!"

"It hasn't, I can assure you, and no one ever stays away." She looked at him coolly. "Not even you, it seems, and Emily tells me that you don't go out too much."

He returned her gaze. "I would do a lot for Emily," he said. They moved and sat on a cane sofa overlooking the cobalt sea.

"It interests me to speculate how many generations it takes to build that kind of confidence. Yours, too. It's a quality you both have, of being totally at home in your own bodies – of being happy with yourselves."

She was amused. All around them lay the evidence of huge wealth and the total peace and privacy that only it can provide – the endless blue sea, the lawns stretching in every direction, the beautiful low house with its treasures and yet they talked of insecurity.

"I thought you knew that it takes centuries, like making an English lawn. But you told me last night that you didn't let anyone tell you how to live, so you are really no different from Emily and me."

"Oh, your confidence is the real thing. Mine is just bluff!"

She reached out and touched his arm. It could not have

been an easy thing to say, and she wondered if he were sincere. Only after she had done it did she realize the intimacy of the gesture. It seemed immediately to create between them a physical bond that she had been anxious to avoid.

"You're kidding me," she said lightly. "Bankers are always full of the most pompous confidence. How long have you been one? All your life? Were you a pubescent banker? An embryonic one? I remember that someone once told me that bankers are not made, but born."

"Are you trying to get my life's story?"

She settled back more comfortably into the deep cushions of her chair. She felt suddenly more at ease. "No one ever tells the truth about that! We all have something to hide, but somehow you don't seem like a banker to me."

"Have you known many?"

"Goodness, yes! Thousands! There was a time when my whole world seemed made up of them; bankers for breakfast, lunch and dinner. Wall-to-wall bankers, and I never really found one I liked. Certainly no one like you; come on, now, what were you in the beginning?"

"In the beginning? BBC? Before Bellamy Corporation? Oh, then I was an idealist, but it didn't work out at all well. I failed miserably at that, so I decided to pay my way in cash. People seem to understand cash better than ideas. Let's have some lunch before the salad wilts."

They sat at a table beneath a pink canvas awning. Charles poured the wine. In spite of the fact that he had been a rich man for some time, and a hugely rich one for several years, Edwina made him feel uneasy. He felt defensive and a little gauche. Look at the way he had blushed last night. My God, he hadn't blushed in thirty years. He knew already that the combination of the ivory flesh that promised so much and the air of cool and aristocratic containment that seemed so effectively to withhold the promise, had captivated him.

Edwina looked around. "Aren't you nervous in a place like this with no one around?"

"Oh, there are people around, but out of sight." He waved a hand at the surrounding lawns.

"At least twenty people on the estate, four bodyguards, two caretakers. This is Miami, not Belgravia. No one is really alone for a moment, particularly a man like myself."

"Bodyguards? Does an idealist need bodyguards?"

"A rich one does. Besides, all that was a long time ago. I am, unfortunately, more vulnerable these days."

"You are still a suspect idealist. Emily tells me you give a huge amount away."

"I get my money's worth," he said. "Do you imagine that I would be dining with your aunt and all those other old crocodiles and snakes and alligators if I were not rich? She does not invite me for the cut of my jib."

"Why not? She's done it before. I suspect that some of her handsome young men are not so loaded with cash. You never know. She may fancy your smile, or your beautiful body."

He laughed. "You mean I've earned all this money for nothing?"

"There are many more amusing places than Emily's house where a man like you would be accepted without question." Edwina observed.

"And that is precisely why I do not wish to go to those places. Do I need to define for you, of all people, the world of the fair-weather friend? Most of the world can so easily be bought; most people are so easily seduced by all of this." He waved a hand to indicate the whole luxurious estate and all that it represented. "I am always impressed by the few people I meet who cannot."

She gave him a long, cool look. She was not pleased to discover that Emily had discussed these private matters of her life with him. "What did Emily say?"

"She mentioned that some of your old playmates were less than stout-hearted after your husband was killed. The fact that you took their dereliction rather to heart I could tell for myself."

"So easily?" For some reason she felt annoyed.

He shrugged. "Don't be offended. No, it was not done so easily, but I am a trained observer in those territories. That's why I like people like your aunt. Once they hold out their hand in friendship, they never take it back. Those are the kind of people I want to know, but they don't always want to know me."

She let out a peal of laughter. "Oh, Charles, what an odd man you are. If you imagine that so-called old families are any kinder or more loyal than new ones, or any freer from all the defects of human nature, let me disillusion you immediately. Look at Sybell!"

"Emily says they all stuck by you, even Sybell Torrington."

"You and Emily seem to have had a very cozy chat," she said rather acidly. "Poppy says it's the wealthy's version of tribal behaviour. It was a comfort certainly, but it's not friendship."

"Maybe, but I'd like to know how to get into the tribe."

She smiled. "I guess it's like the Communist Party in Russia. You're either born into it, or you must marry into it. I've never thought about it."

"Exactly! And I think about it a good deal of the time! What is the point of being rich if you're not a member of the tribe?"

"The tribe of the rich you mean? I enjoyed my poor days. They were a lot of fun. Come to think of it, they're really still going on, in a way!"

"That's because you were already in the tribe. I guess I don't want to go through life like you in the helicopter, with my nose pressed to the window, a kid looking into a pastry shop."

She looked at him in astonishment. Here was a man who was rich and clever, handsome and urbane, and he was worrying about meeting people she knew to be dull and selfish and corrupt. Very few of them were as able as he obviously was, and even fewer as handsome.

"I wouldn't waste my time if I were you. There's some very flyblown pastry in that shop. There are just as many whores in the penthouse as the basement. In the penthouse, of course, they are called ladies, but they're still for sale."

"How do you know?"

Suddenly she felt angry. Reckless and angry. She pushed her plate away from her in the manner that, when she was a child, Nanny had taught her she must never do, and looked him straight in the eye.

"Didn't Emily tell you that, too? She seems to have told you everything else about me. My father was a drunk who died broke, so I've been in the market, you might say. A nice, well-born, well brought up girl with no money. Poor Edwina! And I've been purchased twice. Are you making me another offer? I had pretty well decided to close up shop after all the trouble I had with Marcus, but you never know. Once a whore, always a whore."

She tried, unsuccessfully, to keep the bitterness from her voice. He reached out and touched her arm, but she shook his hand impatiently off her sleeve.

"Just because you've given me a couple of lumps of lobster and a glass or two of Dom Perignon, you don't get my life story," she said angrily. "You can go to hell!"

"Perhaps I'm already there," he said, "and you, too, for

the wrong reasons. If you are in any way mourning Marcus de Trafford, then I must tell you that he was a dishonest pig, and you'd best forget him."

"I am not mourning Marcus. He made me very unhappy, and I am not sorry that he's dead – only sorry about the manner of his death."

Charles shrugged impatiently. "You're not the only person in the world who has made a bad mistake and lived to regret it."

"What happened in London with Marcus," she said, as deliberately and as offensively as she could manage, "is none of your fucking business, and I think it's time I left."

"You can't leave until I give the order for the helicopter, and as it so happens, what happened in London is very much my business, for I am the person who gave the order that Marcus be killed."

"That is not very funny," she said. "You didn't even know him!"

"On the contrary, I knew him well. I am a drug dealer, and Marcus was a drug dealer. I supplied him with the drugs he sold so profitably in that smart set in which he – and you – moved in Europe. I made a fortune for him, and then he thought he was smart enough to try to steal from me. If I permitted that, I would be out of business in a moment – and dead myself, for that matter."

Edwina felt her hand begin to shake and she slowly put her glass on the table and clenched her hands so that he would not notice. She felt a dull throb of a pulse beating in her neck. She knew that if she tried to stand, her knees would buckle, and she would appear shamefully vulnerable. She could not do that, and yet at the same time she felt an unfamiliar, racing excitement in her veins, a terrible and dangerous attraction to this deadly information that she was receiving.

"Even greed is not without its code of honour, you know, and Marcus could not even observe that. He was not only dishonest but he was a fool. I am only sorry that it has all caused you so much pain, but I didn't know you then."

She looked at the man sitting opposite her, making this confession, and she understood quite clearly that he was without morals in the conventional sense of the word. She supposed that she should feel anger, or rage or disgust, or perhaps fear, but she had faced her own demons too often in the past. She did not know whether she was capable of murder, but she knew well enough that she was capable of being ruthless in her own interest, and therefore not in any position to judge this man sitting in front of her and confessing that he had killed Marcus. She felt deeply shocked, but she did not feel able to judge.

"Marcus' death didn't cause me pain," she said slowly. "I would be quite dishonest to say that it did, but all the foul talk and endless gossip because of the way he was murdered – that caused me pain, and shame. Everyone in our set knew that he liked men, but to have it so openly discussed, in all those disgusting tabloids ..." She put her hands to her face, and Charles thought that she was going to break down, but she merely took a deep shuddering breath and took control of herself again. "If you really did arrange it, then why that way?"

He shrugged. "I wanted the police to believe it was a crime of sex, which they instantly did, and still do. I didn't want it tied to drugs – or money. I don't want people making any connection with me, or any of my associates. I am a respectable banker, after all, and a well-known heterosexual."

She looked at him for a long while in silence. She felt in control of herself again, and took a sip of wine. She was pleased to see that her hand was quite steady.

"I am glad he's dead," she said slowly. "So much so that

many people even suggested that I might have had a hand in it. I might have, if I'd known how to go about such a thing. Living with him was very bad." She drank the rest of her champagne and put her glass back on the table. She looked around at the calm, blue sea and the yacht with the red sails bobbing close to the shore, and was amazed that nothing had changed. "So ... I was right, after all. You are not a banker."

"I own a bank, but no, I am really not a banker – or, at least, not only a banker. I am a very successful crook looking for a suitable wife to protect me, and to advance my position in the world. Emily thinks it should be you."

"Does she indeed?"

"Naturally the information I have just imparted to you was not available to her."

"No, I suppose not. And what about the idealist?"

"I believe that he's still there, waiting to be able to do the things I couldn't do any other way, when I was poor."

She laughed softly and sadly.

"I have learned, Charles, at some cost I might say, that the end has never justified the means, no matter what Gandhi and so many others have tried to convince themselves, and the world. There is always a price to be paid. When I married Marcus, everyone approved, in spite of his rather unsavoury reputation. Edwina's being sensible at last, they said. So suitable, they said. The result was a disaster. In the end, one should really always follow one's heart."

"I've not found it to be the most reliable of organs."

"No, but nicer than the brain. Have you killed other people?"

"Yes, when it was necessary."

"And when was that?"

"When they would have killed me, or ruined me, as Marcus threatened to do."

"Does it never worry you?"

"No."

"Do you trust anyone in the world?"

"Yes, two people. A man called Nick Barton and a woman in South America called Laura Tessier. I could trust you."

"You are as much for sale as anyone, then."

"Everyone is for sale," he said, "when the price is right. I was, when I started out. But when there is enough money, a different morality takes over, you know." He stood up and took her arm. Together they walked towards the water's edge and the sailboat with the red sails.

"If I say, stay and sleep with me today for a hundred bucks, and you do it, the world will say that you're a whore. If I say marry me and I'll settle fifty million dollars on you and give you a duplex apartment on Park Avenue and an estate in Virginia and your own jet plane, then you're not a whore at all. You're a sensible and respectable woman, but really you're just being paid more money for the same job."

"Not quite! Wives work much harder than mistresses, and take greater risks. What if I say that I fancy you madly and I'll stay for nothing?"

He laughed. "Then it's not business at all. It's just a guy getting for nothing what guys always want to get for nothing!"

"Bastard! I believe that you're a genuine MCP. If I had the proverbial promethian handbag with me, I'd clobber you with it."

"I'd defend myself."

"I believe you would!" She looked at him shrewdly. "Did you really mean what you said about Marcus?"

"I don't joke about that kind of thing."

"Why did you make such a mess of it?"

"I didn't make a mess of it. I told you it was meant to

look like a sex crime rather than a drug hit. I didn't understand what it would do to you, the kind of problems that it would cause for you, in your world – and, of course, I didn't know you then, so you didn't enter into my calculations."

"No, I can see you wouldn't think of that. In my world you can do and be whatever you like, so long as it's never in public. You made Marcus and his way of life public property. You made my life public property. I find that difficult to forgive."

"Marcus tried to steal from me, and when I wouldn't permit that, he tried to blackmail me. I have come too far to have allowed a louse like Marcus to bring my world down around my ears."

She looked at him for a long while. "Why am I not frightened of you?" she asked eventually. "I was, back there, for a moment, when you told me this, but, deep down, I am not afraid."

"Because you know that you are quite safe. Because you have lived in a hard world yourself. Because you know that I am not paranoid and that I don't go around killing beautiful women. Only gangsters and crooks and blackmailers, and people who don't keep their word."

"And did you mean it about the fifty million?"

"More, if you want it. Think what you could do with five hundred million, a thousand."

"Do you have that much?"

"More, if you want it," he said again. "I could make you the most powerful woman in the world, and the most admired. You don't want to spend the rest of your life serving tea to morons, and watching idiots play polo, do you?"

"I think you're serious. I think you really are an idealist who has lost the way. What you don't understand is that you'll never find it again now. How do you reconcile these things?"

"Easy," he grinned. "I tried being a poor idealist, and I didn't achieve much. I don't like wasting my time."

"No," she said tartly. "No idealist does. If people don't agree with them about what constitutes a perfect world, they shoot them. You are doing nothing new, let me assure you."

"You have a harsh view of idealists."

"I've met enough of them in my time," Edwina said.

"Like your bankers? Well, now I have become a practical man. Somerset Maugham once said that money buys nothing of value but freedom. He was wrong. It also buys power."

"So now what?"

"Somehow I will change the world."

"You know, that frightens me more than the fact that I know you are a murderer. Too many very mad people have believed they could change the world."

"And some very sane ones have tried, too. I am asking you to help me."

"Well, there's nothing like a modest ambition, I always say. And how will you achieve that? By giving money to society matrons, and going to dull dinners because you're flattered to have been invited?"

"You have a waspish tongue, I see. And did you enjoy being snubbed by trashy people in London for whom you've no respect?"

"Did Emily tell you that, too?"

He shrugged. "No need. I read some of the press reports this morning. No one enjoys being trashed by fools. One prefers to be dumped by people one respects."

"But the people I respect didn't dump me."

"They so rarely do, I find. So, having got rid of an arsehole like Marcus de Trafford, why are you walking back into the same world?"

"It's the only world I know," she said, rather sadly, but she knew he was right. Last night she had realized that she no longer wanted all that. She had understood for the first time that it would no longer satisfy her.

"But what else can I do? The women in my world were brought up to please men. That's the world I was trained for and I don't know any other."

"I have been telling you. You can help me change the world."

"Only governments can change the world."

"Wrong. Only individuals can change the world. Remember Chairman Mao and the first step?"

"What's the point of the first step if you never get to the end of the journey?"

"How do you ever know, if you don't start? With my resources at your disposal, you could make huge changes."

"How?"

"By educating more women, for a start. At the moment, we have a few educated women and a new class of female slaves."

"Why should you care?"

"Because otherwise life has no meaning," he said. "Well, what about it?"

"After everything you've told me today, how could I ever trust you?"

"I have never broken my word," he said, and she believed him.

"If you are offering me a job, I need to know the pay and conditions."

"Yes," he said softly. "Someone else once told me very much the same thing, in much the same words, many years ago. I am not offering you a job, I am offering you a contract.

Everything I own, if you need it, and a seat on the board, if you'll marry me. Emily was right. You are the person I should marry."

She laughed, "First you tell me all the mistakes I've made, then you tell me you arranged the murder of my husband, and now you offer me a deal you think I can't resist. Why the hell should I marry you? I don't even know you!"

He held up his hand and counted on his fingers. "One. I am rich and your first husband was poor. Two. I am heterosexual, and your second husband was not. This is certainly an advantage in a marriage, I am told. Three. You can help me achieve my ambitions, and I can help you fulfill your own unrealized dreams. Isn't that what a partnership is all about? And, four, God help me, I am in love with you."

"Nonsense! You've only just met me, and we're not college kids, for God's sake. Do you normally propose on your first date?"

"I don't normally propose at all. I'm sorry to be inept, but this is the first time."

"And what about how I may feel – or do you and Emily, between you, feel that you best know what's good for me?"

"Well," he said with a small smile, "I rather hoped you might feel like falling in love with me, and throwing your cap over the moon, and helping me to change the world. I've told you I can't do it alone."

"You are really quite crazy," she said.

"That's as good a reason for marriage as any I've heard."

"Oh, Charles!" She felt near to tears. She knew that she wanted to accept this man whom she had not even met twenty-four hours earlier, and that knowledge frightened her, for she felt that she was in a realm of emotions that she did not understand at all. The fact that he was dangerous only attracted her more.

"How about sex?" she asked.

"Well, how about it? Now, you mean?"

"No ... I mean, well, you know ... shouldn't we know if it works, first?"

"It will work," he said. "We'll have a blast with it, but that's not what I'm talking about. We can have that any time. Most people spend the first two weeks in the bedroom, and the next ten years in court sorting out the mess. I'm talking about work. I'm talking about power. I'm talking about trust. I'm talking about a real partnership. You have beauty, brains and an impregnable position. I have brains, cash and clout, and balls! Wouldn't it be fun to see what we could do together?"

"You are an arrogant prick!"

"And you have a pretty good opinion of yourself, too!" He leant over her, and put his arms around her and brushed his lips lightly against hers. It was their first intimate contact, and it passed through her body like a message of doom, like an earth tremor that leaves one forever uncertain if one can ever trust the ground again. She clung to his arms for she felt that she might well fall.

"Will you promise never to lie to me, no matter how bad the truth. Will you promise that?"

"Yes!"

"Is Charles Bellamy your real name?"

"Yes. My father was a lawyer in the West Country. He's dead. So is my mother."

"Other than drugs and murder, do you do anything illegal?"

"Practically everything I do is illegal, but as I am so rich, I am the law."

"*L'état, c'est moi*! You sound as if you were offering me a throne," Edwina said slowly.

"In a way, I am," he said quietly. "You'll certainly have

more power than the Queen."

She pulled away from his embrace and walked to the edge of the lawn, overlooking the sea, whose calm tranquil surface seemed to reassure her, although she found that she was still shaking and could hardly stand. What a fool I am, she thought. Just like every stupid heroine from every trashy book I've ever read.

"I can't answer you now. I'll give you an answer tomorrow. Call your helicopter, Charles. It's time for me to go home."

She leant on his arm as they walked back across the courtyard to the landing pad. The blue helicopter was waiting, the pilot behind the controls, the rotor turning slowly. It's like the White House, she thought. All we need is a Rose Garden.

"Until tomorrow, then," he said. "Do you intend to talk this over with Emily?"

She looked at him in surprise. "No. I shall decide for myself."

The pilot closed the door and the helicopter rose from the pad and drifted northwest towards the city and the evening star. The sun was low in the west, over Mexico, and the sea looked dark as wine, and dangerous.

Charles returned to the house. The phone was ringing. This was a rare occurrence, as he never wished to be disturbed here, on the island.

His secretary apologized. "I have the Senator on the line and he said it was urgent."

"Which senator?"

"Senator Brailes, from Idaho."

"All right, Kitty, patch him through."

He waited while she put him on the scrambler. All calls to

this number were scrambled. Nothing could be traced. Suddenly the line was filled with the heavy, hearty country voice of honest Billy Brailes from Idaho, who pocketed $250,000 a year from Bellamy Corporation as a fee to keep Charles informed of what went on in the committees he chaired or attended in the Senate.

"Jaime Ventura is in the States," he said.

"Jaime? You mean Sebastian!"

"No, Jaime," the Senator said. "He's using a US diplomatic passport in the name of Enrique Cordova. These bastards are pretty cool, eh?"

"Is Miami going to do anything? What about that fool Lieutenant Jerkovitz?"

"No. He's been given the word to back off."

"I should damned well hope so, for all the money we pay the police down there, I'm pleased to know we get something for it. What's Jaime here for?"

"To see you, I understand. Or maybe his brother, Jesus."

"Thanks, Billy," he said. "I appreciate the information. You're worth every penny I pay you."

"Cut the shit, Charles!" the Senator said, and rang off.

Charles liked Billy Brailes. He didn't pretend that his consulting fee was anything other than what it was, a bribe for illegal information. This was unlike most of the others in the Senate and elsewhere. They took his money eagerly enough, but wanted to believe in the fiction that these were genuine fees. Charlie was happy to pay the bribes. That was part of his business, but he despised the hypocrisy.

He picked up the phone again, and punched in the direct number to speak with Nick Barton.

"Nick? I've just spoken to Billy Brailes and he says that Jaime is in the States. Did you know that?"

"No!"

"You heard nothing from Laura about that?"

"Nothing!"

"Nick, we can't afford to lose this one, you know."

"I know, Charles, I know. I'll see what I can do."

"If Laura has gone over to the other side, you know what we must do, Nick."

"Laura has not gone over to the other side, Charles. You must trust someone, you know."

CHAPTER FIVE

MIAMI, FLORIDA
APRIL 1979

THE PLANE LIFTED OFF the runway at Los Angeles International Airport and headed east towards Miami. Harry Wellington settled back in his seat and accepted the vodka martini that the flight attendant had ready for him almost as soon as the plane was in the air. He opened that morning's copy of the *Los Angeles Times* and glanced idly through the pages. They were still investigating the death of some gay earl who was murdered in Scotland the year before. It's a pity, he thought, that the police did not have anything better to do than mess around with that kind of thing. If the man had not had a title, he'd have been forgotten about long ago.

No news about Australia. The place hardly seemed to exist once you left its distant shores. Perhaps that was its saving grace. It had been forgotten by the world. A pity it couldn't stay that way, Harry thought, but there was too much going on in Asia. Everyone wanted a slice of that pie, and Sydney was the logical centre for action in the South Pacific. The new power base. The Pacific Rim. Yes, he thought, in 2001 the Pacific Century would begin.

No, wait. Here was some more news about Phil Morgan-Smith down in Melbourne. The poor fellow had drowned recently in Port Phillip Bay. Harry knew him well. They had sat on the boards of several charitable foundations.

BANKER'S WIFE FOUND DEAD
FATAL ACCIDENT IN TOORAK MANSION

Amanda Morgan-Smith, well-known Melbourne hostess, was found dead in her home in Toorak this morning, by the maid. She had apparently died of asphyxiation from a faulty gas heater in her bedroom, although it is not clear why the heater was in use, as the weather was unusually warm.

This is the second tragedy in the Morgan-Smith family. Her banker husband was drowned earlier this month in a yachting accident in Port Phillip Bay and his body has not been recovered.

At the moment the police do not consider that there are any suspicious circumstances although it is possible that Mrs Morgan-Smith took her own life in a fit of depression following her husband's death.

Mrs Morgan-Smith is survived by her daughter, Anne and two grandchildren.

The article went on to describe Phillip's business activities and the companies of which he sat on the board. Amanda was described as a leading socialite with many charitable interests. There was one child. A daughter, Anne, aged 25, married to a doctor.

The whole thing was very strange. He'd never known Phillip to go yachting when he was in Sydney, where it was a lot more fun than in Melbourne. He didn't own his own boat, Harry was sure. He'd seen them both at the Opera Foundation Ball not much more than a month ago, and they had both seemed fine.

The flight attendant returned and handed him an envelope. "This is an urgent message we received from our office in Los Angeles," she said. "It just came through on the flight deck. Can I get you another drink? We'll be serving dinner in a few minutes."

"Thanks. Another martini." Harry unfolded the piece of paper. It was a message from his wife.

"The President of the Board of Alcon Corporation is Charles Bellamy. I told you to check before you left, but it must be a coincidence. It can't be the same Charles Bellamy who worked for us? Surely not. I couldn't imagine our Charlie managing a kindergarten, let alone anything like Alcon, can you? Let me know immediately if it's the same man. If it is, there's something you ought to know before you get involved, so contact me immediately. Take care. Betty."

Take care? What did he need to know? This was the biggest opportunity of his lifetime. Even if it were the same chap, which seemed highly unlikely, he'd never done Charles Bellamy any harm, other than not being very tolerant of a mild flirtation with his wife. Why should he take care, for God's sake? He ate his dinner, watched a movie and dozed off until the attendant shook his arm.

"Would you fasten your seat belt, Mr Wellington. We're just on our final approach to Miami." He looked out the window at the lights glittering around the water, and almost before he had clicked the belt into place, he felt the thunk of the wheels hitting the runway. He felt full of excitement.

Outside the airport a large black man in a uniform approached him.

"Mr Wellington? I'm Aubrey, one of the Alcon drivers. Mr Barton sent me to meet you." Aubrey handed him an envelope that he instantly recognized as the same stiff, expensive stationery he had received in Sydney.

While Aubrey collected his bags he read:

Dear Harry,

Welcome to Miami. Sorry not to have met you, but delayed at the last minute with one of those emergencies with which I am sure you're only too familiar. Aubrey will take you to the Alcon guest apartment where I am sure you will be very comfortable, and he will pick you up in the morning for an early start. We'll meet then.

Welcome aboard!

Nick Barton
Executive Vice President

Aubrey led him out of the airport to a huge, dark red Rolls Royce. From the back seat Harry looked through tinted windows at the impression of palm trees swaying in the balmy air, as they travelled to the city. He had never been in Miami before, and had no idea where they were, so he relaxed into the luxury of the car and enjoyed the ride.

He understood exactly what the Alcon Corporation wanted in Australia. They would undertake a rapacious and destructive programme to make huge profits for their shareholders, and the financial press would hail them as wonder workers in the Australian economy. They wanted him to cover the damage and make them look good. He was excellent at that kind of thing. Alcon didn't give a shit about the environment. They only cared about the bottom line, but they would set up a Foundation that would blow a smokescreen over all the damage and make everyone look like environmentalists. It would all be great fun and a huge bankroll for everyone involved, including himself. Betty was worrying unnecessarily. Women, he thought, always did. They could not see the big picture in the way that men did.

Aubrey drew up in front of an expensive lobby and took

him up to a luxurious apartment overlooking the bay. As soon as he was alone, Harry telephoned his wife.

She said immediately, "Did you get my message?"

"Yes, but I don't understand it."

"Are they treating you right?"

"Just fine. Top of the mark! Chauffeurs, butlers, corporate apartment. What is this, Betty? You've been very strange about this whole opportunity at Alcon."

"When our Charlie disappeared, you remember?"

"Of course I remember, ungrateful little shit! Not one word of thanks."

"Harry, he won the lottery. It was fifty thousand dollars. I stole the ticket from his desk and collected the prize, and then I had him deported as an illegal alien, so that he would never find out what I'd done. That's how we got started in the big time. I never told you, because you wouldn't have done it."

For a long moment he could not even think. Finally he said, very quietly, "You're damned right, Betty. I wouldn't have done it."

"Yes," she said. "I knew that! Well, it's done now and it can't be undone, but if it's the same Charles Bellamy, and if he knows about the lottery he could be a very angry man. But I don't really see how he could know. You remember how vague he was – just a nice, good kid. It couldn't be the same Charles Bellamy, could it? You're sure they're treating you right?"

"Fine, Betty. Just fine. I'll keep in touch."

He hung up. He thought about what Betty had told him. He found it difficult to be angry, for he knew that he had enjoyed every moment of his prosperity and that he had earned most of it himself. Charlie's money had just started them off. Now he could return it, if necessary. He could make amends. If it was the same man, however, and he knew what had been done to him, then surely Alcon Corporation would never have asked him over here to do this huge job for them. They would not be paying him a fortune to look after their affairs. He would be the last person they would have asked. Betty was mistaken, and she was panicking. It couldn't possibly be the same man.

In the morning, Harry felt renewed. He had rationalized what Betty had told him, and was ready for whatever the day would bring. Aubrey returned with the Rolls and tucked Harry into the back seat for his journey to his first appointment. He wondered idly exactly where he was, but the morning haze and the tinted windows made it difficult to see, and he would not have known anyway. He returned his gaze to the agenda on his knee.

CHAPTER SIX

BOGOTA, COLOMBIA
APRIL 1979

AFTER NEARLY TEN YEARS, Laura Tessier had reached the point where she hated Bogotá. She hated the high, thin air and the provincial society. She hated the poverty and the Indians and the Catholics and the drugs. She hated the violence in the streets. Most of all she hated herself for permitting her life to become so circumscribed by greed. She did not blame Sebastian, to whom she had become attached. It was not he who kept her there. She knew the real cause of her imprisonment was her own fear and avarice. For years now, the profits had increased until she was a very rich woman, but so had the fear. She had begun to believe that she would never escape and would spend the rest of her life in her apartment in Bogotá, and what then would be the use of all the money, sitting untouched and untouchable in a bank account in Geneva? There was nothing to buy in Bogotá. She had all she wanted here, and Sebastian paid for everything. After all, what else had he to spend his own money on but her?

Her apartment was on the top floor of a modern building, looking out over the ancient and dispiriting panorama of Spanish colonialism and its ragged and depressing inheritance. Here she spent her days reading, telephoning her few acquaintances, gazing out the window, arranging dinner for

Sebastian and dreaming of America. She smiled bitterly as she thought of the girl who had come to Bogotá ten years ago. Her mind had been filled with childish recollections of her youth in Colombia with her father and fatuous images of Sugarloaf Mountain, Bette Davis on a cruise boat with Paul Henreid, Ingrid Bergman in the movie *Indiscreet* with Cary Grant, and all those gaucho songs in the movies that she had once thought so romantic. What a fool she had been. Now she watched movies about apartments in Beekman Place and Fifth Avenue and dreamed of being back in New York, but no longer in her walk-up on W 78th Street.

And what else did she have to show for it all? This flat in Bogotá was hers, given to her by Sebastian, but she supposed she would have to leave it behind if she ever left Colombia. She glanced around at her beautiful paintings, her furniture and bric-a-brac collected over the empty years, as she filled in the time waiting for Sebastian to visit, or between her few social engagements or visits to the hairdresser or the dressmaker. Her life in New York had been more interesting, but it was far too late to consider that. The first rule was to accept responsibility for one's own decisions. Any other way led to madness, and she felt she had come close enough to that, over the years.

She considered her reflection in the long mirror. A black dress from Chanel which had cost what she had earned in a year in those old days of her youth. Pearls around her neck, the same ones Charlie had bought her in New York. A superb Colombian emerald on her hand; fit for an empress and given to her by Sebastian. Hair a little darker, if the hairdresser didn't lighten it, skin still, at thirty-one, smooth and pale as honey, and an ass and thighs still tight and firm under her pencil slim skirt. She'd had a lot of spare time to kill over the years, to keep herself looking good. She turned away from her contemplation of herself when she heard Sebastian let himself into the apartment.

She kissed him on the cheek and handed him his Tequila Sunrise. They were as accustomed to one another, after all this time, as an old married couple.

"I didn't expect you this evening. Weren't you going to the Finca?"

"I've just come from there. Jaime has gone away for a while."

"Oh? I didn't know. When did he go?"

"A week ago!"

"A week! Why didn't you come here for a few days, then?"

"I was needed at the Finca."

So far as Laura knew, Jaime was unaware of her existence. Perhaps he still thought his brothers went to the brothels in town, although they were boys no longer, and would hardly be satisfied with that, but Laura was still a secret. Charles paid her so well because she was still a secret.

Sebastian took the drink and returned her kiss, brushing her lips with his own.

"Beautiful as ever," he said. "I must ask Jaime one day if we can be married."

"Don't be a fool, Sebastian. He'd kill us both if he knew I'd been here all these years."

They spoke Spanish together. They were comfortable. She liked him well enough. He had kept his fair good looks and his trim body, but she always felt a touch of fear in his presence. As a man he was still an unknown quantity. They knew every inch of each other's bodies, but their minds were still a mystery to each other. Laura often thought that other people's minds, even if one loved them, were always a mystery. Sebastian had started out as an investment and she could never regard him in any other way. She supposed they did as well as most couples that had been together for ten years.

"You know very well it's time you settled down with some nice well-brought-up Catholic girl from a good Colombian family of whom your mother will approve and have some nice, fat little Spanish babies."

"You are Catholic."

"But not the sort of Catholic of whom your mother would approve."

"There's no rush. Not even Jaime is married yet, only Jesus in Florida, so respectable. You know how he feels about all of that."

Laura shrugged. "Sooner or later, surely, there will be enough money to settle down and stop worrying."

"For Jaime there will never be enough money. It's all he cares about," Sebastian said bitterly. "He is obsessed. Jaime is a fool."

"What?" She laughed. "To go off to the Bahamas for a few days to your casino. It's no wonder he needs a break occasionally from that dreary Finca of yours."

"He hasn't gone to the Bahamas this time. He's gone to America."

She raised her eyebrows. "Dangerous," she said. "They'll be on the look-out. Who is this new chap you spoke of in Miami, so keen to make a reputation by arresting one of the big boys, instead of the little urchins who push marijuana on corners of the street?"

Sebastian smiled grimly. "Stanley Jerkovitz. Good name for him, but he won't be looking for Enrique Cordova, will he?" He held out his glass for a re-fill. "But Jaime is suspicious. He thinks that something over there doesn't smell right any longer!"

"Jaime has always been suspicious. You are all nervous.

You tell me that he was suspicious ten years ago when Nick Barton came down here to sell you his business plan for the future," she said. "The airline, the supermarkets, the holding companies offshore. It all worked out exactly as Nick planned. Nothing has gone wrong for years."

"Not since you came to Bogotá, anyway. You have been my lucky charm. There is a reporter. A chap called Peter Francis. He wants to get at Bellamy, at all of us. He is a reformer."

"Get at Charles?" She laughed. "Do you think that's possible any longer?"

Sebastian shrugged. "Our Alcon deal went wrong," he said, "and now there's some trouble over our accounts with the bank at the Vatican. Someone out there is challenging us, and I don't like it. I say leave it alone, and get out with what we have. There's untold millions for us all, but Jaime won't do that, of course. He's obsessed with greed."

"They say that Bellamy is straight," she said.

Sebastian laughed. "Straight? Who are they? He's the biggest crook in the world today. Every operation he touches is a fraud."

"Yes, perhaps, but a cleaned-up and untouchable fraud."

"He makes millions every year from us."

"And so do you make millions from the operations he has set up for you. None of you could have done all that for yourselves – not from Bogotá! As you say, you could get out and be rich forever with the money he's cleaned up for you over the years."

"You are very well informed, my dear Laura. Are you by any chance still in touch with Charles Bellamy?"

Her heart gave a lurch. If he knew that she contacted Bellamy Corporation every week, she would be dead, no matter how much he cared for her. But she never spoke with Bellamy. Never.

"I? I am in touch with no one, Sebastian. You have me here like a concubine in a seraglio, a prisoner. I haven't seen Charlie Bellamy since the night I met you with him in Miami ten years ago."

She was suddenly afraid of all this talk of Charles, whose name had hardly been mentioned in years. She walked around and sat beside him on the sofa.

"No more talk of marriage, Sebastian. We both know your family would never allow it, but couldn't we go somewhere away from here? Paris? Rome? It's ten years since I left Bogotá and I know so few people in this wretched city. Here we can't even eat together in a restaurant, for fear of what Jaime will say."

"I'm not afraid of Jaime," he said.

"Well, I am." Quite suddenly, talking of travel, of Paris, she was overwhelmed with terror at the vulnerability of her position, of the ruthlessness of these people with whom she was involved, of this world in which she lived. Here she stood in this beautiful room she had created, among men who killed every day, who would not hesitate to kill her if they suspected that she had betrayed them for years. And for whom? For Charles Bellamy who was no better than they were. No, that wasn't true! She had done it for herself and for money that she could never spend. A final irony.

"I'm not afraid of Jaime," Sebastian said again. He slapped his thigh. "We shall go out to dinner together! To the Algonquin!"

"Are you sure?"

The Algonquin was the most fashionable restaurant in town.

"Sure I'm sure. Why should I not dine with a beautiful

American lady? You've lived here for years, a rich American lady. Is there any reason why you should not dine with me? I am not a monk. Come, go and get your coat. Tell your cook to give the dinner to the poor."

"And can I go away to Paris, or to Rio?"

"Why not? We shall plan a vacation. Jaime can't stop me from having friends."

The following morning, after Sebastian had left, she walked downtown to the public phones at the Post Office, as she did every week, and placed her regular call to Bellamy Corporation. Normally she was automatically connected to an extension that recorded her messages and information. To her surprise, this time she was connected directly with Nick.

"Nick? Nick Barton! This is like old times," she said. She was delighted to hear his voice. All the memories of New York that she had kept parked in the back of her mind came rushing back. "Do you remember the bar in New York, Nick, on 2nd Avenue, and the good times we had?"

"I remember everything, Laura. Tell me, why didn't you let us know that Jaime was in the States? Charles is very angry."

"I didn't know myself until last night. I've not seen Sebastian for a week until last night, and he's just told me. Jaime is travelling as Enrique Cordova, an American diplomat," she said.

"We know that already. Do you know why he is here? He never comes here. It puts us all at risk."

"I know, Nick. They, the brothers, didn't want him to go. I don't know exactly what it is, but Jaime is concerned. It is something to do with problems with accounts at the Vatican Bank. You know how paranoid Jaime is. He trusts no one."

She heard a sigh come down the line. "That's Jaime for you," she heard Nick say quietly.

"Sebastian mentioned a reporter, a Peter Francis who he says is determined to make some trouble for us all. There is to be a meeting with Jesus. You know I told you that they wanted to get a controlling share in Alcon Corporation for themselves? Well, they are upset about failing there. They believe that someone is leaking their secrets." She laughed bitterly. "They are suspicious and I don't think they trust Charles any longer."

Nick snorted. "Trust him any longer? They never trusted him. There's no trust in this business. Laura, listen to me," Nick said urgently. He had made up his mind to help her. There was only so far he could go for Charles, and now he must save his own soul, such as it was. If there were to be a choice between protecting Charles and protecting Laura, he would choose Laura.

"Laura, Sebastian knows there's a leak. He knows it because Charles has told him who it is."

There was a long silence on the telephone while Laura considered this piece of information.

Eventually she said slowly, "Charles would not do that to me. He knows they would kill me if they knew."

"He thinks that you have betrayed him in some way by keeping silent about Jaime's visit. If you think that Jaime is paranoid, then you must now see Charles. This business does it to them all. They all go mad – even me, I suppose. He has told Sebastian because he knows that they will now kill you. It will save Charles the trouble of doing it himself, and it gets rid of someone who is in his way. You always knew, Laura, that he wanted everything."

"I am not in his way," Laura said. "Charlie would never do this to me," she repeated.

"Laura, you must believe me," Nick said desperately. "This is no longer the Charlie of the bar in New York. We are no longer those people, any one of us! Those days are gone. Forget it! Charlie will do anything to get what he wants. Listen to me! Because in the old days I was in love with you, before we all became mixed up in this, I am telling you the first thing I've said in all these years that is disloyal to Charles. If you ever tell him I have warned you, it will cost me my life."

"Charlie would never kill you, Nick."

"I've told you, Laura. Charlie will kill anyone who gets in his way," Nick said angrily. "He will not let you get away from Bogotá, Laura. He'll let them kill you, or he'll do it himself, if he has to, because it will cost him too much to let you live, and you are too dangerous. You know too much about us."

"No more than you," she said.

Nick ignored her. "Sebastian knows about you, Laura," he repeated.

Laura laughed. "How could he, Nick, after all these years?"

"I've told you. He knows because Charlie told him. You must believe me."

"Has Sebastian told Jaime?"

"I don't know. Jaime is here somewhere, but we haven't seen him. Maybe he doesn't know yet. Are you on a public phone?"

"Of course."

"Listen to me. I have reserved a seat for you to Rio on Aerolineas do Brazil, leaving Bogotá at one-thirty today, and a connection to Paris on the Concorde, leaving Rio this evening. When you arrive in Paris go straight to Switzerland. As soon as you arrive, withdraw your money from whatever banks you have it in. Do you have a valid passport?"

"Yes!"

"Go back to your apartment immediately. Tell the maid

that you are going shopping and to the beauty parlour and will be gone all day. Don't take a thing. Don't pack. Don't go near the bank."

"But Nick ..." The line was dead.

For ten years she had known that she lived at the heart of a conspiracy. She knew it was heroin and cocaine that paid her huge check every month. Charlie had made that quite clear from the beginning. She knew immediately that she had waited all those years to be told what Nick had risked his life to tell her now.

Strangely, now that the moment had come, she was not frightened. She was quite calm. She understood now why Sebastian had taken her out to dinner last night and talked of marriage, and of holidays in Paris and Rome. He knew already that they would kill her, and probably him as well. She was determined they would not succeed, at least as far as she was concerned. Sebastian would have to look after himself.

She returned to the flat. "Bring my long dark mink, Juanita," she said to the maid. "It's cool today, and my bag, please. I've decided to go to the beauty parlour."

"Let me ring for an appointment, Senora."

"Don't bother. They'll fit me in, I know. Tell cook we'll eat late, not before ten thirty. I'll go to the opening at the Galleria Amparo."

"But Senora ..."

"That's all, Juanita. If Senor Ventura calls, tell him I won't be back before ten this evening. Ask him to join me then for dinner, if he wishes."

"Yes, Senora. Let me phone down to the doorman for a cab."

"No. I'll walk. The weather is beautiful."

Laura slipped her passport and whatever cash she could find into her bag. She looked around her beautiful apartment that she knew she would never see again. She thought about her wonderful jewels in the safe deposit at the bank. At least she had her splendid emerald, which she wore always, and which was now on her finger. Maybe one day she would get the rest. They would be no use to her if she were dead. She walked to the lift and the maid closed the door. She did not glance backwards. She had learned long ago never to look backwards.

She took the lift down to the garage level. No one would see her leave that way. She covered her head with a scarf, and walked to the cab rank in the square. It was unlikely that the driver would remember her. They all took her for a native, or perhaps an Argentine, where so many of the women were blonde. There were many visitors these days and no one paid any attention, but she must be careful to find a driver who did not already know her.

She knew that she was leaving Bogotá forever. She knew that she was in deadly peril, but she felt very calm, as if she were viewing her life from far away, down the wrong end of a telescope. At that distance danger did not look very real. She reached the taxi rank, climbed into the back of the car at the head of the rank, and told him to drive her to the airport.

CHAPTER SEVEN

EVERGLADES NATIONAL PARK, FLORIDA
APRIL 1979

HARRY WELLINGTON FELT TERRIBLE. His head ached and he was freezing cold. He had never been so cold in his life. He seemed to be lying on rough grass, darkness above, but he could hear what seemed to be the rustle and murmur of invisible animals in the heavy stillness. Somewhere close he could smell rotting vegetation and the rank stench of fetid plants and stagnant water. He tried to pull himself back to consciousness from this awful dream. He tried to lift his head, but it seemed weighed down with iron and about to break open and split into a thousand pieces. Surely two or three vodka martinis couldn't have this effect?

But, no, he was not on the plane. He remembered arriving in Miami, and the Rolls taking him to the apartment and picking him up the following morning. So why was it now night? With a huge effort he opened his eyes and sat up. Darkness everywhere. Freezing cold. He realized that it was not a dream. He appeared to be lying, stark naked, half submerged in a shallow pool of water, and the buzz he could hear was mosquitoes feasting on his naked flesh in the dark. He curled up into a ball to keep warm and expose less flesh, and tried to think. Where were his clothes? Where were the Rolls and the driver? They must have been attacked. Was the driver lying dead somewhere, concealed in these ragged bushes? He stood up with difficulty and began to jog on the spot, slowly at first and then with increasing momentum, to get his blood circulating.

Thank God his headache, instead of getting worse, seemed to improve with the exercise, and his feeling of isolation and panic receded. He would have to get to the police, to Alcon Corporation. As he jogged, a thin light appeared in the sky. Dawn. It must be about five o'clock in the morning, almost twenty-four hours since he had left the apartment. They must be looking for him, surely.

He realized that he must be somewhere west of Miami, in the swampy Everglades area. He recalled that it was full of alligators. He must get out. He looked around for his clothes, briefcase, and wallet. Nothing! But there were some trees with large flat leaves, which he stripped off and wrapped around himself as protection from the raw morning chill and his own foolish nakedness. He must make his way to the highway, wherever it was. He did not suppose that Alcon Corporation would have failed to notice the disappearance of a VIP visitor in one of their own huge cars. If he could reach a telephone the whole thing could be worked out. What a lousy start this was to one of the best weeks in his career. Things could only get better from here, he thought.

The sun was well up before he reached a dirt road through the swamp. He followed it for some miles in a southwesterly direction. Finally, around midday, he came upon a ramshackle country store and garage repair shop with an old utility van parked outside. No one appeared to be around. He made his way across the dilapidated forecourt and banged on the door. Silence. He went around the back, and heard the out-of-tune voice of a woman singing an old pop song from the fifties. At least someone alive was around. He hoped he didn't scare the shit out of her. He must look terrible.

He called out and the singing stopped. After a moment or two a woman about twenty-five, hugely fat, came to the door, wiping her hands on a filthy apron. She pushed open the fly screen and looked at him.

"Oh, my Gawd, it's one of them freaks," she screamed and slammed shut the fly screen and the wooden door behind it.

"You git along on yore way, or I'll call the police," she said from behind the protection of two closed doors. "You put your clothes back on, and you git along on yore way!"

"Please do call the police," Harry called out. "I've been mugged and left for dead in the swamp and I've been walking for hours and I don't have any clothes. Yours is the first place I've found and I wish to God you'd call the police immediately."

Cautiously the woman opened the inner door. "You English?"

"Australian."

She smiled, showing a line of broken teeth. "Like Errol Flynn?"

"Exactly!" Harry let out a sigh of relief. It seemed he was getting somewhere, although he was not sure where. Thank God she was a movie buff.

The woman pushed the door a little wider, and peered out. "You got some blood over yore face. What you wearin' there?"

"Leaves," he said. "I told you, they stole my clothes. Please ring the police. I'll wait out here until they come."

"Okay," she said laconically. She seemed no longer afraid. She went inside and returned with a pair of old dungarees and a sweatshirt that she threw through the door. "There! Put those on. They belong to my husband. You can give 'em back later."

"Can you give me some coffee?" he asked. "I haven't had anything since yesterday." He went into the shed behind the cafe and pulled on the smelly clothes that made him feel immediately more able to cope with life. He hadn't realized how vulnerable being naked had made him feel, and he recalled, with pity, newsreels of people in Auschwitz, all naked. Poor buggers!

The woman had left a cup of coffee on the table in the backyard and he sat down to drink. The hot liquid hit his stomach with a jolt like whiskey. He felt totally disorientated and confused. He tried to imagine what had happened since he had left the apartment yesterday morning, but he could recall nothing.

After half an hour a police car drove into the forecourt. Two cops got out, one thin and wizened with a skeptical, lined face that had seen and heard everything. The other man was gross, with a fat belly bulging over his belt, and his hat pushed back on a bald scalp. They spoke with the woman and then walked around the back where he stood, the dungarees hanging on him like a tent, but at least they were an improvement on the vine leaves.

"O'Malley," the thin cop said. The fat one said nothing.

"Harry Wellington." He held out his hand, which the cops ignored.

"So, what's the story?"

Harry sat down again. He felt very weak, and somehow these policemen intimidated him, standing there, so supercilious, ready to disbelieve everything he told them. O'Malley jerked his head in the direction of the diner.

"The woman says yore Australian."

Harry nodded. He told them as much as he knew of what had happened. It was very little. They looked at him with a lifetime of skepticism in their faces.

"There ain't been no reports of missing Rolls Royces, or muggings and disappearances of important people. We ain't heard nuthin' from Alcon Corporation. They have their own security guys. You got a passport?"

"They took everything, but I think I left my passport and airline ticket back at the flat."

"Flat?"

"Apartment." He corrected himself.

"Oh? And where's that?"

"It's on the harbour somewhere. It belongs to Alcon, for their guests. The driver took me there from the airport, and picked me up yesterday morning. You must have some report, something?"

"Nuthin'," O'Malley said flatly. "You ain't heard nuthin', Fred?" Fred shook his head. Harry wondered if he could talk at all.

"Okay, well, we'll go back to the station and see what they say." They didn't believe a word of what he said. "Where's this apartment?"

"I don't know. Ring a chap called Nick Barton. He'll know all about it. He arranged everything."

The two cops exchanged a look. "Mr Barton, eh? We know Mr Barton," O'Malley said. "A very big shot indeed." He wandered off towards the police car. "Tell him I'm okay," Harry called after him.

Fred stood and stared with a degree of complacent animosity, waiting for O'Malley's return. He was gone for some time.

When he returned he stared at Harry with some hostility. "You some kind of fruit cake or somethin'?"

"What do you mean?"

"I just spoke with your Mr Barton, and he don't know nuthin' about any missing Rolls Royce, and he don't know nuthin' about any fuckin' Harry Wellington, either!"

"But that's impossible! They asked me here! I have a letter, a ticket, first class. They bought it for me. Check with the flight from Sydney. There's a mistake!"

"We'll do all of those things," O'Malley said grimly, "and in the meantime you'd better come with us to the station. You got a lawyer?"

"Not here! I only arrived two days ago, for Chrissake! I can ring my office in Sydney and arrange one."

They ignored that request while they pushed him into the back seat and drove back, a considerable distance, into downtown Miami, where they left him at the police station.

"Vagrant," they said. "No documents. No money. No clothes. No hotel. Says he was beaten up in a Rolls Royce." They raised their eyebrows and rolled their eyes. "Book him and put him in overnight until we can sort it out. He makes no sense at all. Says he came here to meet with Alcon Corporation. No one there knows anything about him."

The cell door banged closed. An hour later, Lieutenant O'Malley returned. "We checked with the airline. You came in with them all right. No records of who paid, but first class all the way, right enough!" This impressed O'Malley more than any of the previous information. "We had your Embassy in DC check your passport and visa entry. It seems okay," he added grudgingly. "So what's all this crap about Alcon? Man, they don't know you from shit down there and we don't mess around with that place, I can tell you. They call the tune down in these parts. You wanna ring your office in Sydney? Lieutenant Jerkovitz says it's okay."

Harry shook his head. "No good ringing now. They're sixteen hours behind. It's the middle of the night. I'd like to call my wife."

"Call who you like. The Lieutenant says it's okay."

He called home but no one answered. Betty never left the children alone, and anyway, they were old enough to wake up and answer. He couldn't understand why no one was there. Whereas before he'd felt only confusion and disorientation, now he began to feel a terrible panic squeezing his heart, speeding it up to a horrible, jerky motion that left him breathless and feeling slightly ill. His chest felt as if it were gripped by a cold, tight hand. At least, he thought, if I have a heart attack, they will have to take me to a hospital, or maybe, without insurance, they will just let me die here on the floor. He'd heard plenty of horror stories about American hospitals and people who had no insurance and no credit cards and no money. They just left you to die in the parking lot.

He couldn't ring his secretary. He did not have her home number. He would have to wait until morning in Sydney. He went back to his cell.

At ten o'clock in the evening, O'Malley came back. He was a little more polite. Maybe they'd decided he wasn't just a wino or a junkie after all.

"We've got your office on the phone. Janet's your secretary, right?"

He went outside and took the phone in a shaking hand. "Janet? Janet, thank God! I tried to ring Betty last night, but no one was there. Where are they?"

"What do you mean, where are they, Mr Wellington?" Janet asked. "They're in the States, by now, I guess. Are you okay? You sound awful."

"I am awful! I've been mugged and robbed. Where are Betty and the children?"

"Well, I guess they're in Los Angeles," she said as if talking to a backward child. "We had your fax asking for them to follow you immediately and they left yesterday afternoon, just as you asked. Your fax said you'd meet them there. Where are you now?"

"I never sent any fax asking them to come to America," he said angrily. "And I can't meet them in Los Angeles. I am in a gaol in Miami."

"Oh, my God, what's happened?"

"I don't know, Janet, but ring United and see if Betty and the children went to a hotel, and ring the bank and have them wire me ten thousand dollars immediately, here in Miami, and get my lawyer Gordon Frazer to call me here urgently." He gave her a number.

"Something is very wrong."

Betty and the children here? He must find them and take them home, but first he must get to Alcon Corporation. Those bastards! What did they think they were doing to him? He'd never had any contact with them in his life before, except ... Charles Bellamy? Betty had warned him of Charles Bellamy. It couldn't be the same man, not dopey, simple Charles, working with the Aboriginals. He hoped that Betty and the children were all right.

CHAPTER EIGHT

MIAMI, FLORIDA
APRIL 1979

THE MORNING AFTER HARRY Wellington's arrest, Nick had a meeting with Charles, who was in a towering rage. Nick knew he would be. Charming Charlie hated not to have his own way, and the richer and more powerful he became, the worse it got. Nick was barely half way across the carpet from the door when Charlie spoke to him, in the icy tone that always indicated his worst tantrums.

"Laura's gone!"

Nick finished crossing the room and sat down opposite him. "I know," Nick said.

"What do you mean, you know?" His handsome face was flushed and his eyes literally stuck out from his head as they do in cartoons. If it wasn't so serious, Nick thought, it would be very funny. He looked like Tweetypie after a gruelling bout with Sylvester.

"I know she's gone," Nick said. "Because I arranged it. Did you expect that I would allow her to sit in that apartment in Bogotá and wait until Jaime's henchmen, or yours, Charles, came to murder her?"

"You warned her?"

"She is a colleague, Charles. She is on our side and she

had done nothing wrong. She has worked for you for more than ten years."

"She betrayed me," he said. "There is a code of honour!"

Nick stood up to him, suddenly furiously angry himself. "Fuck you and fuck your code of honour!" he shouted. "Let's stop talking as if we're knights from some chivalrous society in the Middle Ages, not that most of them weren't thugs and crooks, and that's exactly what we are. Thugs and thieves and crooks. Laura was better than you and me. She was just a spy for you. You shopped her to Sebastian because you no longer needed her and she was a nuisance, and you don't want to pay her what you owe her. Talk about honour!"

"You are not playing the game, Nick!"

"Whose game? Yours?"

"Mine is the only game there is. Either you play it, or you're out!"

"Not where Laura is concerned," Nick said.

Charles looked at Nick quietly. He was suddenly calm. "You know you've signed your own death warrant," he said softly.

"Have I, Charlie?" Nick settled himself calmly onto the long sofa against the wall, and lit a cigarette. "Have I really? Do you honestly think that I've worked for you for more than ten years and learned nothing? You really think I'm still that same naive, dopey little provincial lawyer who dragged back two suitcases full of cocaine from Mexico and was too stupid to know what he was doing? You think that?"

"So?"

"So, everything that we've done in the last ten years, everything, Charlie, the airline, the supermarkets, the shit on the planes, the dummy corporations, the murders, the bribery – everything I've organized for you is on paper, verified and certified and locked up with a lawyer you'll never find. If I am not alive tomorrow or any other morning in the near future, the whole thing will immediately be released to the media, to Congress and to the FBI."

"And that's your idea of honour?"

Nick shrugged. "You have your idea, Charlie, and I have mine. I don't waste time on regrets, my friend, but there are some things I will not do. If there is honour among thieves, then that's my idea of it."

"Where is Laura?"

"I don't know!"

"I'll find her, you know."

"That's up to you."

"She could blow us all out of the water, you know."

"Yes, I know, Charles, but she won't, unless you push her to do it."

He looked at Nick. "One day," he said, "you'll regret today's work."

Nick looked him in the eye. "Well," he said, "if I do, it won't be the first day's work I've lived to regret, and I don't suppose it will be the last. Is that all, Charlie?"

"No, of course not," he snapped. "What about Jaime?"

The first storm of the day was obviously over. Nick knew that neither of them would ever feel quite the same about each other again, and he felt sorry about that, but no matter. A partnership is like a marriage, he thought. Through good times and bad, if it suits both partners it lasts. If not, it hits the wall. There would be no divorce this time.

"I believe at the moment he's down with his brother, Jesus," Nick said. "So far as I'm aware they are comparing notes and satisfying themselves that we have been robbing them for years. They are discovering that the funds that should be in the Vatican are not there. Thanks to you, Sebastian now knows that Laura has been informing us for years of their innermost secrets."

"Well, he won't tell his brother. It would mean a death sentence for himself."

"Jaime wants out," Nick said.

"Well, we can't have that, can we? I must see him before he goes to Rome, if that's what he has in mind."

"I realize that, Charles. We've put a hold on some information from overseas, but once he goes there for himself, he and Jesus will easily discover that we've been misappropriating his funds for years. Jesus is a banker himself, after all. We have stolen billions of dollars through the European subsidiaries we've set up and the accounts in the name of the fictitious corporations and the Vatican banks, and the accounts in Liechtenstein and the Cayman Islands. If he'd trusted Jesus more, he'd have found out years ago. We can't let it happen now."

"Or ever," said Charles grimly. "I have no intention of letting that little shit get his hands on all those millions. I want to rub the little turd's nose in the fact that he's been paying me from his own money to take over his own operation from him. What about that fool, Jerkovitz, down at the police station?"

"Lieutenant Jerkovitz knows that Jaime is here, but will not touch him at the moment. It's more than his career is worth. You've made sure of that with all the money you spend in Washington and here in Miami on the local police. But I wouldn't underrate the man, Charles, simply because he's honest."

"You are right, as usual, Nick. It's just that I deal with so few honest people these days. I guess I've forgotten how their minds work. How are we going to get Jaime here, then?"

"I suggest that I ring Jesus and invite him here to have an audit and a meeting so that we can transfer all their holdings.

That's what they want, isn't it?"

"And then what?"

"I leave that up to you, Charles. Do what you like. My honour code, such as it is, doesn't extend to the protection of the Ventura family."

Charles walked over and stood by the window, looking down at Miami. Nick knew it was hard for him because he never apologized, but he said, "I'm sorry about Laura, Nick. I made a mistake, but it's too late to go back now."

"Yes, you did. You've made an enemy of the only person in the world other than myself whom you could trust completely, and who trusted you," Nick said. "And now you can't trust either of us. You are all alone."

"Not quite, I think," he said quietly. He turned around and faced Nick. "My position is so strong now, I don't believe anyone respectable would pay attention to allegations from the Ventura family, but you never know. We can't risk Jaime blowing his mouth off now. There's nothing more that Jerkovitz would like, and that bloody reporter, too. What's his name?"

"Peter Francis."

"That's the fellow. Find out more about him, Nick. We can't have him and Jerkovitz making a nuisance of themselves. We can't risk that. Not now. Just get Jaime here, Nick."

"What do you suppose has made Jaime wake up, after all this time?" Nick asked.

Charles shrugged. "The Alcon takeover failure? It was so ambitious. He knew that something went wrong there. He must have known we had prior knowledge. Even Jaime is not so thick as not to see that, but I wasn't going to let him have Alcon Corporation."

"And you stopped him, thanks to Laura," Nick said.

"You know what they'll do to her if they catch her?"

"Of course. You should be protecting her, Charles, when you talk of honour, not chasing her."

"No man has honour when he's disgraced – or dead," he said. Then he laughed. "I'd give a lot of money to see Jaime's face when he discovers that Sebastian had Laura there all those years, and he never knew about it. It'll be a wonder if it doesn't kill him."

"Yes," Nick agreed, "it may well be the death of Sebastian, so I hope he enjoyed all those years. You've killed him, you know, Charles, if Jaime finds out."

"Sebastian will never tell him," Charles repeated. "We're running a business here, Nick. Or are you forgetting that, with this newfound code of your own? What about that idiot, Wellington?"

"He's down at the police station. We haven't finished with him yet. By the time we have, he'll do whatever you want. Jerkovitz is with him. He feels sorry for Harry, they tell me. Thinks he may have been set up!"

"Really?" They both laughed at that. "I wouldn't have thought that Jerkovitz could feel sorry for his own big toe if it were boiling in oil. I wonder what he thinks he'll get out of Harry? What about Betty and the children?"

"Safe in California at the ranch."

"Be careful of Betty," Charles said. "Betty has all the brains and the balls in that family. Have we blocked his funds?"

"For long enough to keep him unhappy."

"Has he come to you to ask for money?"

"Not me. I have denied any knowledge of him to the police for the time being, but sooner or later he's going to ask for you, Charlie. Yours is the only name in this whole company that could mean anything to him at all."

"So we don't want him down there talking too long to our friend Jerkovitz in the police station, do we? Better get him out this afternoon, Nick."

"You still want him?" Nick asked.

"Oh, yes, I want him all right. I've been waiting for him for years. Harry and Betty. My God, do I want them! Have you been in touch with the woman at the petrol station?"

"Everything's been done, Charles."

"Good. Anything else?"

"Monsignor Bland in Rome is concerned about the transfer of Ventura funds to our account. He wants a written confirmation from Jaime this time." Nick coughed. "It's a very large amount of money, Charles. I don't think their bank is very keen to let it go."

"Too bad," he said, "but we're ready to move now, and this whole thing of Laura blowing up like this, we must move quickly to finesse them. Leave Monsignor Bland to me. Send up the papers immediately for all transactions between us and the Vatican Bank and I'll talk to him myself ... and Nick?"

He turned to Charles on his way out of the room. Charles grinned at him. "You know I've asked Edwina de Trafford to marry me?"

"I suspected as much. Has she said yes?"

"Not yet, but she will. Now that we are having all these problems with Rome, it's a pity her family aren't Catholics."

Nick shrugged. "Why don't you marry one of the Kennedy clan – or Senora Ventura?"

Charles laughed. "I think she's a little old. Even I'm not prepared for so big a sacrifice. That's all, Nick. Ask them to get me the Cardinal on the phone, will you? We'll see where he stands. How much did we give them last year?"

"A lot."

"How much of it got to His Holiness?"

"A lot, but then His Holiness gets an even larger amount from Senora Ventura. Jaime sees to that."

"Okay. Have those files sent up. And Nick?"

He turned again. Charles seemed reluctant to have him leave the room. "You know I'll have to deal with Laura before Jaime gets to her?"

"I wish you luck," Nick said. He'd done all that he could for Laura. Now she was on her own, but he was prepared to put his money on her, even though she might bring all of them down in the end. He knew that he would do what he could to protect Laura, even if it cost him his life. He had known that since he first saw her in BJ's bar all those years ago. Charles had made a grave mistake.

CHAPTER NINE

GENEVA, SWITZERLAND
APRIL 1979

LAURA DID NOT RELAX until the Air France Concorde had lifted off the airport at Rio de Janeiro, and was cruising up in the stratosphere, high over the Atlantic Ocean. In a little over four hours she would be in Paris. It was time to work out a plan for her survival.

She understood what Jaime's fury would be like and, for the first time, realized how serious the danger for Sebastian would be if Jaime ever found out. Perhaps last night he had been saying goodbye for both of them. She shuddered. She did not love Sebastian. She had never loved him. They had spent many good times together, and she wished him no harm, but Sebastian would have to solve his own problems.

She wondered whether she would ever see him again. She recalled leaving Miami with him all those years ago, and thinking then that a whole chapter of her life was closing behind her. She felt the same again now, but this time she knew the game was deadly, and she was ten years older, with less time to spare.

The steward placed a glass of Krug on the small table in front of her. A glass of champagne, she considered, would be the perfect way to celebrate her freedom, and her escape.

Laura understood clearly that she could trust no one but

herself. She knew only too well that her own life was worth no more than a passing thought to the men who organized the sale of the Ventura brothers' products throughout the world. She must be as smart and clever and ruthless as they were if she wanted to live. She rang for the steward.

"Please check Air France timetables, and book me a seat on the first plane departing for Geneva after we land. I've no luggage on board. I want the earliest flight you can get."

"Of course, Madame Tessier."

"One more thing. When I travel in Europe, I always prefer to use my maiden name, so would you please make the reservation in the name of …" She glanced down at the magazine in her lap for inspiration, "… in the name of Ellery."

"Of course, Madame."

The crews on the Concorde flights were trained not to blink an eye at any request by a passenger. They were catering, after all, to those few people in the world who were rich enough to be obeyed without question, but whose missions were often questionable.

She would go straight to the bank and transfer her funds to yet another organization, as she had had them transferred every month from the bank into which Charles Bellamy had paid them. Thank God she was now reasonably rich, and might one day be very rich, if Charles kept his word and his contract with her. She did not, however, expect that he would do so. Twelve million or more already paid in by Charles over the years, plus the interest that she had hardly touched, was in her bank account, and she knew that was all she would ever get, no matter what bargain they had sealed together in the New York Deli on 7th Avenue all those years ago.

The steward returned. "There is no Air France flight for several hours, Madame Tessier, but we have made a reservation on Swissair 189 which leaves only 25 minutes after we land. As you are a Concorde passenger, we have arranged for your ticket to be collected at the departure gate. We are on time, as always, so you should make it! You will not have to bother with customs or immigration, of course, as you will be in transit."

"How shall I pay?"

"If you will give me your credit card, I can organize that now, on board." A card would be traced, she knew.

"I prefer to pay cash."

"Of course. Two hundred and thirty dollars. Unfortunately, the reservation is only tourist class, as first class is full, but as Madame said it was urgent ... "

"That's fine, thank you."

She counted out the cash and settled down to her Sole Bonne Femme with more relish than she had anticipated, sipping a little more of their excellent Krug until the plane began to descend into Paris Orly. She felt as she had when she'd left New York and gone to Colombia – that same tense excitement, that stirring in her guts of danger and adventure. She felt alive again. She had been given a reprieve. Nick had saved her life. She was in his debt, and she felt that she owed it to him to escape. He might very well need her help some time in the future and this was an obligation she would never forget. She took out the black scarf and wound it expertly around her head and neck, so that none of her blonde hair showed, and as little as possible of her face. She had once been, as Charles had told her, an actress of sorts. Her talent would perhaps now save her life.

CHAPTER TEN

MIAMI
APRIL 1979

LIEUTENANT STANLEY JERKOVITZ OF the Miami Drug Squad did not see himself as a good man. He was untidy and slovenly and rather grubby and he'd left his ex-wife to bring up the kid in Milwaukee when he sloped off to Miami. He smoked dope himself and regularly let the kids who sold it in the street get off with a warning and a few clouts around the head, which is what he thought they deserved, and no more. He fucked the girls who worked in the streets around the area in which he lived, and he didn't expect to have to pay them for their services. After all, he was a cop, wasn't he? He scratched his head as he let himself into his apartment and looked around with disgust at the untidy mess which greeted him. He went through to the kitchen for a beer before he made his way into the living room.

He was a bad father and he'd been a rotten husband, and he really didn't think that he was anything out of the ordinary as a cop, but he was certain that this Australian, Harry Wellington, was being framed, and somehow this stuck in his throat. The fellow was a nice, innocent guy and he was being given a very raw deal by someone. Deep down, in an area that he had previously studiously ignored, Stanley felt that this was wrong, and that he ought to be doing something about it, but he dared not do anything without authority from his boss. That sort of thing could get him cashiered in a second. When he'd raised the matter of his suspicions about Harry Wellington he'd been warned, and in no uncertain terms, to lay off. It was more than his career was worth to go against that order. Yet, once again, behind it all, Stanley could recognize the fine Machiavellian, and exceedingly powerful, hand of Charles Bellamy, although, of course, his touch was never directly evident. Stanley felt again the thrill that he thought he had long ago lost, the thrill of what it had once meant to him, in his younger and more cheerful days, to be a cop in America.

Harry Wellington was sitting slumped in the window seat, watching some children playing ball across the street in a fenced off area strewn with litter. This was not the Miami of the tourists, but of the poor Cubans and Puerto Ricans, and of underpaid policemen, and if Harry had not already been depressed, the view from the window would have succeeded in doing so. He was thinking of his own family, and whether he would ever see them again. He was thinking he had not spent enough time with them. In spite of the advice from the women's magazines and the feminists, there simply wasn't enough time in one lifetime, to be the perfect husband, lover, father and breadwinner. It would be wonderful if there was time for everything, and then suddenly something happened to bring down the whole world, and it seemed that, like so many men these days, he had all his priorities wrong.

Harry looked up as the cop came into the room. "Thanks for putting me up here," he said. "Until my money gets here tomorrow, I haven't any funds for a hotel, and no credit cards."

"You want the bad news first?" Jerkovitz asked, casually swiping his arm across the coffee table, depositing its contents on the floor, and putting the two beers on the cleared space.

"You mean there's some good news?"

Jerkovitz shook his head. "You get caught up with these power brokers, there's no good news. There's bad news and worse news."

"Well, whatever it is, it can't be worse than what's already happened."

"I wouldn't count on that. It's worse, all right. You know the dame out at the diner?"

Harry nodded. "Fat and dirty," he said, "but she gave me a cup of coffee and a pair of pants, so I'm grateful."

"Don't be! They've just tipped me off down at the station, so I can warn you. She's going to file against you for aggravated sexual assault."

"For what?"

"For rape!"

In spite of everything, Harry laughed. Inside his terrible, smelly, too large pants his belly shook and rumbled with mirth.

"Jesus, Stan, you've got to be joking. Have you seen that dame? I'd been out all night, beaten up and drugged. I couldn't have raped her if she'd been Venus de Milo, and she'd lain down and begged for it!"

"I believe you," Stanley said. "I know you're being set-up, Harry, but at least your lawyer has you out on bail. You can sleep here until we sort it out. The power boys are out to get you, my friend, for some reason that neither of us can work out at the moment, and they will succeed in screwing you into the ground unless you're very smart indeed. Even if the jury finds you innocent, the publicity will screw you. I'd clear out and go home if I were you, before they arrest you!"

"They've got my wife and kids, Stan. Don't the police have any leads on them?"

Stan took a swig of his beer and settled onto the sofa with

his feet on the coffee table. "LAPD isn't even looking for them, man. Your wife came here of her own free will. No one has time to look for them when half the city's falling apart. Anyway, I've told you, the word is out to do nuthin' about it. Have a beer." Stan passed him a bottle. "You say that Alcon invited you here?" Stanley asked.

"Sure, and paid my fare. I had a letter from a chap called Nick Barton."

"Yeah! We know Nick. Nick's okay. You know him?"

Harry shook his head. "Never heard of him until I had a letter inviting me over here to talk with them."

"You don't know no one at Alcon, then?"

"Well, I don't know," Harry, said. "Maybe I know this fellow, Bellamy."

Jerkovitz whistled. "Jesus Christ, Harry! Why didn't you tell me that before? You know high and fucking mighty Charles Bellamy? That's like knowing the King of England around these parts."

"Well, my wife and I used to know a fellow called Charles Bellamy once, years ago. He worked for me in Australia then, but I really don't think it can be the same man. The one I knew was kind of a dreamer, you know."

Stanley shook his head. "Can't be the same fellow. This man is one tough hombre, man. I'm telling you, you can't get near him."

Harry felt a hard knot of despair form in his guts. "Charlie always said I cared too much about the money," Harry said.

"Can't be the same man," Stanley said again, shaking his head and taking a long swig of his beer. "This one cares about nothing else. Generous, though. Gives away heaps to all kinds of good causes."

Harry looked up. "Is that so? Charlie was always going on about making the world a better place." He thought a moment. "Stan, do you believe in divine punishment for your sins?" Harry asked.

"Shit, man! I don't even believe in sins. Are you some religious nut or something?"

"Stanley, a couple of days ago my wife told me something that I didn't know. She told me that she stole a lottery ticket from our Charlie Bellamy, a lottery win he didn't know about. She stole the ticket and she claimed the prize, and then she had him deported so he would never find out what she did. Now I believe we're being punished for it!"

Stanley looked at him sadly. "Oh, man! If it's the same Charles Bellamy, you're being punished all right, and it ain't even started, and it ain't any divine retribution. God isn't interested in you, Harry, but I'm beginning to think that Mr Bellamy is, aren't you?"

"You think it might be the same guy, then?"

"Can you think of any other reason for all of this shit that's going on? I believe that Bellamy is tied in with the Ventura family in Medellin, and that his money comes from drugs, or did in the beginning before he went legit and began to smell so sweet. I can't prove it, though, and I can't investigate, because I've been ordered to stay away from Bellamy and all his concerns."

"If it's the same Charles Bellamy, I don't think he'd be into drugs," Harry said. "This guy was a bit of an idealist."

"Is that so?" Stan asked sourly. "Those sort are always the worst."

The phone rang. It was the station chief. "Hey, Jerkovitz, you got that Australian, Harry Wellington, there?"

"Yeah!"

"Damnedest thing! I've just had a call from Alcon Corporation to file a missing persons report. They wanted to know if we had any reports on a Harry Wellington. They say he just wandered off the other morning. They thought he might have gone off for a couple of days. Then they were starting to get worried, thought he might have had a blackout or some kind of memory loss. They were damned relived that we had him. They thought he might be dead, or something."

"Did they indeed? It took them a while to do anything about it!" Stan said skeptically. "They said they knew nothing about him yesterday!"

"Well, they're sending a car for him now. You'd better bring him back here to the station. I don't want them to know that he's up there with you. That could cause complications for you, you know."

"Everything with Alcon causes complications," Jerkovitz said.

Stanley put down the receiver and looked at Harry. "My friend," he said. "I think you are in twenty-four carat trouble."

Harry looked at him glumly. He couldn't take any more bad news. He was going to be made to look like a criminal and an idiot in front of all his colleagues back in Sydney, in a society too small for him ever to re-establish himself. He would be ruined.

"What is it now?"

"Get your coat. Alcon have just discovered that you're missing and they're sending a car to the station to pick you up. Let's get going."

As they walked out of the apartment, Stan said, "Harry, will you let me know the truth of all this, when you know it yourself? Will you give me your word to meet with me before you leave, and tell me what's going on?"

"Sure, Stan. Of course I will. You're the only one who helped me here. You've been very decent to me. I'll do whatever you want."

"Will you meet with my pal, Peter Francis? He's a reporter."

"Sure, I will, so long as he says nothing about the stolen lottery ticket. That would ruin me. I'd like you to keep that to yourself."

They climbed back into the police car and returned to the station. "I won't say a word about that," Stan said. "Not to anyone." Outside the car the warm, tranquil air of the Caribbean slid by with the palm trees, calm and carefree, soft as a kiss.

The Rolls Royce was waiting outside the police station. Aubrey was standing beside it. "Good evening, Mr Wellington," he said. "It's nice to see you again, sir. We've been worried about you, gone for two days without any message." He held open the door of the car. "I've been instructed to take you back to the apartment to clean up, and then to Mr Bellamy's house for dinner. They're expecting you."

Jerkovitz gave him a shove. "Get in there, Harry," he said. "You came here to work with them so get in and go to it."

Harry climbed into the back of the car. He found another man seated on the far side, away from the door that clunked shut behind him.

"Good evening, Harry, I'm Nick Barton. It's nice to meet you. We thought you'd run away from us."

"When they rang you, you said you didn't know me. You told the police that Alcon had never heard of me," Harry said.

"Yes, I'm sorry about that, but I had my orders, I'm afraid. In these matters none of us is a free man, is he? Charlie thought we needed to soften you up a bit before we talked."

"What do you really want from me?"

"We just want to do a deal, or do we go ahead with the rape charges?"

"There was no rape, and you know it!"

Nick smiled thinly. "Of course I know it, but there are the rape charges. They are quite real, I assure you."

"What kind of a deal do you want?"

"Any kind we tell you!"

"I'm not ready to do anything dishonest," Harry said, immediately aware of the stupidity of his position. Nick simply laughed.

"My dear chap, you're a crook and a thief, and we have the evidence to prove it, so it's a little late in the day to take that attitude with us, don't you think? And we have your wife and children, and also a woman who says that she wishes to press charges for rape. So are you ready to do as we ask, or do you want us to ruin you, and your family as well?"

"I'm ready to do as you ask, of course," Harry said. "I'm not a total fool, you know."

Time enough later, he thought, to extricate himself from this mess.

"Good! I was worried for a moment you might be."

The car drew up outside the apartment block. "Go upstairs and make yourself presentable," Nick said. "You look like hell, and Charles is very fastidious. Aubrey will be back in half an hour to take you over to Charles' house for dinner, and we will talk then. Betty and the children are in California, just in case you give us any trouble. You do what we want and they won't come to any harm."

CHAPTER ELEVEN

NAPLES, FLORIDA
APRIL 1979

JAIME VENTURA SAT BESIDE the huge pool in the garden of his brother Jesus' house in Naples, Florida. The garden sprawled over a ten-acre estate on the edge of the town, overlooking the milky waters of the Gulf of Mexico. It gave the impression of being a part of the countryside until one became aware of the electronic eyes that guarded the perimeter of the estate, and the guards on duty at the gate. Some people questioned the need for such elaborate security for the president of the local bank. However, these were few in number, for the Ventura hospitality at this huge villa was princely and those who criticized him, explicitly or implicitly, were not invited again.

Catherine O'Reilly Ventura, Jesus' wife, had been clever. She had made no attempt to invade the bastions of old money that wintered around Palm Beach and Boca Raton, but among people who lived year round in Florida, along the Gulf Coast, she had become a powerful influence. To be removed from Catherine Ventura's list of those who were invited to her beautiful and elegant house was to close a number of other influential doors in the community. Criticism of the manner in which the Ventura family lived was therefore minimal.

Further, if you were persona non grata with Catherine, you were also removed from that short and special list of those who lunched occasionally with Jesus. Those who were fortunate enough to be on that list received mysterious investment advice that always provided profits considerably in excess of those available in the general financial market. No one wished to be dropped from that list.

Jaime sipped his beer. The day was already very hot, even though the news showed New England and Washington DC to be covered in a blanket of late snow and whipped by gales. He admitted the house and garden were splendid. Catherine had real style. It was a pity she was so devout. As far as he was concerned Holy Mother Church was useful only for business deals, not for spurious promises of paradise. However, she was a good woman, and undoubtedly she had helped create the atmosphere of trust and rectitude that surrounded Jesus and the Credit Naples Bank, in spite of the increasing notoriety of his family name in Colombia. It was generally accepted in the USA now that he had severed connection with the dubious interests and methods pursued by his more notorious brothers.

Catherine's reputation for Christian sanctity and social ruthlessness had been important in creating this trust. Now, for the first time since Jesus had left home, Jaime was here to talk business with his brother. The visit was supposed to be amiable and anonymous. This had not been achieved.

Jaime turned to his brother. He had difficulty in controlling his voice. "You tell me that we have lost millions?"

"Yes," Jesus said. "I do not have the proof yet, but it would appear to be so!"

"And you blame Charles Bellamy?"

Jesus shrugged. He was not afraid of his brother. He was now a powerful and respected man himself, and in the United States of America, where it counted for something.

"I don't know. I only know that our affairs are not being

as properly managed by the Bellamy Corporation Investment Funds as I believed. Now that you are here, we must see Bellamy."

"What do you suspect?"

"Theft, or at least a sophisticated attempt at it," Jesus said.

Jaime was so angry that he had difficulty speaking. He had left these matters in the hands of his brothers while he managed the supply of drugs. They had made a mess of it. They were such fools.

"Well, so we are in trouble. Perhaps Bellamy has betrayed us. Perhaps others. We are very vulnerable. No wonder we failed with the Alcon Corporation takeover. Someone inside our trusted circle is working against us."

"We have made millions over the years, Jaime."

"Yes, but not all the millions to which we are entitled, and I mean to get the rest from that bastard Bellamy. Years ago I said we couldn't trust him, but you and Sebastian would have it otherwise. Where is Sebastian?"

"In Bogotá, I believe."

"He should have unearthed these things. He deserves to be strung up by his balls, but even I don't want the blood of my own brother on my conscience."

"Revenge will not get the money back."

"By God it will," Jaime said. "All these years with no trouble, not even a major bust. We've moved the stuff out of Colombia in our own airline, tons of it, year after year, in the shit cans, and out through the supermarkets. And now, all of a sudden, all this trouble with our accounts."

"Not with the distribution, Jaime. Bellamy still does that to perfection."

"What the hell's the use of perfect distribution throughout the world, if we're not getting our proper share of the profits, Jesus? You and Sebastian should have picked this up. Do I always have to do everything myself?"

"The money's all there on paper," Jesus said.

"But it's not all there in fact, if we wanted it, is it?"

"I don't know for sure. The only way to know that is to ask for it."

"And that's what I intend to do. I shall go to that shit Bellamy and ask for it. I don't think we've seen the worst of this yet. What about the unctuous prelate, Monsignor Bland?"

Jesus laughed. "You needn't worry about him. We've been dealing with him for years at the Banco Vaticano. We have all the certificates for our deposits there in our own name, and the balances are held in the names of a series of our own companies around the world. Nothing to do with Charles."

"And how has this money been placed?"

"Well, first through the First National Bank of Florida, which sends it away ..."

"Exactly. The First National Bank of Florida, which belongs to Charles Bellamy, and which has just misplaced millions of our dollars. Misplaced!" He spat out the words disgustedly. "As if they're talking about the change the maid brought back from the marketplace! And we are beaten to the draw on Alcon. I am becoming very suspicious of this bank. They are our US clearinghouse, and they hold most of our paper, and have done for, what, almost ten years?"

"Charles Bellamy has made our fortune for us, Jaime. He is absolutely reliable."

"No one is absolutely reliable when this amount of money is involved, Jesus, particularly the English, if I may say so. An Englishman's handshake may be his bond, but only when it's given to someone he regards as his social equal.

Otherwise he does not feel bound. How do you think they made an Empire from other people's land? I think it's time I called on Mr Bellamy to give us our money."

"They will need time. We can't just call around tomorrow afternoon for several billion dollars."

"Quite so, but I shall want better evidence of what he holds than we seem to have at the moment. I shall go and call on him tomorrow or the next day."

"I understand that he is going to be married."

"So I see in all the newspapers this morning."

"Edwina de Trafford comes from one of the most influential families in the USA," Jesus said. "Catherine was very impressed."

Jaime laughed rather nastily. "But with a slightly tarnished reputation. Who else would have Bellamy?"

"Come on, Jaime, don't be foolish! This is not some little muchacha from a village in Colombia who has got herself knocked-up by the local cowherd. This woman's last husband was a cousin of the Queen of England, and her mother's family connections here are so powerful that there is no way around them, even with all the money we have at our disposal. They've been there too long."

"With all the money we now have at our disposal, Jesus, we can go around anyone, provided that it is at our disposal. But you assure me that you're satisfied with the securities we have with Bellamy's bank, and in other banks in Europe?"

"Totally satisfied. They constitute a good portion of the capital of this bank, and they satisfy the government auditors."

Jaime grunted expressively to indicate what he thought of anyone employed by governments in America, or elsewhere.

"We shall see what Mr Bellamy has to say to all of this himself. Now what about our share deals? Are all those troubles caused by the brilliance of Charles Bellamy, or is someone betraying us, for some reason? What about that tricky Monsignor Bland? He is worse than Talleyrand!"

"In view of our generosity in that direction, I think we can rule out Monsignor Bland. In any event, he is a cousin of Catherine's."

"And that makes him honest in your eyes? Cousins! My God!" Jaime asked in astonishment, and spat on the ground.

"I am quite as capable as you, my dear Jaime, of seeing the difference between my duties to God and to Mammon, and to Catherine, too, for that matter."

Jaime was undisturbed. "So, we rule out Monsignor for the time being. That leaves you and, of course, Catherine, who could be the cause of the leaks."

"'Not quite!' Jesus said angrily. "I will not have you question the loyalty and integrity of my wife in my own house, nor will I tolerate my own good faith being questioned, for that matter, while the reputation of that little whore in Bogotá goes unscathed. I hardly think Laura can be omitted from this equation. Nor Sebastian himself for that matter!"

"Laura? Laura? Who is this Laura? I know of no Laura in Bogotá!"

Jesus stared at him in complete astonishment. There was a prolonged silence during which Jesus realized that he could not go back, yet to go forward would sign the death warrant of Sebastian, and Laura too, whom Jesus had actually rather liked on the couple of occasions he had met her.

Finally he said, "You mean you really don't know? You don't know that Sebastian has had an American girlfriend in Bogotá for years, and now she has just disappeared? I thought it must be these matters which had finally brought you over here to talk."

Jaime carefully put his beer on the table. For a long time now he believed he had known everything that his family was doing, believed that he had been in control. The Capo! It had been at the foundation of his belief and of his strength that they obeyed him in all things and bowed to his will. His blood pounded so heavily in his neck that he found it difficult to speak.

"Who knows of this?" he asked thickly.

"I know. Catherine knows. We thought that you knew and had condoned. We have spoken to no one."

"And in Bogotá?"

Jesus shrugged. "It's a small city, full of gossip. Who knows? Yesterday Sebastian telephoned that she had gone, disappeared, taken nothing. He has traced her as far as Paris, and after that no more information, so far. He thinks it is she who has betrayed us. He has put out an order to have her killed, of course. Don't be angry, Jaime. Ten years is a long time. He is very upset. He did not believe that she would betray him – all of us!"

Jaime spat again. "No doubt she has been doing it every day of those ten years, and he has been giving her the information to do it. Why do you think, all those years ago, I said no women? You can't trust women. Well, at least she wasn't working for the CIA, or we'd all be dead by now."

Jesus bent his head. "I couldn't bear that you should suspect Catherine or myself. I didn't know you knew nothing of this other thing."

Jaime felt the blood in his neck begin to settle. "What's done is done," he said. "Sebastian is family. You say he is dealing with the woman?"

Jesus nodded. "He is taking steps to remove her."

"How much do you tell Catherine?"

"As little as possible!"

"Trust no one. Everyone will betray you, sooner or later, when the price is right! People are such fools. Everyone is a potential Judas. Foolish wars in which both sides pray for victory to the same God, who must therefore always betray one side or the other! The hypocrisy makes me want to vomit. If we sold drugs for two thousand years we couldn't kill as many people as the Crusades! Don't talk to me of trust!"

"I trust Catherine," Jesus said.

"She will betray you when her conscience tells her to do it."

He spat again. Jesus recoiled. He had become too fastidious after so long in America, Jaime thought. In Colombia, everyone spat. It was worse than he thought. The bile in his belly came from knowing that his authority had been a myth. They had done as they pleased and they had ruined themselves, and him, too, just when they might have been the most powerful family in South America.

"And where did Sebastian find this ... this Laura?" He choked on the name.

Jesus' voice was very low. "I believe he met her in Miami with Charles Bellamy! She was a friend of his, or at least an acquaintance."

"Ha! There it is again! This connection with Bellamy. He's at the centre of the web, believe me! You are all such fools. Why could Sebastian not be satisfied with the whores, as I am?"

"We are not all like you, Jaime."

He stood up. "I am going inside to think," he said. "Leave me alone."

For the first time in his life he felt like an old man, knew what it was like to feel the sap running low in his veins, to grow weak, to die. He must go to this banker, Bellamy, without delay, and find out the worst of it, before it was too late. Before someone wrested control from his hands.

CHAPTER TWELVE

GENEVA, SWITZERLAND
APRIL 1979

LAURA TESSIER HAD NEVER been to Europe, but she had spent ten years in Bogotá learning where smart and rich people spent their time. Air France had reserved a suite for her in the name of Ellery at the Hotel Beau Rivage. Although it was late when she arrived, she could see, in the spring starlight, the Dents du Midi rising majestic and snow-covered on the French side of the lake, and, in front of her, the Jet d'Eau flung its single spout of water high into the chilly air. Directly below her balcony was the pavement along the waterside to the ferry boat, the same pavement on which the Empress Elizabeth of Austria had been stabbed to death with a hatpin through her heart, before the turn of the century. Unaware that she had been hurt she had dragged her dying body back to this same hotel, perhaps to this very room where Laura now stood by the window. Poor Empress Cissy. Laura shivered. She hoped that some similar fate was not in store for her.

She closed the door on the chilly, spring air of the mountains, rang for a wake-up call, double locked the door and went to bed. She felt safe in this hotel. The price protected her, and the bed linen was superb. It is amazing, she thought, the illusion of safety that money can buy.

By nine o'clock the next morning she was with the manager of the Banque des Trois Cantons, which had looked after her affairs since she had first gone to Bogotá, without ever having seen her. The bank was small, discreet and independent. Every month her payments from Charles into her account with Credit Suisse had been transferred to this small investment house and put to work on her behalf on the advice of Monsieur Edmond Braechel, with whom she was now closeted in his book-lined and handsome office that looked more like the library of a handsome private house.

"Madame Tessier, this is a pleasure to meet with you after all our correspondence. May I say that you are considerably younger than I had expected."

"Thank you, monsieur," Laura replied in the perfect French she had learned from the Sisters of the Immaculate Conception in Bogotá. "But we have little time for compliments, I'm afraid. I must rely on your complete discretion."

He inclined her head. "That is why we exist, madame."

Laura smiled. "We both know that in this country mysterious accounts can be created and may also disappear. I, myself, am well aware of accounts manufactured to blackmail prominent persons who have been accused of having accepted ... commissions."

M. Braechel looked saddened by these irrefutable facts of international banking. "We live in a complex world," he agreed tentatively.

"A crooked world," Laura said. "But not much more so now than previously. Now, to business. While I wait here this morning, I want a list prepared of every cent which you hold on my behalf, and I want a receipt from the bank signed by yourself and at least one other senior bank official."

Edmond Braechel looked wounded. "Madame, this is not necessary. With this bank your affairs are fully protected."

"You will permit me to be the best judge of that, monsieur. Please give the necessary orders for such a statement to be prepared."

She waited while he did so.

"From this moment, monsieur, I am no longer Madame Tessier, but Madame Ellery. As I have come here from Colombia, you will understand when I say that my life may be in some danger, and the same may be said to be true of my funds. Other than the person who transfers the funds to me, only three people in the world know that I have an account with your bank. They are you, the operative at Credit Suisse who transfers my funds to you each month, and myself. However, I believe that, in a short while, you may receive a delicately worded request to block my accounts."

The manager held up his hands. "In all my years at the bank I have never heard of such a thing. It is not possible, madame."

"Perhaps your good Swiss clients lead less complex lives than I do," she said. "Should there be any suggestion of a personal reward for such an action, you may be assured I would be prepared to be equally generous."

"Madame Tessier – Madame Ellery, such things do not occur in this bank, or even in Switzerland. Your account and your identity are perfectly safe within these walls, I can assure you."

Laura gave him a cool look. "I am sorry to raise such ugly matters when we first meet," she said, "but I do it only to warn you to be careful."

There was a knock on the door and an elderly clerk brought in a long statement from the computer, and a letter on bank letterhead.

"Here is a statement of your holdings, madame. Bonds, cash deposits and shares. We shall have to check with our brokers for today's prices, but an approximate valuation is in the vicinity of twenty million US dollars. Here is a letter setting all this out as you requested, already signed by our general manager, and now I countersign." He looked uncomfortable. "This is most unusual."

She took the letter and statement. "This is good. It's more than I thought. You have done well. How long will it take to liquidate all these holdings and let me have a banker's cheque for the full amount?"

"Everything? In cash? You will lose some money in selling deposits which have not reached maturity."

"Yes, everything. How long?"

"Forty-eight hours. Do you wish a bank cheque or a transfer to another bank?"

"A bank cheque will be required, monsieur. An open cheque with no payee named. Just a draft on your bank. And I need some cash now, if that is possible."

"Of course. How much?"

"Five hundred thousand francs will be enough for the moment, I think."

When the elderly clerk returned with the cash, she rose to leave. "I shall see you at nine o'clock in two days to collect my draft. Thank you for your help. There is just one more matter ..." she hesitated. "My passport."

"Yes? You have it with you, I think."

"I do, but it is in the name of Tessier. I need to make other arrangements, in the name of Ellery."

"I am sorry, madame," he said stiffly. "I'm afraid I can't help you in such a matter. I would not know whom to recommend."

He held the door open and she passed through. "I am at the Hotel Beau Rivage, under the name of Ellery, if you need to reach me," she said. "Au revoir, Monsieur Braechel."

"Thank you, madame. After all these years, I am sure you will not find your confidence in us misplaced."

"I hope you are right, monsieur." She stepped into the street.

If no one tried to contact the bank, then perhaps she was a little safer than she thought. Perhaps she had lost them in Paris, for she knew it would have been no trouble to trace her as far as that. As she strolled along the quay, she passed a ferry at the wharf, looking like some elaborate toy from the nineteenth century, with a huge paddle wheel, flags flying, and a band playing on the deck. On an impulse, she purchased a ticket for Lausanne and went on board. It was a beautiful, sunlit day. She would have lunch on board and watch the lake drift by.

CHAPTER THIRTEEN

MIAMI, FLORIDA
APRIL 1979

"You're back, Mr Wellington" the doorman said as Harry stepped from the Rolls Royce. "You have a good trip to Brazil? You look like you've still got your working clothes on!"

In the apartment, he found everything as he had left it. He showered and changed into clothes the valet had laid out on his bed, and Aubrey drove him to an immense stucco villa on the inland waterway, a house surrounded by huge lawns, and lit like a palace. They were admitted through the gates by a guard, and into the house by a butler. Harry had time only to notice a superb Renoir and a Picasso, before the butler announced him and he crossed into a room in which the only thing he noticed, at first glance, was Charles Bellamy and Nick, standing together at the end of the room.

Charlie looked a little older to him, but not much. He had, however, a sheen about him, a patina of success, an aura of authority that changed him more completely than any ageing process could have done. Harry found it difficult to realize that this was the callow young man they had met in India all those years ago.

"Hello, Harry," Charles said easily, as if they had seen each other yesterday afternoon. "Nick you've met, I think." The butler passed a tray with drinks and then withdrew and closed the door.

"You've had a nasty time, they tell me," Charles said. "Even perhaps a little undeserved. Had I known that you yourself knew nothing of the theft, then I might have gotten Betty over here and roughed her up a bit instead, but no matter. The end result was the same for me, wasn't it?"

"Where is my family?" Harry demanded.

"Very commendable," Charles said approvingly. "They are at my ranch in California, a very luxurious retreat I may say, and they will be perfectly safe there, provided you agree to everything I want."

"And what is that, Charles, apart from revenge?"

"Apart from revenge?" Charles laughed. "There is no 'apart from revenge', Harry. You, or at least your wife, wrecked my life and now I intend to wreck yours. Fair's fair, don't you think? We need your help."

"Well, you won't be getting it!"

Charles laughed again. "Same old Harry. Bull-headed and stupid. It's very fortunate that you have a wife with brains, or you'd still be working in those dingy offices in spite of stealing my money. You know a chap down in Melbourne called Morgan-Smith?"

"Phillip? Yes, I knew him. He's dead. His wife, too, apparently. It was in the paper when I came over."

"It was, indeed. We knew all about it here, even before it happened, in fact."

"You arranged it?" Harry was shocked. He had understood that Charles and his colleagues were ruthless, but not ruthless enough for murder.

"You must learn not to put things quite so crudely, Harry, but, yes, in a manner of speaking. You know what this man did?"

"He was a banker, very prominent socially; a philanthropist."

"He was a drug dealer, and a dishonest one at that."

"You must be crazy. This man came from a very prominent family, well known and respected. There's no possibility of such a thing!"

"No? You believe that respectable people don't do such things do you, Harry? He was broke. He could no longer afford to live the way he believed he was entitled to live. And so, he headed up the largest distribution ring in Australia, importing drugs directly from Colombia."

"I don't believe you!"

"You would be foolish not to do so, Harry. I am not here to waste my very valuable time, but let's try another tack. What if I told you of two very respectable persons who raise funds for charity, and that I have a copy of a cheque for fifty thousand dollars, which they, or anyway, one of them, stole from me, and deposited to their own account? Would you believe that?"

"Yes," he said. "I would believe that." Nick felt embarrassed to watch him. He was not so much humiliated by this information, as destroyed. His large body seemed to shrink and crumple in front of them and he did not look at either Charles or Nick.

"But I didn't know about it until a few days ago."

Charles laughed sadly. "Vintage Harry!" he said. "You take the praise when it's going, and push the blame onto others when things go wrong. It will bring you to a bad end one day."

"I really did not know," Harry protested. "Not until a couple of days ago."

"Quite so!" Charles said. "But nevertheless we have at least proceeded to the possibility that respectable people can do less than respectable things, even if they are socially prominent in ... where is it, Nick?... Ah, yes! ... in Melbourne. So I think we might now proceed to the fact that I was not happy about being dumped here all those years ago as if I were a common felon. I think we might agree that you and Betty owe me a favour or two."

He turned and spoke to Nick. "Embezzlement and rape, you say, Nick? Dear me! I think that Harry will have to help us now, don't you? Is that not so, Harry?"

Charles was enjoying himself. He thought back to that first terrible, penniless winter in New York, ashamed and derelict. Now he would make them pay for it.

"What is it you want us to do?" Harry mumbled.

"I want you to go home to Sydney, and do what the late and unlamented Phillip Morgan-Smith was doing, only you will do it for me, and not for the Ventura brothers."

"Import drugs?"

"Import them," Charles said, "and create a network for selling them for us in a market which we do not intend to share with the Ventura boys, who very foolishly believed our little stories about Phillip, and relieved us of the necessity of removing him."

"I won't do it," Harry said.

"Of course you will, or you'll be ruined and in gaol and the children will be dead, and then Betty will do it for me without you."

Harry looked at Charles. "And you planned all this?"

"Quite so!"

"You've changed a lot," Harry said slowly. "I think I need another whiskey."

"Then you agree?"

"I don't seem to have an alternative."

"I thought so. Everyone always agrees, once the price is right. Well, tomorrow you can have your meetings with Alcon. We still want all of that. It's a perfect front. Then you can go to California and tell Betty all about our little chat, and she can get back to Sydney and buy a larger house, for entertaining. Poor Betty. She never approved of my dreams for a better world, did she?"

"She might have done," Harry said bitterly, "if she'd known what they truly were!"

"Oh, and Harry ..." Charles said, "no more little talks with our friend Jerkovitz, if you don't mind. Not even a telephone call before you leave! He is a very misguided and untidy fellow who seems to believe that he can single-handedly clean up Miami. Our lawyers will settle up all the misunderstanding with that woman. Jerkovitz has, after all, advised you to go home, has he not?"

"You had the apartment bugged?"

"An unpleasant necessity, but no worse a moral crime than banking a friend's cheque into your own account, I think. And the reporter, too, Harry. No words with our little friend, Peter Francis, either. He and Jerkovitz think they are the conscience of America. We don't want you too close to that, now, do we?"

Harry stood up. "You are an evil man, Charles."

Charlie shook his head. "Harry, Harry! So judgmental. You mustn't be like that. We all do what we must in this world, or we blow our brains out."

"That would always be an alternative," he said.

Charlie shrugged. "You might remember that advice some day for yourself, Harry. You'll always have the choice, my friend."

CHAPTER FOURTEEN

LAKE GENEVA, SWITZERLAND
APRIL 1979

GOD HAD NOT FORGOTTEN her, Laura thought, as she ate a delicious lunch on the ferry and watched the miraculous beauty of the lake drift past the window. Perhaps all those endless Hail Marys and Glory Be's kneeling on the hard floor of the Cathedral in Bogotá, which had smelled of death and treachery, were finally to bear fruit. The horror of that place, haunted and feverish with devotion and despair, and, before that, the memory of awful, shameful confessions in the stinking little confessional in New York, made her shudder. She recalled the feeling of shame that overcame her when, her act of contrition complete, she felt no easing of her conscience, for she knew she had fudged the issue once again. She wondered, as she had wondered so often before, when she would finally realize that she might fool the priest, she might even fool God, but she would never be able to fool herself.

After lunching on board the ferry, Laura left the boat at Montreux, and walked along the foreshore of the lake, under the trees just tipped with a fuzz of new growth, like the beards of adolescent boys. Across the glittering water, the mountains soared up into a limitless sky, and the air was somnolent with leisure that was unlike anything she had known before. She bought a dress and some lingerie, and late in the afternoon she boarded another equally picturesque ferry. It was quite crowded. She asked her neighbour why there were so many people on board.

"This ferry stops at Evian on its way back to Geneva. It is on the other side of the lake, in France, Madame, and in France they can gamble. There is a casino and many will get off to try their luck." The woman smiled. "No gambling in Switzerland. Only banking and clocks!"

On an impulse, when the boat docked at Evian, she went ashore and followed the crowd up to the casino entrance. She changed ten thousand francs into French money and went over to the roulette table. The room was warm and crowded, feverish with activity. It amused her that she could simply cross the lake and be in a country so completely different from the calm town where she had strolled and shopped in the afternoon. There it had been peaceful and somnolent. Here the air crackled with a nervous electricity, with the sharp calls of the croupiers and the click, click of the betting chips, and the tiny balls as they rattled around the roulette wheel.

She watched for a moment while the croupier called and swept the board clear of losing chips. She had played occasionally at the Sports Club in Bogotá, but this seemed more vital, quicker, more exciting, more glamorous and much more fun. She turned to the man next to her.

"*Pardon M'sieur, est-ce que vous savez ce que je dois faire? Je n'ai jamais jouez en France.*"

He smiled. He had a nice smile, she thought. "I'm sorry," he said. "I guess I'm the original ugly American. Do you speak English?"

"A kind of English," she said, smiling. "The New York kind."

He laughed. "Oh, don't worry, I understand that kind well enough.

"I asked, how do you play? I am an amateur really. They go so fast it makes me nervous."

"Best way to be. Just put your chips on red or black, here, or on a number, like this. That's called *en plein*. Or at the end of a row here, to bet on all those numbers in the row."

"It looks awfully easy." She leaned forward and put all her chips on number eighteen.

He grinned. "That's a mighty generous bet, ma'am. You'll be excited if that comes up, but maybe you'll have beginner's luck. Mind if I follow you?"

"I should warn you. I never win at anything."

The croupier intoned, "*Les jeux sont fait! Rien ne va plus!*"

He spun the wheel with a practised flick of his wrist and dropped the little ball into the spinning circle of numbers. Click, click, clickety, click! It sounded to Laura as if it were counting off the wasted years of her life.

"*Dix-huit, rouge et pair,*" the croupier intoned as the ball dropped in the slot of number eighteen, red and even. She watched as he raked away most of the chips on the table and tapped her bet with the end of his rake.

"*A vous, madame?*"

"*Oui!*" She gasped at the pile he pushed towards her, and looked at her neighbour. "Is that right?"

He smiled. "They never make a mistake. You placed a large bet, around a thousand dollars, and the odds are thirty-three to one. You've won thirty thousand dollars, and brought me luck, too. It's the first win I've had all day. May I buy you a drink to celebrate?"

"Well ..." she hesitated, feeling suddenly shy and ill at ease. It was so long since she had been with anyone but Sebastian.

"Come on," he said. "I'm not a spy or a white slaver, you

know. I thought you kids from New York were more adventurous."

"I'm not really from New York. I was just there for a while, years ago. Okay, just a glass to celebrate our luck."

"*Rien ne va plus,*" the croupier intoned again, behind them. Click, click, clickety click. Those years clicking away again.

"Oh, Christ!" the man exclaimed. "We were so busy talking, we forgot to take our original stake off the table."

Laura reached out to take it off, but the croupier shook his head.

"Too late! We'll have to kiss that goodbye. Let me help you with your chips."

Click. Click. "*Dix-huit, noir et pair,*" the croupier said.

The man looked at her with astonishment.

"What is it?" she asked. "Does that mean we've won again?"

He nodded.

"My God, another thirty thousand dollars! Look at all those chips!"

"Give the croupier a plaque for one thousand. Just say '*Pour la table*', or do you want to go on playing?"

"After that I don't think I can go on standing. How much did you win?"

"Not nearly as much as you, but I did fine!"

"I'm so glad," she said, "but the champagne's on me. That's only fair!" They collected their chips and moved off towards the bar.

"I'm Andy Davidson from Atlanta, Georgia – via Geneva at the moment." He held out his hand.

"I'm Laura Tess ... Ellery," she said.

"Well, Mrs Ellery, you're the luckiest person I've been around all year."

"Call me Laura," she said. "After all tha[t] feel we're old friends. Are you a diplomat her[e]

"Nothing so glamorous, I'm afraid. Only [a] banker, sent over by my Daddy to learn how so successfully."

"And do they have a recipe?"

"Oh, sure, absolute secrecy and plenty behind a facade of complete and impregnable

"I'm delighted to hear it. Exactly what I ed. Which bank are you with?"

"Oh, you wouldn't know it. It's very sma[ll] international. It's called the Banque des Trois bankers for all the rich butchers and bakers makers here in Geneva."

"Are you, indeed? Well, order us a nice b[ottle] be right back."

She had never before believed in luck, n[or] and she saw no reason to begin now, in sp[ite of] roulette. She called her hotel.

"Yes, Madame Ellery, I am glad that yo[u] an urgent call from Monsieur Braechel at Trois Cantons. He has rung three times a number, if you wish to reach him after work

She wrote down the number and called

"Monsieur Braechel. This is Madame E[llery."]

"Thank God, madame. You are all righ[t?"]

"Quite. Is something wrong?"

"After this morning, when I was so inc[onsiderate to] an honoured client. You said you'd be at you[r]

"I changed my mind. What is it?"

"I am perhaps being melodramatic, but

...blic phone. Where are you?"

"At the casino at Evian."

"I'll call back and have you paged."

"Before you go, I have met a man here who says he is ...your bank. A Mr Davidson. Is he trustworthy?"

"This morning, madame, I would have said all our staff ...trustworthy. Now I trust no one." He rang off, and she ...ned to Andy Davidson. He stood up. "Everything okay? ...look too serious for someone who has just won sixty ...sand dollars."

"The cashier is preparing a cheque. I think I'll stay over ...cash it at the bank tomorrow. Do you know a good ...l?"

"Grand or simple?"

She laughed. "Simple, but not too simple."

"I stay at the Royale. Why don't you stay there, too, and ...dinner with me."

"Perhaps," she said. "I'm waiting for a phone call."

A page walked through the room carrying a blackboard ...ing her name, ringing a small bell and calling her name. ...aised her hand.

"Madame Ellery? Telephone, madame." She followed ...to a booth beside the guichet.

"Yes?"

"This afternoon, around four o'clock, after we had given ...rders for the sale of your holdings, I received a very prop-...uest to transfer all your funds to the First National Bank ...orida in Miami. Did you send that request?"

"I did not, and I do not have an account there. I trust you ...not sent the money."

"No, madame. I would have done, if you had not been in

here this morning. I went to the manager, and I explained the situation to him. I said I must have further instructions from you. He insisted that I remit the funds. I thought he would have a stroke when I refused."

"What then?"

"We had a terrible row. The first I have ever had in the bank. He insisted I send the money as requested in the cable. I refused again, and now I have until nine o'clock tomorrow morning to have my instructions re-confirmed by you. I would never have believed such a thing could happen here in Switzerland, in our own bank! I think, madame, there is something bad."

"Who owns this bank in Florida?"

"It is owned, I believe, by the Bellamy Corporation."

She felt a flutter of panic in her belly. So Charles knew where her money was, and where she was too, no doubt.

"Tell me, do you trust this young man, Davidson?"

"He has been with us only for a few months – a rather nice young man from somewhere in the South. Atlanta, I think. His father is influential there, I believe. He is training to be a banker, or just having a good time. Perhaps both, if that is possible."

"Has he any connection with the Bellamy Corporation?"

"No, not so far as I am aware."

"I am sending him to you with a letter to ignore that cable and to give the cashier's cheque to him personally. Can you have it ready by nine o'clock tomorrow morning?"

"I shall do it. It would, in my opinion, be totally wrong for the bank to act in any other way."

"I shall wait here in Evian. Do not tell anyone where I am."

"Of course not, and Madame … "

"Yes?"

"The matter of the passport. I shall give Mr Davidson a name and address."

He hung up without further explanation. She understood that he was breaking a lifetime habit as a law-abiding Swiss citizen. She felt badly to have caused him this crisis of conscience.

She returned to the bar and gave Andy a direct look. "I hope you are an honest banker," she said.

"We are all honest bankers," he said with a smile, "within the limits of necessity."

"Unfortunately, I have just discovered that those limits can be stretched quite far." She sipped her champagne. "I have not been entirely straightforward with you."

He shrugged. "Why should you be? We've just met. I am a man. You are a beautiful woman. It's a perfect recipe for a lack of straightforwardness."

"You are a terrible cynic for so young a man."

"Not so young," Andy said. "Merely an illusion of youth retained because I lack a serious purpose in life. A serious purpose is very ageing."

"Well, that small, discreet bank of yours ..." She hesitated, and then decided that she must trust someone. "In fact, I know it very well. I have had an account there for more than ten years, and I have just been speaking with Edmond Braechel, who handles my affairs."

"So you were checking on me?"

"No, not quite. Well, that and other things."

"Aaah – other things. With a beautiful woman there are always other things. You wanted to know if I own a Ferrari and if my Daddy owns a bank?"

She laughed. "That would be nice. Do you and does he?"

"Yes, but not this bank."

"In that case I'm sorry that I'm not a little younger."

"To be much younger, you would be in a school uniform, I think. I prefer you in your little silk Chanel suit. Very chic."

"You will be pleased to know I can buy my own Ferrari, even without my luck this afternoon. This is more serious. Can you be serious?"

He gave the matter his consideration. "It goes against the grain," he said, "but for you …"

She hesitated again. Once more she was drawing another innocent person into her corrupt and dangerous world. She had no choice and, after all, he did work for the bank that was trying to swindle her.

"I know this sounds very dramatic, but I believe that someone is trying to kill me," she said, "and, just about as importantly, I know that someone is trying to steal the funds I have in your bank. I told Edmond Braechel to change the name of my account to Ellery, which is not my real name, and I booked into the Beau Rivage under that name. No one knows this but Mr Braechel and me. I instructed him to sell all my holdings and to prepare a cashier's cheque for me to collect the day after tomorrow."

"Yes?"

She was pleased that he seemed neither amazed nor disbelieving. That gave her a little comfort, for she felt a fool.

"This afternoon, he received a cabled request from a bank in Florida to send all my funds there. That cable is a forgery, but if I had not been at the bank this morning, all my funds would have gone to Florida, and out of my control. I would like your help, as you work for the bank. There may be some risk involved, but I have nowhere else I can go for help."

"Edmond Braechel is totally honest. He would not have given away any information. As for risk, that I don't mind. It is only with stupidity that I draw the line. I believe I have a right to know what I am taking on here."

"Otherwise you won't stick your neck out?"

"Exactly!"

She sighed. "Yes, why should you? Well, let's have another glass of this excellent champagne. The wages of sin should at least be enjoyed."

She was not proud of what she was about to tell this man whom she had only just met. He refilled the champagne glasses.

"Many years ago, when I was very young," Laura said, "I went to Bogotá. I went to live with a man. He was not a man with whom I was in love. I went there as an agent for a business colleague ... as an industrial spy, if you like, and I reported back to this man on the operations in Colombia of the man with whom I was living. I was paid very well, and those funds are in your bank."

"With whom did you live in Bogotá?" Andy asked.

"Sebastian Ventura y Cortez," she said quietly.

Andy whistled but said nothing.

"Yesterday morning," she continued, "I was advised by a friend to leave Bogotá immediately. He said the Ventura family knew what I had been doing, and would kill me, which I knew would be true. I did as this man told me and left Bogotá that morning. In Paris I booked a flight to Switzerland under the name of Ellery. No one knows that name, and no one knows I had an account at your bank. My funds were sent to Credit Suisse and then remitted on to the Banque des Trois Cantons."

"That would not be difficult to trace, for anyone with access to the system. Do you have any connection with this bank in Florida."

"None, but Edmond Braechel tells me it is owned by the man for whom I was working."

"He is a banker?" Andy asked in some surprise.

"He is a man called Charles Bellamy," Laura said.

"Ah," Andy said quietly. "And you are Laura Tessier."

"Yes. How did you know that?"

"You are right. You are in very grave danger," he said. "Charles Bellamy is, I believe, the most corrupt and dangerous man in America today, and perhaps the most powerful, too. Sebastian Ventura was found dead in your apartment in Bogotá this morning. It was on the wire service at noon to-day."

Laura looked at him sadly. She could not even pretend to be surprised.

"I have been a great fool," she said. "But I would prefer that they did not kill me, too. Nor steal my money."

"How did the Ventura family find out about you?"

"I understand that Charles Bellamy told Sebastian," she said.

"Nice friends you have," Andy said. "And what can I do? I'm no hood, you know."

"If you could take my written instructions to the bank tomorrow morning, Edmond Braechel will give you a cheque for my funds. You work there. No one would be suspicious. No one could possibly connect you with me. After that, you need have nothing further to do with me."

She gave him a wan smile. "Unless, of course, you wish to continue to win at roulette."

He grinned. "I guess I do owe you a favour there, and you are a client of the bank. I wouldn't go back to the Beau Rivage, if I were you. I'll pay your bill and collect your luggage."

"I don't have any luggage. Just ring them and have them send the bill to the bank. Don't go near the place. It's too dangerous."

"And you?"

"Once I have the money, I'll get a new passport and disappear."

"Not so easy, with the people you're in business with. Where did you meet Charles Bellamy?"

"In New York, many years ago, when we were all young and ambitious, and thought that life dealt out dreams for breakfast."

"Yes," he agreed sadly. "I've been to that place, too."

The manager came up to the table and gave her a cheque for the equivalent of sixty-four thousand US dollars.

"Congratulations, madame. I hope you will come back and try your luck again. You may put this in your bank, or cash it at our bank in town, but don't lose it. It's a bearer cheque."

They stood up. Andy touched her arm.

"You're in one big heap of trouble, Laura, but if we had to be responsible forever for all the mistakes of our youth, life would be impossible. Let's go to the Royale, check in and have some dinner, and then we can make a plan."

In the lobby of the hotel, he said, "You can't show your passport. They could trace you here with that in a few hours. I'll take a suite in my name. We can get rooms overlooking the lake, and dine on the balcony. It's a nice old hotel. It belongs to the days when life was less dangerous."

"What about not having any luggage?"

He laughed. "They won't care about that! This is France, not Idaho!"

The sitting room did have a balcony, and in the distance, over the lake, twinkled the lights of Lausanne and Montreux, of Vevey and all the tiny villages in the mountains high above the water. They ate their dinner in the window embrasure, looking out over the water.

"I am worried about this thing tomorrow," she said. "It may be too dangerous. I would never forgive myself ..." He put his hand over hers.

"I was in Vietnam for three years, in the early days," he said. "What I didn't learn in that place in three years isn't worth knowing."

"You don't look old enough for that."

"I was nineteen when I went out there, twenty-two when I came back, totally fucked up. I've blocked out those years, but I haven't forgotten how to look after myself. Let's forget about all of that."

"Is it that bad?"

"Vietnam corrupted everyone who touched it, even the Vietnamese. It was a filthy war."

"You mean to tell me there's another kind?"

"We weren't heroes," he said. "More like criminals, I think. At least when you're killing for Christ or to keep the farm, or to stop someone putting Jews into the oven, you understand what you're doing and why you're doing it. I think we were kind of ashamed of ourselves, in some way."

While he spoke, his fist, lying on the table, clenched and unclenched. Fascinated, she watched it while he spoke. He had long, fine fingers with spatulate tips like a pianist, musician's hands, and on his wrist, fine gold hair against the pale, winter skin. In all her life, Laura had never wanted to touch someone as much as she suddenly wanted to touch that hand. Her heart began to beat, and her breath began to come in gasps. She raised her own hand, over which she no longer seemed to have control, and placed it over his own, touched those few golden hairs with the tips of her fingers.

He stopped talking and looked at her.

"For many years now," she said, "I have not made love

with a man I really wanted."

She had thought, once, that she had been in love with Charlie, but she had never felt for him as she suddenly did now for this man whom she hardly knew. Her whole body was overwhelmed with lust.

He turned his wrist and took her hand in his palm. He lifted it to his lips.

"In Saigon," he said quietly, "when I was very young, I married a beautiful Vietnamese, a girl of good family. Her parents objected strongly, as did my own father. We had a daughter. I never got them out of Vietnam. They were both shot. Since then, I've not made love to anyone. That's what 'Nam did for me."

He smiled, a youthful and very sweet smile. "I think I'm so out of practice, I may not be much good any more."

She put her hand against his cheek. The feel of the warm flesh made her shudder, as if she had achieved an orgasm simply by touching him.

"Let me worry about that," she said. "I'll take a risk on it. Just let me make love with you for one night. Just one night with someone I really want."

Andy stood up and took her in his arms and led her to the bed. He undressed her slowly in the warm dimness of the bedroom, lit only by the starlight from the brilliant sky outside over the lake.

"Lie beside me," she said softly. "Lie full length, with your whole body stretched against mine, still ... still ..."

He kissed her breasts, caressed the nipples with his lips and slid his mouth slowly over her belly towards the hot cave between her legs. Touching her he felt the ability to love coming flooding back into his veins. That night, for the first time in years, as he touched her, kissed her and finally entered her slim loins, he began to feel the hard core of hatred inside him begin to melt. The heavy toll of anger and despair that he had believed would be a lifetime burden for him to bear began to drop away, and the tyranny of the past released him, finally, into the reality of today.

Before she slept, she murmured, "Don't go to Geneva tomorrow. Forget the money! What we're finding here together is worth more than all of that."

But when she woke in the morning, she found that he had gone, and a note was pinned to the pillow.

It said, "Wait here for me. You have banished the ghosts. I love you for it," but she was filled with apprehension. Ghosts, she knew only too well, did not always wish to be banished.

CHAPTER FIFTEEN

BENNINGTON PARK, NEW YORK
APRIL 1979

"OF COURSE IT'S A WAR!" Senator William Spencer declared.

He was an older and very senior senator, known for his moral probity and his uncompromising stand on such matters as abortion and drug abuse. He was chairman of the President's Special Commission on Drug Addiction. He was one of twenty guests dining at Bennington Park, the home, overlooking the mighty Hudson River, of Edwina de Trafford's uncle, Ambassador William Bennington and his wife Elizabeth.

They were celebrating the forthcoming marriage of his niece with Charles Bellamy that would take place in June, in a simple civil ceremony to be attended by five hundred guests who would include the President of the United States and a selected list from several countries. From this list, Edwina had struck off with some relish the names of those who had been unpleasant following Marcus de Trafford's murder. Revenge, she discovered, is every bit as sweet as legend proclaims.

"And it is a war the government cannot win, Senator," Charles Bellamy said quietly.

"What do you mean, sir?" demanded the Senator. "My Commission will recommend laws which will end such a war as this, a war against peasants growing drugs."

"Your Commission, Senator, will be told what those in charge of the drug business wish it to hear. It will then recommend measures which are wholly unenforceable, and which, therefore, will never be enforced."

"I cannot accept that, Mr Bellamy," the Senator said, his white mane and his pontifical attitude lending weight to his words. There were nods of approval around the table. The Senator was in control of the situation, and who, anyway, was this Bellamy fellow? An upstart! Not even a junior senator.

"There is only one way," Charles said, undisturbed by the disapproval around him, "to get rid of drugs, and that is to decriminalize them. No profit, no more drugs. Then spend some money on the people who are addicted."

"My dear chap, that would never do. The government couldn't be seen to be condoning drugs! It would cost us votes!"

"There was a time when they thought they couldn't be seen condoning alcohol, and look where that took us."

"There is a moral difference, sir!"

"Ah! I had not quite understood that this was a discussion on morality, a subject on which politicians the world over are experts, I believe."

"If we, as leaders, do not decide what is right and wrong, who will?"

"Who indeed?" Charles raised his eyebrows. "The private citizen has a lamentable tendency to err which politicians manage to avoid, perhaps? But while our leaders make decisions on such issues of morality, how do you stop the drugs, and the crimes that follow in their wake, to say nothing of the corruption? In these matters, the United States has so far been singularly unsuccessful."

The Senator was ruffled. He was not accustomed to being disagreed with on social occasions. "It is our duty, sir, to legislate in favour of a moral society, and of the police to enforce that law!"

"The police in Nazi Germany believed they were enforcing a moral law when they arrested Jewish people."

"I don't believe that is the issue," the Senator said.

"Then we should make it the issue," Charles said. "A law against drugs cannot be enforced, as we see clearly every day. A law that cannot be enforced will be disobeyed, and will bring the system into disrepute. It is happening all around us."

"There are many people involved in working with addicts," Uncle William Bennington said. "Many concerned citizens."

"Yes," Charles agreed. "I support just such a group in Miami, and I know all about its work and its efforts. It doesn't even scratch the surface. There will be drugs aplenty in this country, and elsewhere, while there are huge profits to be made, and there will be huge profits to be made so long as drugs are illegal."

"Are you suggesting, Mr Bellamy, that drug money is being distributed by way of bribes?"

Charles laughed briefly. "I am not suggesting it, Senator, I am stating it categorically, and a good deal of it in Washington, I may say!"

"How could you possibly know such things, Charles?" Uncle William said. "If you can prove such things, you should go straight to the police."

"I am a banker in Florida. I draw my own conclusions, Ambassador. To whom in the police do I go with those conclusions, and by whom would they be taken seriously?"

It gave him some pleasure to pursue this conversation. Around this table there were at least two persons in receipt of substantial payments from Alcon Corporation, and from

Bellamy Corporation, too, and from other sources less public. They assisted these companies to trade in drugs throughout the world and to sell arms and ammunition and related technology. One of these people was the self-righteous Senator himself.

Charles smiled. "I cannot reveal my information without a court order, or I would not be in the banking business."

Uncle William laughed.

"Now, Charles, you are teasing us for being too serious when this is a celebration." He tapped his spoon against his glass for silence. "No more talk of drugs. I give you a toast ... to Charles and Edwina, may they enjoy each other in happiness and much prosperity all the days of their lives!"

"Hear! Hear! Long life and happiness!"

The company drank the excellent champagne, imported from France at considerable profit to both governments in taxes, levies and import duties. Charles considered that this was not the moment to dwell further on these matters. He had had his fun. He had no wish to offend these worthy people who were under the impression that they ran the world.

Later that evening, after the gentlemen had joined the ladies, Edwina and Charles went to the library for privacy.

She poured a cognac for them both. "Did you mean what you said at dinner?"

"What? Long life and happiness?"

"About the drugs?"

"Of course. Another twenty years like this and people like me will own half the world. There's no way to stop it. No one has the guts to legalize it!"

"And why do you want it?"

"Legalization? I've made enough, I guess." He shrugged. "But human beings will always want drugs. It's as old as sex and just as much a part of our nature."

"Are there others who agree with you?"

"Of course, but they have no power, and it's politically safer to spend money on rehabilitation. It looks so good to the voters. The power equation, however, is shifting in favour of those who deal in drugs. We already control a number of small economies. It won't be long before we control larger ones." He sipped his brandy. "And then we shall invest, and then we shall die, and our children who have gone, very respectably, to all the best schools, will inherit the earth. They will become the new aristocracy of the twenty-first century, because they will have all the money!"

"What would happen if you get found out?"

"Don't worry, Edwina, I am already too rich for that! And just as well, too. I looked into the apartment in New York, on the way through, and what did I find?

"A vast improvement, I trust!"

"My darling, a transformation. Archie out the door, and Edwina in his place."

"A touch of Charles, too, I hope."

He laughed. "More than a touch. Three million? Four?"

"It's no use complaining. You said I could spend what I liked, although I must say it did turn out to be a little more than I expected. The place is so huge, Charles! But you have all my own wonderful furniture from London, so it does look like a home, as far as anything in New York can look like a home. You liked it?"

"It's perfect, but we can't do all our entertaining in New York, you know. What about London?"

"Well, the most beautiful private house left in London is Trafford House, naturally, since I had a big hand in restoring it and looking after it for years, but since we can't have that ..."

"Well, it just so happens ..."

He drew a paper from his breast pocket and handed it to her. "It just so happens that I was speaking to his new Lordship yesterday in Ottowa, and he's found that he has one house too many for a simple Canadian lad. We came to a deal. He said he'd sell it to me if I gave it to you."

She took the paper and read it slowly. "I don't believe it! You've given me Trafford House and all the contents."

"Provided you leave them all in England. There'll be a terrible hullabaloo if you try to take them away!"

"But Charles, it must have cost you millions."

He nodded. "He was very greedy, that simple backwoods Canadian lordship."

"But Charlie, to buy it! No one will believe it. It's so wonderfully vulgar!"

"I know," he said happily, "but with you as my wife I can get away with it, you see. You know what they'll all say in England and across the Channel. 'But, darling, isn't it too wonderful to have Edwina back at Trafford House,' and it'll be fine. You are the only woman in the world I could have bought it for without looking a complete damned fool, so it's your wedding present."

"Do you think I'm worth it?"

"That remains to be seen." He pulled her towards him and kissed her on the lips. "Let's go upstairs and see."

"What about our guests?"

"Fuck the guests!"

"I'd hoped it was someone else you had in mind." She returned his kiss passionately. "You know, I could become very attracted to you, Charles. That would be a unique experience, wouldn't it, actually being in love with my own husband?"

"It's a short life," he said. "You should try everything at least once. And now, let us run away from all these boring people and hide upstairs and make love. We'll soon be married and it won't be half so much fun!"

CHAPTER SIXTEEN

EVIAN, FRANCE
AND GENEVA, SWITZERLAND
APRIL 1979

EARLY IN THE MORNING, Andy Davidson kissed Laura softly on the cheek, climbed quietly out of bed, taking care not to disturb her, and dressed quickly. He drove into Geneva and let himself into his office with his keys. He went straight to Braechel's office. Edmond was waiting for him. It was eight o'clock.

"What's going on here, Edmond?" Andy demanded.

"Have you brought the letter of authority?"

"I have. I drafted it myself. It is quite adequate. Have you got her cheque?"

"I am breaking every rule, Andy, because something strange is going on."

"I know what's going on, Edmond. Charles Bellamy is trying to steal her money. We have a moral and legal responsibility to our own client. Do you have the cheque?"

"Not all her investments have been sold, Andy. There hasn't been time for that, but I have estimated what they'll bring. I shall hold back a small amount in case there is a market fluctuation, and to cover any fees. They are preparing the draft now, but I tell you, it may cost me my job. I'm under huge pressure not to do it!"

"You've seen our client. You have her instructions. I don't see where there's a problem."

He shrugged. "Bellamy, perhaps, as you suggest. Certainly someone does not want her to have this money. Monsieur le directeur," he pointed to the ceiling, and made a face, "seems terrified, or hysterical, as if it will break the bank or something." He snapped his fingers. "It is nothing, the money. Not to us. But to her, twenty million ..."

"Twenty million?" Andy asked. "Dollars, or francs?"

Edmond rang through to the accountant, and again demanded that he hurry up with the bank draft for Madame Ellery.

"Dollars!" he said.

Andy whistled. "No wonder she can afford thousand dollar bets at the casino!"

"Perhaps I shouldn't tell you this, Andy," Edmond said, "but yesterday she asked if I knew where to get a forged passport. There is no doubt she is frightened and she has, as I suppose you know, changed her name. I was rather rude, I'm afraid. It's hardly in our line of business, but things have been so odd, I thought she needed help, so I have a name and number. I said I'd give it to you. Are you an old friend? I got the impression, last night ..."

"I am helping her," Andy said curtly.

There was a knock at the door and an elderly clerk entered. "Good morning, Mr Davidson. I didn't see you come in. I have the draft for Mrs Ellery, but all this is most irregular."

"Mr Davidson has a signed authority from our client. He will countersign, and we will both sign the authority to draw the cheque. All is in order, Mr Knopf. Do not worry."

The old clerk handed the paperwork to Mr Braechel and both men signed. He left the room muttering that nothing was done properly any more, as it had been in his day. "Everything's always in a rush with young people. Rush, rush, rush!"

Braechel shrugged. "It's fortunate that our esteemed director is a little late this morning. Knopf will not be able to wait to tell him and then, as they say in your country, 'the shit will hit the fan'. I suggest you disappear smartly, and keep out of the way today!"

"I am sending in my resignation, in any event," Andy said. "I have decided to go back to America, and to please my father for once. Have them clear my desk and I'll send you a direction for my stuff. There isn't much. I'll let my father know, don't worry. Let me know who is pulling the strings here, if you ever find out."

Braechel smiled wanly. "More likely I shall be like you, looking for another job next week."

Andy shook his hand. "If you are, let me know. You can come and work for us in Atlanta. They tell me the Civil War is finally over."

"Thank you, but I am too Swiss for America, I think. Even for the Deep South," he added with a faint smile.

Andy smiled back. He liked Edmond Braechel.

"Perhaps New Orleans," he suggested as he took the draft and put it in an envelope with the telephone number which Edmond gave him for the passport. He wrote Laura's name on the outside, with the address: Hotel Royale, Evian and the number of her room, and put it in his inside pocket. He waved to Edmond's secretary, Laurette, as he left Edmond's office. He suspected she was a little in love with him, poor girl. He went to his office and collected his loaded gun from the desk drawer, and went directly out into the street by the private door without passing through the general office.

He had decided that he would not return to Evian without a little inspection at the Hotel Beau Rivage first. He drove his car across the bridge, turned right onto the quay in front of the Hotel Beau Rivage, and admired the Jet d'Eau, throwing its sparkling column of water high and straight into the sky in the morning light. He parked in front of the old and prestigious hostelry. He was well known there. The bank often sent overseas clients to this hotel.

"Madame Ellery has not returned, Monsieur Davidson," the concierge told him.

"I know, Antoine. She is spending a few days in Evian as my guest." Andy gave him his most charming smile.

"I have her letter authorizing me to collect her luggage and pay her bill, if I may have her key. She is a client of the bank."

"*Bien sur.*" The concierge banged the bell for a bellboy.

"No need," Andy said. "I know this suite well. I'll take myself up." Andy ran up the stairs to the first floor. The double doors to the suite at the end of the corridor were closed. A housemaid was coming from another room.

He gave her the key. "Do you mind? I've just arrived from New York, and I don't wish to startle my wife. Will you go in and see if she is sleeping? No, no, don't knock."

The maid opened the door a little. The room was in darkness. She looked back. He nodded, and waved for her to go on in. She pushed the door open and entered. Before Andy could say anything more, he heard from across the room the deadly spit of a gun with a silencer in place, and the woman gasped just once and slid gently to the floor. He swore silently. Taking his own gun from his pocket, he moved quickly up the corridor and waited. His footsteps made no sound on the thick carpet.

There was silence for a moment, and then quiet footsteps crossing the room. Someone had waited patiently all night for Laura to return, and was now realizing that the woman on the floor was not the one he had wished to kill. Andy heard the single word "Shit!" and then he pushed open the door and shot straight at the figure bent over the dead body of the housemaid.

The man was taken completely by surprise.

"Jesus!" he said, and then, like a trained soldier, as he rolled over, he held up his arm and fired at the man in the doorway.

A single shot, and then he died.

Andy swore savagely as the bullet, fired at almost point blank range, ripped through his shoulder, tearing bone and muscle, and buried itself in the gold and white painted door behind him. What a fool! What a bloody fool! The lessons of Vietnam had been learned too long ago. He had been careless and too slow.

He reached for the light switch and the blazing overhead chandelier sprang into life, momentarily dazzling him. No one else was there. He looked at the two bodies on the floor. Later he would be upset about the maid, but not now. Now was a time for killing, or being killed.

He crossed the salon to the bedroom, and it was only then that he saw the third body, stretched out at the foot of the bed. So they had both come to kill her – the Ventura family and Bellamy, and they had silenced each other. That seemed like justice. He felt no pity for the two men. That was the risk and cost of being a mercenary and working for crooks. He could only think that it might have been Laura lying there if she had not taken a boat ride yesterday and met him at the casino, and won. In such small decisions, he thought, lay the course of one's life. Coincidence. Luck. Nothing was ever the way one planned. There was no God.

Andy understood that he must leave this place, now, and get back to Evian. It would not be long before whoever was in charge of this little operation discovered that the wrong woman had been killed, and then they would all be looking again for Laura. But he was bleeding profusely, and he knew that he could not get back to Evian. He could not, perhaps, even leave the hotel. He knew that he could easily die here on the floor with the rest of them, and never see Laura again, never make love again and chase away the demons. The memories of the previous evening plugged him full of energy. He sat on the bed and picked up the phone.

"You may dial direct by first pressing 9," the telephonist said.

"Please, please. This is an emergency. I am not well. Ring the Prince Albert Hospital. Immediately."

"Will I get the house doctor?"

"No, no, the hospital. Quick!"

He could feel nausea overtaking him, and consciousness drifting away in long pulses, like waves along the shore. He would die, not in the jungles of Vietnam after all, as he had once feared, but right here in a thousand dollar a night suite in a luxury hotel in Geneva. The irony of it did not fail to amuse him.

"Prince Albert Hospital, good morning."

"Dr Curtis, quick! This is an emergency!"

"One moment. I'll try to connect you!" There was a long silence during which Andy struggled to stay conscious.

"This is Dr Curtis speaking."

"Harvey, this is Andy," he whispered.

"Andy? Speak up, old son. I can hardly hear you."

"Andy, come quick. Suite 118 at the Beau Rivage. Come straight up. Don't stop at the desk. I've been shot ..."

"Andy? Andy? Are you there? Jesus Christ!"

Harvey Curtis had known Andy since they were boys in

Atlanta. In Geneva they had shared a flat for a while. He had never known his friend to be anything other than calm. A typical banker, he always said. That he might manage to get himself shot, and in a respectable place like the Hotel Beau Rivage, seemed inconceivable. He grabbed his bag and took a taxi to the hotel. He crossed the lobby and raced up the stairs. The door to the suite was ajar, held open by the two bodies, and in the bedroom, two more. The first man was very dead, and so, he though at first, was Andy, but there was still a faint pulse.

Andy's eyes fluttered open. "Harvey? Great, man! Get me outta here!"

"Let me get this coat off."

His coat? Andy struggled though the fog that enveloped him. There was something important about the coat.

"Lie still, man, for God's sake. You're haemorrhaging like a pig. I'm giving you an injection while I look at this wound."

"Coat pocket. Inside ... an envelope. Give it to her. Tell her ..."

The needle took effect. Harvey removed the coat gently and looked at the wound. He picked up the phone. "This is Dr Curtis. Get me an ambulance and send the manager here," he said. "Immediately!"

"The manager or the ambulance?"

"Both! *Vite! Vite!*"

The manager arrived, out of breath, in two minutes.

He pushed open the door from the hallway. "Dr Curtis! What are you doing here? Is Madame Ellery ill?" He stared down at the bodies. "*Mon dieu!*"

"Just so! We do not want every newspaper in town here, do we Marcel? There are three dead bodies, and one dying. I have called an ambulance."

"And Madame Ellery?"

"I know nothing about her. The only woman here appears to be one of your housemaids."

"We must ring the police."

"After we remove Mr Davidson."

"Mr Davidson? From the Banque des Trois Cantons? He is here?"

"Dying in the bedroom."

"*Mon Dieu!* This is terrible. There will be a big scandal! I know him well!"

The manager stood wringing his hands while the ambulance team pushed past, removed Andy to the hospital and left the manager to telephone the police. At the hospital, Andy went straight into surgery.

At Evian, Laura waited for him, looking out over the lake, so full of light and promise. She waited with a heavy heart until late afternoon, and then she rang the bank.

"Mr Braechel, please."

"Who is this speaking?"

"Mrs. Ellery. I am a client of the bank."

The girl on the telephone burst into tears. "Oh, madame, it is terrible. Mr Braechel has been murdered. He was shot in his office this morning by one of our managers, Mr Davidson. And our poor director, killed, too, in his bed at his home with his wife."

Laura felt the afternoon cold creep up her arms until they were heavy enough to stop her heart from beating. Anything was possible now. Anything.

"And Mr Davidson?"

"We know little, madame. It seems he, too, was shot, at the Hotel Beau Rivage."

"He is dead?"

"I do not know, madame. He is at the Prince Albert Hospital. Oh, madame, the scandal. It will be in all the papers. Nothing like this has ever happened to our bank before. If only we could keep it a secret!"

Laura replaced the receiver. She was shaking with shock and fury. The fool! The bloody fool! He went to the hotel! Much good Vietnam did him there. But he could not be dead! God could not desert her now. Andy could not have killed Braechel. Not possible! Nor the director. He'd been with her all night. It was Bellamy, or Jaime. With luck they would destroy each other. But not soon enough, she thought regretfully. Not soon enough.

She turned distractedly into the room. The television? The news reports. She switched it on.

" ... three bodies discovered in the large suite occupied by a mysterious American, Mrs Laura Ellery, who seems to have disappeared. One was a housemaid employed at the hotel, and two others have not been identified. The fourth person found at the hotel is Monsieur Andrew Davidson, an American citizen who is an official of the Banque des Trois Cantons. Monsieur Davidson, who was discovered by Dr Harvey Curtis, a resident at the hospital who is believed to be a friend, is in a critical condition at the Prince Albert Hospital. He is the last known person to be seen with murdered bank official Edmond Braechel before his body was discovered in his office at the bank a little before nine o'clock by his secretary. Bank sources state that a considerable sum of money ... "

Thank God, she thought. Not dead yet, at least! Now they will try to frame him for the murders and for the theft of her money. To exonerate him, she would have to identify herself, and once again, they would be waiting.

They would find her, and she would die, she thought, and

Andy's life will be wasted, too. However, she was not entirely without resources, as they would think. She had most of the five hundred thousand francs she had drawn from the bank and she had the money from the casino. She sat down and rang the hospital.

"Dr Curtis, please?"

"Are you from the press? Dr Curtis is not permitted by the police to speak with the media."

"No, no. This is a personal call. Tell him it is from Evian."

"One moment, please." There was a silence, and then ...

"Yes?" The voice was cultivated, cautious.

"I am a friend of Andy Davidson."

"Yes, from Evian. He mentioned Evian, or I would not have taken the call."

"Thank God. How is he?"

"He is dying, madame."

"I will not allow it," she said. "He will not die. He killed no one. The money is mine. He did not steal it!"

"Ah! You are the mysterious and missing Mrs Ellery? I have an envelope for you. He had it in his pocket."

"Yes, yes," she said impatiently, "but you must understand that it is I whom they wished to kill, not Andy. It is my fault that he is dying. I must help him!"

"People die all the time, Mrs Ellery. It is not so difficult as you may think. It is living which requires the effort."

"It is an effort I cannot make without him," she said.

As she said the words, she knew that they were true. She would not let him die.

"Ah, so! It's like that! Well, Andy is my friend. I'll look after him. Ring me tomorrow. If he's alive tomorrow, we'll see what's to be done. Don't come here. The morons from the media are here like flies, and God knows who else as well! I'll look after your envelope until I see you."

"Be careful. Whoever killed these people wants that envelope ... or, at least they want to prevent my getting hold of it. They won't hesitate to kill you if they know you have it."

"What does it contain?"

"A bearer cheque for more than twenty million dollars."

"A lot of money, but surely whoever is orchestrating all of this cannot be short of funds?"

"No, but they think I am, and they want me. If I have no resources, I am an easier target, you see. Andy is in this mess because he helped me, and now I must help him."

"Yes, I see that. Ring me tomorrow at this private number." He gave her the number and rang off.

Laura sat down and looked out at the lake in the fading light. It was calm and beautiful. She might have failed the nuns who raised her, she thought, but nevertheless they had known the difference between right and wrong, and they had implanted those values in her. She understood clearly that it was her duty to save Andy. The Church gave its believers an alternative in many matters. They could sin and repent and sin and repent again, but in matters such as this, there were no alternatives. To fail to act properly now would prevent absolution, and she would be damned.

Finally, after considerable time, she picked up the phone. "Operator, will you find me the number for the Miami Drug Squad, please? I wish to place a person-to-person call to a Lieutenant Jerkovitz."

CHAPTER SEVENTEEN

MIAMI, FLORIDA
APRIL 1979

As HE WAITED IN HIS office to meet with Don Jaime Ventura y Cortez and to begin the fight for the control of their empire, whose glittering rewards could now rival those of ancient Rome, Charles thought back to that day when he had been thrown out of Australia like a common criminal, and had landed penniless in New York, humiliated and full of fury and ambition.

In spite of being broke and angry, he remembered that was a time when he had begun each day with a high heart. He tried now to recall when the stones accumulating beneath his breastbone had begun to weigh him down. He supposed death would be like that, when it came. Not a disease, but simply going down under the weight of accumulated woes; of mistakes and regrets; a drowning in the brackish tide of ancient sorrows and the lakes of unshed tears which life provides.

He tried to think when he had become aware that the first stone had lodged? When had he first noticed that the weightlessness of youth with which he had once soared so effortlessly each morning was gone? Had it begun with the knowledge that the happiness of another human being was not within his gift? No, not then. With his stupid infatuation with Betty in the days when he had roamed the world believing that his own goodwill and passion could change the ugliness and sorrow of it all?

No, not even then.

He knew that the first stone had lodged when he discovered, back in America, what Betty had done to him; when he realized that she had thrown him to the wolves in search of her own greed and ambition. That was the moment when he had ceased to believe in love, and when all the other starry eyed illusions of his youth had begun to die. That was when he had started to understand the rules by which the world is really managed; when he had become aware that he must get power, and for that he would need money. And with that knowledge the weight in his chest had begun to feel a little heavier every morning than his ability to ignore it.

It had seemed to happen so quickly at the time, like the speed of those jerky old movies racing frenetically towards death and rescue under a train or on the wings of a bi-plane. Now, looking back, it was all in slow motion, not preordained in any way, but inevitable all the same, like so much that happens in life. Each step had appeared at the time to be the logical sequence to the one before it. It was only by looking back that he could see that there had been the forks in the road and other paths he might have taken, but by then it was too late.

By that time it had become evil, and the only possible road had lain ahead, or there would be no road at all, simply a precipice over which he would tumble and fall, or be pushed by the Ventura family and the other greedy and ruthless rivals for his territory and the fortune he was building. In this game there was no turning back, but he had learned that lesson too late for it to matter.

If he had known about the lottery win and the theft at the time it would, he thought, have given him an acceptable reason for Betty's treason. It would have softened the blow of her betrayal. In its plain human greed and dishonesty, it would have been the one explanation that would have obtained his forgiveness, but he had found out too late for that. By then he had started selling drugs, and the fork in the road had been passed which might have led on to another kind of life.

They hadn't seemed so bad, at first, the things he did. Selling some marijuana, arranging a few dates for out-of-towners. A little happiness for others, a moment or two of escape from reality, and some urgently needed cash for himself. He'd seen so much desperation in the sad places in the world where he had worked that he had come to define an escape from an unbearable reality as a small gift rather than a crime. And when the serious money started to come in – a better apartment, a more comfortable life, it was easy to find excuses. He'd seen, in India, in Africa, in the Philippines and Thailand, a struggle for survival that was so basic and so ruthless that it justified everything.

He had easily and quickly identified the same desperation here, in the American cities. There had been no difficulty there. There was little room for preaching in a twilight world. They wanted food, sex and forgetfulness in that order, and he provided them. Survival and its attendant necessities, he had understood even then, had their own uncertain dignity.

Now, at the times when the weight in his chest grew unbearable, he had his excuses ready for himself, but he knew they were lies. He knew that his great strength in the lethal world into which he moved, and the reason for all his successes, was that he never believed his own lies, but sometimes, he thought wryly, they offered a spurious comfort. At times, such as now, when he must deal with Jaime, and even worse, with Laura. Her reward for years of loyalty, well-paid but nevertheless delivered to him, had been an order that she be killed because she was one of the few people in the world who could identify him personally with the Ventura interests. That was a risk he could never take. Certainly not now, when he was so close to achieving everything he had worked for. He sighed. How far down the path he had come. How long ago it seemed that, like Caesar, he had crossed the Rubicon.

Mahatma Gandhi had said, "Look after the means, and the ends will look after themselves." Fine words, but Edwina, with her aristocratic disdain for dissimulation, had warned him that the corrupt means would taint the achievement, when it came. He hoped she would not be proven right, or his life would have been wasted. Today, in this meeting, he intended to complete this work, and to make himself the richest man in the world. The price he had already paid was far too high to contemplate either failure or compromise. He must either win or disappear.

He knew only too well that a man can never go back. He shook himself. It was a mistake to even look back. It made you weak and sentimental. In June he would marry Edwina de Trafford, and that marriage would be his final step to the acceptance of his power by the powerful. It would make him free to do as he pleased. It would open the last few closed doors into the world of the mighty. Edwina was above suspicion of fraud and dishonour and she would place him there beside her on that pedestal. Before that marriage took place, he must tidy his affairs. There could be no mistakes now.

His secretary buzzed the intercom and interrupted his thoughts.

"Mr Cordova is here, Mr Bellamy."

So, after all these years of planning and manipulation, of savagery and revenge, the moment of truth comes. He thought of Ernest Hemingway, down the road in Key West, obsessed with the hubris of the bullfight. Well, he would not end like that!

"Ask him to come in."

Jaime Ventura y Cortez was not what he expected. He vaguely recalled a tough and swarthy and rather muscular man, a punk in spite of his Harvard background and his alleged aristocratic blood. There was still the dark hair and olive skin, yes, but now a man taller than he recalled, and more slender, with a far-away expression which might belong to a monk or a mystic, or perhaps a idealistic lawyer in a small, provincial town. Charles reminded himself that it was always men such as these who caused revolutions. Dangerous dreamers like himself, he thought wryly.

Charles crossed the room and held out his hand. Jaime ignored it.

"I do not shake hands with a man whom I do not trust," he said quietly. "And I do not trust you, Mr Bellamy. We have done millions, billions of dollars of business together. We could both have been rich, but you do not want that. You plant a spy in Bogotá. You murder my brother Sebastian because you know I will not do it! Stupid and greedy!"

Charles smiled grimly. Here was an adversary who belied his mild and academic looks. "Greedy, yes. Stupid, no," he said calmly. "It has brought you here to me, as I wished."

"You wish to see me? You deal with my brother Jesus, and his little bank. You run the airline and the supermarkets and all the distribution networks. You dealt with Sebastian on the takeovers and the European corporations. You do all our dirty business with all the other dirty bankers all over the world. Why do you need to see me? It is I who wish to see you!"

"Because, Senor Ventura, you are the boss, and on matters of real importance I only deal with the boss."

Jaime bridled slightly. It was a very small gesture of vanity and the only one that might have identified him for what he was, a clever and ruthless criminal, and a South American.

"And what is this important matter?"

"I intend to take over all your European and American assets. No, not all. I will leave you the Finca and the refineries in Colombia. Your ancestral lands."

Jaime laughed. He bent over double, enjoying the joke hugely, but with no humour in his cold, fanatic's eyes.

"My assets are not for sale, and even if they were, you could not afford them, and I would not sell them to you."

"Quite so, but then, you see, I do not intend to pay for them."

Jaime stood up. "This farce has gone on long enough. I am closing all my accounts and dealings with this bank and with you, Mr Bellamy. I want a full accounting. There is no doubt that you are good at your work, but for the price you charge I can always find someone else."

"I think not," Charles said quietly. "For one thing, you cannot leave this room without a signal from myself, and if you try to touch me, armed guards will be here in five seconds. Sit down and listen to what I have to say."

Jaime continued to pace up and down the room. "You'll never get away with this," he said. "There are three guards in my car who will come up when I do not return, and another in your outside office, waiting for me now."

Charles shook his head. "They are all gone, as is your car. You have disappeared, Mr Ventura, and you will not return until I say so."

"I am kidnapped by my own banker? That is novel. Well, what do you have to say for the short time during which you will remain alive?"

"Let me explain some matters which I am sure Jesus understands completely but which you may not. In addition to this bank, which is now the largest in Florida, we own the Banque des Trois Cantons in Geneva, another in Liechtenstein, the Sweicherbank, another in Luxembourg, the Banque Caroline, one on the Cayman Islands, the Albert Bank, and one in the Bahamas, the King George Bank. All of this you may know. Or Jesus does. These banks all handle funds belonging to you. All of them act as trustees, for obvious reasons. Through these banks, and our contacts at the Vatican, we know of every share which you hold and where every dollar of yours has been invested. We know the names of all your dummy corporations and illegal bank accounts. Further, the huge sums which you have placed with us are, at this moment, no longer available to you, as they are being transferred to me, together with your funds deposited all over the world."

He paused and looked at Jaime who stared silently back.

"We have stolen your liquid funds," he said, "and now all that will be required are some signatures on documents my lawyers have prepared for us, and all the rest, everything you own outside Colombia, will be in my name. We will be happy to continue to deal with you for raw materials, and to pay top price into whatever accounts you nominate, provided they are safe. We could go elsewhere, but why should we?"

Jaime stared at him for a moment. "Over my dead body," he said.

Charles coughed. "Well, I am hoping it will not come to that!"

"You're crazy! I could walk out of here and denounce you."

"Really? To whom? And who would you say you were? In any event, the authorities would find our affairs in perfect order. Only a total international audit of every company and bank we own would reveal what we are doing, and that is impossible. The transfers of cash will be electronic, and all quite proper. I have only to pick up the phone and call that idiot Jerkovitz, and you will be in gaol in two minutes. You would not get out of gaol for forty years."

"We can undersell you," Jaime said, "and send you broke. After all, we grow the stuff! We supply it!"

"But you have no access to the distribution networks, all those supermarkets I have bought to get rid of the stuff, all that is controlled by me. We'd simply tell our people not to touch your stuff and you'd have no market."

"And you'd have no goods to sell."

Charles shrugged. "There are other suppliers, and I have stockpiled for more than five years. We could afford to give the stuff away to gain control, if we had to do it."

Jaime laughed scornfully. "Jesus says our affairs are in proper order. I have no proof of what you say and I shall sign nothing. You'd be dead in five minutes if I did. You will be, anyway."

"Perhaps, but first you must leave this office."

Jaime stared at him. "Have you any idea how much money is involved?"

"But, of course. We are your bankers. The bearer bonds and cash deposits would amount to around twenty billion dollars. Your assets in shares in the offshore corporations we have set up over the years, probably another twenty billion, and then there are your shares in the airline, and Diggely-Doggely supermarkets, and in this bank, and the Alcon Corporation, and the little stockpile of drugs I have accumulated. Maybe another thirty billion dollars. It is a very nice little pile, but you will still have all your assets in Colombia, plus the farmlands and the factories. Not bad, really."

Jaime looked at him with his mad monk's eyes. "You are quite crazy," he said. "I will never sign anything."

"Then you will never leave this building, and after you are dead, we shall simply buy your assets with your own money and transfer them to my own holding companies. Who will complain? Jorge? Jesus? And to whom? The police? The government? They will be satisfied with what will be left in Colombia. It is still a very substantial fortune."

Jaime stood up and screamed. All his academic calm was gone now. "You are a dead man! Dead! Dead!" He looked like a South American drug dealer now, Charles thought, or a psychotic patient, with his face suffused with blood, and his mouth distended with rage.

"We all die in the end," Charles said. "Even me! It's what happens before then that interests me."

Jaime stared at Charles. Now he said calmly, "Jorge will come for me. He will send someone."

Charles shrugged. "He will wonder, no doubt. He will ask around. But in our business, as we all know, people disappear all the time. He will make millions more for himself, with the farm and the factories. He will have all he needs. He will have all the girls he wants, and the boys, too, without you to stop him. No one needs all that money."

"Then why do you?"

"To change the world," Charles said.

Jaime laughed sadly. "Now I know that you are truly crazy," he said.

Charles went to a cupboard and took out a thick folder. "Here are all the transfers we shall need, together with the power of attorney. I trust that our lawyers have done a good job. They should have. God knows we pay the thieves enough. Jorge and Jesus will get substantial dividends. We shall make sure of that. They will be happy." Charles pressed a button and a wall rolled back to reveal a room furnished like a hotel suite, modern but anonymous.

"This room is quite inaccessible. It is thirty-three floors up, and has no windows. Food comes up on an elevator. You could live there for twenty years and no one would be any the wiser."

Jaime looked at him, amazed. "You are a respected man of business, a leader of the community," he said. "You are about to marry a beautiful and famous woman of the world. Do you mean to tell me you would imprison me here in your office, in the middle of Miami?"

Charles laughed.

"Don't talk rubbish, Jaime. Let's not believe our own lies. I am just a thief and a drug smuggler like you, no matter what I pretend to be. I am just better dressed. Have you ever hesitated to give an unpleasant order to get rid of an enemy? How many men have we killed over the past eight or ten years? Why should you be surprised that I would do it to you? You would do it to me without a moment's hesitation. A man in a well-tailored suit can commit a murder as easily as your Colombian peons down there in the back streets of Medellin. It's just that people, even the police, find it harder to believe. Why do you think I pay so much money to my tailor?" He looked critically at Jaime's awful clothes. "You should try it sometime."

The phone on his table rang. "Lieutenant Jerkovitz is here to see you, Mr Bellamy."

"How very convenient. Ask him to wait." He turned to Jaime. "Well, do you go into my guest room and sign these documents, or do I introduce you to the incorruptible Lieutenant Jerkovitz?"

"You asked him up here?"

"Not at all. That is merely an unhappy coincidence. I have no wish to see you in gaol."

Jaime picked up the share transfers. "I shall go in and study these papers. I have no wish to be arrested, but I shall never sign them. You are dead meat, Bellamy. Dead meat!"

"Aren't we all, my friend," Charles said, pleasantly. He ushered Jaime into the room and closed the door. He buzzed his secretary. "I am releasing the security from inside. Show Lieutenant Jerkovitz in."

Stanley Jerkovitz entered the room with the aggressive assurance of one unaccustomed to luxury, but determined not to be impressed or intimidated by it. He was unsuccessful on both counts.

Charles shook his hand and sadly noted his appalling cotton and nylon suit, and his shoes with soles half an inch thick. He winced. He wondered vaguely about a nation in which the police looked more like criminals than the criminals.

"What can I do for you, Lieutenant?"

"What do you know of a man named Harry Wellington, Mr Bellamy?" Stanley demanded aggressively.

"Am I to understand that this is an official inquiry, Lieutenant?"

"No, not exactly. I am simply concerned about the man. I met him here. It's more personal."

"Ah, personal. I see. Well, I know very little, I'm afraid. An Australian consultant whom we are using, who got himself into some local trouble, I understand. Are you not our local drug chief? Surely he is not involved with drugs?"

"Certainly not, but I understand that Alcon denied any knowledge of him?"

"Did we? Dear me, but Alcon Corporation is a very large company, Lieutenant. We employ hundreds of thousands of people around the world. I thought all that had been sorted out. We told our lawyers to deal with it, and I understand that woman has withdrawn charges."

"He was mugged, and accused ... " Jerkovitz was so

angry he couldn't speak for a moment. He took off his spectacles and wiped them quickly on a rather grubby handkerchief. "He was set-up! I let him come to my apartment while he waited for money to be sent, and now ... now, " he spluttered. "Now he has disappeared."

Charles raised his eyebrows. "Disappeared? Dear me! Have you come to warn us, then, that he is not a suitable person for us to employ? It would certainly seem so. I shall tell Nick Barton to look into it. Has the case been tried?"

"Of course not! The charges were withdrawn."

"All of them? How nice. Then he is innocent of any wrongdoing? Excellent! I trust there will be no more problems. Are the Miami Police able now to look into the future and reassure me?" Charles lifted his eyebrows to indicate his surprise. "Now if there is nothing else, Lieutenant ...?"

"I've told you. He has disappeared."

"I think not. I believe he had meetings with our corporate advisors yesterday or the day before, and now he has now gone to California to join his family for a vacation. If you believe there is more to this than I can see, then you are the police. I'm sure you can find him. " He pressed a button on his desk.

"The lieutenant is leaving, " he said.

"Not so fast, Bellamy. What about Ventura?"

"What about him?"

"We followed him here. We have followed him since he arrived in the States, calling himself Mr Cordova."

"Is that so? And are you aware that Senor Ventura has been a customer of this bank since before I owned it? He has every right to come here. He discussed some business with Nick Barton and left."

"Are you aware that he has illegal interests all over the world?"

"We all know what the media says about him, Lieutenant. Is there a warrant for his arrest? Do you have some proof of malfeasance? Has he been charged with some crime in Florida?"

"Not yet!"

"Then you must excuse me, Lieutenant. This is a bank, not a court of law. It is not my job to decide who is guilty and who is not. I know nothing of Mr Wellington, and I never see private customers."

"But you saw Ventura!" Jerkovitz said triumphantly.

"On this occasion, yes, briefly. He is a very large depositor in our bank and has been for many years, as I've already told you. He rarely comes to Miami. I am a banker, as I said, and not a moralist, Lieutenant. You are a policeman. When a customer of this bank has been proved to have committed a crime, I will be happy to co-operate with you. Until then ..." He shrugged.

"Where is Ventura?"

"He has left!"

"He has not. We have been watching this building."

Charles looked him up and down, with some distaste. "Jerkovitz," he said. "If you don't mind my saying so, you are a prick, and a very tiresome one at that. Do you see Mr Ventura here? You will note that there is a private elevator in the corner. It takes me, and others who wish to use it, straight to the basement car park. Senor Ventura used that elevator. Where he is now, I have no idea."

The phone rang. "I have Monsignor Bland on the phone."

Charles picked up the phone. "Yes, Monsignor?"

"We have transferred those funds to the Banque des Trois Cantons, as you requested. Do you have the necessary authority from Ventura?"

"Yes, we have it, Monsignor, as I've already informed you," he said and hung up.

"Is there anything else, Lieutenant? I am very busy."

"There is no one here."

"So I have observed myself."

"Would you ask Mr Wellington to contact me when you hear from him?"

Charles looked at him in amazement. "I am not a secretary for the Police Department. I shall not be seeing Mr Wellington. He will be working for Alcon Corporation in Australia, not for the bank. I suggest that you contact Nick Barton. However, if Harry Wellington does not wish to see you, Jerkovitz, I'm afraid there is nothing that we can do about that. And now, I really am very busy."

He opened the door and the Lieutenant departed. Charles sighed. Corrupt people were so easy to deal with. It was only a matter of how much they would take. Honest men were another matter. It was fortunate there were so few of them or he would be out of business, and out of patience, too.

Stan Jerkovitz went out into the street. He was not a happy man. He knew that Harry would not ignore him like this. They had agreed to keep in touch. Harry had promised to report to him on what had happened, and he had heard nothing. He drove down to the Central Police Station where Harry had been taken the morning they found him in the Everglades, to check the records there. The outer office was full of the usual collection of sad and disreputable Cubans and blacks, sitting around waiting for help of one kind or another that no one would bring them. He found the officer in charge in a small back room, which smelt of urine and stale hamburger meat.

"There is no record of any arrest here in the name of Wellington," he said to Stan, consulting his record book of arrests.

"But there must be," Stanley insisted. "I was called in on the case myself, in case there had been drugs involved. Can I talk to the men who were on duty that day?"

"Not a chance," he said. "They went out flying to the Aero Club yesterday. They were student pilots, you know, and they were both killed when their plane crashed. It's terrible. They both had young families, you know. It was in the papers this morning. Didn't you see it?"

Jerkovitz drove slowly back to his apartment and took a cold beer from the refrigerator. He switched on his answer phone. There was a message. Perhaps it would be from Harry.

"Lieutenant Jerkovitz?" A woman's voice that he did not recognize. "I believe I can help you if you will help me. Do you want to know about the Ventura family? Isn't that your job? I'll ring back in twelve hours. Your phone is bugged so I can't talk or we shall both be dead. Have another number ready on which I can reach you."

Stan sucked thoughtfully on his beer, and stared around at the untidy mess of his apartment. Who the hell was that? The last thing he needed was some hysterical bitch who thought she had valuable information for the police. Miami was full of nutcases like that. Stanley wondered what she could tell him, and why she would think his phone might be bugged. If it was, there was now someone, somewhere, who would know this woman had been in touch with him. He hoped, if she knew anything useful, that that someone would not find her before he did.

CHAPTER EIGHTEEN

LOS ANGELES, CALIFORNIA
APRIL 1979

THE ALCON CORPORATION RANCH was a sprawling Spanish Californian spread in a pretty curve of the hills east of Los Angeles, and surrounded by eucalyptus trees that had come originally from Australia, and now grown huge in the benign climate of southern California.

"Where have you been?" Betty demanded, as soon as the helicopter landed on the pad in front of the ranch house and Harry emerged exhausted and disheveled from the cabin.

In the few days she had been at the ranch, her skin had acquired a light, pretty California tan, but her eyes were anxious and her face was drawn.

"It's beautiful here, but I couldn't get through on the phone to Sydney or to Alcon in Miami. I began to wonder if they were keeping us prisoners here." She laughed at the absurdity of such an idea.

"Betty, why didn't you tell me about the lottery?"

Harry had arrived from Miami on the Alcon jet and transferred to the helicopter at Los Angeles airport for the trip to the ranch. He was exhausted physically and emotionally from the trauma of the events in Miami. The effort of trying to protect Betty from the consequences of her action seemed not so much beyond his imagination as beyond the energy that such protective action would require.

She looked at him belligerently. "I tried to warn you before you left on this crazy trip," she said.

"I didn't mean now," he said wearily. "I meant then, when you did it."

"You wouldn't have agreed," she said. "We would still be back in that horrible little cottage, scratching for a living."

He looked at her sadly. He knew what she said was true. He understood that he wanted life to come out right, to be great; he wanted to be successful, but he never wished to pay the price. He let others do that for him. It would be difficult enough to think up stories for his colleagues back in Sydney. There would be no point in lying now to Betty. They were in this thing together, and he suspected she would have more stomach for it than he did.

Betty interpreted his silence as unwillingness to talk, as an accusation.

"Why the hell did you bring us all this way, anyway, if you weren't even going to be here? We could have come later!"

"I didn't bring you," he said. "Alcon did. I didn't know at first that you were even here. And you are right to feel like prisoners. You are, or were, hostages. If I hadn't agreed to what they wanted, they would have killed you all."

Betty stared at him. "So," she said softly, almost to herself. "It is the same Charles Bellamy after all." She took a deep breath. "One never gets away with anything in this world, does one? You'd better tell me everything."

They were sitting on the terrace of the ranch house. Below them, the scalded, yellow land of the hills east of Los Angeles dropped away in rounded, brown folds towards the distant metropolis, like the wrinkled skin of some prehistoric animal. The city itself was defined, at this hour, only by the low cloud of smog that hung over it, lit now by the wondrous pink haze of the sunset, a poisoned halo that resembled a giant cap of floss floating over the city.

The haze is typical of the age in which we live, Harry thought. Corruption dressed to kill. No one wanted smog, but everyone wanted cars. Everyone wanted to travel, but no one wanted an airport nearby. Everyone wanted convenience food, but no one wanted litter. Cheap power was demanded, but no atomic energy or pollution. They would stop driving their millions of cars only on the day they could no longer breathe, he thought; on the day when there were not enough forests left to cleanse the air, and there was no oxygen. Then everyone would be an environmentalist, and it would be too late. We are no brighter than the dinosaurs and would come to the same end, sooner or later, he considered.

He stirred lethargically in the warm, still air. What was the point of being angry, with the motorists or with Betty? He had always known, in his heart, that he could not avoid the truth forever. No one did.

"They were holding you hostage here until I agreed to become their drug distributor in Australia."

"And you agreed?"

"They had copies of the cheque, Betty, with your endorsement. They had framed me with the police. There was a rape charge. They had you and the children held here as captives. Of course I agreed. I didn't want you all buried here in these bleached hills."

She stared at him. She knew he was speaking the truth. "I have been in gaol in Miami," he said, "Charges of rape and vagrancy and God knows what other fraudulent charges. We must do as they say or we shall be ruined, or dead."

"And Charles? You saw him?"

"Of course. He looks the same, even more of a shining

knight than before, but he is quite changed. He is a ruthless killer, a billionaire, and a law unto himself."

He told her all that had happened in Miami. She listened without interruption.

Finally she said, "I'm sorry, Harry. How could I know?"

He shrugged. "It's no good being sorry," he said. "That's too easy."

"What do they want you to do?"

"Because of my outstanding record in the field of national and international philanthropy, I am unlikely to be suspected," he said sadly. "I am too respectable. They have my balls in a vice, and they will go on squeezing until it kills me."

"What do they want you to do?" she asked again.

"Not me – us!"

"Well?"

Far below them, the city came alight like a distant icon; beckoning them, like a wayward star, towards God knows what remote and corrupt Valhalla.

Betty spoke, her voice dry and firm. "Whatever it is, we shall do it all, of course. Just as they want, and we shall do it so well that no one will ever know. There's no going back now."

He shook his head. "I can't believe that Charlie has turned into this man. Our Charlie has disappeared."

"There is nothing so dangerous as a disillusioned idealist," Betty said. "Never mind that now. Our Charles is dead, just as the people that you and I were in those days are dead. In their place are a drug baron and two corrupt and hypocritical philanthropists."

He stared at her. "My God, you're being pretty cool. Come to think of it, you've been cool about it since the day you banked that cheque."

"Would you rather I had hysterics now, and we were all murdered here in the hills? I will do anything – anything – to save the good name we've built up and the life we've created, and the children's future. Anything! It's far too late for regrets. That's a luxury we can't afford. What do they want?"

"Do you remember Phillip Morgan-Smith?"

"The banker who drowned?"

"He was murdered. He was double dealing while running an Australian operation for the Ventura family. Charles wants to take over, and for us ... or rather, me ... "

"Us," she interrupted harshly. "You could never do this alone. You are too soft at the core, too full of conscience. We can't afford that now."

He stared at her. It was as if he found himself married to someone he didn't know, had never known, and now did not want to know.

She accepted his stare calmly. "You must toughen up, Harry, and do as they ask. Otherwise we're finished."

"Yes, finished. Alcon Corporation is shortly moving to Australia, armaments, petroleum exploration, mining, logging and a whole mass of environmentally sensitive issues. There will also be the drugs, heroin, cocaine, whatever. They want the market for themselves. Alcon will provide the smokescreen. They will set up a charitable foundation of which I shall be the director. The drugs will come into Australia on regular flights of their freight airline, which now has landing rights out there. They will be labelled as public relations literature and philanthropic publications, whatever. We will set up an operation to sell the stuff. We shall be rich if we succeed, dead if we don't."

"And my role will be to place the operation beyond suspicion?"

"You're very quick at this game. Yes. Sell the house and

buy a much bigger and smarter one. Money is no problem. Entertain, support charities, be publicly involved in good causes of the utmost respectability. The foundation will deal with the rest of it." He sounded tired.

She took his hand. "Harry," she said quietly, "I never thought when I stole that cheque that it would come to this," she said.

"No, I'm sure you didn't," he said, "but it always does, doesn't it?"

"We'll make a success of this, too. You wait and see."

She shook herself. The desert night was closing in and the air was suddenly cool. Inside the children sat watching the television beside a huge log fire. The scene was very tranquil, a Californian version of the perfect family. Betty took his hand as they walked inside.

"Don't look back, Harry," she said. "It will only break your heart."

"You realize that we have sold our lives," he said.

"We'll get them back again, one day."

"No," he said sadly, "that's something we must face up to here and now. We shall never get them back. If we don't understand and accept that fact, we shall never survive."

CHAPTER NINETEEN

MIAMI, FLORIDA
APRIL 1979

STAN JERKOVITZ WAS TIRED. He hadn't slept much since his meeting with Charles Bellamy, and reading about the forthcoming wedding in every newspaper had not improved his disposition. With the weather getting hotter his skin felt itchy and he supposed, morosely, that it was all psychosomatic.

Stanley knew Nick well enough and rather liked him, so he telephoned him.

"Nick? This is Stan Jerkovitz down at the Miami Police. What's all this about employing Harry Wellington?"

Nick laughed. "Don't tell me you've become involved with that business, Stan? I thought you were in drugs? There are no drugs in this one. Harry just seems to have made rather a fool of himself. He got drunk, and got himself mugged, too, it seems. We almost dropped him from our plans, but he does have a good reputation in Australia, so we went ahead with our contract."

"Come on, Nick. There must be more than that. He told me he spent a night in gaol," Jerkovitz said, "but when I checked, there was no record."

"Well, you're the police," Nick said. "Don't ask me how you run your business."

"The two cops who were on duty at the time were killed in a plane accident yesterday."

"Is that so? Extraordinary. I didn't read anything about a plane crash."

"A small trainer, apparently. They were learning to fly. And Wellington?" Jerkovitz persisted.

"He has gone back to Australia as far as I know. We've had our meetings with him and he's fully briefed. He left a day or so ago. He's probably back in Sydney by now."

So Harry Wellington had left without another word. It was very strange of him. Stanley had rather liked the Australian, and he didn't believe that he would voluntarily have dumped him like that. Stanley took his worries to his superior, who was even more ill-tempered than himself, and scratched himself, too. Two police dead, he reported, and no record of the arrest, and now Harry Wellington, to whom he'd shown some kindness, was gone without a word. It was all tied in with Alcon Corporation and that bastard Bellamy. What should he do?

His boss said, "Drop it!"

"Drop it? Captain, I know the guy was framed! Why, even the woman who alleged rape has disappeared. The diner is closed and there's a FOR SALE sign on the door."

"Drop it, Lieutenant. That's an order. Drop it! I don't want to hear another word about Mr Wellington and his alleged disappearance. We are not going to get on the wrong side of Alcon Corporation and Bellamy here in Miami, over some bloody Australian visitor who behaves badly. We have to live with Bellamy every day of our lives."

So Stanley had dropped it. He knew when there was too much pressure from somewhere up above. He went home for a beer, and now there was a message from some crazy dame who was going to ring him at six in the morning, and why would she think that someone would bug a cop's phone? If she was right about that, then maybe he should talk with her. Maybe she was not just another Miami nutcase, after all. That night, in spite of his troubles, he slept well, until the phone rang at six.

"I am the woman who rang yesterday. I need your help. Do you have another number ready?"

He gave her the telephone number for the public phone in the diner where he had his breakfast. She hung up immediately. Stanley pulled on his jeans and jogged down to the diner. He ordered coffee. In five minutes the phone rang.

"Is that you, Lieutenant Jerkovitz?'

"Yes, ma'am."

"You know your home phone is being tapped?"

"No, I didn't and how do you know?"

"Never mind that, but I hope that the fact that I do know proves my bona fides. Check it out! Get out your notebook. I'm only saying this once. My name is Laura Tessier. You know that name?"

"The woman in Bogotá?" Jerkovitz woke up fast and began to pay attention.

"I lived with Sebastian Ventura for ten years. I am in Geneva, where three people are dead at my bank and three more in a hotel. That's how I know your phone is bugged. These people never make a mistake."

"There are three dead people in the suite of a Mrs Ellery at the Beau Rivage Hotel in Geneva, is what I read," Jerkovitz said.

"I am Mrs Ellery," she said.

"Shit!"

"An innocent man is dying, because he helped me. Now I am going to help him, Jerkovitz, and you are going to help me do it! In return I will tell you about the Ventura family and Charles Bellamy. Is it a deal?"

"What do you want?" Stanley asked. He knew this was the break he'd been waiting for.

"A man called Andy Davidson is in the hospital here. He was shot in the hotel, and is accused of murder and embezzlement. He is innocent, but he will be convicted, or killed, unless I help him. As soon as he is able to move, you and I are going to get him out of that hospital. You will deal with the police here, using as much of my money as you need."

"In Switzerland?"

"Forget the squeaky clean image. They call it discretion here, but it's business as usual, the same as anywhere else. You will come over here and do what's necessary for me to get Davidson out of the country, and I shall tell you all you want to know about the Ventura family and all their contacts, which is a very great deal."

"Where can I meet you?"

"Fly to Geneva. Go to Evian, across the lake in France. Be at the casino in two days time, at four o'clock in the afternoon. Go to roulette table number four, and place three consecutive ten dollar bets on number eighteen. Don't try to reach me before then in any way at all. At least five people here are already dead, although some of them deserved it. I don't want you to be one more ... or me, either, for that matter. Any mistakes, and you or I will be number six. I will book a ticket for you on a flight out tonight." She rang off.

Stanley went to the counter and ordered a double helping of fried eggs and toast. He drank two cups of coffee. He went to his doctor and got a certificate that he was ill and needed a break. He left it at his office, and told his secretary that he was going fishing in the Adirondacks. That night he picked up a pre-paid ticket from the airport and left on a flight to Geneva.

By morning he was in the office of Dr Curtis.

"Will he die?" he asked. He knew if Andy Davidson died, he'd get no help from Laura Tessier. She would simply disappear.

"He will if another policeman tries to talk with him," Dr Curtis said.

"Okay, okay, so I don't get to talk with him. When can we move him?"

"When the Swiss police say so."

"Fuck the Swiss police. Is he a friend of yours?"

Curtis nodded.

"I know who is responsible for this," Jerkovitz said. "The longer he stays here, the greater the chance that they'll have another go at getting rid of him. You, too, probably. You want that?"

Dr Curtis simply stared at him.

"So when can I move him?" Stanley asked again.

"In two days, in a properly equipped ambulance plane, and if I come with him. It's still a 50-50 chance. He is guarded all the time, you know."

"Don't worry about that. I'm a policeman so I know how dumb they are. Schedule him for surgery at two in the afternoon day after tomorrow, in a theatre with two entrances. Let me know where it is."

"Are you seeing Mrs Ellery?"

"Tomorrow."

"Give her this," Dr Curtis said, handing over the envelope he'd found in Andy's pocket. "It's a bearer cheque for more than twenty million dollars. It seems to be the reason the men at the bank were killed."

"Are the banks here so desperate?"

"It's a lot of money." Dr Curtis shrugged. "Bankers

always like to get their money back."

The following afternoon, Stanley went to the casino and put his ten dollar bets on number eighteen. He lost each time. He hated to lose; except for the ticket, he was paying his own way on this jaunt.

"I should put fifty on number ten," a voice beside him said. "It's the number of years I spent in Bogotá. I think it owes me something."

"Other than twenty million dollars," he said, giving her the envelope. She was very beautiful. For some reason he was surprised at that. He always expected these women who consorted with criminals to be tough and ugly, but this one was quite obviously a classy broad.

She looked at him calmly. "Other than that. That I earned," she said. She looked at the small envelope. "So! After all that killing they didn't get the money, but it won't be worth much if it costs his life. Or mine!"

He stared at her. She had a soft voice with some kind of accent, very slight and attractive. He would have to learn that you can look good and be bad, but it was hard.

"It won't cost his life," Jerkovitz said. "Not if I can help it."

"Maybe I am being punished?"

Stanley breathed deeply a couple of times to give him patience. "I think maybe you've earned the money, as you said. If anyone is going to be punished, it will be me, if my boss finds out that I'm not fishing in the Adirondacks."

The croupier called, "*Faites vos jeux. Rien ne va plus!*" Jerkovitz placed a fifty dollar plaque on number ten.

"You do this often?" he asked.

"Only when in extremis," she said.

He wasn't sure what she meant, but Laura felt a feeling of panic pass through her like a cold needle. If she did not get this man to help and Andy died, then she would also die, and it would all have been in vain. She could do no more.

"*Numero dix, pair et rouge!*"

"There, you have won fifteen hundred dollars." Absurdly, she felt she could trust him because he had won, and that everything would be all right. "Don't make another bet! We can't be so lucky twice."

They sat in the restaurant and Laura ordered tea. "You knew my phone was tapped," he said. "I checked it out and you were right. Who can do that? Tap a cop's phone?"

"It's Bellamy. He's very thorough."

"But I am a police lieutenant," he said.

"He can do anything."

Jerkovitz shrugged. "Then they will know you are here."

"They knew I came to Switzerland for the money. They killed the men at the bank to prevent my getting it. They didn't know about Andy. They will be looking for me, but we shall be too quick. Dr Curtis rang me and told me what he said to you. The plane will be at Geneva Airport, domestic terminal, at two o'clock tomorrow.

"That was quick work." He sipped his tea and winced. "Do you mind if I have a beer?"

"You'd be amazed what money can buy," she said. "I certainly am. The pilot will file a flight plan for Berne. I want you to arrange a place to land outside Switzerland, but not too far. An ambulance will be waiting at the service entrance to the hospital to take him to the airport. Can you get him out?"

"Yes. The Swiss will think he has gone into surgery. We shall be gone before they know."

"Gone where?"

"What other cards are you putting on the table, other than winning at roulette?"

"How about all the Ventura business contacts in Colombia? Manner of delivery of drugs from the factory? Delivery to America and Europe? World contacts? Visitors? Contracts for disposal of unwanted persons? Money laundering schemes? Corporations they own? Just for starters."

"And Charles Bellamy?"

She sighed. "That, too. He is the boss. I was working for him. Now he is trying to kill me. He should have trusted me, and I would never have let him down. Men are such fools. So, where do we go?"

"A small airfield in Austria, and then, when he's well enough, back to America. In return for your help."

"It's a deal!" She held out her hand. "Do you want it in writing."

He smiled. "Not yet. It's nice to trust someone occasionally. Otherwise you can get too cynical in this game. Besides, I'm on my own time now. Officially, I was told to keep out of this."

"I'm not surprised to hear that. Charles is well protected in very high quarters."

CHAPTER TWENTY

GENEVA, SWITZERLAND
APRIL 1979

IN THE AFTERNOON, TWO days later, Laura stood by the ambulance at the service door of the hospital. She knew that if Andy died, a part of her would die, too. Certainly the best part, she thought, and perhaps the only part worth keeping. He had made a gift of himself. He had helped her as no one else had, and it had almost killed him. She owed him his life.

The Swiss police had been told never to leave him alone. They still believed he was guilty of murder. They thought he could give them information on the other murders. They believed he would be killed if they did not protect him, and there, at least, they were right.

In the operating theatre, another patient was substituted for Andy Davidson, while Stanley wheeled him out the back way, down in the lift reserved for garbage disposal and dead bodies. Close enough, too. Half his shoulder and most of one lung were gone, and all that blood. Laura hoped the Swiss were screening their blood for AIDS. You could never tell. In Switzerland, everything was so kosher on the surface, but behind the scenes all too often, she now understood, it was another matter.

By the time the other operation was finished, and the police discovered that Andy Davidson was not in the operating theatre, they would be gone, slipping over the border to Austria at the last minute, and down to the small airport Stan Jerkovitz had found in the Tyrol, a private field used sometimes for military aircraft, or for the occasional plane of the very rich, coming in to ski in the Tyrol in the winter.

Laura had new passports for them both. They would use them until the police, or Andy's father or the Swiss government, decided that he was innocent. Then he could again become a respectable banker in Atlanta, and not a half-crazed victim of a nasty war, who went around gunning down innocent victims in law-abiding Switzerland. That's what the papers were saying. She wondered if that was Charles' work, too, the careful placing of these evil stories in the world press.

Law-abiding Switzerland! That was a joke! During the past two days, while she waited for this moment, she had told Stanley everything she knew. The airlines, the distribution through the Diggely-Doggely chain of supermarkets, the operation in Colombia, enough to put them all behind bars for a hundred years. If Charles thought he knew about revenge, he hadn't even begun to learn yet, Laura thought, with some degree of satisfaction.

"Did you speak with Charles Bellamy when you reported from Bogotá?" Jerkovitz had asked.

"Never! It was always a recording, except the last day, when Nick warned me to get out. I have not seen Charles Bellamy since I left the States to go to Bogotá with Sebastian ten years ago. I liked him, then. I thought he was very straight."

"Were you lovers?"

She smiled. "That was the sixties, Lieutenant. Let's say we were good friends. I didn't mean straight in that sense, though of course he was that, too. I meant in the way he dealt with me. No crap, no bullshit. I trusted him. I'd have done anything for the man, but I was proved wrong in the end. In the end he tried to kill me as Nick Barton said he would."

"Who killed the people at the bank?"

"Charlie's people, I would think. He didn't want me to get my money. It makes me too independent."

"Well, the police are still very anxious to blame Andy Davidson, for that fool of a secretary says no one else came into the bank, but it wasn't Andy's gun. He had that with him, and there is another entrance. Anyone could have come in. The police have no real case. It's all circumstantial, but they're out to make trouble. Believe me, I know when someone powerful is pushing from the top, and what they can achieve. That's what's happening here. If they want Andy, they'll have him, guilty or not!"

"It's me they want, and when they know that you have talked with me, it will be you next."

"They won't dare touch a policeman," he said.

She laughed. "They think they are above the law," she said. "Be careful."

"I'll nail these bastards," he said.

"Yes, and then they'll get themselves a smart lawyer, and you'll end up wearing a cement waistcoat off the coast of the Bahamas."

"You read too many crime stories." He smiled. "You don't have much faith in me, do you?"

"Yes, Lieutenant, but you are a decent man, and the others will stop at nothing. It does give them an unfair advantage."

"You know, until they found Sebastian Ventura murdered in your apartment, you were the best kept secret of the century."

"And the irony of it is that they weren't keeping the secret from you, Lieutenant. They were keeping it from Jaime! If Jaime had found out, he'd have killed us both. He may have killed Sebastian. I don't know who was responsible for that."

"Jaime? He may have. We won't know if we can't find him."

"What? Have you lost Jaime? He went to the States."

"Yes, we know. He went to visit Charles Bellamy at the bank, and just disappeared."

"A man can't disappear in the middle of Miami, in a perfectly respectable bank," she said with a small laugh.

"No, not in a perfectly respectable one. I find it very suspicious that it should be that bank!"

That had been yesterday. Now Laura leaned forward suddenly, forgetting her talks with Stanley. They were coming out of the hospital. Stanley was with him, wheeling the stretcher, dressed as an orderly.

"Is he okay?"

Stanley shrugged. "I'm no doctor, but he's still breathing. Let's get going!"

"Where's Dr Curtis?"

"He'll meet us at the airport. Come on, quick!" They climbed into the back of the ambulance, which started immediately. She sat beside Andy, shocked at how ill he looked, but he opened one eye and winked.

"They haven't got us yet, the bastards," he croaked, "and they bloody well never will, with you around!"

The siren screeched above them, and they cut through the traffic as they wailed across town. Cointrain Airport is only seven kilometres from Geneva alongside the autoroute to Lausanne, which skirts the lake. It is tucked under the mountains that form the western border between Switzerland and France. The ambulance drove straight onto the tarmac, right under the tail of a medium sized two engine jet painted with the colours of the International Red Cross. As the flight plan stated that the plane was bound for Berne, there were no customs formalities. In two minutes they had boarded and the doors were closed.

"Red Cross Flight 110 to Geneva Tower. We have our emergency patient now on board. Are we cleared to taxi?"

"Tower to Red Cross 110. You are cleared to taxi to runway 9."

"We cannot leave without the doctor," Laura said. She looked at Andy. He seemed already dead to her.

"Red Cross 110 to Tower. We cannot taxi without the doctor on board."

"Tower to Red Cross110. Are you an emergency or not? We have recorded an emergency, and have cleared the runway accordingly. Please confirm."

"110 to Tower. Confirm emergency. Doctor now boarding. We are ready."

"Tower to 110, immediate clearance to taxi to runway 9. We are holding other traffic."

Harvey Curtis ran across the tarmac as the pilot lowered steps from the rear of the plane. He climbed on board, and the plane immediately moved towards the southern end of the runway as the steps drew back up into the plane behind him.

Harvey shook hands with Laura.

"It's not too good. They are very suspicious. They saw me leave the operating theatre, and wanted to know why. They'll be checking. We should get off immediately."

He moved over to sit beside Andy. The nurse took his blood pressure and shook her head. Dr Curtis gave him an injection. The plane stopped. Ahead of them were a Swissair 747 and a Lufthansa Boeing 727. They heard the huge roar from the engines of the jumbo as it began to roll down the runway, and their own plane swung into position behind the

Lufthansa jet. A minute passed and then the higher scream of the Lufthansa's jets. Their plane swung around again to face straight down the runway, facing north into the cold, grey light of the alpine sky, in a position for take-off. Another wait.

"Geneva Tower to Red Cross 110. You are cleared to roll."

"Thank you, Tower. We are rolling." As their pilot said the words, the twin jets on either side of the tail roared into screaming life, and the jet gathered speed down the long runway for take-off. Laura breathed a sigh of relief. They had escaped. She could hardly believe it. They were free and Andy was still alive.

The radio suddenly cracked into life. "Tower to Red Cross 110. We have emergency police request to abort. Abort take-off immediately. Immediate confirm. Abort take-off."

The plane continued to hurtle down the runway. Neither the pilot nor the co-pilot paid any attention to the message until, seconds later, the plane lifted off the tarmac.

"Red Cross 110 to Tower. We cannot abort. We have lifted off runway."

"Tower to 110. Swiss police demand you circle and land. We are holding all traffic while you circle."

The jet passed over the periphery of the airport, gaining height rapidly in a steep climb, but not yet more than five hundred metres off the ground. A rapid series of explosions rocked the jet, and flak appeared around them in the grey afternoon air.

"Jesus Christ, someone's shooting at us!" the pilot screamed. "Tower, are you there? This is a Red Cross emergency flight. Tell those bastards to stop shooting at us. What the fuck is this? Fucking Russia?"

"Tower to 110, we know nothing of shooting. Police say it is not them."

Again the plane rocked violently. It was hit by a rocket fired from below as it passed across a field beyond the northern end of the runway. The pilot pulled back on the stick and the Caravelle shot almost vertically into the air, the jet screaming with the strain of so steep a climb.

"110 to Tower. What the fuck is going on down there? We have received direct hit and are checking for damage. We have sick patient on board, possibly dying. We will not – repeat not – circle and land. Proceeding according to our flight plan to Berne. Advise police accordingly. We intend to file formal complaint."

"Tower to 110. Roger. You are cleared to ten thousand feet. Police advise that you will have a fighter escort to Berne. Look out for visual contact."

"Like bloody hell we will," the pilot said to himself, and to the tower, "Confirm climbing to ten thousand feet. Over and out."

He turned to the co-pilot. "Get Mrs Ellery up here," he ordered.

When she entered the cockpit, he said coldly, "I know we are being paid fifty thousand dollars for a few hours work, so my co-pilot and I both understand that what we are doing is illegal, but you said nothing about being shot down, madame. Fifty thousand is no good to us when we are dead."

"I did not know, but I tell you now that these people will stop at nothing."

"Not even shooting down a plane with innocent people on board?"

Laura gave a bitter laugh. "They know who is on board and do not consider us innocent," she said, "But even if they did, it would make no difference."

He looked at her, sitting so calmly in the damaged jet as

it shot upwards. "Are you not afraid, then?"

"Of course! Only a fool would not be afraid, but what good does it serve to show it?"

"If we keep this heading we'll have the whole Swiss Air Force on our tail, but we're not cleared for any other. There's always the risk of a collision. Do I have your instructions to change course?"

"Life is full of risks," Laura said. "Do what you must to get us out. I care only that this man on board is given a chance to live. If anyone on this flight is innocent, it is he!'" She stood up and returned to the passenger cabin.

The captain watched her with admiration. He had not been brought up to understand that women, in moments of crisis, could be quite as cool-headed as any man, and it constantly astonished him.

"We'll go straight up to thirty-five thousand feet," he said to the co-pilot.

"What about control?"

"Bugger control. They were happy to have us shot down. Keep your eyes open for other traffic."

They started to climb, in a wide arc over the city of Lausanne, and headed south east.

"There is a plane at two o'clock," the co-pilot said. "It's closing fast. Jesus! They're firing at us!"

The Swiss Air Force fighter jet was coming up from beneath them, across the lake, and a spray of bullets arced out from the guns of the fighter towards the Red Cross plane, ripping across the wing.

"Mon Dieu, they really do intend to stop us, even if they kill us all! It's completely mad!" the pilot exclaimed.

He pulled the jet into a tight steep climb, and hauled its nose around to the south so that, almost immediately, it entered a thick and heavy bank of clouds hanging over the Dents du Midi.

"We'll keep climbing," he said, "and stay in these clouds and hope there's nothing else in here with us! There's enough moisture to confuse their radar with any luck. Are we losing fuel?"

The co-pilot shook his head. "There's some damage to the wing, and maybe the landing gear. What was that all about?"

"God knows! Will we lose them?"

The co-pilot grinned. "How much did she say? Fifty grand?"

"And now another ten, for the current danger, the lady says."

"We'll lose them, just so long as we can clear the tops of these mountains in these clouds."

"Just keep going up until it's time to come down."

"Are they expecting us at Graufchen Airport? It's mainly used for drugs and contraband, and the military. It's a very short runway."

"They're expecting us. Everyone is being well paid, except the Air Force. Or maybe the Air Force most of all!"

They both laughed. "The Air Force won't follow us up here. They'll be too afraid of hitting a jumbo and making a scandal."

At twenty thousand feet they shot out of the clouds into a brilliant sunlit sky with the clouds spread beneath them like a fat white carpet, penetrated here and there by mountain peaks. They turned east towards the Tyrol. No one would be looking for them here, but they would never be able to land in this cloud.

"Maybe it will break," the co-pilot said philosophically,

Half an hour later, having overflown Graufchen, the pilot

turned west again, in scattered cloud. Weaving in low between the peaks of the Austrian Tyrol they dropped down onto the tiny strip, stopping just short of the end of the runway. An ambulance was waiting, and a black sedan. Laura gave a fat envelope to the pilot.

"What shall we do with the plane, madame?"

"Leave it and get away from here before they start asking why we have not landed in Berne. The owner will fly the plane out. He has been paid for that. No trace of it will ever be found."

"And the Red Cross?"

Laura laughed. "Don't worry about them. They never heard of this plane. We did a paint job on it. Look after yourselves!" She shook their hands. "And thanks! Sorry about the excitement!" She climbed into the ambulance.

The pilot shrugged. "We are sixty thousand dollars richer and still alive," he said.

The two men watched as the ambulance drove away and then got into the car.

CHAPTER TWENTY ONE

BENNINGTON PARK, N.Y.
JUNE 1979

THE SPLENDOUR OF THE wedding was almost, but not quite, marred by the representatives of the media, who swarmed around the gates of Bennington Park like flies around a carcass. Only those with the required engraved card were permitted to enter.

In an age bereft of heroes, the media beat the airwaves with platitudes enough to create an illusion of mystique. For one afternoon reality was dissolved, and princes wed in lily-padded rooms in castles high, assured of that perfect bliss that would elude lesser mortals in cocktail bars across the nation. A hundred years of genocide in the twentieth century had bred a touching belief in a happiness whose languorous content is the product of a sophistication denied to all but a very few. It is a world of illusions.

Not perhaps since the wedding of Grace Kelly in Monaco had the popular mind been so intrigued. This was a liaison between a dashing buccaneer from Florida, a veritable keeper at the gates of a modern Lyonnesse, and the beautiful, sad American whose star-crossed dark beauty seemed haunted by tragedies whose roots went back into the recesses of history which echoed to the tramping feet of Norman peasants following their duke to adventure and fortune on English shores.

Only the most arrogant of the gutter press dwelt on the unfortunate manner of the demise of Marcus de Trafford, while the glossies dealt more happily with the home-grown aristocracy of the bride, whose cousins lurked in every corner of the East Coast establishment. As her family was rooted firmly in the dark and aggressive soil of American democracy, it was generally agreed that the bride, while bringing no material contribution to this union, could hold her head quite as high as any bride in the land, fortified by the genealogy of those previous aristocratic unions of her youth, the wealth of her forebears, and the distinction of her cousins.

The setting left little to be desired to enhance the hysteria that such events generate in lands devoted to the concepts of freedom, equality and the pursuit of happiness. Bennington Hall stood on a high bluff overlooking the Hudson River, and its sweeping lawns, now occupied by five hundred guests, commanded broad views of New York State. The dollars that had built this faux-chateau were liberally stained with immigrant blood, but time and money had adequately cleansed those stains, and they could bear as close a scrutiny, now, as any in the land. The fortunes made by Crusaders and Norman conquerors were also stained with ancient blood that had, once upon a time, been that of the freshly dead. Old blood is more respectable than new money.

The same could not be said of the wealth, real or imagined, of the bridegroom that seemed to have arisen, fully fledged like a phoenix, from some mysterious Florida spring. Considerable speculation took place among the guests as to the possible source of Charles' prosperity. Only the beauty and prestige of his new wife, and the even greater, and far less scandal-scorched reputation of her aunt, Elizabeth Bennington, prevented such speculation reaching the height of vulgar comment, in spite of the blue-blooded background of the assembly.

The general consensus, as both Charles and Edwina had known it would be, was that the Bellamy fortune was sufficiently immense to be beyond criticism, and that he was fortunate to have so elegant a consort as Edwina on whom to lavish it. Therein lay the power of the popular fascination. A union of power and prestige in two persons, both handsome and popular, easily clouded the popular mind with the hysteria of unobtainable dreams.

The immense house, built in honey coloured sandstone in the style of Louis XIII, had witnessed seven generations of the Bennington family's purchase of suitable brides with their ill-gotten gains of nineteenth century plunder. Only rarely, however, could such gatherings have equalled the distinction of the guests assembled on the lawn this early summer afternoon. This was a union, like that of John Fitzgerald Kennedy and Jacqueline Bouvier, which might change the face of the modern world. There was an air of expectation. The guests were there not only to celebrate, but also to witness an historical event. They would speak of it when they were old, and the glamour was gone. They would tell their grandchildren that they had been there and watched this union take place.

Edwina wore a long Chanel dress of dark blue lace, chosen by her friend, Ines de la Frissange, the beautiful model at Chanel, and on her head a circlet of diamonds and sapphires which had been made for Princess Pauline Borghese, the legendary, licentious and greedy sister of Napoleon Bonaparte. The guests were gathered on the south lawn, and Edwina walked between them on the arm of her uncle, Ambassador William Bennington, to meet Charles at the altar of carnations and lilies erected at the end of the lawn.

"With this ring I thee wed, with my body I thee worship, and with all my worldly goods I thee endow."

At the last moment Edwina almost pulled back her hand before the ring could slip over her finger, overwhelmed suddenly by a feeling of panic as frantic as anything she had ever experienced in her life. Did she want this huge wealth and the burden of this power? Did she want this man, so handsome and seductive, whom she hardly knew, a murderer for whom she felt so dangerous an attraction? Where was he leading her, down this path scattered with such generous gifts, such splendid prestige, so much gold? But she did not pull back her hand, and the ring, which had arrived that morning from Cartier in New York, slid over her finger.

"I now pronounce you to be man and wife forever. Those whom God hath joined together, let no man put asunder," the clergyman intoned.

Charles bent and kissed her on the lips as a string quartet began softly to play the airs of Bach in the background. She returned the kiss and felt emotion flood her veins, but in the background of her mind, she also heard her dead mother's gin-soaked voice telling her that this adventure might well be the ruin of her, unlike her previous marriages which had led, instead, to the ruin of her husbands. It was difficult to see Charles Bellamy ruined, Edwina thought. If he were going down, he would take the world with him.

They signed the register, turned, and as the music of Bach flooded across the lawn, they walked between the serried rows of guests into the house, where the reception would take place in a huge suite of rooms which had held kings and presidents, which looked over the Hudson River and the green and rural pastures, marching all the way to the glittering ghettoes of New York in the distance.

Later Charles said, in his speech:

"It is not given to many of us to wed in the splendour of a fairytale castle, and I thank William and Elizabeth Bennington for the use of their palace for this occasion. Nor is it given to many husbands to find favour with a bride of such style and beauty as she who has chosen to risk her future with me today. I have given much thought, therefore, as to how I might distinguish Edwina, who has already been rewarded so liberally with life's gifts.

"Edwina knows, as few others do, of my concern that so few people are rich and free, or live in a country that is rich and free, as ours is. Too many in our world yearn without hope to eat, to think, to speak freely, indeed even to survive. All my life I have believed that these things must change, and I believe they will only change with the further education of women. Not necessarily in the manner in which we educate women in America, to be the equal of men, but in a manner which will make them powerful as themselves, to think and argue and rule as women in a world where, much to the constant surprise of men, at least one half of the inhabitants are female.

"Edwina agrees with me in many of these ideas, and she has her own reasons for understanding that our hypocrisy in these matters can wound deeply indeed. I do not wish, therefore, to give my wife any material possession today to remember me in the years to come, but instead to place a weapon in her hand with which, I hope, she will be able to set free the women of the world.

"From this afternoon she is President and sole trustee of the Edwina Carlingford Bellamy Trust for the education of women and children throughout the world. This trust is underwritten by a number of banking houses in Europe and America. It will permit her to begin to provide facilities for women and children everywhere and will, one day I hope, give us all a better and more peaceful world. I ask you to raise your glasses and wish for my wife, Edwina Bellamy, success in making this world a place which will be safer and less despoiled than that which we inherited and live in today."

"To Edwina Bellamy!"

Charles raised his glass and smiled. He toasted his wife

whom he had just made, although she was not yet aware of it, the richest and most powerful woman in the world. What he had not told the celebrating guests was the fact that the stolen and yet to be stolen billions of the Ventura family were now at her disposal. It would be the greatest single fortune the world had ever seen, and she could use it as she pleased. With it she could achieve his ambitions for him, salve his conscience, and satisfy those yearnings with which, as a young man, he had set out to India so many years ago believing that he could change the world. Now he would merely provide the resources to do so. Edwina would provide the genius.

CHAPTER TWENTY TWO

MIAMI, FLORIDA
JULY 1979

AT FIRST JAIME HAD not been unduly concerned at being locked into the guest suite at the bank. He was furious, but the whole thing seemed so impossibly ludicrous that he regarded it as nothing more than an elaborate joke, albeit one that he would never be able to forgive. There were plenty of books, television, and good food arriving in the little food elevator. Jaime knew that in a day or so, Charles would open the door, and tell him to forget the whole thing. Not that he would do so, of course. There would be neither forgetting nor forgiving. Charles Bellamy would have to go. The man was clearly mad.

Jaime would remove his funds from Charlie's bank as soon as he could, but this would not be quite so easy as he wished. The amounts were now so huge, and there were many banks, even perhaps most banks, Jaime conceded to himself, which might not wish to deal in money so suspect. However, there would be some who would be prepared to do business with him. Enough. There was always someone, somewhere, who would do these things. The Nazis had found perfectly respectable bankers. So would he.

For many hours he worked on his plans. He would take over his own distribution again. They had allowed themselves to get much too dependent on Charles and his organization. He realized now how far he had lost control. He must never allow that to happen again. He seethed with fury to think how arrogant Charles had become, how much in control of their vast wealth. Revenge, or at least the planning of revenge, is sweet, but slowly he began to realize that Charles had meant what he said. There would be no release until he signed the papers.

He could not believe that he, Jaime Ventura y Cortez, descended from conquistadors and one of the richest and most notorious men in South America, feared in Medellin and in Bogotá, feared by the Colombian Government itself, could be locked up here like a common criminal, in a bank that, after all, he partially owned.

No one must ever find out about this, or his prestige would be gone forever. He would be a laughing stock. Meanwhile, on the television, he followed the almost royal progress of the newlyweds through their much feted honeymoon tour in London, Madrid, Paris and the South of France, being entertained by presidents and kings as if they were rulers of their own country.

News began to be leaked of the Edwina Carlingford Bellamy Foundation, and its plans to acquire properties and to establish educational plans that were revolutionary in their scope. Jaime planned their downfall every day. It sustained him. But by July, after he had been incarcerated for almost three months, he finally began to accept that if he did not sign the papers, he would spend his life in this apartment.

So why not sign? he reasoned eventually.

Once away, he could employ the best lawyers and the best assassins. He could bribe the highest in the land with sums so astronomical that not even honest men could refuse. Until he was out he could do nothing. He wrote a letter to Charles and put it in the little elevator that brought up his food. The next day the house phone on his desk rang. The sound, so unfamiliar, so unexpected, made his heart pound.

"Well, Jaime?" Charles asked.

"I am going crazy enough to sign your papers," he said. "Here are my terms. I go from here to the airport, and I sign on board the plane, after I am through customs and immigration. The plane is Colombian territory. I want Jesus to be with me. Otherwise I do not trust you to permit me to leave when I have signed all that stuff over to you. I want my own lawyers from Bogotá on the plane. I want them to witness that I sign under duress."

"Very sensible," Charles said. "I would do the same. Trust no one, least of all myself. I will make all the arrangements."

Charles was pleased. He had thought it might take longer to break Jaime, to get him to see that he had no alternative, and the longer he was locked up, the more dangerous speculation there might be as to his whereabouts. Already there were many who believed that he had disappeared, been murdered, perhaps, by some rival gang and turned into shark food. Jesus was already pressing to approach the Probate Court for an order to investigate and administer his assets, although such a move was, of course, hopelessly premature. The only thing stopping Jesus at the moment was his desire to avoid the curiosity of the tax authorities and the police.

And worse, Senator Brailes had informed Charles that Lieutenant Jerkovitz and that damned reporter, Peter Francis, were working together on a document about his activities, although no support was being given from the Police Department. And Laura could still not be found. He had failed to bring their plane down, even with the help of the Swiss Air Force, and although it had subsequently allegedly disappeared in the Alps, no wreckage had been found. No bodies. He began to feel that, at the moment of his greatest triumph, when even the United Nations was beginning to pay attention to Edwina's plans for her Foundation, Stanley Jerkovitz and his associates would be able to compromise him. Peter Francis had even had the impertinence to ask him for an interview. He'd had to grant it, and the man had insinuated that his vast wealth was based on something less than honest practices. Charles didn't believe he would have dared such a comment unless he had collected some concrete evidence from somewhere. The man was becoming a serious nuisance.

Now Charles put a call through to Jesus, and while he waited, he stood and watched his favourite view over the Caribbean, imagining his planes winging those empty skies, bringing him the fortune which was protected by the highest authorities in the land.

"Jesus? This is Charles. I have found Jaime!"

"Jaime? You've found Jaime?"

Jesus was not pleased. He had begun to believe his brother dead, and to plan the right moment to claim the mantle of power, now that Sebastian, too, was gone. Only Jorge, stuck back at the Finca in Medellin, was left, and he posed no threat.

"Where the hell has he been?"

"He has been in a retreat. Meditating. He wants you to return to Bogotá with him."

"Meditating? There is something very strange about all of this, Bellamy," Jesus said. "I don't like it at all."

"Nor do I, my dear Jesus. I am afraid that Mother Church may have her claws into him, and perhaps he is considering asking the Church for absolution – in return for a very large gift. You need to talk with him!"

Jesus was horrified. "My God, Charles, we can't have that. Do you think he might talk to the press, or even worse, the authorities?"

"I don't know, Jesus, but I am arranging for him to return to Bogotá tomorrow evening, on the regular flight. He may be in a very unstable frame of mind, and we can't run any risk that would compromise your reputation – or mine. We all wish to avoid any form of scandal, don't we?"

"Do we fucking ever!" Jesus thought with horror what his wife might have to say if her own impregnable position were threatened by scandal.

The whole thing with Sebastian had been bad enough, being found dead in that woman's apartment in Bogotá. All the media sniffing around! That bloody Jerkovitz and his mate, Peter Francis, cooking up stories without a single element of truth in them.

"In retreat you say, Charles? *Madre de Dios!* The Church has already had a fortune from us. Not another penny!"

"There's a Colombian Airlines flight from Miami to Bogotá tomorrow evening at nine o'clock. Can you be ready?"

"Sure!"

"I've prepared some transfers and a power of attorney so that I shall be able to act quickly to protect your interests and mine. He has agreed to sign them at the airport before the plane leaves. Leave everything to me. Just be there. You will be alone?"

Jesus laughed sourly. "You must be joking! I don't even get to crap alone these days. There will be three of us. Me and my two heavies."

"Okay. Jerkovitz will be the only problem. If he gets wind of it ..."

"That fucking Jerkovitz. He seems to know far too much these days. He seems to know the way we think."

"Well, that would not be difficult, even for Jerkovitz," Bellamy said.

"And what kind of a smart-ass remark is that? Just because you had lunch with the Queen in London, don't think you can patronize me. We can buy and sell you twenty times over, Bellamy, just remember that!"

"I think of it all the time, Jesus. It is one of the motivating forces of my life. I also remember that Sebastian had a girl in Bogotá who has disappeared, and I strongly suspect that a lot of Jerkovitz's information comes from that source. Have you discovered anything?"

"We can't find her. If she's alive, then someone who knows his way around must be helping her. It's as much your fault as mine. You couldn't even stop her getting her money from a bank that you own. If she didn't have those funds we'd have caught her long ago."

Charles sighed. "I know, Jesus, I know. The problem is always an honest man. Find me an honest man, and I'll find you some trouble."

"Well, we got rid of that honest man at your bank in Geneva for you."

"Yes, my friend, but too late! Too late!"

"Your friends couldn't even bring the plane down with the help of the Air Force, and that must have cost a pretty penny."

"A pretty penny indeed, but not as many pretty pennies as it will cost if Laura has been talking with that policeman and his reporter friend. Leave that to me. Just get on that plane tomorrow. I'll make the necessary reservations."

"You'll be lucky. That flight is always full."

"We do own the airline, Jesus," Charles reminded him.

He rang off. Jesus was smart but because his wife had been so successful in creating an ambience of cultural and social power around him he had an inflated idea of his own charm and intelligence. A fatal flaw in a business where a cool assessment of reality was the basic necessity for success, Charles thought.

He lifted the receiver and dialled. "Lieutenant Jerkovitz? This is Charles Bellamy. You've shown a considerable interest in the activities of the Ventura boys recently. Would you appreciate a tip from me?"

"I would appreciate anything from you, Mr Bellamy. Have you found Jaime Ventura?"

"As a matter of fact I have. He has been in a retreat."

"A religious retreat? With monks?" He laughed coarsely. "I find that difficult to believe."

"We are all more complex than you give us credit for, perhaps. I am ringing to tell you that he will be on the Colombian Airlines flight from Miami to Bogotá tomorrow. It might be very useful to you and your friend Peter Francis to be on that same flight. I'm sure that you could find out some very interesting information."

"Thanks Bellamy. And to what do I owe this sudden interest in my affairs?"

"I am in support of truth and justice, my friend; it's a pity that you have never understood that!"

"And the American way, too, I suppose?"

Charles laughed. "Of course. That is what has allowed me to prosper over the years," he said. He hung up. He dialled Colombian Airlines.

"Carlos Sanchez, please ... Carlos? This is Charles Bellamy."

"Charles, this is a privilege to hear your voice. You must want a big favour."

"Your flight to Bogotá tomorrow?"

"We have two. One leaves at two in the afternoon, and the other at nine in the evening."

"That one. I want the whole first class."

"That's a 747. We have twenty first class seats. Sixteen are booked. I can give you four. How about that?"

"How about ratshit, Carlos? I want the whole compartment, or are you deaf this afternoon? The Venturas are travelling, with guards and their lawyers, and I am guaranteeing their safety. No one else is to be in the compartment. Put the other passengers on another flight, put them in business, give them a free hotel suite, kiss their arses if you have to, but I don't want to see another face in that compartment tomorrow evening when I go on board. Is that clear?"

"You are going, too?"

"Not bloody likely! I'm farewelling!"

"Okay, Charles, but you'll owe me. That flight is almost full. It's the football in Bogotá!"

"Fuck the football, Carlos. This is real life we're talking about now. What's the flight number?"

"Four six eight."

"Thanks, and remember, no press, no VIP treatment. Total silence. Absolute discretion. Is that clearly understood? Total!"

He rang off and dialled a number on his direct private line.

"Airport Maintenance? David Mathieson, please ... Davie? I want my special parcel on Colombian Airlines 468, leaving nine o'clock tomorrow evening. You can collect your twenty thousand the following morning from teller five, here at the bank. If you fail, you're dead."

"Don't sweat it, Charlie. It's as good as done."

Bellamy's voice was cold as a knife. "And don't ever call me Charlie."

"Sorry, sir. I forgot it isn't the old times."

"The old times were finished a long time ago, Davie. Just get the job done."

"Yes, sir, Mr Bellamy, sir! It's as good as done."

Charles replaced the receiver. For a moment he had allowed himself to be disconcerted. It was imperative never to lose control, to be afraid. That's when mistakes were made. Charles loathed making arrangements himself. He eased his conscience by delegating life's more disagreeable tasks, but occasionally it was imperative that no one but himself knew what orders had been given. No one at all.

The following evening Charles boarded the Colombian Airlines jet ahead of all the passengers. He waited in first class with his lawyer. At seven-thirty Jaime came on board, accompanied by three of the bank's security officers, and his own lawyers, who had arrived from Bogotá that morning. He did not look good. His clothes hung shabbily on his muscular body and his swarthy skin was pallid, his hair long and unkempt. He did not offer Charles any greeting. Charles produced the folio of papers and handed them to Ventura.

"You've seen copies of these to brood over," he said shortly. "This is Stephen Black, my lawyer. He is senior partner at Black, Cottismore and Davies. He will witness the signatures."

"You understand what you are signing, Mr Ventura? These papers transfer your assets outside Colombia to the bank until further notice, with all your voting rights. There is a personal power of attorney to Mr Bellamy."

"I understand fully, Mr Black. And how much are you being paid to participate in this deceit?"

Mr Black appeared offended that any kind of unprofessional conduct should be imputed to him.

"What deceit can there be if you sign of your own free

will?" he asked stiffly. "I am advised that these transfers are being made to protect you against any possibility of ..." he coughed discreetly, "of future prosecution in the United States and elsewhere, which could involve sequestration of assets. Is that not so?"

"Of course, it's so," Charles interrupted. "We have agreed all this. The bank will hold the assets in trust until the present situation is resolved. Come on now, Jaime, sign up, and we can leave the plane and let it take off on time."

"Where is Jesus?"

"In the lounge. He will board when we leave."

"You will not get away with this, Bellamy," Jaime said, but his voice was tired and he was too determined to get home to argue the matter further. He would work out the solution when he was back on his own territory, at the Finca. He signed the papers and his signature was witnessed by Mr Black, whose reputation was beyond dispute, and by the man from Bogotá, his own lawyer. When they were all signed, Charles prepared to leave immediately, taking the documents with him.

"That wasn't very intelligent, making a scene in front of Stephen Black," Charles said to him.

Jaime looked at him with deadly eyes. "You have just robbed me of the profits of ten years' work. I will get it back."

Charles smiled at him coldly. "It is going to help pay for my wife's work to make a better world."

"You are crazy as a cat, Bellamy. A better world?" He laughed bitterly. "You're kidding yourself."

"You should be happy to contribute to it, Jaime. Both of us have plenty left for anything we could possibly want for ourselves."

"Fuck you, Charles. I'm sorry we ever met you."

"You would not have made all this without me," Charles said. " You would have nothing but peanuts to give away. Now here is your brother Jesus. My chaps will stay at the door until the plane leaves, so do not attempt anything foolish. Hasta la vista, Jaime! Oh, and your friend Jerkovitz is on board. Talk to him if you want. I suspect that Laura has already told him plenty!"

"That bitch!"

Charles went downstairs to the exit and climbed into his car. "To the bank," he said wearily to the driver. He wished that Edwina were with him, but she had gone to India. He missed her more than he would have thought possible. He was now rich enough to outdo many a thriving national economy. Throughout history, governments had fought to gain such wealth, had called men to arms and asked them to lay down their lives to protect it.

Now that he commanded such assets, had not he, too, the right to demand such sacrifices? Was he, too, not a monarch of a kind with a right to demand fealty in the protection of his realm? What greater right than he, he thought, had those governments who called their citizens to arms and sent them to their death?

But the feeling of triumph he had anticipated was sadly lacking. Perhaps kings felt like this as they stood at the windows of their palaces, and watched a nation's youth march off to war, bedecked with flowers, to die alone in distant fields in the mistaken belief that, thus, men might remain free. Was that not what he intended to achieve with all this money? A better, freer world? He would go up to his office and spend the night looking out at the sea. The view over the sea always made him feel better.

Earlier that day, when Stanley Jerkovitz had finished talking with Charles Bellamy on the telephone, he went around to the precinct station to talk with his boss, Captain Franco Martinez. He took with him the report he had been preparing on Charles Bellamy.

"Read it, Franco. It'll tell you everything you need to know about this bastard." He threw the report onto Franco's desk.

Franco tapped the report with his horny forefinger. "You want to know what I think? I think that if this goes any further than my desk, you're a dead man, Stanley."

"Come on, Franco, whadda we doing? Wanking? We arrest people who don't count for shit. We throw into gaol a whole lot of little pipsqueaks pushing a few ounces of dope on the street corner, and all the big guns go free."

"Maybe," Franco said, "but you can't prove it. Where's Wellington? Will he give evidence? Where's Tessier? Will she? I doubt it! Where's Jaime Ventura? Will he come here and give evidence? No!"

"Ventura will be on the plane to Colombia tonight, and so will I!"

"Drop it, Stan!"

"Jesus, Franco, I do a report which involves some of the biggest names in the country, and you won't send it up the line."

"I like you, Stan. I don't want to see you dead! Whaddya have here? Names! Fuck me, Stan, you've got enough names here to blow the whole of fucking Washington apart! This is enough to start World War III, but you don't have proof!"

"At least it would alert them that something stinks!"

"They know something stinks, Stan, and you know what it mostly is? Mostly it's themselves they smell, so it all smells pretty sweet to them. Whaddya think they're going to say? Now here's a nice little report from some little turd down in Miami, and it's all true, so we'll just give up our consultancy fees, and we'll resign our jobs and get rid of our houses and our girl friends and our cars and our boats, and go off to gaol for a few years because that'll make the world a better place? Jesus, Stan, it's too hot to handle. Burn it! Take it home and put it in the incinerator. Fuck, Stan, you're a cop for twenty years and you bring me this?"

"So what's the point, Franco? The kids out there go on shooting up, and stealing, and bashing up old ladies for small change, and beating up shopkeepers, and we can't ever touch those who are behind it because they're too rich and too successful and too prominent? So we spend the rest of our lives catching the little guys, not one of whom matters one grain of shit, the poor little buggers!"

Franco looked at him sadly. "Yes, Stanley, I guess that's what I'm telling you, and you know it, and you've always known it. So what's bugging you now?"

"I tell you what's bugging me now. I've seen these bastards. I know their self-satisfied, well-fed, hypocritical faces. I've seen their wives and their houses, and they don't just have a little bit more than the rest of us. They have it all! If someone doesn't have the guts to do something about it soon, the world will be owned by monsters like these people, who have the moral responsibility of a neurotic slug. I can't go to bed at night because I know that Harry Wellington will eventually end up down a disused mine shaft. Laura Tessier would already be dead in a hotel in Geneva if it weren't for Andy Davidson. I think of them all, and I can't sleep anymore."

Franco said gently, "Stan, take the report home and take a Mogadon. We all feel like this sometimes. It's an occupational hazard."

"No, Franco, not this time. This time I'm going to Bogotá and I'm getting more information and I'm sending in that report."

"Well, while you're in the Miami Police Force, it must go

through me and if you send it to me again, it'll end up in the trash can."

"In that case, I resign!" Stanley took his badge off his coat and placed it on the desk, and picked up the report. Franco looked sadly at the badge lying on his desk.

"Don't do it, Stan. Don't do this to yourself. It won't do any good. Not for you. Not for nobody."

"It'll do me good," he said, "and all the rest is ratshit!"

He walked out and closed the door behind him. He rang Peter Francis.

"You coming to Bogotá on the plane tonight, then?"

"Stan, I'd love to, but I can't. I've a breaking story in Washington, and I need the dough! Shit, man, since I lost my job on the paper, I've been scratching for a meal."

"It'll all be worthwhile in the end, you'll see. In the end, you'll get a Pulitzer for this."

"In the end I'll probably die of starvation. You go and then we'll get together when you come back and see what we can do. If you've got the goods, I'll print it."

"Okay, but I want to tell you, I've done a report. The police won't use it. I want to send it to you, just a copy for your records."

"OK, Stan, send the report. And have a good trip. I hope you get all the stuff you need."

Stanley rang off. He walked down the road to the post office and sent a copy of his report to Peter. He kept a copy for himself.

※ ※ ※ ※ ※ ※

Charles Bellamy was still in his office the next morning when his secretary brought him the morning papers.

COLOMBIAN AIRLINES JUMBO HITS MOUNTAINSIDE REPORTS INDICATE NO SURVIVORS

Early reports indicate that there are no survivors among the four hundred and twelve passengers and crew of Colombian Airlines Flight 468 from Miami to Bogotá, which slammed into the side of a mountain seventy miles north of Bogotá on its approach to land. There had been no indication of any problems. The pilot had, moments before, contacted the tower for landing instructions.

The passenger list has not yet been released, but it is understood that many of the passengers are from the Florida area, and were travelling to Bogotá for Saturday's big football match. There is a rumour that members of the notorious Ventura family were on board, and police and investigators say that sabotage cannot be ruled out at this stage. Miami police report that a senior member of the local Drug Enforcement Squad, Lieutenant Stanley Jerkovitz, was also on board the plane.

Charles read the report again, and then he telephoned Nick.

"Nick? You've seen the news? A man named David Mathieson will come to Teller 5 today to collect twenty thousand dollars in cash. See personally to every detail of that transaction, will you? Every single detail, please. And personally!"

It was done. He sat down in his chair. He felt very old. At last he had what he had wanted since he had landed penniless in America – the power of unlimited wealth. He wondered, for just a moment, if it was all worthwhile. The weight of the stones beneath his ribs seemed almost unbearable this morning. Almost, but not quite.

PART THREE

Rich Rewards
1980 – 1984

CHAPTER ONE

INNSBRUCK AND NEW DELHI
JUNE 1980–FEBRUARY 1982

Laura still wondered how Andy had survived. She knew now that he must be tougher than he looked, but it still seemed like a miracle. Their plane had manoeuvred so violently to avoid the gunfire at the airport that the stretcher had become dislodged. He had begun to haemorrhage as he was thrown from side to side in the compartment. By the time they had landed at Graufchen, Andy was in a coma in spite of the transfusions they had given him.

They took him immediately to the Clinic Franz Joseph on the outskirts of Innsbruck, where Laura sat with him for seven days, willing him to live, forcing strength into him from her own body. At the end of seven days, he opened his eyes and she knew that she had saved both their lives.

He winked at her.

An undutiful and skeptical Catholic, Laura thanked the God in which she had such an unreliable belief, but she avoided making any promises to Him. She had made that mistake too many times before, and had no wish to be further compromised.

"So we made it!" he said. "You are one smart lady!"

Then he slept. Laura went to her room and wept. It was the nicest compliment she believed she had ever received.

The Tyrol province of Austria is a mountain land lost in time. It seems lost in some kinder and more picturesque era that has no relation to the violence of the twentieth century. Innsbruck is the capital. It was once the favourite resort of the Emperor Franz Josef, when people danced to Strauss waltzes and gay meant that you were having fun. Somehow the streets and houses, the flower-filled window boxes and the imperial vistas still preserved an aura of peace and plenty, of kindness and security, and a belief that violence had been foregone in favour of more civilized pursuits. Yet the beautiful city was haunted, too, by today's knowledge that the dream was doomed.

With the snow-covered mountains towering over it, and the air crisp and cool, the town resonated with the ghost of that enormous hope of a better world with which the twentieth century had begun after one hundred years of the Pax Britannica. A faded imperial dream that would end disastrously. Here, surrounded by the mountain pastures of Austria, and by fields filled with edelweiss and grazing cows, and the laughter of young men and women, Andy had gradually come back to life. It was not an easy journey.

One lung had been destroyed and removed. The shoulder and rib cage had been extensively damaged by the dum dum bullet of his assassin and had been extensively repaired with transplants. The blood loss had been severe, the trauma immense, and the patient was hardly filled with an overwhelming desire to live. But live he did, in spite of that.

Harvey Curtis stayed with them for six weeks. He supervised the operations when it was decided to remove the damaged lung and undertake cosmetic surgery. He prevented Laura from dying of exhaustion.

"There's no point in his recovering only to find that you have died beside his bed," he said. Every morning he sat with Andy while Laura rested. Andy continued to breathe in her absence, because Harvey could not have borne the responsibility of telling her that he had died while she slept. This woman, Harvey knew, had willed him not only to live, but also to want to live, a much greater and more complex task. It was a miracle.

After eight weeks, they moved him to the apartment that Laura had rented. By the beginning of September, he was well enough for walks along the mountain paths. Through the winter he skied a little, on the lower slopes, and by spring of 1980 he had decided that he would like to remain in this world a little longer.

This idyll might have lasted forever, but in June, Peter Francis called from Vienna. Harvey Curtis had returned to the States, where he was less likely to be arrested than in Switzerland, and no one else knew this number except the hospital. Laura was surprised and suspicious.

"Jerkovitz told me where you were going, and what names you are using, so I called the hospital," he said. "If I can find you so easily, anyone can," he said.

"No one else knows what name we use," Laura said cautiously.

"They are very powerful, Laura. Omniscient. I'd be very careful if I were you. You knew I wasn't on the plane?"

"What plane?"

"You don't know about the plane?"

"We don't know about anything up here. All I think about is keeping Andy well and happy," she said.

"Last year, a Colombian Airlines jumbo hit a mountain near Bogotá. It was not an accident."

"No? I wonder why I am not surprised to hear that! Who was on it?"

"Aside from four hundred and twelve innocent soccer

fans and other assorted travellers and staff, the whole first class was occupied by just eight people. Jaime and Jesus Ventura, their lawyers and their bodyguards. In the tourist class was Stanley Jerkovitz."

"No! Not poor Stanley? So they killed him, too?" She stood looking out the window of the chalet at the serene and tranquil alpine countryside. It seemed impossible in this idyllic countryside that evil could be taking place anywhere, but she knew that Austria knew as much about human catastrophe as anywhere. "A whole planeload of people," she said sadly to herself. Now she knew for certain that Charles would stop at nothing, that he was totally consumed by his ambition and that he had become evil. "Well, I guess I'm responsible for that! Everyone who helps me dies, it seems."

"He was a policeman, Laura. He knew what he was doing, and the risks he was taking," Peter said. "I'm in Vienna. Can I come and see you?"

"Does anyone know you're here?"

She was frightened by the idea of a visitor, as if his presence in the house would reveal its location to others, would bring the world to their doorstep. She only knew this man, other than by reputation, as a colleague of Stanley's. She did not know if she could trust him, but since he had the address anyway she did not suppose that a visit could do more harm than might already have been done.

"No, I've told no one. Even I am learning. Is Andy Davidson still alive?"

"So far we are both still alive. How much do you know?"

"I have all Stan's notebooks and I have his report. He mailed it to me before he went on that plane."

"Aaah! Then you know it all. If you want to start a crusade, don't come. We are too tired and I, for one, am too afraid."

"No crusade, but the truth if I can find it."

"You can't print it," Laura said.

"No, not now, but it may be useful some day, in saving all our lives."

"Or it may kill us."

"Laura, there were more than four hundred people on that plane. Don't you think you owe them something?"

"Yes, Peter, I do. But tell me, will they be better off now, if Andy and I, and you, are also dead?"

"You know that the Swiss police have dropped all charges against Andy? They understand that he is a hero and they're real embarrassed about that Air Force shooting. Someone paid plenty for that!"

"Well," Laura said, "we can all take an educated guess who that was, can't we?"

"It wasn't the Swiss police, anyway," Peter said. "They still had their noses glued to the window of the operating theatre."

She laughed sadly. "I'm not surprised. Stanley said they would."

Since he had received the news of Stanley's death, and the package of information containing his report, Peter had worked quietly at home, gathering information on Charles Bellamy and all of his interests. He had no wife and no family and he lost interest in going to bars and picking up one-night stands on the nights when he had once needed the human comfort of another body close to his own. The pursuit of vindication for Stanley's death became for him an all-consuming cause, and the small legacy he had received from Stanley, including the man's life insurance, enabled him to live while he researched. It was a lonely life, but he was obsessed, and an obsession is always enough to keep loneliness at bay, at least for a while.

He had moved to a larger apartment with better security and he kept all his files and information at home, where no one could access any of it, and made sure that the security was excellent. Stanley's death had shocked him badly, not only because he could well have been on the plane, but because he understood that Charles had wanted him to be and had expected that he would be. He felt, because of all these things, that he owed Stanley a debt that could only be repaid by the continuation of his investigations.

Peter arrived on the afternoon train from Vienna the following day. He was a pleasant, nondescript, untidy fellow who, Laura thought, did not resemble a hero. Rather to her surprise, he and Andy liked one another. Laura was concerned. She did not want Andy drawn back into world affairs. He looked fine again. Thinner, a little older, a bit drawn, but well. Only Laura knew how fine was the line between his health and a breakdown, and she nurtured him every day.

"There was a bomb on that plane?" Andy asked. "How do you know?"

"I have the reports from the police. They know that Stan and I were working together on this, and they feel badly about it all. If they hadn't told Stan to bugger off, he may well still be alive today. I'd have been on the plane with him, but at the last minute I couldn't go." He stopped. "Bellamy rang and gave us the tip that the Ventura brothers were on board, and we could get a good story," he said slowly. "He suggested that we go along for the ride."

"So are you going to do anything about this?" Laura asked. She read all the material he had brought, both his own research and the report that Stan had mailed to him before he went on the fated plane. "You could get a Pulitzer."

Peter laughed sadly. "That's what Stanley said, but it would come with a bullet in the head, I think. I'm not quite ready for that," he said. "Laura, you know better than anyone that these people will stop at nothing. Stan is dead, and so now are Jaime and Jesus Ventura. Sebastian, too, as you know. Only Jorge is left, hiding out in Medellin, and you are our only witness, and their biggest worry! I am saving it all up for later. There will come a time, one day, when we can use it to better advantage. Now, it would simply mean a death warrant for us all." He turned to Andy. "As it is, you're lucky to be alive."

Laura laughed. "He reads, he sleeps, he makes love. He drinks the local beer."

"What more can one ask? It sounds like a good life to me."

"It's good," Andy agreed, "but it's not enough. What kind of a world do we live in when scum like this can get away with murder? You know, Peter, my old Dad is a very patient man, and he's put up with a lot of shit from me since Vietnam, but one day he hopes I'll go back to Atlanta and do something worthwhile, and maybe one day I will. I can't run away forever."

Laura looked at him with huge, sad eyes.

"Why not?" she asked. "I like running away. I'd make every mistake all over again, just to have had these few months here with you. I wish that it could last forever."

He grinned. "Well, why not? Did you ever read any Somerset Maugham?"

She shook her head. "I don't know. *Rain*? *Cider with Rosie*?"

"I think that was Laurie Lee, but old Maugham was a great storyteller, you know, and he said every good story must end either with a marriage or a death. Since we cheated death, it looks like it'll have to be a marriage. Peter here can be a witness."

Laura laughed rather shakily. "God, Andy, you don't want a girl like me. I'm nothing but trouble!"

"You mean to tell me that there's another kind of girl?"

"You are fooling me. You'd better be careful or I might take you seriously," she said, shaking her head.

"Not at all. This is only the second time I've proposed. It's not something I do lightly, I can assure you."

"With my past," she said sadly, "I don't think I'd make the ideal wife for a banker."

"How about a politician?"

"Even worse."

"Don't you think," he said seriously, "that I am the best judge of that? Are you saying you don't love me?"

"Of course I love you, you idiot. I never intended that you should get away from this chalet, even if I had to chain you to the bedpost."

"And I love you," he said. "Before you picked me up in the casino ... "

"You picked me up!"

"Don't interrupt! Before you picked me up at the casino, I was a good-for-nothing neurotic. Now, after just a few murders, one near plane wreck, and hiding for our lives for several months, I am finally a good-for-something neurotic. That has to be an improvement, don't you think? And it's all due to you."

She burst into tears. Andy looked across at Peter. "I think that means yes," he said. "Don't you?"

"It's been my experience that when they cry, you've won," Peter agreed dryly.

"Yes," she sniffled, "but ..."

"There are no buts," he said firmly. "Do you realize that you are the most beautiful, gutsy, intelligent and sexy lady that I have ever met? Did you think that I would ever let you get away? Whatever you've done, it's made you what you are.

You will be a very refreshing breeze in the banking community."

"And what's this about politics?"

"It's just a thought," he said. "If no one decent ever gives it a shot, we get what we deserve, and the Charles Bellamys of this world continue to prosper."

Peter coughed. "Before you two get completely carried away," he said, "I came here with a proposition I'd like you both at least to consider. It would only take a year, eighteen months at the most."

"A year!" Laura exclaimed.

"You could be together," he said. "Have you heard what Edwina Bellamy is doing with that Foundation of hers?"

Laura shook her head. "I told you, we've heard nothing."

"They've given up trying to persuade the men in India to have vasectomies, and she is now going to educate the women there."

"It's about time someone thought of that, if she's rich enough," Laura said.

"Oh, she's rich enough, all right. I've been trying to follow the money trail, but that's not easy since I lost my job and my credentials as a journalist, but I suspect she has a pile of the Ventura cash at her disposal. Typical of Bellamy that he wants to change the world with someone else's money."

"Change the world? Is that what he's still saying?" she laughed.

Peter grinned at her. "That's what he's saying now."

"But that's what he's always said. My God, how that brings it all back to me! You know, years ago, when we were all young together, that's what Charlie used to say he wanted to do. He was going to change the world. I was going to be famous, and Nick wanted to be a free man. I remember we laughed and told him he would be the only one who'd fail.

How strange life is."

"I want you to go to New Delhi and work for Edwina Bellamy," Peter said flatly.

"Hell, Peter, she wouldn't have me," Laura said.

"She won't know who you are," he said. "You will use the same names you are using here – Jack and Anne Lacey. I have a friend who can arrange it. I think you owe it to Stanley," he said. "He helped to save you."

"No, it's asking too much." Laura was angry. "It's too dangerous, and I'm finished with spying. Look where it got me."

"Very rich," Peter said caustically.

"You really are a bastard," she said. "Will I never be free of this?"

Andy interrupted. "Never," he said. "It's built into your future, like all of our pasts. I think you ought to do it. I think we ought to do it together."

"Oh, Andy, you're not ready. You're not strong enough."

"I'm strong enough," he said. "I'm tired of sitting here in this paradise, doing nothing, while the world is run by shits! And it will be a stepping-stone back to the world, Laura. Let's pay our debts and then perhaps we can really be free." He turned to Peter.

"What do you have in mind?"

"Edwina has set up her headquarters in the old Imperial Hotel in Delhi. She needs a top grade assistant to work for her. Laura, you could find out what the hell she's doing. Is it clean, or is it more dirty work? Is it just opening up markets for Bellamy Corporation and their filthy drugs? I think we ought to know."

"Can't the police do it?"

"No. The Bellamys are too powerful."

"So I am to spy again?" She looked at them both rather sadly.

"Let's look on the good side of it," Peter said cheerfully. "At least you won't have to sleep with her. She has, I believe, an established reputation for men."

Andy laughed. "Laura will have me there for that," he said.

"Well, when you two guys have finished carving up my future, I think I might like the idea of working for a woman who believes in women," Laura said tartly.

"I think we ought to do it," Andy said again.

"And we've fixed a little job at Barclays International in New Delhi for Andy, too," he added sweetly. "Just for verisimilitude."

"All that information I gave Stan Jerkovitz. Has it done any good at all?" Laura asked.

Peter shook his head. "None, so far. The police would not handle his report. They wouldn't touch it! There are too many people getting paid, and no one wants to shit in their own pants. Plenty of arrests, of course, but only small guys and they know nothing except their orders. One day I'll do a report and try to get it to someone honest. It killed Stan Jerkovitz and if I did it now, I'd be dead in five minutes. That would be pretty pointless."

Andy said, "Okay, we know that Bellamy is tied in with the Ventura interests still, but bankers will bank for anyone. That may be all he does. What else can we prove?"

"Why not go to India and find out," Peter said. "You ought to get out of here, anyway. You've been here too long, and if they're still looking for you, they'll find you here without too much trouble, just as I did."

"You knew what name to look for. Besides, don't they think we all went down with the plane? They never discovered what happened to it, did they?"

"Maybe the police swallowed that, but remember they

never found any wreckage. I doubt that Charles would be so naive. You know him better than any of us, Laura. What do you think?"

She laughed rather sadly. "I used to know him, once. Not any more. I think the man I once knew has disappeared."

"Well, whatever you do decide, I don't think it's safe here any more. You must go somewhere else, and quickly."

Laura looked at him. "This is a lonely kind of life, this crusade, Peter. Are you married?"

"No, not married. I was once, but she died of an overdose."

"Oh, I'm sorry. Is that why you are so interested in all of this stuff?"

"No, not really. There will always be drugs, and she'd have found them somewhere. I'm interested because I'm a reporter, even if I haven't got a job at the moment, and this is what a good reporter does. He ferrets out the story!"

"Using what for money?"

"I still have a little of what Stanley left," Peter said.

"Let me help you. I'm a rich man – or at least my father is, and we'd be helping ourselves, too!"

"Thanks, but no thanks. I'll manage."

"Better than that," Laura said, "why don't you fix him a job. Didn't you tell me your father has some connection with the *Washington Post*? That would give him the kind of credentials he needs, and give him a legitimate income as well."

Peter looked at Laura, and then at Andy. "Could you do that? Could you fix something like that?"

"Consider it done – if you'll stay and be my best man," Andy said.

Two weeks later, they were married at the Town Hall in Salzburg, and they went to New Delhi and moved into an apartment in Golf Links, near the centre of the city, overlooking a huge maidan where the kids played cricket in the evenings. Delhi, Laura thought, was like moving back to biblical times, if you could imagine those times with a modern airport and plenty of exhausted taxis. In Golf Links there were no crowds, only a few beautiful sari-clad women drifting around in the parks, and the occasional servant shopping on his bicycle.

Laura had to remind herself that she was in the middle of one of the largest and poorest cities in the world. Only the occasional half-starved cow wandering across the maidan reminded her of that. Otherwise all she heard in the sunny afternoons was the soft click of the cricket balls that the white-clad players on the maidan hit back and forth.

India, ancient, sophisticated, old when Europeans still lived in the forests and painted their faces blue; old when emperors ruled in Rome and pharaohs in Egypt; India, beautiful, ragged, shocking, but somehow sane in spite of it all, Laura thought. Poor, but nothing wasted. Women in biblical rags with fine, proud eyes and heads held high as empresses; men arriving at work immaculate and cheerful, laughing, yet who had come from some distant suburb where they had bathed in a river and vacated their bowels beside the railway track. She thought of the snarling crowds in New York. This, she thought, is a nation undefeated by poverty and hardship. It made her feel alive. Vibrant and full of energy. She was glad, now, that they had come.

Each morning Laura walked through a lane behind the Imperial Hotel, onto which backed the gardens of the huge villas of the rich. Every morning she would find a high pile of garbage, with an old crone plucking papers from it. Later in the day the old crone would be gone, her franchise agreement exhausted, and others would be there, extracting those items to which they had some secret pre-emptive right. Towards evening the cats and dogs were rooting in the pile, and finally the birds. By nightfall the street would be clean. In the morning it would begin again, as eternal, as determined, as ruthless and as justified as India herself. There was always someone further down the pecking order who would need what was discarded.

Laura had feared that she might be repelled by this ant heap of deprivation, by the starving people crowded against the very rich, but she was not repelled. She was beginning to understand what Edwina Bellamy wanted to change; why five million children died every year; why women submitted even while they dominated and held the country together. She was fascinated by its curious balance, its economy, its dignity, its proud past and absurd future, its crazy democracy. It was like a balancing act defying gravity, yet still up there above the circus crowd in spite of its insane bureaucracy, riddled with corruption which seemed endemic, tragic, inevitable – yet it all worked.

Laura found she liked Edwina Bellamy very much indeed, and it did not take her very long to be impressed by her sincerity. Wherever the money was coming from, from whatever corrupted source, Edwina was using it powerfully for good. Without bigotry, she possessed a passionate belief in the rightness of her plans, and she pursued them with a demonic energy that removed all obstacles form her path. She possessed that aristocratic trait which simply assumed that all details would be dealt with by someone else, and she would remain free to concentrate on important issues, and to have her own way.

On the afternoon she arrived, Laura had discovered Edwina under a huge umbrella on the lawn of the Imperial Hotel, talking with Ramesh Singh, a millionaire businessman who lived in Delhi.

"Thank God you're here," she'd said, briskly, indicating a chair. "It's Anne Lacey, isn't it? I have heard all about you. Welcome to this madhouse. We are going to educate the women of India. Are you organized?"

"Very!" Laura said. She had no idea whether she was or not.

Ramesh Singh was the Indian president of Edwina's Foundation. A cousin of rajahs, and a descendant of gods, he had gone to Cambridge and then to the Harvard School of Business. He spoke English with a perfection never achieved by English people. He was beautifully dressed in a cream linen suit. In Nice or San Sebastian he would have passed for a Spaniard or a Provencal.

Edwina was inflamed by the immensity of her task, a job finally suitable for her energy and her intelligence.

"You must understand, madam," Ramesh was saying to her, "that India has defeated every foreigner who has come to change her. She has taken their wealth and their bones and their jewels and their palaces and remained unchanged."

'Yes," said Edwina, "and where has it got her? Poverty, civil war, appalling hygiene, filth, disease and an uncontrolled population explosion which keeps everyone poor."

Ramesh held up his hand and laughed. "Edwina! Edwina! This is not Boston or Cannes, you know. If we had not bred so much we'd be a rich nation!"

"But, my dear friend, you have bred so much. Unless that stops, you will soon be going backwards!"

"Backwards, forwards, we do not necessarily think in these western terms. Money is not so important as in the West."

"That is true only for those who have plenty of it," she said, tartly. "The rest of India wants work and cash and homes and television sets and cars, just like Americans."

"And you believe your money can achieve this? It will disappear into India as if it never was. My dear Edwina, you spend a few weeks here, and think you know the place."

Edwina was annoyed, although she did not permit herself to show it. The rich were the same everywhere, she thought.

They did not want any change that might threaten their secure power base. But in England or America or here, change came whether it was wanted or not. She would not allow India or its establishment to deter her. Laura was impressed.

"I'm not saying I know India yet, Ramesh, but I know human nature.'

"In India everything is different."

"Nonsense!"

Edwina was no longer just a fashionable woman, photographed by the magazines, but someone whose decisions could affect the destiny of nations. She wanted not so much to teach women to compete in a man's world, but to create a women's world. It's time, she said to herself, that we stopped begging to be allowed into the priesthood, the boardroom and the marketplace. She meant to change the fundamental rules.

At first she had not quite understood the huge sums at her disposal, sums so enormous that the very moving of them could affect exchange rates and topple banking houses. Once men had been polite to her because they wished to be invited for dinner or maybe to sleep with her. Now they did so because they feared for their livelihood, for the very existence of their businesses.

"If you can show me Indian women who would prefer to have ten children and watch seven die, rather than have three healthy kids and rear them all, then I shall believe that India is different from other countries."

"Indian women are already having smaller families," he said.

Edwina laughed. "Oh, yes. The women you know, Ramesh. The educated women who go to Paris for their clothes, and the South of France for the winter. But not the women out there." She gestured towards the immensity of India beyond the civilized garden in which they sat.

"You will never change them," he said, shrugging.

"Why not? Your wife has changed. How? Because she is educated. Why is it not possible for others? My God, this country is ruled by a woman!"

"And what has she done? Tried to geld a few men, very unsuccessfully!"

Edwina tried not to smile.

"A reaction which could hardly be defined as exclusively Indian," she said. "We must start with the women, not the men!"

Saying these things, Edwina thought suddenly of Charles and was moved by an intense physical desire for him, for his lovemaking, for his touch. It had been a marriage of convenience between two worldly people, each with his own agenda, yet she had never before felt so alive, so moved by a man's body, so fulfilled. With some effort she dragged her mind from these images.

"I have already made offers to purchase land for three educational centres," she said.

"You will need permission from the government," Ramesh said, nibbling a cucumber sandwich being handed around by a turbaned footman. "To buy land, to import funds, all require permission from the government," he repeated with some satisfaction, as if such a statement should finish all further discussion on the matter.

Edwina smiled sweetly. "But, my dear old friend, that is exactly why you are president of my Foundation here in India. Your job is to untangle the red tape."

"And when do you want it untangled?"

"How about next week?"

"Oh, bah bah, bah," he muttered, shaking his head, becoming Indian suddenly, in spite of his beautifully cut Western clothes. "Nothing in India is solved so quickly."

"We are talking about a lot of money, my friend. There will, of course, be a commission for your services. Say one per cent of what we spend?"

"One per cent of what?" he asked rather rudely.

"We are talking of a total of, say, one billion dollars." Edwina's voice was very calm. She knew when talking about sums like this that she had no need to raise it. "A commission of ten million dollars, payable where you please – Switzerland, the Bahamas. Reporters will be here in September to see what I am doing. There is an election in October, you know, and it may surprise you to know, Ramesh, that half of the voters in your amazing democracy are still women."

Ramesh was sitting straight and listening. He had known that Edwina was formidable, but – one billion dollars? And that was apparently just for starters. This was very considerable indeed. This could change the government. This was a very powerful equation. Suddenly he was very interested. He could see that he could not afford to ignore Edwina Bellamy.

"What will this programme be, which you are initiating?" he asked cautiously.

"Basic training. Hygiene, vaccination, post-natal care to prevent infection and dehydration in the babies, practical and simple methods of contraception. Management. It will all be done in a non-threatening environment that village women will understand. Then they will train others." She gripped his arm, suddenly very serious indeed.

"It can be done. I can tell you that there is no woman born who wants to see her baby die in agony. We got rid of it in Europe two hundred years ago and we can do it here!"

He sighed. He knew when he was beaten, but he said, "Why do you do this, Edwina? You want to establish universities for women in America and Europe? Fine! Why do you spend your money and your energy in a country which is not even yours?"

"Ramesh, the whole world is mine – and yours, too. That is how it must be in the future!"

He heaved himself out of the low wicker chair. "India does not need another Mother Teresa, you know, Edwina."

"I am interested in prophylaxis, my friend, not cures," she said shortly. "By the time it has to be cured it's too late."

She walked across the lawn with him to where his car and chauffeur waited. Edwina was pleased. She returned to the table where Laura waited.

"Indians understand crazy people," she said pleasantly. "Your name is Anne Lacey, isn't it? I shall call you Anne and I am Edwina. Welcome to my crazy world. I'm so glad you're here. You will be in charge of everything that I can't do, which is most things, I'm afraid," she said with a laugh.

Laura did not believe her, but it turned out to be true. Edwina was in New Delhi only every second week. The rest of the time she spent with Charles in London, or New York or Miami or Paris. The Bellamy jet, that seemed to Laura to be the last word in travel luxury, arrived every second Sunday evening, and returned the following Wednesday evening. When Edwina was not there, Laura stood in for her. It was very challenging. They liked each other. They trusted each other. They soon became friends.

"She is doing just what she appears to be doing," Laura reported to Peter Francis when he came to Delhi. "It is the best kind of philanthropy. There are no drugs involved. I see all her papers. Nothing is concealed and she is often not there. And she trusts me, Peter. I can't do this forever."

"Just one year. How much money is she spending?"

"A great deal. More than one billion dollars in India alone."

"And that doesn't include what she's spending in Mexico, and in Venezuela, and on the universities for women. Just hang in there for a while. It's good experience for both of you, especially if Andy is serious about going into politics when he gets back to the States. If this work is all on the level, it's fine, but where is all that money coming from?"

"They're rich people, Peter!"

"My dear girl," Peter said irritably, picking up a cucumber sandwich and gazing at it with critical concern, " you are a rich woman. Rich is an estate in Virginia and a penthouse on Park Avenue. This is enough money to support the entire Cuban economy. We all know governments can throw it around, but these are private funds, or so we are led to believe."

"They know other rich people, Peter," Laura said. "Perhaps they're kicking in, too?"

"Perhaps. Get Andy to check how it comes in through Barclays Bank."

Laura was indignant. "Andy has done enough already."

"No, Laura. If you don't get to the bottom of this, you may be spending your married life together inside a cement overcoat."

She spoke about it to Andy, expressing her reservations about his being involved, and finding out information from the bank. He laughed at her.

"My darling Laura, they tried to kill you. They tried to kill us all. I'm happy to find out whatever I can."

"But who would ever suspect a woman like Edwina Bellamy?"

"Exactly!" said Andy. "Who would?"

By the end of the year, the project was on line and Edwina was being widely praised. In spite of objections from the Vatican, the Indian government and leaders in Indian life, the courses would include contraceptive methods that could be used by either men or women. By the time Laura left to return to the United States in February 1982, Edwina was a famous woman. She was a powerful and famous woman with a spotless reputation. She was unassailable.

Andy reported that the funds came in from their old friends the Banque des Trois Cantons, among many other banks, all of which were controlled by the Bellamy interests, or formed a part of a loose group of associates. The funds came almost exclusively from Ventura accounts and investments, of which Charles Bellamy appeared to be the trustee.

In December 1981, Edwina begged Laura to stay. By then she had been there almost eighteen months.

"I can't, Edwina. My husband wants to go back to the States. He is thinking of going into politics. He won't go back without me."

"Can you stay until the end of January? Charles and I go to Australia next month to launch the Alcon Foundation there."

Laura agreed reluctantly. Although Charles Bellamy never came to India, Laura lived in a constant state of anxiety that he would turn up one day and of course he would recognize her.

"But tell me, Edwina, because I think we are friends. I see how much money you spend. How can you keep this up long enough to have a real effect?"

Edwina took Laura's hand in hers.

"We can keep it up for a hundred years, if necessary. I am telling you this in complete confidence, as no one knows it but me. Charles says the capital of the Foundation is seventy billion dollars, so we are only spending income. We can do anything we want! I wish you'd stay with me and be a part of it all."

"Edwina, I must help my husband. Besides, surely you've made a mistake. No one has seventy billion dollars."

"No! There's no mistake."

"My God," Laura said. "You're like an empress."

"The money is not mine."

"The power of it is yours," Laura said.

When she told Andy this information he said, "I'm a banker, Laura, and there's something wrong here. No one gives away seventy billion dollars of their own money."

"You know what's happening, don't you, Andy? This woman is becoming a secular saint. We will never be able to attack Charles, because it will be attacking her, and people won't stand for it. He's been very clever."

"Very," Andy said. "But we'll find another way. Now, what do you want first, a shower or a drink?"

"Let's make love first, and then a shower and a drink."

"Why not? We haven't done anything as irresponsible as that since yesterday," he said.

He took her in his arms. "I love you very much," he said.

She looked at him. "Has it all been worth it?"

"Every moment," he said, "and it's just the beginning."

CHAPTER TWO

SYDNEY, AUSTRALIA
1980–1982

IT HAD NOT BEEN as difficult as Betty Wellington had envisaged, once they had both accepted the inevitability of it. When they returned from America, Harry's associates were so thrilled by the volume of work, and the contracts that he brought back that, no matter what rumours had circulated about events in Miami, no one had dared to ask embarrassing questions. The story of an accident and a temporary loss of memory had sufficed.

Everyone in Sydney who heard any rumours simply shrugged and said, "Well, Miami! What can you expect?"

They all looked at the bottom line and no one felt inclined to investigate further. Greed is a wonderful panacea, Harry thought.

Betty had been fortunate, too, with the house. One of the oldest and largest mansions in Sydney, Slowes Court in Darling Point had come onto the market. Without waiting for the auction, she had made a very generous offer and obtained the house immediately. Charles had said money was no object. Fine! At least that would be a compensation. The house was a mess. She told her builders it must be ready by 30 June, and she then made a very substantial donation to The Pink and Gray Committee, which organized the most fashionable charity ball of the year. She offered the use of her house. She was invited to join the Committee.

The tickets were oversubscribed by one hundred percent, and the interest of the media in the house and its generous new owners was immense. Harry and Betty Wellington became fashionable. Even more so when it became known that in January 1982 the Alcon Foundation would be launched from their home, and they would be entertaining the fabulous and glamorous Charles and Edwina Bellamy.

On the evening of the ball, Betty stood in the hallway with the president of the Committee, General Sir Charles Hornsby-Smith. Splendid flowers had been arranged by Bloomey's, the most fashionable and trendy florist, and a string quartet played in the minstrel gallery. Later, two bands would play in the ballrooms until three o'clock in the morning. The ball, she had been told, would make more money than any previous event. Betty was triumphant. In less than two years she had created the perfect camouflage for Harry and herself. They must never be suspected, let alone found out. It would be fatal. There must never be a breath of any scandal.

The rooms were full, and Betty was looking with satisfaction at the fashionable crowd in her house when a woman grasped her arm. Her grip was so intense that she removed her hand with some difficulty. She turned to the woman, surprised to find that she was quite young, pretty and very fashionably dressed. "Can I help you?"

The girl shook her head. "No. I can help you," she said. "I am Anne Morgan-Smith. They killed my mother and father, you know. No one will listen to me. Not the police. No one, but I know they killed them."

She seemed distraught, possibly drunk, Betty thought. She led her into a small sitting room and closed the door.

"I'm so sorry," she said. "I met your mother and father

once or twice. They were charming."

Anne stared at her. She looked quite demented.

"Never mind that," she said. "There was no accident in Port Phillip Bay. There was no accident with the gas in my mother's bedroom. They were murdered. And now your husband is involved with them. They will kill you, too."

Betty stood very still. "Who? Who will kill us?"

"The Americans. The people from Alcon. The people from that bank. I don't know. My father didn't take me into his confidence. He thought everything was fine, and then he died." She looked helplessly at Betty. "Daddy was doing so well, and then he died!"

Betty put her hand on the girl's arm, but she brushed it off. "Don't patronize me," she said angrily. "You are part of it all, too, because I see that you aren't frightened. He wasn't either. There is something wrong here. I shall tell everyone in Australia."

She stood up and walked to the door. "I'll tell them," she said. "I'll make them listen."

She went through the door and closed it behind her. Betty rang for a maid. "Find Mr Wellington, Mona. Ask him to come here. Tell him I'm not feeling well."

When Harry came, she said, "Anne Morgan-Smith is here. She's quite crazy, but she's right, of course. She's telling everyone that the Americans – Alcon and whomever – killed her parents." Betty caught his arm.

"What if she starts talking to someone who'll believe her? What happens if they find out what we're doing? Where the money is coming from?"

"Get control of yourself, Betty. There are five hundred people in this house and every one of them is important to us. Get hold of yourself. No one will listen to her. The police have said the deaths were accidental. Go upstairs and bathe your eyes. You don't want people to see you like this! And don't worry!"

"That's easy to say, but how does one stop?"

Betty was frightened. She was always afraid of whatever she could not control. The five hundred people in this house were not friends. They would turn their back on her if there were so much as a breath of impropriety. We are not old rich, like the Morgan-Smiths, she thought. We are arrivistes. Betty knew that, in this world, she could not, for years to come, afford an adverse comment, let alone a disaster.

Better than Harry, she understood the subtle and Byzantine complexity of snobbery in an apparently egalitarian society. If there were a scandal, nothing would save her children from an ostracism that would last a lifetime. Betty vowed that she would never allow that to happen.

CHAPTER THREE

SYDNEY, AUSTRALIA
FEBRUARY 1982

EDWINA BELLAMY WAS ANGRY. She was alone and tired and, inexplicably, a little frightened, an emotion with which she was not familiar. She did not like this large and pretentious house, so perfectly decorated as if it had been purchased, fully fledged, from the pages of *Vogue Living*. She did not like Betty Wellington, and she did not like being alone in Australia. Charles had left her with the responsibility of making speeches, handling the media, and doing all the honours for the opening of the Alcon Foundation. He had pleaded work pressure, but they travelled always with two or three servants and secretaries. She understood that he had lied to her about his reasons for not wanting to go to Australia, and that worried her, for in spite of everything, their relationship up to now had been an honest one, no matter how bitter the truth had been.

So here she was, with a damned dinner party downstairs, in this ghastly house, with no maid to help her dress, in a country that seemed to her to be at the ends of the earth. And none of this would have mattered if she had not known that Charles had lied to her. She looked across the garden to the sea that glittered relentlessly in the February heat. She had heard so much about Australia and now she was here it was not the least as she had imagined. It was not like California, as everyone had said, nor the Mediterranean. It was not like the Caribbean. Sydney was not in the least like San Francisco. It was not like anywhere she had ever been before. The endless suburbs of this huge city, ugly and insidious, depressed her. The glittering light made her eyes ache. The huge, brown land seemed to stretch forever under the wings of her plane as she inspected the mines and the forestry operations being undertaken by Alcon Corporation in the name of progress. This was a part of the wealth that supported her philanthropy, but she found it difficult to relate one to the other.

The great country seemed deserted, neglected, betrayed by time, huge, desolate and lonely. She could not assimilate the distances, the perspectives, nor feel comfortable under the high arch of the empty sky. The distant low mountains looked as if they had been filed down by disasters so ancient that even the woe of their destruction had long since been dispelled, leaving only the ashes and the ghosts of some long dead civilization.

The splendour of the red emptiness rejected people. She felt alienated, challenged and inadequate, and she resented this land which so threatened her sophisticated confidence. She recalled reading somewhere that in the heart of every Australian there is an empty space that is his country. Now, as she criss-crossed the eternal emptiness she felt such a space growing in her own heart, and it frightened her. This ancient southern land quelled her spirit. She longed to leave. The dinner this evening for the Alcon Foundation, being given in this splendidly grotesque mansion of the Wellingtons, would be her last engagement. Tomorrow she could get on her beautiful plane and fly back to the crowded and competitive world she understood. Australia was an enigma, and even in the heat of the summer evening, she shivered.

She had done what Charles had asked of her. She had opened the factories, dined with the lord mayors, attended the

The Honour Code Of Greed

media briefings, and apologized again and again for the fact that it was she doing these honours and not her husband. No one seemed to mind. They loved her.

Now this dinner would give her the opportunity to tell them what work the Alcon Foundation would support to recompense Australians for the destruction to be wrought in this lovely, lonely and sad old land. She felt badly about it all.

At eight o'clock, with the sun still red in the sky, she descended to the huge drawing room of Harry and Betty Wellington's house, with its apricot walls, and its mirrors, and its disturbing Australian paintings by Arthur Boyd and Brett Whiteley and William Dobell and others whom she did not recognize. The paintings were beautiful, strange and fey, and they seemed to catch that quality of Australia that she found most mysterious and threatening.

She looked magnificent, but she knew it was all a trick, a complex deceit, a sleight of hand wrought with money, a good dressmaker, and the right kind of advance publicity. If people expected to see a legendary beauty, that's what they would see. Every film star knew that.

She wore her dark hair piled high on her head and pinned with diamonds. She wore the splendid emeralds Charles had given her on their wedding day, emeralds which had been set for the Empress Josephine – legendary jewels, legendary beauty, legendary lives. The black chiffon from Chanel fell softly around her legs and the jewels felt huge and warm against her breasts. Some day, she thought, I will create a legend myself, a legend of reform, and wisdom, of change and progress, a generation of women educated to govern, and confident to do so in their own right, as women and as human beings.

They were in a huge, striped marquee, twenty tables of ten people all clapping, looking towards her. The last speech of the tour. She rose from her seat.

"My husband Charles who, like all husbands, should be with me this evening and is not, has asked me to say to all of you that it is with great pride that he brings to this exciting new country and its young and vibrant civilization all the skills, resources and experience of the Alcon Corporation of Florida.

"He hopes, and I join him in this hope, that the combination of our know-how and expertise with your energy and ambition will serve the mutual interests of all who participate and share in our joint ventures in Australia.

"However we all understand, these days, that nothing can be taken from this earth of ours whereby it is not diminished, its beauty tarnished and its future ability to serve and support us tainted. It is the responsibility of all who use those resources to replenish them for the generations yet to come.

"For this reason, so that this strange and beautiful country might remain intact while we take some of its treasures and turn them into prosperity for both our countries, we have established the Alcon Foundation which will be endowed with an initial gift from my husband and myself of … " she paused. " … of fifty million dollars."

She paused again for the applause and for the gasps, for she knew the figure to be far greater than they had expected. "… and the Foundation will do everything in its power to help Australia preserve a natural beauty which has been uniquely preserved by time and isolation from destruction over the millennia."

"The first award from the Foundation will therefore be made to …"

"Murderers!"

The cry came from the middle of the room, thin and hysterical. Edwina stopped speaking and looked around. The room was suddenly silent, the guests frozen in their seats with shock and embarrassment. A slight, blonde young woman stood up and turned towards Edwina. In a clear and very precise voice she said again, "Murderers! You speak of preservation but they killed my parents. They are all murderers!"

The thin, high voice crackled through the hot silent air like electricity. Edwina heard Betty Wellington say in a sibilant whisper, "For God's sake, Harry, get her out. She's crazy as a loon."

Edwina saw Harry cross the room and take Anne Morgan-Smith by the arm.

"Anne, my dear," he said softly. "It's all right. Please sit down!"

But she would not sit. Instead, she looked straight at him.

"You are a fool, Harry! I have warned you. They will kill you, too, when it suits them. They ruined my parents and then they killed them. They will do the same to you, unless, of course, you are one of them!"

She turned again to Edwina, standing at the microphone.

"Your husband, madam, is a murderer. Do not speak here of generosity and preservation. You should speak of destruction and of vengeance, for that is what you are involved in!"

"Anne, you must leave," Harry said urgently, and this time she allowed him to take her arm and to lead her from the room. Edwina's eyes followed the straight, white-clad back until Anne Morgan-Smith disappeared through the door of the silk-hung tent.

The silence was complete. The hot, humid air in the tent swirled like a miasma around the silent guests. The candles smoked in their sconces. Edwina waited, saying nothing. The two hundred guests stared at her and she stared back at them while Anne's hysterical voice echoed and faded away into the heavy night.

Finally Edwina spoke into the thick and suspicious silence. She put her hand to her throat and touched her immense jewels.

"These emeralds," she said softly, "were the gift of the Emperor Napoleon to the Empress Josephine on another summer night almost two hundred years ago. They are supposed to be warmed for all eternity by his undying love for her, by the kisses from his burning lips. Yet, not long after he gave them to her, for want of an heir, he divorced her and married Marie Louise of Austria, the niece of the beheaded Queen Marie Antoinette. The French people, who loved Josephine and hated the Austrians, predicted that his luck would leave him, and so it did. Within three years he was in exile, never to return."

She stopped speaking and looked into the silent, hot and crowded room. No one stirred.

"We all have our private grief to bear. I do not know that woman who has left, but my heart goes out to her, as it does to that lonely Empress when I wear her emeralds. It is a lonely journey we all undertake, my friends, and none of us wishes to make it alone, as in the end we all must. The awards will be announced tomorrow in the press. I know they will help to preserve this unique country of yours in which I have been so briefly a guest. Thank you all."

She sat down.

There was a smattering of applause. This was not what they had come for, and the guests did not know how to react. People never do, Edwina thought, when their roles are suddenly changed. She felt utterly drained, wrung with pity for that poor creature shouting insults, and equally ashamed for herself for she knew the awards were only to distract attention from the damage which Alcon would do to make its huge profits and pay its generous dividends.

Betty was distraught.

No sooner had Edwina departed for the airport the following day than she said to Harry, "I knew we shouldn't have invited that woman. She's made a fool of us twice now in our own house. I don't give a damn how well-connected she is, she won't come here again. She's mad as a hatter, and she's out to destroy us with her crazy lies."

"Let's keep a sense of proportion, Betty," Harry said quietly. "You and I know they are not lies. We both know to our cost that Alcon will stop at nothing to get its own way. Anne's parents were murdered, but only her mother by the Alcon Corporation, I think. Her father was killed by the Ventura family, who were tipped off by Alcon."

"But why?"

"To make room for us. Charles wanted all opposition out of the way, and he wanted to take his revenge on us."

"Do you think Edwina knows anything of this?"

"I'm not sure how much she knows, but you can rest assured that she is happy to use the money as she does. In that way she protects Charles. She is making him untouchable."

"All the more reason to be concerned," Betty said. "Sooner or later someone might begin to listen to Anne Morgan-Smith and her crazy talk."

"What do you suggest we do?"

"How the hell would I know?" Betty shouted. "Have her certified? Report the matter to Miami and let them worry about it! After all, she's just been slandering the wife of their President. Did Edwina say anything to you?'

"Not a word. I thought she handled it very well."

"So did I," Betty agreed grudgingly. "There's no doubt that a few hundred years in the ruling class gives you confidence, but unfortunately you and I can't wait quite so long. "

"She's bound to mention it to Charles," Harry said.

Betty shrugged. "I think he's tough enough to handle it, don't you? Alcon Corporation is investing a lot of money out here in order to maintain a very clean sheet."

"Charles' name is never mentioned in anything to do with the drug operation."

"Of course not. If anything ever goes wrong there, you can rest assured he will be a long distance away. He's far too rich to have to do any of the dirty work himself. Those days are long gone, I bet. It will be you and I who take the rap unless we are very smart indeed."

"In the meantime," Harry said, "we take a leaf out of Edwina's book, and simply ignore the whole incident."

Betty put her hand on his arm. "You know Anne could put us in grave danger. People may listen to her."

"My dear, we have been in grave danger ever since we became involved in this, and we shall be in grave danger now until we die," Harry said. "Anne Morgan-Smith didn't put us there. We did that ourselves, and now there's no way out."

Betty put her face against his shoulder and wept. She was not a sentimental woman, and she did not weep for the high price they were paying for the fulfillment of her ambitions, but for the fact that she knew that the accounts for their current splendour were far from being paid. She had a premonition that the largest bills were yet to be rendered.

CHAPTER FOUR

WASHINGTON DC
1982 - 84

LAURA AND ANDY HAD returned to the United States in February 1982, as soon as Edwina had finished her tour in Australia for the Alcon Foundation. All of the charges against Andy had been withdrawn amid considerable publicity praising his actions and reminding America of his role in the Vietnam War.

His father was pleased. His son would now join him in the banking business, he believed, but Andy had other ideas. A very powerful man had tried to kill him, and worse, had tried to kill the woman he loved. The score was far from settled as far as he was concerned. In fact, Andy thought, as far as he was concerned, it would never be settled, and he felt that he could no longer stand aside and allow his country to be run by people he did not trust, and that he knew were not trustworthy.

"If you go into politics," Laura said, "our lives will become public property, and we shall be made scapegoats for the public morality. Every bit of dirt will be unearthed. You know what politics is, these days. Filthy!"

"Oh? And what will they discover? You lived as a private citizen in Bogotá and a notorious man was murdered in your apartment when you were not there? By whom? Perhaps by the CIA. We can make you a heroine."

"A heroine?" she laughed sadly. "And you? Three murders at the Bank in Geneva, three dead bodies in the hotel, and your escape. How do we explain that to the *National Inquirer*?"

"I think that's all been done – and my father is quite a powerful man, too," he said.

"Powerful enough, maybe, but not, perhaps, quite ruthless enough," she said thoughtfully. "However, if you are determined to do this, then when the time is right, there is an even more powerful man who we might use. Charles Bellamy."

"Bellamy? Are you crazy? He would never help me."

Laura smiled. "Perhaps not, if he had a choice. We shall see. He owes me a great deal. You are sure that you really want to do this thing?"

"America is powerful and rich, but there is something wrong. There is a belief that what's good for America is good for the world, when it should be the other way round, I think. I want to try to put it right."

Laura sighed. "Why do I always get mixed up with evangelists? All right, my darling, if that's what you want, then go for it! I'll be right there with you. You saved my life, so maybe I shall be able to save yours."

"You've already done that," he said.

She shrugged. "Maybe once is not enough for a girl like me."

Andy had joined his father's bank on his return to the United States, and two years later, in 1984, when the midterm elections were held and one of the sitting Democrat senators for Georgia was felled with a heart attack, Andy was selected to replace him and very quietly, without fuss and without any national publicity, he became a junior senator.

No one outside Atlanta paid any attention to the fact that

there was now a new, young senator from Atlanta, Andrew Davidson, whose father was Chairman of the Georgia Bankers' Association. The new senator's lovely blonde wife, Laura, was the daughter of a Swedish diplomat who had retired in the United Sates and who was now deceased. She had been brought up and educated in Minnesota after spending time with her father in various foreign missions. Laura had been an aspiring actress in her youth, but she now kept a very low profile, as she had recently had a baby son. The new senator was a family man, and a good liberal, with a fine war record, a sound grasp of economics and an excellent mind. From the very beginning he was regarded as a coming man, a man for his time. A winner.

Before they moved to Washington, Laura said to him, "Charles Bellamy will do everything in his power to stop us, Andy. He would not hesitate to try to kill us again, particularly as we begin to exert some influence in public life."

"I'm surprised he hasn't tried already. I can only assume that he's too busy these days being an international figure to pay any attention to the arrival in Washington of an obscure Georgia banker to the Senate, in a mid-term appointment to which no one in America has paid any attention. When he does find out, he'll go to work. What will we do then?"

"We will use the information we have about him," Andy said. "We will use Peter Francis. He has more information on the Bellamy operations than any living person."

Peter was excited when they contacted him.

"My dear Andy," he said, "this is wonderful news. We can make you President! You have everything the country wants – or perhaps I should say, needs. You have brains, independent wealth, glamour, intelligence, a modern attitude to problems, a considerable knowledge of the world and a beautiful wife. In addition to all that, I suspect that you might even be honest! What more could America want?"

"And we have an unhealthy past," Laura said. "I think the Presidency is a little too ambitious, Peter."

"Charles Bellamy has a far more unhealthy past than yours."

"True, but he's not planning to run for President, and the media love him and Edwina," Laura said.

"They are running for secular sainthood. If we have to play dirty, they have more at risk than you do," Peter said flatly. They were lunching at the Watergate Hotel, as he was now living quietly in Washington DC and working as a financial journalist at the *Post*. In his spare time he continued his research into the Bellamy Corporation and its worldwide consortium of linked companies. "Charles Bellamy has spent almost twenty years of his life building up this image of a great, aristocratic philanthropist. He can't afford to risk it now."

Peter turned to Laura. "You must contact Edwina. You must tell her that you and the girl who worked in Delhi are one and the same. We must start to lay plans that will keep Charles quiet. We must start now."

"I would feel terrible about that. I like her very much and she will think badly of me if she knows that I tricked her in Delhi."

"Edwina may be straight, Laura, but you can take it from me that she knows where the money comes from, and she is unlikely to be as easily shocked as you seem to think. You need her on your side, believe me."

"And what if the media learns the truth about Geneva?" Laura asked.

"We will turn the pair of you into heroes," Peter said. "Just leave it to me. I will handle all the media for you. I will be a genius," he said, laughing.

"So you would consider dumping the work you're doing and taking on the job as my press liaison officer, or whatever it's called?" Andy asked.

Peter jumped up from the table and shook his hand. "You're really offering that to me? I wouldn't miss it for the world," he said. "You are the first decent man I've met in politics in twenty years. With a President like you, we can go anywhere."

"Peter, Peter! Calm down! I'm not the President. I'm just a junior senator from Georgia! Let's not go too fast."

"We must have a vision for the future!"

"And already we must start that vision by playing dirty tricks," Andy said sadly. "Does anyone, I wonder, ever get to the top uncorrupted?"

Peter shrugged. "We start by telling the truth. Oh, not all of it, but enough. You have never done anything wrong, Andy. We play the game we have to play if you want to get there, because that's the kind of world we live in. I think the first thing we do is call a media conference and come clean straight away, and the second thing we do is contact Edwina."

"I really hate to do it," Laura said. "She was so damned decent to me in Delhi. She trusted me. I just hate to tell her that I was there under some kind of false pretence."

Peter laughed. "Toughen up, Laura. Edwina is extremely intelligent, hugely successful, very rich and very aware of the somewhat sordid ways of the beau monde, and of her husband, too, I'm sure. If there is one woman in the world who will not be surprised by what she is about to discover, I'd put my money on Edwina Bellamy."

"You are very reassuring," Laura said rather acidly. "All of that makes me feel really great about having behaved like a rat in Delhi!"

"Don't exaggerate, Laura. Like a mouse only – not a rat. Now that you are in Washington, you'll soon learn how rats behave!" Peter said sourly. "You are a very small mouse by comparison, I can assure you."

"Well," she said with a small smile, "I suppose a mouse isn't too bad, is it?"

"And I," he said, "shall visit the lion in his den and let him know the new rules of the game. I can't tell you the amount of pleasure that will give me."

Laura smiled at the thought of the scruffy and untidy Peter fronting up to the immaculate Charles. That would be an interesting meeting.

* * * * * *

"Not you again, Peter," Charles Bellamy exclaimed, as Peter was ushered into his office overlooking the whole of Miami, a few months after his conversations with Laura and Andy at the Watergate Hotel. "I thought that we'd managed to get rid of you – or at least to shut you up."

"If you wish to be so famous, Charles, you must put up with the attention of the media hounds, and I do apologize for missing that plane to Bogotá."

"What on earth do you mean by that?"

"Wouldn't it be more convenient if I were dead?"

"Certainly not. You are not important enough for that. So what is it this time, then? My wife has arranged a party in New York this evening, and she has told me that I am to be present on pain of death. I must leave for the airport in half an hour. Are you married?"

"I was once."

"Then you will understand the importance of my being

there when I have promised that I will be there."

"That's why I'm no longer married," Peter said. "I won't keep you too long. I'm doing a story on the new senator from Georgia."

"Georgia? Is there a new senator from Georgia? What on earth has that to do with me? There have been no elections. What happened to the old one?"

"He had a heart attack and died. You should keep your finger on the pulse a little more, Charles. You would never have made a mistake like this in the old days when we first met, back in the days when Stan Jerkovitz was alive."

"Mistake? What mistake are you talking about? Who is this new man, then?"

"His name is Andrew Davidson. He is the son of Willie Davidson, President of the Georgia Bankers' Association, with whom I'm sure you've had dealings of one kind or another in the past. Andy was involved a few years ago in a small fracas in Geneva, which you may recall. He is now married to a very beautiful and intelligent woman who was once a great friend of yours."

"And who is that?"

"I believe her name in those days was Laura Tessier." Peter stopped. This was enough for starters.

Charles sat down and stared at him. It was the first time since Peter had known him that he had seen Charles Bellamy lose his composure.

"They are dead," he said. "Their plane crashed out of Geneva back in 1979."

"That was what you and the French police, and the insurance companies involved, all mistakenly assumed, but they are not dead," Peter said. "They are dining, in fact, with you and your wife in New York this evening. I thought you might like to be prepared. They have very ambitious plans for the future."

Charles laughed. He was back in the saddle, a rich man to whom nothing happened that he did not want to happen, a man in total control of his life.

"With a past like those two have, they'll not achieve anything. I can ruin them in two minutes."

"Of course you can, but you will not do so, Charles, for if you do, then I shall ruin you and Edwina in an even shorter time than that."

Charles stared at him. "Are you daring to threaten me?" he asked quietly. "You're a brave man, Peter. Reporters are very dispensable, you know."

"Let's not waste each other's time playing games, Charles. You've said you are in a hurry, and you don't need trouble. No criminal charges were ever laid against Andrew, and now he has been completely exonerated. He has been made a minor American hero, in fact. Certainly, to my knowledge, no charges of any kind were ever even contemplated against Laura Tessier."

"Who gives a damn about that in Washington? Or among the American electorate? The rumour mill would destroy them in a flash – a few nicely destructive articles here and there, full of innuendo – would finish them in a week."

"And you, too. Edwina's chance of a Nobel Prize would fly out the window, along with a good deal else, like your good name."

Peter held up his hand. "No, no, Charles, don't protest. It ill becomes you. In the old days you never fooled yourself. It was your greatest strength. Let me have just five minutes of your time, so you and I can come to an understanding about the young Davidsons and their future. In 1981 a Colombian Airlines 747 crashed. I am sure that you will recall this, as a company controlled by you owns this airline. Jaime and Jesus Ventura were on board, along with my old pal Stan Jerkovitz, who was there at your invitation, or at least at your suggestion. I would also have been on board if your plans had gone properly. I must say that would, indeed, have saved you a great deal of trouble."

Peter walked over to the window and turned towards Charles, his voice suddenly hard.

"You made all those arrangements, from your phone right here in this office. You also telephoned a man called David Mathieson, an employee in the maintenance department of your airline. He placed a bomb on that plane and subsequently collected twenty thousand dollars from this bank for his trouble. He is now dead, of course, but I know where we can locate his body, if necessary."

Charles was very calm. "You can't prove any of this," he said.

"On the contrary, Charles, I wouldn't be wasting your time or mine if I couldn't prove it. And I can prove that you have transferred the Ventura investments under your own control, and these are the monies being used to fund Edwina."

"To make a better world," he said calmly.

"That may be so," Peter agreed, "but the American people have their own ways of deciding who makes a better world, in what is laughingly called this democracy."

He held up his hand. "And don't bother to imagine that you will be able to lock me in your little hospitality suite up here as you did with Jaime. If I am not at my lawyer's office by six this evening, all this information will be released to the press. Then whose reputation will be destroyed by the Washington gossip mill?"

"What do you want?"

"My dear fellow, I don't want anything. It is Andy and

Laura who want something, and I think they deserve it. They want your support, both financial, and political, in a campaign to make Andy President of the United States of America in 1992."

"How much?"

"How much did you promise Laura back in 1969 if she went to Bogotá and spied for you? I believe that the deal was twenty-five per cent of the profits if you got rid of the Ventura family. A gentleman does not go back on his word, surely, Charles? Particularly one who wants his wife to win the Nobel Prize for good works?"

"That would be a very large amount of money."

"Quite! It would be more than enough, I think, to secure the Presidency for an eminently qualified man.'

"And if I refuse?"

"Come on, Charles," Peter snapped with authority. "We are not here to waste each other's time. We both know you cannot refuse. Andy and Laura go to Washington shortly, and this afternoon, before flying from Atlanta to New York for your wife's dinner party, they gave a media conference, organized by myself. Can you guess what they said?"

"Not the truth, surely? America can't be ready for that!"

"Amazing, isn't it? I don't believe it's ever been tried in politics before, has it?"

"Are you telling me that they told the media about Laura's money and where it came from?"

"No, Charles. We didn't tell them the whole truth. This is America, remember? We told them enough to be in the clear later on; when these matters are raised again as they are bound to be. You may rest assured that Charles Bellamy was not mentioned. Nor will you ever be, if you keep your side of the bargain. Total support, financial, moral and political, and as much of Laura's money as she needs. Otherwise ..."

Charles rose heavily from behind his desk. "And if I do all of this, what security do I have that if, one day, he is President he will not compromise me?"

"I think he could hardly do that, without causing serious problems for himself ... and for Laura."

"How did you find out all this information?"

"I have had many years of not believing that Charles Bellamy is everything he appears to be."

"How much of it came from Nick?"

"Nick? Nick Barton?" Peter looked amazed. "No, I have never been given anything by Nick Barton."

"From now on, you will deal only with him. I never want to see you in this office again." Charles felt the stones again in his chest, high up under his breastbone, weighing him down. "Now get out!"

Peter walked to the door. "Don't fool yourself that being angry with me will do the trick, Charles. Don't blame the messenger. The rest is fate!"

Charles looked at him with a gaze so chilly that Peter felt as if a razor blade were being drawn slowly across his eyeball. The blood around his heart coagulated.

"One thing further ..."

"There will never be anything further," Charles said. "I am sure you understand."

The guard held open the door, and Peter passed through.

Charles looked at his watch impatiently and asked his secretary to have his car brought around to the basement elevator. He was running late, and he must consider how to control this situation. Andrew Davidson must never become President. Laura must never be First Lady. God forbid! How in God's name did they get themselves invited to his house tonight? Edwina did not know them, surely. He was a fool to have ever persuaded himself that this matter was over. Nothing in life was ever over, until you were dead, and often not even then.

Charles went down in the elevator and stepped into his car. At the airport, the chauffeur drove past the terminal and drew into the special lounge reserved for travellers with private jets. The Bellamy Corporation 727 was waiting on the tarmac. Charles went on board and ordered the captain to take off immediately.

"I'm sorry, Mr Bellamy. You are later than you said you would be, and we have lost our slot. I have spoken to the Tower. They say that air traffic is very heavy and we may have to wait almost an hour for another take-off slot."

"Just go up front and start the engines as you were told," Charles said coldly. He picked up the phone and punched in a number with an aggressive forefinger.

"Hello? This is Charles Bellamy. Connect me with the Chief Administrator immediately." He waited a moment.

"Hello, Hanson? I am down here in my plane waiting to take off." He listened for a few seconds.

"Yes, I am aware that the airport is busy, but you see, I don't give a tiger's fart if there are one hundred 747s lined up out there. No, twenty minutes will not be convenient. I wish to leave immediately."

There was a moment's silence.

"No, you listen to me, my friend. I am aware that you receive an annual consultancy fee of one hundred thousand dollars from the Bellamy Corporation. What do you think you get paid for? Your expertise?" Charles laughed sourly. "If I am not in the air in five minutes not only will that fee be cancelled, but the IRS will be advised that it has been paid into an account in the Cayman Islands since 1978 ... Thank you,

Hanson."

A moment later the pilot popped his head into the cabin.

"Just had confirmation that we are cleared for immediate take-off, sir. We are to proceed straight to the head of the queue on Runway 2-9. They are holding all other traffic. I must say, Mr Bellamy, you do know how to cut through the red tape around this place. It's a real pleasure to work for you."

The big plane was already taxiing across the tarmac.

"Yes," Charles said, fastening his seat belt while the steward prepared a martini. "Cutting the red tape is my specialty, Captain. Now, if you'll excuse me, Kurt has a martini for me already and I've had a rather difficult day!"

Yes, difficult, certainly! And it is not yet over, he thought sourly.

The jet with the huge dark blue B on the tail trundled across the airport, passed down the long line of commercial planes waiting for clearance at the top of the runway, and swung into position in front of a Lufthansa 747 bound for Bonn that had waited patiently for half an hour to get to the head of the long queue.

With a thrust from its huge Rolls Royce engines the plane hurtled down the runway and lifted into the late afternoon skies. Behind them twenty six planes from all over the world with maybe ten thousand passengers waited patiently for their departure. It was exactly five and a half minutes since Bellamy had spoken to the Chief Administrator.

CHAPTER FIVE

NEW YORK CITY
1984

"THANK YOU, SHILLINGTON," Edwina Bellamy said to her butler as he closed the door of her New York apartment behind her.

"How was everything in Delhi, madam?"

"Just fine, thank you. Is Mr Bellamy here?"

"No, madam. They phoned from Miami to say that his plane was late taking off. He hopes to be here by seven, at the latest."

"Well, I hope he's not any later. I don't want to have to manage all these people by myself. What time have we invited them?"

""For eight o'clock I believe, madam. Shall I send Lucy to you?" Lucy was Edwina's secretary.

"Yes, to my bedroom. I'll rest a while."

Lucy came in while she was sipping her tea.

"So what's happening with our bankers' dinner this evening, Lucy? I must have been crazy to organize anything for tonight. I'm exhausted."

"Well, tomorrow you have dinner at the White House and then you fly to Europe for meetings in Paris. This was your only free night for weeks, so there it is, Edwina. You're simply trying to do too much."

"All right, Lucy. No lectures! How about the dinner tonight?"

"Everyone you wanted to come has accepted. The fellow from the International Monetary Fund, and the President of the World Bank, and all the others. Crawford and Guest are doing the catering, and the Club is sending two extra waiters. Oh, yes and the Davidsons have arrived. I must say he's very cute. I've put them in the Blue Room. I hope that's okay?"

"The Davidsons?" Edwina said vaguely, and sipped her tea. "Staying here in the Blue Room? Who on earth are the Davidsons? Are they friends of Charlie's?"

Lucy looked puzzled.

"Come on, Edwina. You remember you specially asked me to invite them. He is the new young senator from Georgia and you said she was your secretary in New Delhi several years ago. I hope I haven't made a mistake."

Edwina laughed. "Heavens, no, Lucy. She rang me the other day. I was just confused for a moment. In those days she called herself something else. Lacey, I think. I wonder why? Perhaps she wasn't married then? They seem to be making a bit of a stir in Washington, but they always love someone young and new and pretty down there. Her husband's family owns some little bank down in Georgia, I think."

"What bank in Georgia?" Lucy asked suspiciously. Edwina was very casual about protocol, and could never understand why her guests became upset if they were not given their proper consequence.

"I don't know what bank," Edwina said. "It's probably the First Interstate Bank of Wattamolla Junction, with two customers from the local Baptist Church. You know the kind of thing they have down there. That kind of person always has an inflated idea of his own importance. I don't believe I ever met him in Delhi, if he was there. He'd been sick or something, now that I think of it. She was rather pretty as I recall, and a huge help to me. I liked her very much, but I haven't seen her since I went on that lousy trip to Australia. She promised to keep in touch, but I didn't hear anything until just the other day, when she rang me again. Strange, really!"

Lucy said, "There are forty-eight people. We have six tables of eight. I've opened the doors between the dining room and the library. Parkers have finished the flowers. I've put the Davidsons here, on table five, but I think I ought to check ... "

She picked up the phone and called the Public Relations Department at Citibank.

"Yes, that's it, Sandy. Yes, the new young senator. Yes, yes, that's it! Okay, thanks."

She replaced the receiver, and gave a short, rather mirthless laugh.

"Really, Edwina, you are the pits, you know. Andy Davidson's father owns the First City Bank of Atlanta, which is the largest bank in the South, and he is Chairman-elect of the Association of Southern Bankers. They are one of the richest families in Georgia, and very powerful. Senator Andrew Davidson is President-elect of the Bank, and he is very highly regarded in Washington among the junior senators as a coming man, very much a man with a future. He will be practically the most important guest here this evening. I'll have to put him at your table, and she will have to go with Charles."

Edwina giggled. Lucy was not amused.

"Really, Edwina, sometimes I wonder why I work for you!"

"When she rang the other day and told me her husband worked in a bank, I though I was doing them a favour. She was great fun in India, so I hope she hasn't become a bore, like all those awful political wives in DC, pushing and shoving for their husbands all the time. Charles hates dowdy, boring women, but I seem to recall that she was very competent. Well, not to worry. Charles will also have the Countess Markevitch, who is very naughty and amusing. Tell Linda that I'll wear the red Oscar de la Renta with my rubies, will you. I'll just have a little rest."

She woke to find Charles standing beside her, shaking her shoulder.

"Thank God you're here in time," she said, sleepily. "Did you have a difficult day?"

"Terrible," he said. "I must talk with you about these Davidsons you've invited."

"Oh? Is there a problem? Too late now to do anything about it. They're already here."

"Lucy says she worked for you in India."

"Yes, but she called herself another name. Not Laura Davidson."

"I'm not surprised," Charles said sourly, striding up and down the room in a manner that Edwina did not recognize. He was normally so calm and controlled. "Do you remember, about the time we were married, all that fuss with those murders at the Bank in Geneva?"

She sat up and rang the bell for her maid. "Vaguely," she said. "Some problem with a woman in an hotel, and an American who saved her or something."

"Yes," he said grimly. "Well, that woman was Laura Tessier who lived with Sebastian Ventura in Bogotá, and the American was Andy Davidson, to whom she is now married. I knew her years ago here in New York when I was just starting out. It was I who sent her to Bogotá to be my spy in the Ventura camp. They are the only two people in the world today who could bring us to ruin."

"Ruin?" she asked. "Financial ruin, you mean?"

"Hardly, Edwina. That's not possible, but the money for your Foundation comes from drugs, as you have always known, and as, of course, they know. We would not look good if the world also knew. Even your reputation might not be able to save us, or keep me out of gaol."

Linda came in with the red dress and Edwina's jewels. She looked at Charles. "Shall I come back, madam?"

"No, let's get started," Edwina said. She bent over and kissed Charles on the cheek.

"Don't worry, darling. I've flown close to the flames just as often as you have. Neither you nor I is fated to be an Icarus! I'll make sure there's no problem. Just go and have a swim in the pool before dinner, or you'll be getting fat, and stop worrying. It makes you look so old!"

"Exercise has killed more Americans than food or drink," he said, morosely, getting up. The maid was in the bathroom.

"Edwina," he said urgently, and quietly, "don't treat this too lightly, my dear. This is the worst problem we have ever faced. Don't underestimate it. The fact that Laura went to work for you anonymously in Delhi makes her very dangerous. She must have nerves of steel."

She touched her hand to his cheek. "When you asked me to marry you, you told me what you did and what you wanted to achieve. You were honest with me and I took the risk. I won't let you down," she said. "When it comes to protecting you, to protecting us, I, too, have nerves of steel. After being married to Marcus, I can assure you, there's no situation which I can't handle."

"I love you," he said.

"Yes, my dear, I know that. We make a very good team." He took her hand in his.

"No," he said, "No. That's not what I mean. I mean I really love you."

She kissed him gently on the lips. "Oh, Charles, you do pick a bad time to tell a girl important things. Tell me again later, when this evening is over. Oh, and incidentally, those awful people from Australia, Harry and Betty Wellington, are in town."

"I know. You didn't invite them tonight?"

"Good God, no. The bankers are trouble enough. We can have them for lunch maybe." She turned to look at herself in the mirror.

"How strange life is," she murmured. "You'd think that our stuffy little world of bankers would be free of drama, and yet we are in the middle of it. It was the same with Marcus, too. Perhaps I bring it on myself? Do you think so, Charles?"

Charles said nothing. He went out and quietly closed the door.

* * * * * *

In New York there are many fabulous apartments, suites of stupendous rooms high in the sky over Park Avenue and the East River, their long windows filled with that fabled view. There are modern apartments with plate glass walls; splendid old apartments on Riverside Drive, Gracie Square and Beekman Place, whose walls are splattered with Old Masters hauled back from a pillage of Europe. There are the huge mausoleums on West Central Park favoured by the Jewish families who had made it big a hundred years ago, and then there is the Bellamy apartment, forty rooms on two floors, with the pool and solarium on the roof.

The staircase had come from a famous ante-bellum mansion in Louisiana, and the linenfold panelling from an Elizabethan manor house in Suffolk. The rooms would not have shamed a small palace, but it was, above all, the 'Edwina touch' that made it perfect. The furniture was worthy of a museum, but this was true of many New York homes. In Edwina's house, however, the human element shone and took precedence, and made her guests more amusing and more glamorous than they were elsewhere. Here and there a chair was shabby with wear, a little frayed perhaps, as if many lives had been lived in its presence, and old woes and joys had mellowed it. The place was a palace, but it was a palace in which real lives were being lived, every day, and in which guests felt happy, and displayed their talents to best advantage.

Laura felt it that evening as she descended the stairs on Andy's arm. She was not nervous, for it was too late for that, but she felt cautious and a little apprehensive, like a well-trained soldier going to a battle. She was thirty-nine and she knew that her future and that of her husband, whom she loved, would depend on what happened tonight in this powerful and frightening apartment. It was a quelling thought.

Laura did not outshine her hostess whose dark beauty, faultless chic and splendid jewels were already legendary, but she made a formidable rival. Her shining, pale hair was drawn back in the manner made famous by Evita Peron, and swept into a high chignon. In her ears and at her throat she wore perfectly matched grey pearls set with diamonds, a gift from that old buccaneer, her father-in-law, Willie Davidson. Willie was growing old and he clearly understood that his son would succeed only if Laura wanted this to happen, and was prepared to help him. He moved in powerful circles, but they did not include the Bellamys' international set. He was both curious and impressed that Laura had that entrée, which was open to relatively few. He did not intend that, on such an occasion as this, his daughter-in-law would be outshone.

Laura's dress of pale grey organza, flown from Lanvin in Paris, floated around her like an evening cloud from which rose her splendid head, and the superb glittering necklace and earrings of pale grey pearls.

My God, she thought angrily to herself as she stood at the doors of the long reception room, if that bastard Charles Bellamy tries to do any more harm to Andy, or to me, I'll give him a good run for his money! The thought of such a battle brought to her pale cheeks just that touch of colour needed to enhance her Nordic beauty. She would not be beaten now, with such a winning post in sight. If Andrew wanted to be the President of the United States, then by God, if she could help to get it for him, he should have it! And no one, least of all Charles, would stop him!

Edwina looked up just as her butler Shillington announced, "Senator and Mrs Andrew Davidson."

Even she, so experienced a barometer of the social scene and of the human heart, was a little taken aback by the pale and perfect vision which stood in her doorway on the arm of one of the most handsome men she had seen in a very long time indeed. She detached herself from a group from the Deutsche Bank and kissed Laura warmly on the cheek. It was a gesture of intimacy that she knew would not go unremarked. This woman had been her friend in New Delhi. Edwina now understood that Laura was, and had always been, playing a complex and dangerous game, but no more so than she herself. She admired her for that. Whatever Laura had done, Edwina did not feel herself in any position to judge, and nor she did want so obvious and formidable a rival to become an enemy. They must be on the same side in whatever game was to be played, or there would be serious trouble.

"Edwina – so long! Too long!" Laura said. She very much liked and admired this woman. "This is my husband, Andrew. I don't believe you ever met in Delhi."

Andy bent over her hand. "I already know you by repute," he said, "as a perfect employer."

Edwina laughed. "And I you, as the perfect husband. Anne – Laura, I mean. I must call you Laura now – that dress is a dream." She noted the pearls and the diamonds. This was not the dowdy woman who had helped her so efficiently in New Delhi. This new Laura was beautiful and dangerous.

Laura looked at Edwina. Here was the woman with whom she had worked for more than a year, standing before her now in this fabled house, in her Nizam's rubies. Edwina was a woman whose competence she admired, and who believed passionately, Laura knew, in the work she was doing. She was a woman, perhaps like her namesake Edwina Mountbatten, who had come late in life to unselfish goals, and who was now achieving them with an apparently effortless style and an extraordinary dedication. She tried to imagine how the Charlie Bellamy she had known in New York could command such a woman as this. He had been an attractive man, God knows, she remembered, but Edwina was a prize fit for a king. She and Andy must be very careful of this woman. In her own way she was as formidable as her husband if, Laura hoped, not quite so ruthless.

Edwina took her arm. "Charles tells me that he knew you once, in New York, many years ago. How amazing it all is!"

Edwina spoke in the bantering tone of one who understands that such coincidences were to be found only in fairy tales, and castles on the Rhine or the apartments of the very rich in New York. So, Laura thought, Charles has told her everything, as I have done with Andy. It will be very interesting to see who wins.

"You know, Laura," Edwina said as they crossed the room, "I am rather a connoisseur of jewels, and that emerald you are wearing on your hand is probably the finest I have ever seen."

Laura held it up to catch the light. The mystical jewel, huge and dark as the Brazilian jungle, glowed there like a symbol. Her own cool, grey eyes looked straight into those worldly blue orbs under the halo of black hair.

"Thank you, Edwina. It's very fine, I know. It was a gift from Sebastian Ventura, a man whom I knew well in Bogotá some time ago. He's dead now."

"My God," Edwina said under her breath. "You've got guts!"

We must never be enemies, she thought.

"And now here is my husband Charles, but then you know each other already, he said, from when you were young here in New York!"

Charles bent over her hand. "Beautiful Laura. More beautiful then ever, I think, and much more deadly. I do not like to be blackmailed," he said softly.

She smiled. "Dangerous Charlie, more dangerous than ever, and so rich. You broke your word to me, Charlie, and that's something I'm told a gentleman does not do. I did not like the idea of being killed when you tried so hard to do it."

"We'll talk later," he said softly, "and now may I introduce Lord Charles Herbert and Lady Charles, from InterBank in London, and Monsieur and Madame Francois Belhomme of the Banque de France, and Senor Carlos de Mendoza from Banco Espaniola in Madrid, and Senora de Mendoza."

Laura spoke her perfect, almost too perfect, French and her fluent Colombian Spanish. She began to enjoy herself. She noted the looks of admiration in the eyes of the men and those of envy in the faces of the women. She had escaped from Bogotá and Sebastian, from Charles and from the vengeance of them all, and she discovered in doing so that she had the strength to go wherever Andy wished, even to the Presidency of the United States, if that was what he wanted. Damn these people! She needn't be worried about any of them, all of them so pompous, so secure, so frightened of change behind the complacent masks.

She understood enough of their world, however, to know what they did and how they thought behind the facades and the protection of their jewels and their apartments and villas. She would never allow herself to be defeated by people like this. One world was soon to be ending and a new one growing in its place. She belonged at the top of that new world. She and Andy had paid their dues.

When all the guests had gone, the four of them were alone together in the library.

"Well, then," Charles said, "what is to be the bargain? We all have too much to lose for there not to be a bargain. Unlike Israel and Palestine, we cannot afford a war which would destroy us both!"

"Laura has told me a great deal about you, Charles, and about you, too, Edwina," Andrew said. "I know how you are using your drug profits to make what you both believe to be a better world, and therefore you believe you are justified in what you do. Well, I too think of a better world. I want to be President in 1992, and I want your unqualified support. That will pay me back for the murders and the fear and the fact that you almost killed me."

"You mean money?"

"I mean every way. Money, publicity, support from all your companies, speeches ..."

Laura interrupted him. "You broke your word, Charles. The deal was twenty-five per cent of the profits. You not only didn't pay it, but you tried to steal back what I had already earned."

"Andy's father is rich enough to buy an election," Charles said.

"Perhaps, perhaps not. A successful election is a very expensive operation, and it is you who will do it, Charles," Laura said. "That is what you owe us."

"And then I have an enemy in the White House. Why should I do that?"

Edwina stood up and walked across the room. "There is only one person in this room who is truly innocent," she said, "and that is Andrew Davidson! All he has ever done is try to care for the woman he loves. Each one of the rest of us is already compromised by greed or selfishness – if there's a difference! Let's have no talk of enemies. We are colleagues whether we like it or not. We must sink or swim together. If we fight each other, we'll destroy everything that any of us believes in, and perhaps even our country as well. If we all believe that we can make a better world then why not try, each of us in our own way? No one else is making much of a fist of it, and drugs haven't killed as many people as wars – not yet!" She turned to her husband. "So … Charles?"

Charles looked at her.

"Yes, you'll have our support," he said heavily. "You know, Andy, your wife and I started out together in this venture. It's ironic that we should end up the same way."

Laura said, "I had your word once before, Charles. It wasn't worth much."

Edwina stepped forward in front of Andy and held out her hand to Laura.

"This time you have mine," she said. "I pledge our support. I give you my word. If we can help you to win the Presidency, it will be yours, no matter what it costs."

Laura looked at her. She took Edwina's proffered hand.

"Yes," she said. "I will accept Edwina's word. But I want Nick, too. I want Nick to run our campaign."

"Nick? I can't do without Nick!" Charles said.

"You will have to try. Nick knows where all the bodies are buried, and I want him on our side," Laura said. She crossed the room to Charlie and kissed him lightly on the cheek.

"Cheer up," she said. "Andy will make a marvellous President, and he, too, has no pimples on his ass."

Charles looked at her and burst out laughing. "My God, Laura, don't you ever forget anything?'

"No," she said. "Nothing!"

Upstairs in their room, Andrew said, "Do you trust him?"

Laura looked at him in amazement. "Damn it, Andy, of course I don't trust him! You're as bad as all the others. Because he's handsome and behaves like a gentleman, you believe he is one. But Nick will keep him honest, and I do trust Edwina."

"Who is Nick?"

"He's the third man on our team." She laughed rather sadly. "Nick's the one who wanted to be a free man. We said he was the only one of us who would fail. I wonder if he did?"

Andy put his arms around her. "I think there is only one man who can protect us from Charles Bellamy," he said. "Tomorrow we go to Georgia. Willie Davidson will keep him in line. I'd put my money on him against Charles Bellamy any day."

"Do you think he'd help us?"

Andy looked at her with astonishment. "Of course he'll help us," he said. "He's my father."

PART FOUR

Checkmate
1992 – 1997

CHAPTER ONE

ATLANTA, GEORGIA
NOVEMBER 1992

When Andy and Laura returned from their visit to New York with Edwina and Charles Bellamy in 1984, they went to Willie Davidson to ask for help. Laura liked her father-in-law. Her own father had always been a rather distant figure, and he had died while she was in Bogotá. Willie was, in a sense, the father she had never had, but her affection and admiration for the old man went a good deal deeper than that.

"What will we tell your father and what do we leave out?" she had asked Andy before their meeting.

"Leave out? We don't leave out anything. If he's to help us, he must know the whole story."

"What about Sebastian? What about all that?"

"You told me. It didn't make any difference to me."

"But this is your father. He's older. He belongs to a different generation. He expects so much from me!"

"He knows you," Andy said. "He loves you. He sees how happy I am. He credits you with bringing me home again, making me well, giving him a grandson. You know his attitude. If you're good enough for me, you're good enough for him, and if you're good enough for him, you're good enough for Atlanta and if you're good enough for Atlanta – by God, you're good enough for anywhere."

So they told him the whole story. He listened without interruption. When they finished, he said, "Everyone makes mistakes. Life's full of them. You'll make plenty more before you die. Don't waste your time on regrets. Today is all that matters. Today and tomorrow, if it comes – and if it doesn't, well that's the end of your worries, isn't it?"

They were dining at his farmhouse outside Atlanta. Laura was wearing a long dress of fine white wool, which she had bought in New York. Her hair was drawn back from her forehead and she wore no jewellery except her emerald ring. Willie Davidson thought that she looked beautiful. He knew that his son was a lucky man.

"So you lived with a crook in Bogotá and educated yourself. You speak fluent French and Spanish. Not bad. You go and lift up the rugs in any drawing room in Washington and a lot worse than that will come crawling out. You've got style and you've got guts. So has Andy. Between us all we've pots of money. I think Andy would make an excellent President, and you will make a perfect consort. I think you should go for it. After all, what more do we need than that?"

"Freedom from scandal? Protection from Charles Bellamy?"

"Yes. Bellamy is a dangerous man. You say he's agreed to help?"

"Yes, but only because we've threatened him with his own past. I don't trust him," Andy said.

His father laughed. "Nor should you. Don't trust anyone if you want to be President. Leave him to me. I'll help you deal with Bellamy. What about his wife?"

"Edwina?" Laura asked. "I worked with her in Delhi for more than a year. She has nothing to do with the business of drugs, but I'm sure that she knows where the money comes from. She is like him in many ways. She likes the prestige and so long as she can use it to some good advantage in the world she doesn't really care where the money comes from – and it gives her great power, too."

"Then they are very vulnerable. Dangerous and crooked idealists."

"She is a realist," Laura said.

"Do we have anything we can use against him?" Andy asked his father.

"In the banking world? Not that I know of," the old man said. "The operations we have conducted with his banks have always been undertaken with the utmost probity, but we will find something, never fear. I'll stand by you, and so will everyone on my team." He looked at them both and smiled with some satisfaction. "That will count for a lot. You'll be surprised." He raised his glass. "Here's to a future President of the United States, and to the most beautiful woman in the South."

"When do we start?" Andy asked.

"Right now. You're only a junior senator with one successful election behind you. If we want to get you elected in 1992, then we start right now."

"We already have Peter Francis who has agreed to handle the media, and Nick Barton is to be seconded from Bellamy's operation to manage the campaign."

Willie frowned. "Do you think that's wise?"

Laura said. "I'd trust Nick with my life. In fact, I already have, and he saved it."

Eight years, and two senatorial elections after that dinner with Willie, they were all gathered at the farm again, watching the retiring President concede defeat, and Andrew

Davidson become the new President, and Laura Tessier Davidson the new First Lady of the United States. Nick watched quietly from across the room while Andy made his acceptance speech, with Laura standing by his side. He couldn't help remembering her, all those years ago, in BJ's bar. She had wanted to be the most famous woman in the world, as famous as Marilyn or Jackie – well, he thought, now she was. Charles was the richest man and Laura the most famous woman, just as they both had wished all those years ago

But am I a free man, as I had wished? Nick thought. Well, maybe not free, but freer than most men. He wasn't doing too badly. He believed that he could settle for that.

Peter came over to stand beside Nick. They smiled at each other. From now on, they would both be only one step from the seat of power. What would they do with that?

CHAPTER TWO

CANALA CITY, CANALA
FEBRUARY 1994

THE PLANE SKIDDED SLIGHTLY as it landed on the greasy runway at Canala Airport. The rain was torrential. In a few minutes it would be quite dark with the sudden tropical night. Because of the storm the airport was closed to all commercial traffic, but as Charles Bellamy was the personal guest of General Thomas Balthazar, President of Canala, his jet had been given special permission to land.

Charles could see that the perimeter of the airport was ringed with soldiers, and there was a special extra guard at the terminal, although no evidence of passengers or of any activity. When the steps were brought to Charles' plane, a colonel of the Canala Armed Forces came on board immediately without requesting permission.

"Mr Charles Bellamy?"

Charles was annoyed. He disliked and resented this aggressive interruption.

"Yes?"

"I am Colonel Manuel Lorca, adjutant to the President. I am to escort you immediately to the Palace. You have brought a secretary?"

"I always travel with three assistants, Colonel Lorca."

"They may not come. A car will take them and your crew to a hotel in town. Come!"

Charles remained seated at his desk in the main lounge of the big plane.

"I think there is some misunderstanding, Colonel Lorca," Charles said with frigid politeness. "I am here as a guest of the President and at his particular and urgent request. My valet and my personal secretary will come with me while the rest of my people go to an hotel, or we shall re-fuel and leave immediately."

"I have my orders, sir."

"I am sure you do, Colonel Lorca. However, I am not a citizen of this country, and you are on my plane, and therefore on United States territory, without my permission. I am quite certain neither the American Government nor your President will be pleased if you remove us under duress."

Colonel Lorca stared. "Very well," he said abruptly.

Charles said to the captain, "Have the plane refuelled immediately, then go to an hotel, and let me know where you are. Be ready to leave at thirty minutes notice."

An airport attendant held a huge umbrella, under which they walked in the torrential rain to a waiting limousine that flew the presidential standard. The soldiers opened the gates and the car passed through. The soldiers were dirty, undisciplined and dangerous looking.

"I am pleased to be able to assist the President," Charles said to Colonel Lorca, "but I have received no briefing papers for this meeting."

"I am not in the President's confidence in this matter."

His tone indicated that he was both angry and jealous at this situation, and he retreated into silence. Charles stared through the window at the tropical suburbs and nondescript Central American Spanish architecture. There were soldiers at the intersections but no traffic. He supposed this to be normal in a country like Canala, although it was difficult to imagine what might be considered normal in a country torn constantly by revolution. It was ruled by a President who had refused to depart when democratically rejected by his people, and who seemed determined to bring his country to chaos and destruction.

The car raced through a pair of huge gates, drenching the guards as they presented arms. They drove up a wide driveway and stopped under a porte-cochere. Inside, another adjutant, with a heavy, ill-humoured face, came forward.

"Mr Bellamy? The President will see you immediately."

"I would like ten minutes to change."

"That is not possible! The President wishes to see you immediately."

Charles followed the overdressed back of the adjutant up an elaborate stairway and through a room whose shelves were stripped of books and into an office where President Balthazar sat behind a cheap copy of a Louise XIV desk. Once styled the saviour of his people, and leader by popular acclaim, he was now a feared and detested dictator supported by a network of corruption that made his predecessor look like an angel. He was surrounded by a private police force of drug smugglers who knew their lives would be forfeit if anything happened to their leader, and who were prepared to fight even their own people to keep their jobs.

The General remained seated. He watched Charles' progress across the room with lizard eyes set in a grey and pockmarked face. A pulse beat in Charles' temple but he controlled his anger. The doors were closed behind him.

"You may be seated, Mr Bellamy."

"General, unless I have your assurance that my crew and staff will be treated with greater courtesy than I have as yet received, I shall find it quite impossible to be of any help."

"We are in the midst of a crisis, Mr Bellamy."

"The crisis is yours, General, not mine. If you wish to have my help, then there must always be courtesy."

The General looked at him with small, hard eyes. "I am informed you are available, Mr Bellamy, if the fee is sufficient, with or without courtesy. This visit is not expected as a favour."

"Indeed I should hope not, but we have yet to establish whether the fee is, in fact, sufficient. So far, in coming here at all, it is I who have extended the favours, such as they are."

The General grunted. "Cut the crap, Bellamy. You came because you could smell money all the way from Miami. Let's get down to work. You've heard what's happened in Bogotá and Medellin?"

"You mean the escalation of the war between the Medellin cartels and General Masa in Bogotá?"

"Are you aware that yesterday a bus was driven into General Masa's headquarters? It was detonated and killed three hundred people."

"Yes, I know about that. Neither the General nor his senior aides were killed, in spite of the fact that there have been several attempts on their lives."

"You are well informed. This latest news is not common knowledge."

"I would not be in business if I depended on common knowledge. What is the point of all this, General?"

"You know that Jorge Ventura is the leader of the cartel troops."

Charles shrugged. "He has a great deal to lose."

"As do you."

Charles smiled sourly.

"Now that Communism is no longer a threat, the United States will increase its anti-drug offensive," Charles said. "They will give greater support to the Colombian government's initiatives in that direction. I have made my own arrangements to manage this situation."

"Your President assured me that I would have an adequate supply of cocaine. My country and indeed, my own survival, depend on this income."

"That undertaking was not made by President Davidson, General. The new President in my country does not agree with this policy. He is giving his full support to the initiatives in Colombia, as I'm sure you know."

"He breaks the word of the United States?"

"General, I am not here as a representative of the government of my country. I cannot speak for the President."

"Why not? You helped to put him there!" The General laughed disagreeably.

"I had my own reasons for supporting President Davidson."

"Are you aware that your President is to blockade the whole coast, starting in two weeks?"

"I know of all this, although I am surprised that you do. It is highly classified information."

The General laughed again. "You and I, Mr Bellamy, must be paying the same people in Washington. However, the unhappy result of this activity is that my supplies are drying up, and so therefore is my cash. What will you do when this blockade starts?"

"General, we are bankers to the Ventura family, but we have no other connection ..."

General Balthazar interrupted angrily.

"Come on, Bellamy, let's not fuck around here, for

Christ's sake. Time is too valuable for this kind of crap. And you needn't worry that the CIA bugs my office. Here at least we can speak frankly. I've known for years that you control the Ventura distribution. You bring tons of their stuff into America and Europe every year, although I wish I knew how. I know who sent that plane into a mountain all those years ago. You got rid of that fool, Jerkovitz, because you couldn't buy him. Now you've helped to make a President. If I didn't know these things I wouldn't be talking to you." He took a deep breath and lit an enormous cigar.

"Now, shall we start again? What are you going to do to stay in business?"

"Nothing! It's too risky at the moment and I have at least three years supply stored in America and Europe. After that I will look for new sources if the Ventura family are out of the business. Under this President, I think Colombia is finished. Maybe he'll even find a way to put a stop to the whole trade, in which case we are out of it. My assets are re-invested elsewhere. The drugs are no longer necessary. They merely put the icing on the cake."

"Ah, an idealist in the White House. That will be interesting!"

"Not an idealist, General. We have not elected anyone quite so dangerous as that. The President is an honest, practical man. A realist! And finally it seems that there are apparently enough honest men in Bogotá. Don't waste your time, General. You are to be indicted in the United States for drug offenses. This new administration wants your scalp, and I believe they'll get it. Don't make it worse by trying to deal any more with Jorge Ventura who is, anyway, a dangerous fool."

"Easy for you to say, my friend, but the Americans have cut off my money supply, and my arms shipments. I am no longer on the CIA payroll. If I cannot raise funds I'm finished.

I want you to sell me some of those supplies you have stockpiled against a rainy day."

Charles shook his head. "The rainy day is here, General. Why should I sell my umbrella? Besides, with what would you pay?"

"I have funds in Switzerland."

"Indeed? Have you been reading what the Swiss are doing with the dubious accounts of Eastern bloc leaders? They are embargoed until proven legitimate. They will do the same to you. They could tie up your money forever."

The General rolled back in his chair and rocked with laughter, slapping his meaty thighs at Charles' little joke.

"Those Swiss bankers are really something else, aren't they? First they have their banking secrecy so they attract all the illegal cash in the world, all the money stolen by politicians, all the drug money, all the illegally exported funds from the Communists. They know how high it smells. That's why it's there. Now the Communists have no power, so what do the Swiss do? Steal their funds! Ha!"

"This is done by the government, not by the banks!"

"Total sophistry! Total hypocrisy. The point of the matter is that I am still a head of state and they dare not touch my money, no matter how crooked they are!"

"Not until you are deposed," Charles said.

"And that will not happen!"

"Perhaps your excellent sources in Washington have not yet informed you that an invasion of your country is planned for the fifteenth of this month, in order to free your people from the yoke of tyranny," Charles said with heavy sarcasm. "They intend to take your person back to the States for trial."

General Balthazar slapped the table with his enormous fist. "Lies!" he bellowed. "My sources of information are impeccable!"

"Not so impeccable, perhaps, under the current regime. And in the event that such an invasion takes place, you will no longer have funds in Switzerland with which to pay me."

The General jumped up and paced around the room, muttering to himself.

"No, no, they wouldn't dare to invade a small country like this, to depose the legitimate," he corrected himself, "the de facto, government. The United States would not dare. The UN would never permit it!"

Charles gave a bark of laughter.

"And what will the UN do for you, General? Pass a resolution?"

"The Church? What about the Vatican? After all, this is a Catholic country!"

"The Church?" Charles asked incredulously. "You have insulted Rome consistently ever since you came to power. I should imagine they would support any opposition they could find. You have robbed the Church of its property here. You have given no funds to its works for years. You have abolished its rights and removed religious toleration. The Holy Father will be pleased to see you go. You'll get no help there.'

"They would support me for money."

"I doubt it. Even Rome is not so cynical!"

"I do not worry. How do I know you tell me the truth?"

"I see it in your face," Charles said.

"I have my troops. I have my secret police! There will be a popular uprising, like Vietnam. My people do not like Americans!"

"And if these things do not happen, what would you do to pay me?"

"You could trust me!"

"General, I have not trusted anyone since 1965, and in

that period, as a result of such a policy, I have become prosperous. I am a banker now, Balthazar, no longer an idealist, and certainly not a revolutionary. I want payment up front or no deal. I do not trust revolutionaries."

"I am a head of state, and can guarantee payment as such."

"I do not trust governments, either, for that matter. I have more chance of getting money from my gardener than from a sovereign state that decides it does not wish to pay. Cash or nothing!"

"How do I know you will deliver?"

"You don't. You will have to trust me!"

"Trust!" The General spat in a cuspidor beside his desk. "You do not trust me!"

"It is not I, General, who asks for the favour."

General Balthazar looked at him. "If I give you my Swiss funds now, and I am deposed, will you have to declare the transaction?"

"If the Swiss government were suspicious, and if the funds were still in Switzerland. However, they could be moved immediately to the Cayman Islands, and then back to Liechtenstein, then to Monte Carlo, and then ..."

"And your fees?"

"Fifty per cent ... and, of course, payment for the drugs you want sent here. You will pay twenty per cent above the current bulk price, and you will be responsible for transport. I suggest you send Canala Air Force planes while you still can. We will move the funds out of Switzerland as soon as they are deposited in the Banque des Trois Cantons."

"And if I decide to use someone else? Someone cheaper?"

Charles looked at him with contempt. "There is no one else, cheaper or otherwise. Take it or leave it!"

"If I ever find out that you have swindled me ..." the General said.

"General Balthazar," Charles interrupted with icy politeness, "I'm not accustomed to dealing with people who use this kind of language. However, if there is no invasion and you remain head of state, I am prepared to cancel the whole deal, and charge a five per cent fee for cancellation. Can I be fairer than that?"

"Who tells you about the invasion? Who has access to it other than President Davidson?"

"My dear sir, I can only tell you that I do not receive any information from President Davidson, who is an honest man. More than that I cannot say."

"You are an evil man, Bellamy. You are greedy and evil. In the end you will do more harm than me."

"And perhaps more good, as well. The evil, yours and mine, will last only as long as we do. The good? Who knows? It may last forever. When you seized power here, you did some good."

"I did much good."

"Then who knows? Perhaps history will forget that your good was paid for in drugs and misery. Look at Napoleon. Only the glory remembered! Look at the Church. So much death to prove that Christ was right."

"The Church!" the General interrupted. "That is what you must do for me before you leave. Go to the Papal Nuncio, and ask him to receive me in sanctuary, if I need it. Ask what it will cost. If there is trouble I could still go there."

Charles shrugged. "I doubt they will have you, but I will ask. Then I want immediate clearance for departure."

"You are not concerned about a bomb?"

"While I am still useful to you, General, I am sure that your airport security will make sure that there is no bomb on my plane. Have your driver take me to the Archbishop's Palace."

"And if I am defeated and arrested and taken to America and tell them of this meeting?"

"You may do that if you wish. My flight plan shows that I flew to Nicaragua to meet with my representatives who will, of course, say that I was there. There will be no trace of banking records, and certainly no trace of any more dubious transactions. The members of my crew are paid enough to know nothing. You would not be believed."

"And the Papal Nuncio?"

"The Church is wiser in the ways of deceit than either you or I can possibly imagine. She has had two thousand years of practice. My advice to you would be to keep your mouth shut, otherwise your scarce resources may be even more depleted."

It was after eleven o'clock when Charles reached the residence of the Papal Nuncio. The night was dark and stormy and the streets barricaded and manned with surly soldiers. The car was not stopped, but the way was devious and slow.

At first the frightened servants would not call the Cardinal, who had retired for the night. Finally his secretary was located and persuaded that Mr Bellamy came directly from President Balthazar and required an urgent audience of His Eminence. A little after midnight, Cardinal Frederico Montiniero appeared in his drawing room in his dressing gown, but not in any way bereft of his dignity, which was bestowed by his great height, his intelligence and his biretta.

He extended his hand and Charles kissed his ring, not without amusement. Everything has its price, he thought wryly.

"So, Mr Bellamy, we meet again, and once more under rather unusual circumstances."

"I had forgotten that Your Eminence had been with the Vatican Bank before your elevation.'

Charles had forgotten no such thing. Cardinal Montiniero, then a bishop, had been privy to the transfer of Ventura funds to the Banque des Trois Cantons after Jaime Ventura's death. A considerable percentage had gone back to Peter's Pence and thence, no doubt, to Solidarity in Poland. The Pope, Charles himself and Cardinal Montiniero had all been satisfied with the deal. Parish priests, even bishops, may not meddle in politics, but no such restriction applies to the Pope himself. John Paul II would one day be recognized as having changed the face of Europe, with a little help from funds derived from drugs. Charles had little doubt that that particular debt would not be acknowledged, but he knew that everyone who mattered was well aware of his contributions.

"May I congratulate Your Eminence on your elevation? The Church shows its wisdom in many ways."

"That will do, Charles. No flattery! We all have to compromise to achieve our ends and what's past is past. To what do I owe the honour of this surprising late night visit?"

"To the question of sanctuary, Eminence."

"What?" Even the old prelate's urbanity was shaken. "Don't tell me that you, my dear sir, are asking for the protection of the Church?"

Charles laughed. "No, not I. I come as an emissary from the President, who requests it, should the necessity arise."

"How could it? He rules with a rod of iron, the opposition is all in gaol, and the Church in Canala reduced to penury. I have been insulted publicly by the General, as has His Holiness himself."

"But in the event that an American invasion changes these matters?'

"Ah!" The Cardinal thought a moment. "In such an event I believe the Vatican would find it difficult to offend the American government. The question would have to be referred to the Curia, of course. It would be a matter concerning our relationship with a foreign power."

"Eminence, General Balthazar is a Catholic."

"Long since lapsed and ex-communicated!"

"But if he were to repent, and ask for absolution, can the Church withhold Her mercy, or would you have him murdered on your doorstep? Think how that would look in the world's media."

"The world's media, as you very well know, Charles," the Cardinal said sourly, "has an unpleasant tendency to dramatize."

"Nevertheless, Eminence, on your doorstep? It would not look too good!"

"I take it your information about an invasion is reliable?"

"Reliable and confidential. However, as I know that you will immediately inform Rome, I ask that you do not identify the source. Regard it as having been told to you under the seal of the confessional."

"Charles, do not make fun of our institutions."

"I'm sorry, Eminence, but what would you have done with this vital piece of information if you had received it under the seal of the confessional?"

"I would have sent it to Rome, as you very well know," the Cardinal said with a slight smile. "What will happen to all the Church property which has been confiscated by the General over the years?"

"Unofficially, I imagine that President Davidson would pressure any new government in Canala to restore Church property."

"You know him well?"

"Andrew Davidson? I know him well enough to assure you that he is a decent and honourable man. However, on a more private and delicate matter, I am authorized by the General to make a personal donation directly to you in the sum of fifty million dollars in the event that the General needs help and that he can find it here in an emergency."

The Cardinal was too urbane a churchman, and too experienced a banker, to even so much as raise his eyebrows, but he could not forbear to ask, "From his personal funds?"

"I have just this evening been appointed as his banker and he has authorized me to make this visit on his account."

"Tainted money, Charles. Tainted money!"

"Nevertheless, Eminence, money returning to a source where it can do most good for the poor people of Canala, would you not agree? It could hardly be said to be the first tainted money the Church has accepted in two thousand years."

"You are very cynical for a young man, Charles!"

"No longer young, I'm afraid, Eminence."

"I shall seek advice from Rome and advise the President. I assume you do not remain?"

"I leave immediately. It would not be wise if this visit became too widely known."

"My lips are sealed as if by the confessional," the Cardinal said with a slight smile.

As the servants had long since retired, the Cardinal's secretary waited in the hall to show Charles out. At the airport the tropical night was still thick and dark, but the rain had ceased. The crew was already on board, and the plane left immediately, climbing straight into the heavy clouds. At fifteen thousand feet, it broke through into the black starry velvet of the night sky. Charles undressed immediately, and fell into a deep and dreamless sleep.

CHAPTER THREE

SYDNEY, AUSTRALIA
1994

Betty Wellington was in the hall of Slowes Court, about to leave for her lunch with the members of the Sydney Opera House Committee, when Harry's car stopped under the portico and he came into the house.

"What are you doing home at this hour?" Betty asked. "Are you ill? You look awful."

Harry ignored her and threw the paper on the table. "Have you read the *Herald* this morning?"

"Invasion of Canala by the Yanks, and about time, too. That creep General Balthazar is in hiding. The dollar is up and the share market is down. What's upsetting you?"

He riffled through the pages of the *Sydney Morning Herald* until he came to a picture of Anne Fielding (nee Morgan-Smith) with two small children. It was obviously an old studio portrait, in which Anne looked younger and prettier, and more carefree than the way that Betty remembered her.

"Killed in a car accident yesterday, with both the children. Oh, my God!"

Betty touched his arm. "This is awful, but it's happening all the time. She's been very odd these last few years. She was probably driving badly."

Harry brushed her hand away from his sleeve. His face was white and furious. He looked at her with contempt.

"You don't seriously believe this was an accident?"

"That's what the paper says. She lost control on the greasy road after the rain and went over the cliffs at Mornington. It's something that could happen to anyone. Why are you taking it so hard? You hardly knew the woman."

"Betty," he said slowly, as if talking with a very small child. "Let's not get any further into the habit of believing even our own lies. It's very dangerous. We both know this was not an accident. Anne has never stopped accusing the Bellamys of corruption and murder, and finally they grew tired of it, or maybe someone important was beginning to listen. So now she's dead, and those two poor kids as well. They are dead because of us."

He sat down on a chair in the hall, placed there for the use of weary housemaids. "It's no good, Betty. I can't go on doing it. I thought I could, for you, for our children, but I can't."

Betty put her bag down on the table. "Doing what?"

"This whole business that we're in. Shit, we're helping to corrupt a whole generation, just so we can have all this." He waved his hand around the immense hallway. "But this is straight out murder, and they killed the children, too."

Betty stood up and took his hands in hers. "Get hold of yourself, Harry. You don't know it was murder. You're hysterical."

He stood up. "I am not hysterical. I'm thinking clearly for the first time in years and I cannot, and will not, go on with this. I wish to God you'd never seen that lottery win of Charlie's. I don't care whether this was an accident. It's all a part of the same evil pattern, and I can't live with myself any longer and be a part of it."

"Listen to me, Harry! I don't like it any more than you, but we're trapped. If we stop now, we lose everything, and we'd never be able to hold our heads up again. We'd be finished."

"Quite so, even if we managed to stay out of gaol, which is unlikely."

She grabbed his arm in a vice-like claw. "Gaol," she whispered in an awful voice, full of fear. "We can't go to gaol. What about the children? Harry, think! You haven't thought this through – how terrible it would be."

"I have thought it through all morning," he said quietly, "and I cannot do it any longer. Nothing that happens could be more terrible than what I am now doing."

She stood up quietly, accepting the fact that he was serious. "Are you going to the police?"

He shook his head. "No, not here. Here they would only catch the minnows. If I am throwing my life away, I want to catch the shark."

"And my life, and the children's lives, which I do not concede you have the right to throw away."

"I have the right to do what I must do. I am going to America to contact that reporter, Peter Francis, who is a friend of poor Stanley. I will give evidence, and I will catch that bastard Charles Bellamy and bring down his whole pretty house of cards."

"And you will be making this magnanimous gesture which will ruin us, in order to stop something which has been going on for centuries and will still be going on long after you and I are dead."

He ignored her. "I've already spoken with Peter. He thinks my evidence, added to what he has, may clinch the deal."

"You've told him already?" She felt the room sway around her as her dreams collapsed in shards in the hallway. "You've done this already, without even consulting me? Does my life mean nothing? The children? Don't we even rate a discussion after all these years?"

He looked at her with hatred.

"If it were not for you, we would not be in this position."

Finally it was out. After all this time, growing like a cancer in their marriage, and in their lives, it was said. It lay between them now like something alive, an aborted foetus, but he felt better.

"So," Betty said, looking at him with utter contempt. "The final resort of the weak man. Blame someone else! I despise you and I do not agree that, after so long, this option is any longer open to you!"

She picked up her bag and gloves and opened the front door. The chauffeur waited there beside the Rolls Royce parked under the ornate portico.

"I am now going to the Opera House lunch. Go to America and talk to your friend Peter Francis. Go to Alcon! Go to hell for all I care, but make sure that you are no longer in this house when I return at five o'clock."

She stepped into the back of the huge car, and listened as the door closed with that heavy clunk achieved only by a combination of money and good engineering. The door, she knew, was closing on a whole phase of her life. It was closing on her youth.

When she returned, she found the note.

"I am taking a Qantas flight this afternoon to Los Angeles, and then to Miami. I'll make sure there are some funds for you somewhere. I suggest that you make plans to leave Australia. Alcon will find somewhere safe, I suppose. I'm sorry. I will not be coming back. Harry."

She stood quietly in the hall. She should have known all those years ago that he would not have the guts to see it through. Every action has its price, she thought, and no one gets through life without paying it. Harry wanted the prizes, but he was a coward. He wanted to clean up his own conscience, and that would be enough. Never mind the litter and the debris of other people's lives. She wondered if that crime would ever weigh down his conscience. No matter. It would be too late and the damage would be done. She thought of the women she now knew in Sydney who would be pleased to see her lose her beautiful house and her wealth, who would gloat to see her fall.

The anticipation of such humiliation rose in her like a tide of bile. She thought of her children who were to be sacrificed on the altar of Harry's conscience. Two innocent lives for the price of one already corrupted? No, that would be a very bad bargain. She picked up the telephone and called Qantas.

"You have a flight to Los Angeles today?"

"QF110 via Honolulu left this morning, madam. Our direct flight QF001 to Los Angeles left on schedule at five o'clock. It has just taken off."

"Oh dear. My husband left for Miami, and I need his ongoing flight number so I can arrange for someone to meet him. Is that possible?"

"What name?"

"Harry Wellington."

"Yes, Mrs Wellington. We have him first class with a connection on United flight 430 departing from Los Angeles at six o'clock, local time."

She went upstairs and lay down. She felt very calm, as if all her life had been moving inevitably towards this moment. The East Coast was fourteen hours behind Sydney. At eleven o'clock she made her call to Miami.

"Bellamy Corporation, good morning."

"May I speak to Mr Charles Bellamy?"

"And who may I say is calling?"

"Mrs Betty Wellington."

"One moment, please ..."

"This is Mr Bellamy's secretary. Mr Bellamy is not taking any calls this morning."

"Please inform him that this is Mrs Harry Wellington and that this call is urgent."

"One moment, Mrs Wellington, please hold ... I am connecting you."

"Betty? I'm very busy. What is so urgent?" Charles asked impatiently.

"You know that Anne Morgan-Smith died yesterday?"

"As you have taken the trouble to make this call, Betty, then I assume you understand that I would know."

"Harry is on a Qantas flight to LA. He has just left and will go on to Miami on United 430 tomorrow afternoon, your time. He is not going there to see you."

"Peter Francis?"

"Exactly!"

It was so satisfactory talking with Charles. Nothing required any explanation.

"Who will manage his affairs while he is gone?"

"I can assure you that I am quite capable of running everything, now and in the future as well, should that be necessary. Everything," she repeated, with quiet emphasis.

"Thank you for your call, Betty. I'll be in touch." The line went dead.

Betty lay down again on her bed. In Miami a new day was beginning. At least, today was beginning again. It was as if God was forcing her to live this day twice, but she had made her decision and she was not a woman who changed her mind.

The Honour Code Of Greed

She rolled over in the large bed and closed her eyes. She slept.

In Miami the following evening, Peter Francis waited at the airport for Harry. He had waited for ten years to get this evidence, and with an affidavit from Harry Wellington he would finally be able to make his move. Every week Peter saw the dead bodies, and the freaked out junkies, and knew of the murders and the rapes and the break-ins and the babies born addicted. He knew of the whores, worn out at twenty, and of the disease and the destitution. He saw it all first hand, as he collected his stories and his evidence.

He knew that in those palaces along the inland waterway, or in New York, or Paris or Cannes, lived the men and women who made the marionettes dance. Perhaps now he could reach behind that golden curtain of money and power, and bring at least some of them onto the street with all their victims. Finally, now he would have enough evidence to catch the puppet-masters.

But Harry was not on the plane when it landed in Miami. Peter felt a dull weight in the pit of his belly. Harry had said that he was telling no one about coming to America. United said he was still in Los Angeles. Peter returned to the parking lot and sat in his car, away from the happy crowds of people welcoming friends. He knew that there would be no affidavit. There would be no evidence. He drove slowly back to his apartment.

The following day Fedex delivered a thick envelope from Harry Wellington, written by hand on the plane from Sydney and sent from Los Angeles Airport.

CHAPTER FOUR

WASHINGTON DC
1994

SENATOR GORDON MANCHESTER WAS pleased with himself. The senior senator from Florida occupied an imposing suite of rooms overlooking Washington's parks and gardens, with the Potomac River winding its way through the city. With a thin film of early spring snow covering the landscape, the Senator thought that his view of this centre of power and influence looked as good as he had ever seen it in all his many years in Washington.

Yes, he was very pleased with himself. Yet again he had managed to help to block the President's initiative for the legalization of drugs. He knew this would please an influential group of his conservative supporters who had no interest in seeing this lucrative trade handed over to legitimate chemists or the supervision of the medical profession or, God forbid, to the do-gooders and trendy liberals of the world. However, at the same time he had firmly established his anti-drug position with a vote in favour of continued US sanctions against Colombia and a vote in support of the invasion of Canala to bring the notorious General Balthazar back to Miami to be tried for selling drugs.

The situation was delicate. For some years the USA had supported the General. In return Canala had supported and favoured American interests in the area. Now the position had changed. General Balthazar's freely and democratically elected opponent was supported by the new government in Washington and by President Davidson. They were no longer prepared to turn a blind eye to the General's drug trafficking and his blatant breaches of international law.

What makes foolish men like the General turn against the USA, the Senator wondered. Vanity? The illusion that they can get away with anything? A feeling of invincibility? Ego? The fool must have known that support from Russia and the Soviet bloc would cease with the collapse of Communism. Even Cuba could no longer help him. Too late he had come crawling back to beg help from a new President who did not care to listen.

The invasion had been a complete success, although condemned by the United Nations, as President Davidson had expected. However, the world found it difficult to sympathize with a leader who had refused to depart when he lost a free election. Now the General, much to the amusement of the world, had been refused entry everywhere, including Cuba. He had sought refuge at the residence of the Papal Nuncio in Canala City, which had been temporarily granted.

The Vatican and the government of the USA were placed in an awkward position. If the Church continued to offer sanctuary against the wishes of the United States and public opinion generally, it would reflect badly on Rome. On the other hand, how could the Church expel from its protection even so lapsed a Catholic as General Balthazar, if he begged for sanctuary and for absolution?

Senator Manchester, a descendant of pilgrim stock and a lifelong Episcopalian, found his sense of humour tickled by this situation. Rome had two thousand years of somewhat devious diplomatic experience behind it and a solution would no doubt be found, he knew. However, following the play in so complex and subtle a game had put him in an excellent mood this sunny morning. It was not destined to last long.

On his desk was a thick envelope marked PRIVATE AND CONFIDENTIAL. TO BE OPENED BY ADDRESSEE ONLY. He shrugged and slit it open. With his reading of the title page, his whole enjoyment of the morning and of his own political shrewdness disappeared.

A REVIEW OF THE CONNECTION BETWEEN ORGANIZED CRIME IN THE SOVEREIGN STATE OF COLOMBIA, DRUG DISTRIBUTION IN THE UNITED STATES AND ESTABLISHED LEGITIMATE BUSINESS WITH PARTICULAR REFERENCE TO THE OPERATIONS OWNED AND/OR CONTROLLED BY CHARLES BELLAMY AND ASSOCIATED COMPANIES.

Prepared by Peter Francis.

A covering letter stated that the document was being forwarded to the Senator in the hope that some action might finally be taken in respect to the facts revealed in the document. It further stated that, until the Senator decided what action, if any, he should take, no further copies of the report would be distributed. All of this information made the Senator feel distinctly unwell. He told his secretary that he would take no calls and to cancel all his appointments for the morning.

Then he read the report. He was aghast. Peter Francis named names, companies, connections, diplomats, banks, bureaucrats, government officials, senators, members of the House of Lords and members of Parliament in England and Australia, an immense and complex network, but so far as the Senator could see, there was no concrete proof. No affidavits. There were no witnesses in custody, but the Senator knew that sooner or later these would emerge if an official inquiry were launched.

He thought for a long time. He had been in receipt of considerable consulting fees and campaign contributions from Charles Bellamy over the years. However, he clearly understood that his first job, if he wished to be able to live with himself in the future, was to protect the institutions of this great country. If those institutions were undermined by a document such as this ever seeing the light of day, he felt that the structure of freedom in America would be threatened, could even disappear. He had a clear duty to act, whatever his allegiance might be to Charles Bellamy, and whatever the financial cost would be to himself.

The Senator was not a fool. He knew better than anyone that his ranch in Arizona, and his house in Georgetown, and the funds which enabled his wife to be one of the most powerful and influential hostesses in Washington, all came from Bellamy. He was very reluctant to take any rash steps that might result in the loss of these trophies. On the other hand he had been a senator for many years, and had tried more or less honestly to manage a democracy that he believed was rapidly spinning out of control.

He was a democrat in the truest sense of the word, in that he believed in the freedoms offered by the United States to its citizens. He thought that his country had an enviable record of providing a good life for those who lived in it. He believed, within the scope of his own failings, that he was an honest man and a good American. If he took fees from established businesses to further their interests in the Senate, this was no more than was regarded as normal practice by most of his colleagues.

The Senator did not like Mr Bellamy. He thought it was men like him who had brought the American system into disrepute with their fathomless greed and complete amorality. Bellamy and men like him were destroying the America of the Founding Fathers, an America that the Senator truly believed had given so many millions of people a hope and succor that their own countries and systems had so significantly failed to provide. He despised that kind of man.

With some reluctance, and a very painful awareness of what it would cost him, but without hesitation once his mind was made up, he reached for the phone and asked his secretary to call the President.

CHAPTER FIVE

NEW YORK, N.Y.
1994

CHARLES BELLAMY WAS IN his apartment in New York when the President called.

"Good afternoon, Charles," Andy said.

"Good afternoon, Mr President."

"I need to see you in Washington, Charles. Something has come up."

"I would like that. I shall be there Wednesday of next week, if you have time, sir." Charles had to swallow hard on the 'sir'.

"That will not be convenient, Charles, I'm afraid. It is now five o'clock. I think you can be here by ten if you have that excellent plane of yours up there."

Charles was annoyed. The arrogance of these Washington people! In a year or two they would be thrown out of office, and retire into anonymity, while he would remain powerful and rich.

"I'm sorry, but I have a board meeting in half an hour and then a dinner with the Museum Trust. I could perhaps get to Washington at five tomorrow, if the matter is truly urgent."

President Davidson sensed his anger and was grimly amused.

"My dear Charles, even as President I am not in a position to order you to come to Washington. I merely suggest that in your own interests you get here as soon as possible, or your empire, and very possibly even mine, will be in serious jeopardy."

"And I suggest, Mr President, in view of the very considerable fortune which I have invested in your future, that if the matter is so urgent, you could use Air Force One to come to New York."

"Ah, Charles, if only it were as easy as that! Just let me say that I have, on my desk, an extremely compromising report prepared by our mutual friend Peter Francis. It was brought to me today by Senator Manchester, to whom it was sent by Peter. Have you by any chance seen this document? No? I thought not! I think you might consider taking my advice, by cancelling your appointments in New York this afternoon, and coming here as I have requested."

Charles Bellamy rarely lost his temper. He knew it was almost always a fatal mistake, which cost a man the advantage in an argument. But now he did.

"Mr President," he shouted furiously. "My money and my power and my support over the past several years have put you where you are, and you will do what I say or I will ruin you, and that bitch of a wife of yours as well."

Andy Davidson's voice remained cool. This was the same man, he reminded himself, who had done all that he could to kill both him and Laura. He owed nothing to Charles Bellamy. Nothing at all.

"You made a bargain years ago with Laura," he said, coldly and calmly, "and you broke it! You supported my candidacy because you had no choice, and you paid for it because you owed the money to Laura. If you recall, Charles, when I was first elected as a senator, Peter Francis, as my press secretary, made a statement which told the American people a good deal about my past, and Laura's, too. There is very little they do not know about us, and they still elected me to this office. Unless you are here by ten o'clock this evening, I shall release this report to the media, and we shall then see who the people of America are prepared to support."

He cut the connection and sat back. He was sure that Charles Bellamy would come, and that certainty gave him a great deal of satisfaction.

After Senator Manchester had delivered the report to the President, and returned to his office in the Senate Building, he spoke again with his secretary.

"Cancel my appointments for tomorrow, Stella, and get me on a flight to Atlanta this afternoon out of National. Give me two hours in Atlanta and then get me on a flight to New York. Book me into the Yale Club. Mark my diary that I went directly to New York, and forget that you ever heard any mention of Atlanta."

As Stella would willingly have thrown herself naked into the freezing Potomac River in the month of January and in full sight of the entire population of Washington if the Senator had requested her to do so, she merely said, "Is everything all right, Senator?"

"Perfectly, thank you, Stella. Just deal with those reservations. It's very important."

In five minutes she rang back. "I have you on Delta 245 leaving from National in forty minutes. There is a taxi waiting downstairs now. The seat is reserved in my name, as you wish to have no record of this trip. I have made the same arrangements on the flight from Atlanta to New York. I have charged them both to my own credit card. I have reserved a seat to New York in your name from DC this afternoon that I shall use myself, and leave the return portion at the Yale Club."

"Thank you Stella, you think of everything."

"Will you require transport in Atlanta, Senator?"

"No, I shan't be leaving the airport."

On his way to National Airport he dialled a number on his own cellular phone. The phone was answered immediately.

"Willie Davidson speaking."

This was his private line. There were very few persons who could reach him so easily and directly.

"Willie, this is Gordon Manchester."

"How are you, Gordon?"

"There is a problem here. It may affect you. It certainly affects the President."

"I'm sorry to hear that."

"You recall the Goldthorpe deal? I want to thank you, Willie. You got me off the hook there, and I owe you."

"You do, Gordon. Indeed you do!"

"I am repaying. Meet me in the Delta Lounge at the Atlanta Airport at six-thirty this evening. I'm on my way to the airport now."

"What's this all about?"

"Charles Bellamy!"

"I'll be there!"

* * * * * *

At three o'clock that same afternoon, Nick received a call at his office at the bank in Miami.

"Mr Barton? Mr Nick Barton?"

"Yes."

"This is the White House. I have the President on the line. Please hold."

Nick, of course, knew the President well. In accordance with the deal that Andrew Davidson and Laura had struck with Charles, Nick had run the campaign for his second term as Senator, and then for the Presidency, but since Andrew Davidson had been elected he had returned to his full-time work in the Bellamy companies. Nick had not heard from the President since he and his wife had received an invitation to one of the Inaugural Balls. He had not gone to the ball.

Now, he was pleasantly surprised and pleased to hear from the President. Nick had a family of his own now, and lived discreetly but very well indeed. However, he knew that he was still a little in love with Laura, even after all these years, and he hoped he might see her again occasionally. She was becoming very famous. She and Princess Diana hogged all the limelight.

The President came on the line. "Nick? Are you free?"

"For you, sir, always."

Andy Davidson was a damned nice man, and the only one Nick knew who apparently really was as honest as he seemed. Nick was not much of a romantic. How could he be after all these years of running the dirty works department for Charles? But he would have done anything for Andrew Davidson. He was the kind of man, Nick had long considered, who made America worthwhile, and there were very few of them in politics.

"We have a problem here. How much do you know of Charles Bellamy's affairs?"

"I know everything there is to know, Mr President."

"Would you be prepared to use it against Charles, if necessary?"

"You're asking a great deal, sir. We have worked together for almost thirty years. If he is compromised, then so am I – and so, by implication, are you, sir. I have no desire to put a rope around my own neck. Can you tell me more?"

"No, not on the phone. Have you a plane down there?"

"Charles has the big jet in New York, but there is bound to be something in the hangar."

"How quickly can you get here?"

"How serious is this?"

"It could be finite for us all."

He looked at his watch. "By ten o'clock," Nick said.

"Perfect."

The President hung up, leaving Nick disturbed and rather frightened. He knew that there had never been a time, since the beginning, when he had not thought that they were flying too high and might burn their wings on the sun, but their success had been so stunning and the rewards so glittering over the years that he had ignored these warnings from within. This afternoon his gut feeling told him that moment of truth had come. He tried to reach Charles in New York, but Nick discovered that he had cancelled all his appointments and left for Washington.

Nick rang his secretary and told her to have them get a jet ready for an immediate departure and to file a flight plan for Washington National. He would be at the airport in one hour. He rang his home and told his wife that he had been called to the White House for an urgent meeting with the President. She was more excited about it than Nick could bring himself to feel. He knew only too well, these days, when a problem was serious.

CHAPTER SIX

DELTA LOUNGE AT ATLANTA AIRPORT
1994

GORDON MANCHESTER MET WILLIE Davidson in the Delta Lounge at six-thirty. The commuter crowds had thinned out and there was plenty of room for privacy. They got down to business immediately.

"As a senator from Florida," Gordon said, "who do you think is the largest contributor to my campaign funds, and, ah, other expenses?"

"Bellamy, and his various companies," Willie said without hesitation.

"Exactly! So in this matter, I have had to tread carefully."

"Or else you lose all your additional fees and other emoluments and possibly your seat in the Senate. Come on, Gordon, this is hardly news to me. The whole world works this way. So?"

"This morning I received from Peter Francis a confidential and very damning report on Bellamy and all his business affairs. It seems that Peter has been working on this stuff for years, even with that chap Jerkovitz before he was killed in that plane crash in Colombia. You recall that?"

"Of course I recall it," Willie said impatiently. "I haven't got Alzheimer's disease yet. Get on with it, Gordon, for God's sake."

"This report would ruin Bellamy himself, but it would be also very bad for the President. In fact, in view of the massive and close support his campaign received from Bellamy, he would not, in my opinion, be able to survive impeachment. After some very careful thought, I gave the report to the President himself."

"Very sensible and correct," Willie said, "but I thought that Peter Francis was a supporter of my son!"

"He is, but this concerns a much broader range of issues. The report is not at all critical of the President. In fact, it doesn't concern him at all, but it could be very dangerous for him if it is released, because, as we all know – as the whole nation knows – Bellamy and his associates were vociferous supporters of his campaign."

"Yes," said Willie, with some satisfaction. "We blackmailed him into it, on the basis that it was better to have him on side unwillingly, than off-side and dangerous. We always knew it was a risk."

"Good God! Did you? I had no idea." He reached into his briefcase. "Before sending the report to the President, I made a copy. While I appreciate the support I've had from Bellamy, I feel that I also have a debt of gratitude to America, to the people."

"Yes, yes," Willie said impatiently. "So do we all. This is not a political meeting, Gordon. We can take all that as read. Now what is it?'

Gordon handed the copy of the report to Willie.

"This is probably the most dangerous document I have ever handled in my political life. As I've said, it would ruin Bellamy and many others. It could well bring down your son's Presidency, by inference. There is no allegation at all that the President is directly or even indirectly involved in any of Bellamy's schemes. I believe that if this President were to be sent packing, it would be a very bad thing for America. The document actually proves nothing concrete, even against Bellamy himself. It's all allegations, but I believe that Peter Francis wrote it because he is an honest man, and I believe it is the truth. Unfortunately, with these men who see themselves as crusaders for the truth, they often do more harm than good, in the end."

He sipped his whiskey before he continued.

"Before Andy was first elected to the Senate, he very shrewdly released the details of that affair in Switzerland, and his wife's connection with Sebastian Ventura, who by then was dead. It was very cleverly done, and brilliantly handled by this same Peter Francis. It turned them into heroes and paved the grounds for the campaign for the Presidency and it meant that all of the information was already in the public domain and could hardly be used as destructive ammunition by the opposition."

"But they didn't say that Laura went to Bogotá for Bellamy and that he paid her a fortune to do so," Willie said.

"No," Senator Manchester agreed. "They didn't say that!" The Senator looked at Willie with surprise and some admiration.

"Nor," the Senator continued, "did they say that the Bellamy fortune is founded in drugs and money laundering, although most of it is far removed from those matters today. Nor did they admit that Edwina Bellamy's Foundation is funded totally with funds that he stole from the Ventura family."

"All of this is in this report?" Willie asked.

"It is, and if it is all true, then it is the most shocking denunciation I have ever read about our political leadership, our business ethics, our banking system and the manner in which we run our democracy," Senator Manchester said. "I believe that we could be brought to the brink of a civil war. As two men from the South, I need hardly tell you that we do not want to see that again!"

"Who else has a copy of this report?"

"From me, only the President and yourself. From Peter, who knows. I haven't been able to speak with him since I received my copy this morning. However, at the moment, I believe I have had the only copy that has left Peter's possession. Things will not remain that way!"

"Why do you give it to me?"

"You are a powerful man. The President is your son. Use it to protect him, and our country and such freedom as it still has. God knows, reading this, it's less than I thought!"

"Thank you, Gordon."

Willie reached out and put a hand on his friend's shoulder. "Don't be ashamed that America is not perfect. Nothing ever is. The raw material for our institutions is so faulty, like everyone else's, but I do believe that we do better than most! I will tell you frankly, my family has been threatened more than once from this source, and I will use this document if I must."

"Do what you believe to be right, my friend. And now I must catch my plane to New York. No one except my secretary knows that I have been here, and she is completely loyal."

"I shall go to Washington immediately, Gordon. I want you to know that in giving me this document, you may well have saved the Presidency, and perhaps even Andy's life. Bellamy has tried to kill him before now. The slate is clean between us. You owe me nothing more."

The two old men walked down the corridor towards the departure gate for their flights to New York and Washington.

CHAPTER SEVEN

THE OVAL OFFICE AT THE WHITE HOUSE
1994

At ten o'clock Charles Bellamy was shown into the Oval Office. Laura was there, with Willie Davidson and Nick Barton. Charles greeted them briefly, and raised his eyebrows slightly at Nick.

"Sit down, Charles," the President said. "You intimated to me earlier on the phone, rather unpleasantly, that you considered you had bought the Presidency. I pointed out to you, as I must do again, that it was Laura's money, not yours, that financed my campaign. Be that as it may, you are mistaken. You may believe, rightly or wrongly, that you have bought me, the President, but you have not bought and cannot buy the Presidency. The job is larger than the man, Charles, and it is not, and has never been, for sale."

He tapped the report on his desk. "And it will never be for sale – not even to someone as rich and powerful as you."

He picked up the report. "This document was brought to me today by Senator Manchester, a man who is, I gather, in your employ, Charles?"

"We use him as a consultant, occasionally."

"Come on, Charles. Let's not beat around the bush here. Do you or do you not pay money to the Senator?"

"I do. May I ask what all this is about?"

"All in good time, Charles. This document is a report prepared by Peter Francis, a good friend, you might think, of this administration. Therefore, insofar as it can harm me, and it can, I can only imagine that Peter believes that the contents of this document are more important to the future of this nation than I am. That is his right, in a free country." The President sighed heavily. "In it, Charles, he accuses you not only of massive trading in illegal drugs over many years, of laundering of cash, of murder and blackmail, but, most recently, of treason, in that you are dealing with ex-President Balthazar of Canala. Nick has read the report. He confirms its truth. I shall shortly give it to you to peruse. What do you say?"

Charles looked around the room. He allowed his gaze to rest quizzically for a moment or two on Nick. He was very calm. Nick had never admired the man so much as in this moment of his possible destruction.

"All true, Mr President," he said calmly, "with the possible exception of General Balthazar. I had dealings with him, certainly, but only when he was the legitimate head of state of Canala. I have had no further contact with him since then, other than the fact that at the time of our last meeting he appointed me to be his personal banker and financial adviser. I am not, therefore, guilty of treason. As for the rest, each one of you in this room is implicated to a greater or lesser degree as accomplices. If you bring me down, down comes the United States with me, and all of the rest of you along with it."

"We all agree with that analysis," the President said. "We are here to discuss, not your crimes, Charles, but how we can save the administration, and the American people, from their consequences. If this report goes public it will appear that I am in league with the drug cartels. As you know, I am not, and never have been. We can't have that. You will be permitted to get away with your schemes, because we cannot put the whole of America at risk to punish only one man. It's too great a price to pay."

"What do you suggest?" Charles asked calmly. He knew that he was going to win.

"First we must speak to Peter Francis. We all know that he is a patriot, and an excellent investigative journalist, and an honest American, but he must see that he will do more harm than good with this report, particularly with so much of it apparently unsubstantiated by any hard evidence."

"You will find that difficult to do, Mr President," Charles said calmly. "He is already dead."

There was complete silence in the room. "I am not quite sure what happened," Charles continued calmly, "but I think the police will find that he committed suicide. It's very unfortunate!"

"You had him killed," Laura said. Her voice was shocked.

Charles stood up and let his gaze move slowly around the room, from one face to another, and when he was satisfied that he had held the eyes of each person in the room he spoke.

"My God, you people make me sick," he said quietly. "All of you! You want all the prestige and pomp of wealth and of power, you want all of its privileges, but none of you has the guts to pay the price for what you want."

"You had no right to act without discussing the matter with me first," the President said.

"Oh? Is that a new item in the constitution of our wonderful democracy? Thou shalt not act without the approval of the President, in person, because he is a saint who has done no wrong?"

He walked angrily over to the desk behind which the President sat, and leaned forward.

"I have saved your Presidency for you, Andy, make no bones about that! This death will never be traced to anyone, let alone to you. Now you do owe me a favour, for we destroyed all his papers in his apartment and all the information stored on his computer, and on his floppies. There is no copy of this report except the one on your desk."

"Yes, there is," Willie Davidson said quietly. "I have a copy, and if any action of yours ever compromises either my son or his wife, or if any harm comes to me, that report will be made public immediately."

Charles turned to Nick Barton. "Nick, we are leaving. I believe this discussion is finished."

Nick stood up and crossed the room. "I'm sorry, Charles. You and I have gone as far together as we are going. I am leaving Bellamy Corporation and I am going to work for the President."

Charles looked at Nick as if he had just crawled out from under a heap of shit on the pavement. "For peanuts, I suppose?"

"Thanks to you, I can afford to do it for nothing if I wish."

"What for? To try to build a better America?" Charles asked scathingly.

"Why not? It's not such a bad way to end my life. Isn't that what you and Edwina are trying to do with all your ill-starred gains?"

The President stood up. He was remarkably impressive, Nick thought, for so slender a man. He seemed suddenly not only good, but strong and good.

"I want the word of everyone in this room," he said quietly, "that nothing which has passed between us will ever be spoken of to anyone? Unlike some of my predecessors, no record will ever exist in the White House of this meeting."

One by one the company nodded.

"I want an oath," the President said. He called for a Bible and they all solemnly swore themselves to secrecy. Nick wondered how bound by such an oath a man like Charles Bellamy would feel.

"Am I free to leave now, Mr President?" Charles asked with scathing politeness.

"Yes, Mr Bellamy. Please give my regards to your wife, and goodnight."

In spite of himself, Charles said, "Good night, sir," before he turned and left the room.

"He has no religion," Laura said. "He won't keep his oath."

"I think he will," the President said. "He does have a religion, of a kind. It is the work that is being done by Edwina. He will do nothing to compromise that."

The President was right. Charles would never compromise the work of the Edwina Bellamy Foundation.

The following morning this headline appeared in the *Washington Post*:

Dateline 24 March 1994
PRESIDENTIAL AIDE SUICIDES

Well-known reporter Peter Francis, who had worked with President Davidson as his media liaison officer on all his campaigns since 1986, was found dead in his apartment in Georgetown late yesterday afternoon by his cleaning woman. A suicide note was found in the apartment but police have not yet released the contents of the note. The apartment does not appear to have been disturbed and there is no evidence of a break-in. Mr Francis had a long history of working on controversial stories, and was well-known for his interest in matters relating to the importation and distribution of illegal drugs in the USA.

A computer was found in the apartment, and police are

disturbed by the fact that no information is apparently to be found on the hard disc, and there are no back-up files or other related material in the flat. However, at this stage, the police are regarding the death as a suicide, while awaiting a coroner's report (see obituary notice page 27).

CHAPTER EIGHT

MIAMI, FLORIDA
1994

THE DAY AFTER HIS meeting with the President, Charles flew to Miami for a meeting with Monsignor Carter, the Bishop of Miami, a position of growing importance and influence within the Catholic Church in America. Most of the immigrants to South Florida were Catholic, from Cuba and South America, increasing the size of his flock and, equally important from Rome's point of view, the size of his purse. The Church in Florida had used Charles' bank for many years. He made sure the Bishop received excellent terms for his deposits. The Bishop's account brought those of many affluent Catholics to the bank. Each man clearly understood his benefit to the other, and so they had dealt amicably for several years.

Charles was surprised to have received a rather peremptory request for an appointment, and even more surprised to find His Grace a little ill at ease when he arrived at the bank.

"Come now, Bishop," he said, for Charles liked this old and sophisticated prelate. "We have done business for long enough together for there to be complete honesty between us, surely?"

He was, however, wary. He did not wish to antagonize so influential a barometer of local Catholic opinion. It would cost him a great deal of valuable business.

"I hope you are not unhappy with the service from our bank?" Charles asked.

The Bishop held up his hand. "No, no, my friend. It's nothing like that. We know, and so does the Vatican, that we get excellent terms from you. Last year we sent more money to Rome than did Chicago, thanks largely to you. No, I am here today on a much more delicate mission. A diplomatic mission which closely concerns your government. There must be complete discretion."

I seem to be more closely concerned with this government than I would wish, Charles thought wryly. Having helped to bring it into being, I would be happy to be shot of it at this moment.

"Bankers are more discreet than lawyers," he said, "or for that matter, than priests. We cannot afford to be otherwise. Whatever is said between us will be more sacred than the confessional."

"I should hope so," the Bishop said wryly. "I am here to discuss General Balthazar – a matter which is currently exercising the ingenuity of Washington and Rome."

"Ah, yes! The General."

"As we know, The United States has invaded Canala, offering for its justification the purpose of bringing the General to justice and, incidentally, of liberating the people of Canala and restoring, or more properly creating, a democratic government in that country."

"Quite so!"

"In the Church, we do not yet know why your government changed its attitude, but we do know that over many years it has offered much assistance to the General, and has always tolerated the disgraceful attitude of the General to the Church."

"President Davidson has changed the policy in this matter, I believe," Charles said.

"Quite! That is obvious. Do you mind if I smoke?"

"I guess the Lord is looking after your lungs."

"I doubt it, but since I must join him sooner or later, I may as well enjoy a few worldly pleasures before I go. I am reliably informed there is no smoking in heaven!" He opened his brief case and withdrew a sheaf of papers.

"We have some information," said the Bishop, pulling on his cigar and releasing a cloud of acrid smoke. "We know, for instance, that you were aware in advance of your government's plans. Perhaps you also know why they acted when they did?"

"I do not. However, I suspect they grew tired of paying the General when he was refusing to do what he was being paid for."

"He had been doing all that for years," the Bishop said. "Clearing the Medellin cartel's drugs through Canala City, using his Air Force, laundering money through his banks, perhaps even some of your money, my dear Charles. None of this would have been possible without the active co-operation of the US government, and of the world's banking system. Even President Bush, when he was head of the CIA, had this man on his payroll."

"Yes, Your Grace. I knew of the invasion plans. I warned President Balthazar, and assisted him in certain plans."

"Quite so! He asked you to get his funds out of Switzerland and put them somewhere really safe, and you have done so."

Charles was taken aback. This operation had been so discreet he did not believe that anyone could have traced it. The Bishop gave a small laugh at the look on Charles' face.

"Don't be so surprised. We have our own ways of getting this kind of information. We have been doing it for two thousand years, my friend. We don't care what you are doing with the General's investments, but there is a little matter which does concern us, and which His Eminence Cardinal Montiniero has raised with me."

"Ah, now I understand you, Bishop. You are here to discuss the matter of fifty million dollars."

The Bishop laughed. "You people from the new world are so blunt. I understand there was a conversation during a certain visit which did not take place, in which you negotiated some protection for the General."

Charles nodded. "His Eminence was so gracious as to indicate that he did not feel he could refuse sanctuary to General Balthazar if his life were in danger. I told the Cardinal that the General would, if this event took place, consider a refund of assets to the Church in Canala as compensation for property confiscated. You are right in stating that a sum of fifty million dollars was mentioned."

"Exactly so. And everything occurred as you had advised the Cardinal that it would and, considerably to our embarrassment, General Balthazar sought sanctuary in the Episcopal Palace in Canala City, and is still there."

"Yes, I am aware of these matters, but I am also aware that the US government is placing extreme pressure on both His Eminence and on the Vatican authorities to surrender the General. If this should happen, it would constitute a breach of our agreement, don't you think?"

"This is exactly the matter which I have been asked to discuss with you. His Holiness is very anxious that there be no breach of faith with the United States."

"Which is, after all, one of the richest and most populous Catholic countries in the world," Charles said, annoyed.

"Exactly so! However, His Holiness is equally adamant that sanctuary cannot be broken except under very specific circumstances. Both the Cardinal in Canala and the Curia in

Rome have considered the matter and come to the conclusion that the General is, in fact, a common felon, and therefore not entitled to the protection currently being extended to him."

"Come, come, Your Grace. You are no better than people like that reporter Peter Francis. How can the Curia come to this conclusion when the General has never been tried, let alone convicted, of any crime?"

"The Church has its own methods of deciding guilt."

"I am aware of that, but they do not necessarily accord with modern legal practice in a democratic state. The General has been charged with crimes, certainly, but he is not guilty under US law, or Italian law for that matter, until convicted. He cannot be convicted unless he leaves Canala and is tried. It would seem, Your Grace, that whatever you do, you will be in trouble."

The Bishop puffed his cigar. "Unless we can persuade the General to voluntarily leave the Bishop's Palace and consent to submit to the due process of the law here in America where, if he is innocent, he will be acquitted."

"And what you wish to know today is this. If you are successful in getting General Balthazar to take such an action, which gets both the Church and the US government off the hook, will I pay the fifty million dollars promised by the General in return for sanctuary?"

The Bishop laughed. "You are in a very blunt mood today Charles, but you are quite right. Under those circumstances, do we get paid?"

Charles leaned back. This was a situation he very much enjoyed. It took his mind off the recent unpleasant events in Washington. This feeling of power over so prestigious a supplicant compensated him for all the failures and frustrations of the past, for poverty and humiliation and for the guilt and disappointments of his life. He loved it.

He was silent. The Bishop waited. The Church was accustomed to waiting. It was better at it than most organizations for it measured time in a longer dimension, and therefore it usually won in the end. One lifetime was nothing to Mother Church.

Finally Charles said, "There are several matters to be considered here, but let me review them. Firstly, the money is not mine. I can only dispose of it in accordance with the General's instructions. Secondly, the sum is considerable, and I am not sure that it was meant as a reward for so short a period of protection as the General has currently enjoyed. I think he envisioned a more permanent solution. Thirdly, there is the delicate matter of whether the General actually volunteers to surrender or is simply handed over to the US authorities in Canala City. Finally, we must consider whether even so short a period of protection actually saved the General's life, and whether, without it, he might possibly have ended up as did Mr Ceausescu in Romania or the late lamented Il Duce, in spite of his good relationship with Pope Pius. Also," Charles paused, "there is another small matter of which you may know nothing yet, in spite of being so well prepared for this meeting.'

"Yes? And what is that?"

"Some years ago Senor Jaime Ventura y Cortez and his brother Jesus were unfortunately killed in a plane accident, you may recall?"

"I do, but what has that to do with the matter in hand?"

"Because, Your Grace, prior to his death, Senor Ventura signed his property into my protection and transferred his assets to me. Most of these assets have been transferred to my banks long ago, but not those that were held in the Vatican Bank. I have a feeling that if these funds were now transferred to me, then General Balthazar might look kindly on transferring some of his funds in return for the fact that the prompt action of the Cardinal probably saved his life in the recent insurrection and invasion."

The Bishop puffed one last puff and stubbed out the butt of his cigar.

"Thank you, Charles. I understand the position perfectly, and, as always, it has been a pleasure doing business with you. I shall advise you of our position in this matter shortly."

Charles kissed his ring, and the Bishop raised a hand in blessing. He smiled. "I understand, Charles, that you are to become a father later this year."

"That is so, your Grace. It is a great surprise to Edwina and myself after all these years. Edwina is no longer young, and we had long ago given up hope of a family."

"The Lord works in mysterious ways," the Bishop said.

"Well, I don't know about the Lord," Charles said, "but women are a constant surprise! She must now take a rest from her work. India is no place for her at the moment."

"She is rapidly gaining the reputation of a saint."

Charles laughed, but he was pleased. These were the opinions that counted in such matters. The Vatican could be a very powerful lobbyist in Oslo. He buzzed the button on his desk. The automatic doors to his office slid open, and Monsignor Carter passed through to the reception room, where one of the bank's aides accompanied him to the street door. Charles sat down and smiled to himself. So, he might finally get his hands on the rest of the Ventura billions merely by trading off some of General Balthazar's cash. Excellent! He stretched his legs and picked up the new edition of *Time Magazine*, delivered that morning.

On the cover was a photograph of Laura Tessier Davidson, First Lady of the United States, wearing splendid diamonds and looking stunning. She never seems to grow any older, Charles thought resentfully. Laura's beauty seemed like a personal reproach of some kind.

The cover story stated that the First Lady's popularity rating was higher than any who had preceded her, even Jackie Kennedy. The Americans loved her. They considered that she brought both glamour and family values to the White House. Charles threw down the magazine in disgust. All those years ago, when he had paid her to go to Bogotá, he had created a monster that might yet devour him and everything he had spent his life to achieve. He recalled wryly that, long ago, when he had rejected her, Laura had told him that perhaps, one day, she might be powerful enough to be of assistance to him. Well, he thought, she has the power now. It remained to be seen whether she would assist him or destroy him.

WASHINGTON POST
30 March 1994

General Tomaso Balthazar today voluntarily surrendered his person to the representatives of the United States government in Canala City, and left the sanctuary of the Episcopal Palace where he had been the guest of His Eminence Cardinal Frederico Montinreio since the invasion of Canala by United States troops in February. The decision of the General to surrender himself to US justice is credited to the intercession of international businessman and philanthropist Mr Charles Bellamy, who has worked tirelessly in the interests of both the Catholic Church and the US government to reach a satisfactory conclusion in what might otherwise have developed into a matter of international dissension. (See editorial page 18)

The General is to be flown to Miami to stand trial for crimes committed while he was in the employ of the government of the United States, which is now accusing him of illegal arms and drug deals.

It was uncertain just who would be on trial, Charles

thought, but that was the business of lawyers, not bankers. In the end most of the relevant evidence would be excluded on the grounds of national security, for it would compromise the United States as much as it would serve to convict General Balthazar. Everyone would, in due course, be released with a clean bill of health, including the State Department and the CIA.

CHAPTER NINE

WASHINGTON DC
1994

O N THE MORNING OF the arrival of the General in Miami, Nick Barton received a letter at the White House, where he now worked as a special assistant to the President. It was delivered by special messenger, and was marked to be placed in his hands only.

"Mr Nick Barton?"

"Yes?"

"I am authorized to deliver this letter only to you, from the legal office of Dumbarton Chellerton Smith and Freestone. May I have a signature of acceptance?"

He signed. He knew of this firm of lawyers, of course. Everyone in Washington knew of them. They acted only for the most prestigious and wealthy individuals and companies in the United States. They represented the interests of governments all over the world. He opened the letter with some trepidation.

It contained a single sheet of paper, and a small key.

1224 L Street
Georgetown
WASHINGTON D.C.
23 March 1994

Dear Nick,

    I know you live in the lion's den itself, but having worked with you on the President's various campaigns since 1986, I believe you are the only person whom I can trust, except the President himself and this is hardly a matter for him. I have today finished a long report on your boss, Charles Bellamy. It is made up from sources that include not only my own investigations, but also from facts given to me by Stanley Jerkovitz (now dead), Harry Wellington (disappeared, presumed dead), Sebastian Ventura (now dead), Senator Brailes (now dead, although from natural causes, I believe, if alcohol and sex can be considered natural causes!) and many others, including Laura Davidson, now the First Lady. I doubt that it contains anything that will come as a surprise to you, my friend, but it is a damning condemnation of both Charles Bellamy and of many of those who lead our nation, including regrettably, your good self.

    I have delivered this report to Senator Manchester, senior senator for Florida, as you know. Of course, he is in the pay of Bellamy, like many of them, but I think he has some decency and honesty. What he will do with it I do not know, but I do know that my own life may well be at considerable risk. I have run off one complete copy of the report that I have lodged in Box 7506 at Union Station, together with all my back up tapes from which the information in the report was drawn.

    I have wiped all records off my computer, and I have lodged all my files in a place they will not find, and which you will be told about if they kill me. They will find nothing. I am leaving this letter and the key to the box with Freddie Chellerton who was my roommate at Yale and the best friend I have. If anything happens to me, I have instructed him to wait six weeks, and then to have this letter and key sent to you by private delivery. If you receive it, it means almost certainly that I have been killed. No matter what you hear, I have not killed myself. Do with it what you will.

I enjoyed our work together for Andy Davidson. He may yet save America, he and Laura, if they can stay clear of scandal, but no one can know better than you that both of them are seriously compromised by the past, particularly Laura. Get out if you can, my friend, but be careful. America is in deep shit!

Peter

Nick looked at the letter for a long time. Back in 1967 Nick knew that he had been weak enough, and frightened enough, and, let's face it, poor enough, he remembered, to allow Charles to pull him into his world. Now he would pay the price, by being the only person in the world to possess sufficient evidence to convict Charles Bellamy and perhaps to bring down a good president with the scandal that would follow. Nothing is for nothing in the world. Nick wondered how long it would be before he finally learned that simple lesson. Even after all these years he was still learning that there is no free lunch! He smiled grimly to himself.

He buzzed his secretary. "I must go to New York, Martha. Cancel my appointments for today and tomorrow, please."

"Will you take the shuttle, Mr Barton?"

"No. I am going by train. Find out the schedule, will you? And order me a car to go to the station."

He had no idea what he would do with this information,

but it frightened him to have it, for he knew now that it had killed Peter, and Stan Jerkovitz and God knows whom else. Nick had no intention of letting it be his own death warrant as well.

CHAPTER TEN

MIAMI, FLORIDA
1994

UNREPORTED IN ANY NEWSPAPER, a sum of fifty million dollars was transferred from the Banque Caroline in Liechtenstein to the account of the Archbishop of Canala at Citibank in Canala City. A considerably larger sum was transferred from the Vatican Bank to the Banque des Trois Cantons in Geneva.

These events would have made an excellent day for Charles if he had not also received an invitation to lunch with Willie Davidson. He felt this might well be the most expensive lunch of his career. However, in view of the fact that Willie, so far as Charles was aware, had the only known copy of Peter Francis' report, he felt it wise to accept.

Willie was in an expansive mood. They sat at his table at the Miami Yacht Club, in the same room where Charles had dined with Laura and Sebastian Ventura all those years ago. They demolished two lobsters and a couple of bottles of excellent Chablis. Although New England was in the grip of a late snowstorm, here a balmy wind blew from the Caribbean, smelling of spice and salt. A white liner, slim as a yacht, was taking on provisions and would leave shortly to cruise those old pirate seas. Nowadays, Charles thought, the pirates are inside the clubhouse. It was the best place to do business.

Finally Willie put down his glass and looked at Charles.

"Did you know that my father was a sharecropper from Louisiana? He drank himself to death, but not before the cheap liquor had driven him out of his mind, and he had beaten my mother and raped my sister."

He signalled the waiter and ordered two cognacs, as if these matters were normal conversation between two rich men lunching at the Miami Yacht Club.

"When he died the authorities came down and threw my sister and me out into the street. They chucked our miserable possessions at our feet. I was twelve and my sister was a year older. I won't bore you, or spoil an excellent lunch, by telling you everything that happened after that, but I swore that neither I, nor anyone I loved, would ever be poor and vulnerable again. I won't tell you what steps I took to ensure this, but I do not regret one of them, and if necessary, I would do it all again. We only make one journey, Charles, and without the right luggage, it is not a pleasant one."

"Why do you tell me these things?"

"For two reasons. One, I know you, Charles. You are the other side of myself, and I do not stand in judgement. The other reason? I am a family man, and have worked all my life to be respected. I made a loveless marriage work, as I have no doubt you did, too. I did so because I could not spare the time for four generations of social climbing, which would have been necessary if I had married the girl I loved. I watched my only child go off to Vietnam strong and healthy, and return a wreck. Laura cured him, and turned him into a President. I wanted you to know that if you harm either of them again, I shall kill you. I have done it before. I would not hesitate, any more than you would."

He sipped his cognac and looked reflectively out of the window at the calm and wealthy scene along the marina.

"We both know that Laura could destroy you, as could I with my copy of Peter Francis' report. Laura is too clever to do it, and I am too old, but if anything happens to me, that report will be made public. The President, I happen to know, has destroyed his copy together with all records of the meeting we had the other night. I believe that Edwina is doing good work. I do not wish to destroy you or her, or the child that I understand she is about to bear you. You are very rich. Why don't you get out of drugs – leave it to the crooks – and just go straight?"

"Is that all?"

"Not quite. After all, you did once try very hard to kill my son and the woman to whom he is married. I think I deserve a little compensation."

Charles smiled grimly to himself. He had known this would be a damned expensive lunch.

"It has come to my ears that you have finally managed a small exchange of funds with the Vatican regarding the ex-President of Canala and sundry loose change which belonged to the Ventura family. A very risky business that, Charles. Very risky!"

"The Venturas ... "

"No, no I didn't mean those louts from Medellin who are all dead now anyway, without legitimate heirs. They were amateurs and fools or you could never have stolen so much from them. No, I mean meddling with the policies of the US government and with the Vatican. One day they're your friends, the next day your enemies. Look at poor old Balthazar himself – sold down the river, so the good old US of A can look squeaky clean again."

Willie sat back in his chair and sipped his brandy with some satisfaction.

"Nevertheless, you did manage a very advantageous

exchange. Shall we say that perhaps twenty per cent of those funds might turn up in Atlanta? Just as a matter of insurance of course, and as a nice belated wedding present for Andy and Laura. After all, you did give Edwina billions of dollars of someone else's rather dirty money. Why discriminate against me?"

Charles threw back his head and laughed as he had not laughed in years. He laughed, in fact, as he remembered Laura laughing in the Deli on 7th Avenue, when he had tried to get her to go to Bogotá for peanuts. Here they were, two old buccaneers, dining grande luxe in a very exclusive club, respected, admired, envied by the world, and over their brandies he had just been blackmailed out of a very considerable amount of money that he himself had stolen.

Charles held out his hand to the older man. "Okay. You get twenty per cent and we both keep our mouths shut."

"I knew that we could do a deal," Willie said. "We have always had splendidly successful joint ventures. Why should this one be any different?"

"Why indeed?"

They finished their brandies and retired, well satisfied, for a post-prandial nap in the smoking room.

The following morning, as Charles rode up to his beautiful office on the top of the Bellamy Corporation Building in downtown Miami, he felt more at peace with the world than he had felt for many years. His fortune was immense and intact. Jesus, Sebastian and Jaime were all dead, and Jorge, hidden away in Colombia, stupid and ignorant, would never be a threat to him. His wife was beautiful and admired throughout the world, and she had borne him a son to carry on his line. He crossed over to his huge glass windows and looked again at his cherished view across the water, and his gaze, in his imagination, wandered over the Caribbean, across all those islands in the sun that had co-operated in the making of his fortune.

Then he made a tour of his favourite pictures, kept in this glass eyrie for safety and for his own personal pleasure. He stood for a moment in front of his Picasso from the Blue Period, splendid as anything in St Petersburg; his lovely Goya, the equal of anything in the Prado in Madrid; his Utrillo, his Rubens – all of them evidence of his wealth and his success and the inviolable privilege of his present position. He felt impregnable, but not entirely without concern.

Two Kennedys had been assassinated. It was not impossible that it could be arranged for President Davidson to meet the same fate. Charles was satisfied that his money could buy anything that he wanted and Andrew Davidson and his wife Laura were becoming altogether too much of a problem, as he had known from the beginning that they probably would. Yes, it was time for something to be done about that.

He turned towards his desk and its bank of telephones, and as he did so, the whole huge sheet of glass looking out across Biscayne Bay shattered into a million shards and dropped away in a crystal cascade down the side of the building into the street far below. At the same moment as his stunned gaze took in the sight of a helicopter hovering not fifty yards away, Frederick, his senior security man from the bank down below, burst into his office and raced across the room, throwing himself bodily onto Charles and knocking him full length on the floor as the room filled with the spray of machine gun fire from the helicopter hovering in the sky. The canvases of the beautiful, irreplaceable pictures tore into shreds and one by one dropped from the walls.

Charles tried to push away the heavy body of the guard, which lay across his own. He could hardly breathe.

"You can get up now, Freddy. I'm okay."

"He can't get up, Charles," a voice from above his head said into the cordite-laden air. "He's dead."

Charles moved out slowly from underneath the guard's corpse and swiveled his head around to see the huge figure of Jorge Ventura y Cortez towering over him, and pointing his automatic straight down into Charles' face. Jorge laughed. It was not an agreeable sound.

"You thought I was too dumb to manage this, didn't you?" He rasped unpleasantly. "Never believe your own publicity, Charles. It's the only mistake that you and I can never afford to make." He lifted his arm and slowly shot three bullets into Charles' upturned and angry face.

"Once of those was for Jaime, once for Sebastian and once for little Jesus," Jorge said slowly each time he fired, and then he opened his flies and urinated on the body of Charles Bellamy. "And that is for my family, and for the honour of my family," Jorge said quietly, "which you pissed on so arrogantly in order to become so filthy rich! So much for your wealth now, Charles!"

The mobile phone on his belt rang. He zipped up his flies and answer the ringing tone.

"For Christ sake, Jorge! Quit messing around in there and get your arse over to the window! If we don't get away from here soon we'll have the whole fucking US Air Force blocking the way."

Jorge walked slowly to where the great window had been and waved to the pilot whose huge machine hovered outside. The helicopter moved as close as the pilot dared to the side of the building and the door opened. A rope catapulted from inside the chopper over to Jorge, who secured the buckle around his waist. Then he stepped from the edge of what had been Charles' beautiful office into the void, twenty-nine floors from the street below. The helicopter moved away from the building, swung heavily to the right and raced away towards the Florida Keys. Slowly the rope was pulled into the cabin with its burden, and the door closed.

CHAPTER ELEVEN

WASHINGTON D.C.
1994

When Nick collected the material that Peter Francis had left in the box at Union Station, he did not take the train to New York. Instead he rang Laura at the White House.

"I need to talk urgently."

"It's almost impossible for me to get away. What's it about, Nick?"

"Not about anything that we can discuss on the phone – particularly this phone."

"Bad news?"

"I need your advice."

"Well, I can hardly refuse that, after all the things you've done for me."

He laughed grimly into the rather smelly receiver of the public phone he was using. "Not so much, really, Laura. All things considered, not so much. I am checking into the Mayflower for the evening. Come there."

"Nick darling, I'm the wife of the President, and the best-known face in the United States. I can't just wander around to people's hotel rooms. What about my goons?"

"I'll take a suite, never fear. The goons can come up, if they wish!"

"I'll be at the dinner for the Daughters of the American Revolution this evening. I'll come by on the way home."

It was after eleven when Laura arrived. She looked magnificent in her evening dress and jewels. She had always been a beautiful woman, but power and wealth, and love, too, he guessed, had made her outstanding. Mysterious, too, and sexy in a way she had never been when she was younger. She had been lovely then, but cool and distant. Nick wondered why so many women were more erotic looking as they grew older. Young men never saw that aspect of women, he thought. Or never appreciated it.

She came inside, leaving her bodyguard at the door.

"What is this all about, Nick?"

"Do you want a cognac?"

She shook her head. "Maybe a glass of champagne. These dinners are heavy going and I am always on my best behavior. Hardly a drop passes my lips!"

"Do you ever think, Laura, about those days at BJ's in New York when we were all young?"

She looked at him with those clear, honest eyes, which had won America's heart.

"Yes, Nick, I think of them often," she said, "but they are gone forever. Don't romanticize the past, my dear. Any fool can do that! It won't come again!"

"You wanted to be more famous than Jackie O, and you are. Charlie wanted to be richer than Croesus and he is, and I ..."

She smiled. It was no wonder, he thought, that America loved her. It was a cliche to say that her smile lit up the room, but that's exactly what it did for that dismal hotel suite.

"And you said that all you wanted was to be a free man, and we both laughed at you."

Nick nodded. He felt close to tears.

"And are you not, my dear Nick? You saved my life in Bogotá, when it could easily have cost your own. I suspect you've done many good and kind things behind the scenes since then."

"Some," he said, "and many bad and dreadful ones, too."

"You ran a campaign that ended up with Andy as President, in spite of all the dirty linen that might have prevented that. Andy is a good man and he will be good for us all, for everyone in this country. You have every right to be proud, Nick! I don't know anyone in Washington or in America, for that matter, who has more right than you to call himself his own man. But free?" She laughed sourly. "Well, of course, free is another matter." She indicated the secret serviceman outside the door. "Is any of us free? Perhaps it is an illusion for the young and brave."

Behind them the music on the radio was interrupted:

"We bring you an urgent news bulletin from the Miami Police Department. There has been a terrorist attack earlier today on the building of the Bellamy Corporation, headquarters of the well-known Miami business leader, Mr Charles Bellamy. It is believed that Mr Bellamy is dead in the attack, together with several members of the security force in the building. Further news will be brought to you as soon as it comes to hand."

Nick looked at Laura. "Is that the FBI? Is that Andy's doing?"

She shook her head. "You know as well as I do, Nick, that Andy does not order people to be murdered."

"You must ring him immediately, but first we must discuss why I asked you here. This makes it more important than ever."

Nick took out the box with the report and the computer discs in it. He showed her Peter's letter, which she read quietly.

"Laura," he said, " you were always smarter than me. You knew from the beginning that I would not really be tough enough for this road. I want you to make a decision. What do I do with this? Peter died for it, and he has not been the only one."

Laura looked at the contents of the box for a long while in silence. Finally she said, "I don't think Peter would want any more damage done, do you?"

"He believed that those of us who have perpetrated these crimes should be punished. And he died because of that belief. He did not believe that punishment would damage America, Laura."

"Of course not, because he was a good man, like Andy, and they do not always see the damage that can be caused by doing the decent thing. Do you know I read somewhere that, in 1934, the British Ambassador in Berlin sent a secret report back to Westminster saying that Hitler was a maniac, and that Britain should arrange to have him assassinated. Do you know what happened?"

"Yes. Baldwin recalled him immediately. That report probably ruined his career."

"Imagine," Laura mused, "if that advice had been taken, how much human misery could have been avoided – how many lives saved? This is an old hotel, with huge furnaces in the basement. After I leave, why don't you take all this down there? Charles can't hurt us now, and there's his small son to think of – and my son, and yours. Let's not visit the sins of the fathers onto them, shall we?" She leaned over and kissed him full on the mouth, for the first time.

There was a heavy knocking on the door of the suite. Nick opened the door to the two detectives who had accompanied the First Lady.

"We have an urgent request for the First Lady to return immediately to the White House, sir. President's orders."

"I'm coming right away." Laura said. She put her fur around her shoulders and turned in the doorway. "Goodbye, dear Nick," she said. "Take care. Life is so extraordinary, isn't it?"

EPILOGUE

In March 1996 His Eminence Cardinal Frederico Montiniero was nominated for the Nobel Peace Prize for his work in bringing the war in Canala to an early and peaceful conclusion by having negotiated the voluntary surrender to the United States of General Tomaso Balthazar, former President of Canala. His Holiness declined the honour on behalf of the Roman Catholic Church, stating that peace was the everyday work of the Church and no further recognition was required of its servants.

The award went instead to Mrs Charles Bellamy for her work in the education of women everywhere, but most particularly in India. It was stated that Mrs Bellamy's work was directed towards the control of population and an increase in public health and nutrition by ignoring traditional attitudes of men towards these matters, and training the ordinary women of India in hygiene and contraception.

"Prevention is the best cure, and a firm step in the march of all nations towards a peaceful world," Mrs Bellamy said in accepting her nomination. Mrs Bellamy is the widow of banker and philanthropist Charles Bellamy, who was murdered in a terrorist attack on his Miami headquarters two years ago. Mrs Bellamy is now President of the Bellamy Corporation and its associated banking and armament interests in the USA and Europe.

* * * * * *

In April 1996, General Masa led an armed force in an attack on the Finca de la Madonna de la Luna some miles to the west of the city of Medellin in Colombia. It is understood that this action was taken with the covert support of the government of the USA. After fierce fighting, in which thirty-seven government troops were killed, including General Masa himself, the Finca was occupied and burnt to the ground. Jorge Ventura y Cortez, the last survivor of the four notorious brothers who had formed their own drug cartel in the 1960s, and known locally as "Armpit George", was thought to have been at the Finca at the time. However his body was not found when the building was occupied by United States troops and the Colombian Militia and his present whereabouts are not known. Government sources, however, believe that he is still alive, and that he may have been implicated in the terrorist attack two years ago on the Bellamy Corporation headquarters, but there is no evidence to support this theory.

* * * * * *

At the end of November 1996, President Andrew Davidson was re-elected for a second term by a sweeping majority of electors. The First Lady is considered to be partly responsible for his overwhelming victory. She is one of the most popular and respected figures in American national life, and widely admired for her work in many areas of health and support for the elderly.

* * * * * *

In January 1997, the American *Business Review Weekly* nominated William Davidson of Atlanta, the father of the President, as Banker of the Year.

On 15 February 1997, a small paragraph appeared on the eighth page of the *Los Angeles Times*, which anyone could have missed. It stated that a human skeleton, partly clothed, had been discovered in a shallow grave about ten miles east of Los Angeles International Airport. The man appeared to have been dead for at least three years. There was no identification on the body except for a label on a piece of clothing which bore the name of a well-know men's store in Sydney, Australia. Police are investigating.

In March 1997, Mrs Harry Wellington filed an application in the Supreme Court of New South Wales, Australia for permission to administer the estate of her husband, Harry Wellington. The application stated that Mr Wellington had left for a trip to Miami in 1994 and disappeared in Los Angeles while on his way to Miami. It asked the Court to rule on a presumption of death and to appoint the widow as administrator of the estate, which was considerable.

Mrs Wellington has taken over as Managing Director of the public relations and fund raising firm founded by her husband. She is also currently President of the powerful and well-known Alcon Foundation of Australia. Mrs Wellington lives at Slowes Court, Darling Point, one of the largest and most historic mansions in the country, and is a leader of social and charitable life in Sydney.

In November 1997, on his retirement from the Senate, Senator Gordon Manchester was appointed United States Ambassador to the Court of St James in recognition of his years of service to the country, and his experience in foreign affairs. His wife has long been known as one of Washington's leading hostesses, famous for her receptions in her Georgetown mansion. It is anticipated that they will be one of the most distinguished couples to represent the United States at the Court of St James for many years.

THE END

Also from Sid Harta Publishers

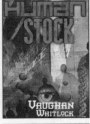
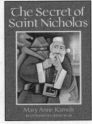

OTHER BEST SELLING SID HARTA TITLES CAN BE FOUND AT
http://www.sidharta.com.au
http://Anzac.sidharta.com

HAVE YOU WRITTEN A STORY?
http://www.publisher-guidelines.com
for manuscript guideline submissions

LOOKING FOR A PUBLISHER?
http://www.temple-house.com

New Releases...

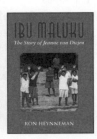